BLUE BOY: THE BOXED SET

BULLET, BONES, BOLD

GARRETT LEIGH

VOLUME 1 — BULLET

CHAPTER ONE

A trickle of sweat ran down the center of Levi Ramone's chest. More beaded his brow. He shook his head, flicking his dark hair out of his eyes. It was too long for working on broken-down motorbikes, too long for his momma's liking, and *definitely* too long for porn.

Hot, lube-slick fingers dug into his hips, jolting him back to reality. He looked down at the boy writhing beneath him. *Boy.* Levi smirked. Zeb was twenty-six, like him, but his smooth, hairless body and baby face made him appear much, much younger. The barely-legal-twink thing didn't really do it for Levi, but it wasn't like he was fucking Zeb for fun. Nah, this was work—this was his *job.* At least the only job he had that paid real money.

Zeb pulled on his hips again. "That all you got, cowboy?"

Cowboy. The word was his cue to move things along. Levi bent and scooped Zeb's much smaller frame into his arms and lifted him from the back of the leather couch. He glanced at the watching cameras, checking the angles, before he deposited Zeb on the fake bearskin rug. "Hold on tight," he warned, sliding back into Zeb's tight body hard and fast.

Zeb moaned and arched his back. "Fuck me, damn it. Fuck me."

Levi obliged. It was getting late, and he had stuff to do. He put his hands flat on Zeb's chest and pounded him until he was a jabbering wreck. They took a break for Zeb to work himself hard again. Levi switched off, almost detached. His mind drifted when the scene resumed, and he barely noticed when Zeb came with a ragged cry. After that, it didn't take long for him to find an absent release in Zeb's talented mouth.

They wrapped the scene, and Levi hit the large communal wet room, left over from the studio building's factory roots. At Blue Boy Studio, showers were a communal thing where models came together to clean up and compare shoots. Today was no different. Levi found himself sharing his space with Caleb, another regular top. Out of habit, he chanced a glance over Caleb's long masculine body. It was very similar to his—strong, subtly defined, and dusted with real body hair. No tattoos, though. The twinks had more ink than the tops at Blue Boy.

That was one of the differences between this place and most of the gay-for-pay studios out there. Blue Boy wasn't about bronzed, muscled, *straight* men pretending to be gay, or vice versa. The models were genuine gay men who loved fucking and/or really needed the cash. Levi reckoned most fell into both categories. He knew he did.

He rubbed shampoo through his dark hair and rinsed it out before reaching for the shower gel to wash the remnants of sweat and other bodily fluids from his skin. Beside him, Caleb went through similar motions. Levi turned to him with an amiable grin. Though pressed for time, he felt genial enough to be polite. "Good shoot?"

Caleb leaned back against the tiled wall with a lazy, shit-eating grin. "Hell, yeah, I had Theo in the weight room. Dude, I nailed him so hard he ain't gonna sit right for a week."

"Yeah, I got Zeb pretty good too." Levi swallowed his disgust and played his role to perfection. He'd learned long ago life was far easier if he said what people expected him to say.

"Damn straight." Caleb held up his hand to high-five. "Saw your scene with Diego last week. You're the motherfucking man."

Levi smirked and slapped Caleb's hand. He'd heard that before. With his unshaven jaw and chest, dark hair, and brooding brown eyes, he was one of the studio's most popular models. "That shoot was kinda cool. Not sure about the barn setting, though. It was a bit cliché, even for hard-core porn."

"Gotta give 'em what they want." Caleb shrugged. "With that accent, you're like the ultimate cowboy fantasy."

"I'm a mechanic," Levi said drily. "I've never touched a damn horse."

"Yeah, but you sound like one, and you're hung like one. It's a no-brainer."

It was true on both counts. He had a big dick, *and* he could trace his roots back to a tiny farming town just east of Austin, Texas. His accent was as deep as his momma's, but he could barely recall the time he'd spent in the South as a child.

"Not like it matters, though," Caleb went on. "Folks just want to see a twink get rammed. No one cares about the rest of it."

Levi grunted in reply. He didn't give much consideration past the actual filming of his scenes. He just wanted to get laid and paid.

Other models began to drift into the showers. Levi acknowledged them all with a grin. Many faces he no longer knew. After dabbling in other studios, he'd worked exclusively at Blue Boy for three years, but models came and went a lot, and turnover in the business was high. These days, he couldn't separate the faces he'd already fucked from those he'd never met.

The wet room filled with naked men, all fresh from a round of filming. The atmosphere was relaxed and jovial. A few had been posing for photo shoots and were still horny and game for some fun. That was the other thing about most of the models lacking normal work-colleague boundaries. Inhibitions were nonexistent, and Levi had enjoyed some good times in the shower room lately. But he wasn't in the mood today. He turned down a blowjob and left them to it.

He dressed in loose, faded jeans and a T-shirt, stepped into his flip-flops, and made his way out of the dressing area. He nodded good-bye to some of the crew and the pretty chick who worked the reception desk. She waved and smiled a rueful smile. Levi knew she was fonder of him than she wanted to be.

"Levi, can I see you for a moment?"

He stopped, his hand on the exterior door, and turned to face Jon, Blue Boy's director and owner. "Right now?"

"If you can spare the time," Jon said with a grin. He tapped his checkbook on the door frame, the universal sign that he wanted to talk business. "It won't take long."

Levi bit back a sigh and let the door swing closed. He had stuff to get done at the garage, but Jon wasn't a guy who took no for an answer, especially when he was waving his checkbook around. He was, after all, the man who paid Levi for his work, and Levi knew he paid him well.

He followed Jon into his office and shut the door behind him. Jon pointed at a chair not too dissimilar to the ones used as props in the studios. "Have a seat."

Levi sat, glancing around the office as he slouched down and stretched his legs out in front of him. Like the rest of the building, it was fairly utilitarian, save the fancy computer. "What can I do for you?"

"What can *I* do for *you* is more the question," Jon shot back. "I'm putting together next month's schedule, and I wanted to talk to you about changing it up a little."

"Changing it up?" Levi sat up, instantly wary. He'd heard that phrase before. In fact, he heard it every time he stepped into the office and Jon offered him increasingly crazy sums of money to perform in one of the bespoke scenes that made the studio unique in the industry. The scenes where rich clients could pretty much write the script.

"Yeah, I know we've talked about it before, but I was wondering if you'd thought any more about the offer I made last time. I know bottoming isn't your thing, but I'm getting requests all the time to put together a special scene. There's a lot of money on the table, Levi. There's gotta be something we can do to make it happen."

Levi shook his head, the refusal already on the tip of his tongue. He didn't bottom. Never had. Never would.

Jon knew that all too well, but he spoke again before Levi could get the words out. "Okay, okay, let me put it this way. What about if we got together a three-way? We could put the scene together so you only had to bottom for a few minutes, get it over and done with, hard and fast. You wouldn't have to come, or fake it. Just let the camera see you take it. Play it up, make it special. That's all they want."

For now, at least.

The rich dudes who had the money to request specialized scenes were like an angry mob. The more he gave them, the more they wanted. He'd done it all—three-ways, four-ways, orgies. If he agreed to this, what the hell would they want him to do next? Get fucked by a damned horse?

"What if I paid you something like this?"

Jon wrote a figure on a page of a notepad and slid the cock-shaped scrap of paper across the table. Levi glanced at it, expecting to see the usual amount, an amount he could bring himself to ignore. The extra zero stopped him in his tracks.

What the fuck? Is he for real?

The ridiculous sum of money was enough to pay off his momma's credit cards, maybe even enough to make a dent in her medical bills. It was too much, too good to be true. It had to be. "You want to give me that much money to bottom for just a few minutes?"

"I'm not *giving* you the money, Levi. I'm paying you to do your job, and giving you a way to carry on doing it. You've been doing this shit a long time now. You have to know you can't go on forever. The way I see it, this is a good way to keep you fresh in your twilight years. You have a huge following, and the prospect of you bottoming has started a bidding war. Seriously, take a look at this. This could be the most profitable scene we've ever done."

Jon spun his computer monitor around, but Levi averted his gaze. The less he knew about the co-op of porn fans clubbing together to make his life hell, the better, and he didn't want to think about the fast looming end of his porn career. It wasn't the job of his dreams, but he needed the damned money. He sat back in his seat and rubbed at his dark beard. It was getting long, growing beyond the buzz of stubble he liked to wear on his face. "Who else have you got in mind for the scene?"

If Jon was surprised that Levi hadn't flat-out refused him, he didn't show it. Instead, he leaned forward with eager eyes. "What about Rex?"

"Rex? Are you kidding me?" The words were out before Levi could stop them. Rex? No fucking way. The dude was massive, from his broad shoulders and tree-trunk legs to his mammoth nine-inch cock. Levi had never filmed a scene with him, but he knew his magic numbers. Each Blue Boy model had the size of his dick recorded on the wall of fame.

"If you're nervous, I'm sure we can—"

"It's not that," Levi snapped, though, of course, it was. Even if he liked to bottom, any sane man would balk at the prospect of having Rex's monster cock crammed into his ass. "I just..."

"Just what?"

Silence. He didn't have the ending to that sentence, and Jon knew it. What was he supposed to say? That he was scared? Yeah, because that would be the quickest way to unravel his hard-earned rep as one of the industry's most ruthless tops.

There was a whispered saying in the industry that you weren't a real star until you'd taken as much dick as you'd given out. He didn't care much for accolades, but he cared about the money—he had to—and without giving the viewers what they wanted to see, the cash would soon dry up.

Jon was a pretty cool boss—the kind of boss who kept him at one studio when others appeared to offer more money. Levi had faith he wouldn't even try to force him to do it, but Jon was one of very few souls privy to what had lured him into the porn industry in the first place, and he wasn't above making Levi an offer he couldn't refuse.

Levi knew what he had to do—he had to roll over and take it like a man. Trouble was he just didn't want to. "Let me think about it," he said reluctantly.

Jon grinned, sensing victory. "Don't think for too long. I was considering getting Sonny on board too, and I want to get this schedule wrapped before I head out to Vegas."

Great. This shit just got better and better. Sonny was a dancer from Silver, the club Jon owned across the street, and one of the industry's rising go-go boys. Bigger than the average twink, he was tattooed and compact, a perfect package of stunning beauty, and totally fucking annoying. He'd never so much as glanced Levi's way, and they'd never filmed together. As far as Levi knew, Sonny stuck to solo scenes and promotional photo shoots.

It wasn't going to happen. There was no way he was shooting a scene with Rex and his monster cock *and* some kid who couldn't hide his disdain. Screw that, or rather, no chance in hell. He opened his mouth to say as much but was cut off by a light tap on the door. The door opened, and there he stood—all five feet and seven inches of Sonny fucking Valentine.

CHAPTER TWO

Levi stared at Sonny. For some reason, the sinuous dancer was the last person he'd expected to see. Sonny glared right back through his sharp and soulful hazel eyes. In fact, Levi found himself musing that Sonny's eyes were his best feature, aside from his tousled blond hair, taut abs, and smooth inked skin, hidden by his hip-hugging jeans and tight T-shirt...

Stop it, jackass. You don't even like the kid. Why are you eye-fucking him?

He reined himself in and averted his gaze. Sonny let out a sound that was halfway between a sigh and a vexed puff of air, but before Levi could respond in kind, Jon shut his desk drawer with a bang.

"Hey, Sonny, we were just talking about you. Levi's gonna think about being the third man in on that three-way I mentioned to you. You two haven't shot together, have you?" He glanced between them. Sonny shook his head, but Levi maintained a mutinous silence. Jon knew full well who had shot with whom. The whole studio was set up around his own perverted fantasies. It had to be. Why else would a man own a porn company? "Okay, well, why don't you hang for a bit, swap numbers or whatever? Be good to get to know each other, eh? Might help Levi here grow some balls to match that huge rod."

Jon laughed like he'd made the funniest crack he'd ever heard, slapped Levi on the back, and left the room. Levi watched him go, knowing he should get up and follow, but something had left him frozen in his seat, caught between fury and a building sense of apprehension smoldering deep in his belly.

Sonny waited for the door to shut, then turned back to Levi with an elegant, arched eyebrow. "Did I hear that right? *You're* going to bottom?"

"Looks that way," Levi replied tersely. Sonny ventured farther into the room. Levi noticed he was barefoot, like he'd come straight from a shoot too. "Did you film a scene today?"

"Yep." Sonny leaped like a cat over the back of the chair Jon had just vacated and slid into the seat. "Some crappy jerk-off scene with Jay and Nico. Man, that shit is so contrived."

"Why do it, then?" Levi snapped, irrationally feeling the need to defend the profession he was growing to loathe. "I thought you were just a dancer?"

"Just a dancer?" Sonny shot back. "I'm not *just* anything, asshole, and maybe you should answer your own question. You're the one all torn up about a bottom scene you obviously don't want to do. Maybe you should worry more about yourself than me. Looks like you're about to get a taste of your own medicine."

"Excuse me?"

"Oh, please." Sonny reached forward, snagging a shiny green apple from the bowl on the desk. The movement caused his shirtsleeves to ride up. Levi caught sight of the script tattoo on his inner bicep. He'd never gotten close enough to read what it said, and now that he was, he could see it wouldn't have done any good if he had. The whole thing was in a language he didn't know.

"Please what? You got something you want to say to me, kid?"

"I'm not a kid, dude. I'm twenty-two."

Levi kept up his sullen, challenging stare. He had four years on Sonny, and he'd been doing porn for even longer. That made Sonny a kid in his book, or at the very least, a cocky little shit who needed to say what he wanted to say or shut the fuck up.

Sonny bit into the apple and chewed thoughtfully. He didn't seem in any hurry to elaborate. He fiddled with a few things on Jon's desk, eyeing Levi with a speculative gaze. Levi let the silence hang for a while before he snapped.

"For God's sake, *what?*" He honestly didn't know why he was still in the room, let alone allowing a little prick like Sonny to yank his chain.

For his part, Sonny shrugged. "I think it's ironic that you're gonna get pounded by Rex. He's probably the only top here who's a bigger douche bag than you."

"Fuckin' whiny twink bitch," Levi muttered, as much to himself as to Sonny. "Listen, *kid*. I don't care what you think of me. I don't need to get fucked by Rex. I've got nothing to prove."

"Haven't you? Even if that's true, seems to me you've got a lot to learn. You've been here, what? Five years? And you hardly let anyone so much as rim you. What are you? One of those gay-for-pay rejects? Or are you just in denial?"

Sonny's beautiful face twisted into a sneer. Levi stared at him, wondering how the conversation had taken such a nosedive so quickly. Then again, it hadn't exactly begun well. "I ain't no straight-assed punk."

He shoved his chair back and made to stand. He'd had enough of this shit. He didn't bottom, but that didn't make him straight. He'd never so much as looked at a woman or denied his sexuality.

"Prove it."

Sonny's words gave him pause. He stopped on his way to

the door. "Prove it to who? You? You're gonna get nailed too, you know. I don't remember seeing you get fucked on-screen before either."

"Maybe you haven't looked hard enough. Besides, I haven't agreed to anything yet. Your name in the hat put me off."

"Feeling's mutual." Levi turned back to the door, not wanting to admit that Sonny was probably right. He never watched any of the scenes that came out of Blue Boy, not even his own. Hell, especially not his own. Now that he thought about it, he had no idea what Sonny had and hadn't done on-screen.

Sonny snorted. "Figures."

"What does?"

"That you're bailing," Sonny said. "Everyone round here knows you're not man enough to take what you're due. If this 'whiny twink bitch' can take Rex, why can't you? Like you said, I'm the one who's gonna get it both barrels. Face it, dude. *You're* the bitch."

"Whatever." Levi pushed open the door. Something, though he wasn't quite sure what, made him turn back. "What is it, exactly, that you think I can't handle?"

Sonny shrugged. "You're a selfish top. A bottom is just a piece of ass to you, a hole to drill so you get paid. Have you ever stopped to consider the person you're throwing around the set?"

Levi scoffed; he couldn't help it. "You twinks ask for that shit."

"Yeah, because that's what we get paid for, what the audience wants. It doesn't mean we always enjoy it. Have you asked? Or even cared?"

"What makes you such an expert on me?"

"I've seen the way you work. The other twinks might think you're a stud, but I think you're an ass. I'm not scared of you. I'll do the scene, but if you think I'm letting you abuse me the way you did Diego last week, you can think again."

The venom in Sonny's tone surprised Levi, but his complaint wasn't without merit. The kid was right when he accused him of never stopping to consider the person attached to the ass he was fucking. To him, that was the point of porn—that it wasn't personal. To him, it really was just a job. "Yeah, well. Don't force yourself on my account. There are plenty of bottoms who'd happily take your place."

"True," Sonny said. "But I wouldn't miss this for the world. Trust me, whatever Jon says, Rex's gonna pound the life out of you, and I'm gonna enjoy every scream that comes out of your arrogant mouth."

Levi drove home in a pissed-off daze. He couldn't believe he'd let that little prick get under his skin. Jon wanted them to get to know each other, but Levi didn't need confirmation that Sonny really was the annoying little fuckwit he'd always assumed he was.

And he had the nerve to call me arrogant?

He pulled up outside his apartment block and went inside. It was early evening, and he still had a stack of bikes at the garage to work through, but for some reason, despite showering at the studio, he felt like he needed another. He got cleaned up and headed back out to the small auto shop he co-owned downtown. The place was deserted. AJ, his business partner, was done and gone for the day. Levi unlocked the shutters and let himself in, pulling off his T-shirt and stepping straight into his coveralls. AJ had left him plenty to do. The garage specialized in maintaining custom and vintage motorcycles, and business was good.

A '77 Triumph Trident kept him busy for a while, but as he worked, he was frustrated to find he couldn't get his conversation—if you could call it that—with Sonny out of his mind.

"Why are you even here?"

Sonny had spat the words to him as he'd pulled himself together and left the office, but he hadn't bothered to reply. He didn't need to. *He* knew why he was there. Why the fuck should he explain it to anyone else, especially that little prick?

Little. Yeah, right. Somehow, he'd found himself glancing at the unofficial wall of fame on his way out of the studio and discovered that Sonny was in fact anything but. If the wall was to be believed, the kid had a thick eight-inch cock hanging between those muscular dancers' thighs.

Damn. Since when did he care about the other model's vital statistics? Life as an exclusive top rendered the size of another man's dick practically meaningless. Maybe Sonny was right, and he *did* have a lot to learn.

He packed his tools away and spent an hour going over the accounts. AJ was a badass mechanic, but he left the bookkeeping to Levi—a job Levi loved and loathed in equal measure. Loved because the garage turned over a pretty tidy profit, a profit he was ridiculously proud of, but loathed because however much money he made, it wasn't enough.

"Why are you even here?"

"Because my daddy shot himself, and my momma's a gambling drunk with more debts than I'll ever be able to pay."

Even after all these years, it still sounded pathetically cliché. The garage was supposed to be his ticket out of porn, his ticket away from annoying douche bags like Sonny, but each time he got close something would happen to drag him back. His momma totaled her car just a few months ago, breaking her arm and cracking some ribs. The medical bills had wiped out three years of hard work. AJ often told him he should just leave her to rot. It wasn't like she cared that he busted his balls to keep a roof over her head, but in his mind, that made him no better than his father. No better than the man who'd blown his brains out in the garden shed without so much as a note.

Levi pushed aside the maudlin thoughts and shoved the box containing the garage accounts back on the shelf. He'd had a long day, and it was getting late. All he wanted was a cold beer, something spicy for dinner, and to crawl into his big, empty bed. On impulse, he backed his truck into the garage and searched out the keys for his battered old Harley XR750. He didn't ride her much, but today, with the blistering LA summer still burning strong, the freedom of the wind in his face was too good to pass up.

Shame it took him all of six minutes to get home.

He parked the bike and went inside to forage in the refrigerator for dinner. He was a good cook, a skill born of greed more than anything else. It didn't take him long to throw together some turkey-chili quesadillas.

After, he sat back on the couch and cracked a beer. He stared at the sports channel for a while, but his afternoon at the studio remained on his mind. Usually, even if he spent a few days at a time shooting various scenes, he could still come home and close the door on them all. Occasionally, some buddies from the studio would drag him out to Silver, but other than that, his life as a porn star remained somewhat separate from his real life.

Not today. Today, he couldn't seem to switch it off. Much of his exchange with Sonny echoed in his mind, but there was one thing in particular.

"Maybe you haven't looked hard enough..."

Maybe it was time he did.

CHAPTER THREE

Levi rummaged under his bed, searching for the box of goodies Jon had given him when he'd signed his first contract at the studio. He had an exclusive, all-access membership to the studio's Web site. All the models did, but he'd be damned if he could remember the password. He hadn't had the urge to use it before. Why would he? He lived the life of most men's fantasies. Why would he need to watch it on the screen of his laptop?

It took a while, but eventually, he unearthed the box buried behind an old suitcase and a stack of CDs. The box contained a bumper strip of condoms, various lubricants, and a selection of sex toys that made even his porn-hardened eyes water. He'd never used the toys, and it had been a *long-assed* time since he'd touched the rest of it.

He retrieved the business card with his log-in information and took his laptop back to the couch. He brought up Blue Boy's Web site, logged in, and was greeted by an image of his own completely nude body. Fascinated, he stared at his naked form. The image was a few years old, back when he had shorter hair and kept his face clean shaven, but the rest of him was much the same—long and strong and covered with a buzz of dark body hair. His dick hadn't changed much either.

Though he was alone, he felt an alien flush of embarrassment creep over him. It had been a while since he'd last felt so self-conscious. He wore the cocky grin like a second skin, but somehow it didn't seem real—like the face staring back at him wasn't his own.

Shit, is that really me?

Levi shook himself. It felt odd to be staring at his image, too odd. He turned his attention to the task at hand, bringing up the search option and tapping in Sonny's name. His Internet connection was slow. He got up to fetch another beer while he waited for the page to load.

A few minutes later, he came back to find the laptop screen lit up with Sonny Valentine. He set his beer down on the coffee table, picked up the laptop, and leaned closer, taking in the lithe, beautiful body that filled the screen. Sonny slouched against a pure white wall, his skin smooth, fair, and inscribed with a web of intricate tattoos. The ink was delicate and eclectic, somehow more subtle and refined than any he'd seen on others. He didn't usually care for tattoos, but on Sonny...

Stop it.

Chewing hard on his bottom lip, he let his gaze travel up Sonny's torso to his face, taking in his sharp, masculine jawline, high cheekbones, and mischievous smirk. Tousled dark blond hair and sparking hazel eyes completed the picture, set off by the diamond studs he wore in each ear.

Levi swallowed. The Blue Boy logo scrolled across the top of the page. He watched it go round in a loop a few times, drumming his fingers on his thigh, procrastinating. The image of Sonny was cut off just above his hips, hiding the lower half of his body. Levi took a long, slow pull of his beer. Did he really want to see Sonny's dick? If Jon had his way, he'd be seeing it soon enough, but he felt kind of strange. Like he wasn't sure he could face it.

Weird.

He tore his eyes away from Sonny's sculpted chest and scanned the scant, obligatory bio information, but it didn't tell him anything he didn't already know. He glanced down the list of movies, and down, and down, and down. His eyes widened. It seemed while he'd been busy *brutalizing* his way through Blue Boy's extensive list of bottoms, Sonny had been moving in the opposite direction, bottoming for nearly every top there was. He'd even done a scene—several scenes—with Cam, a fellow top Levi considered a friend.

Every top except me.

The scenes with Cam looked *hot*. Levi felt a stirring in his belly as his cock hardened. The feeling surprised him. He supposed it was a normal reaction for any man perusing a porn site, but for some reason, it shocked him.

Some porn star you are.

He shut the laptop with a bang. Whatever he'd hoped to achieve had been lost in the memory of Sonny's mocking, humorless laughter. His cell phone beeped. He didn't bother to look, knowing it was the first of many messages from Jon, pressing him for an answer over the three-way. He sighed and closed his eyes. Rex had already signed up, and Sonny had made his decision clear.

With his momma's bills still stacking up, one way or another, he was going to get fucked.

A week or so later, Levi drove forty minutes outside of the sprawling city to check up on his ailing mother. Leaving the clutches of LA behind, even for a few hours, usually refreshed him, but not when he paid his momma a visit. Bella Ramone was hard work; she always had been. A decade of liquor and gambling had hardened her bitter heart and made her tongue impossibly sharp.

He let himself in the back door of her ramshackle home, following the trail of early-morning chaos to the living room where she sat on the couch, drink in hand, and watched talk shows. The house stank of gin, her drink of choice these days. With her car gone and her license suspended, neat vodka was old news.

"Mornin', B." He leaned against the door frame. He'd stopped calling her Momma a long time ago. "Liquid lunch?"

"Very funny." Bella tore her eyes away from her dusty TV. "What are you doing here?"

Levi sighed. What did she think he was doing here? The same thing he did every week—checking she wasn't dead or homeless. "Lookin' in on ya. Not a crime, is it? Where's the mail?"

"Over there."

He retrieved the mail and flipped through it, setting aside the envelopes that required his attention. At the bottom of the pile was a handwritten note addressed to him. It was from Mr. Draper, Bella's ridiculously tolerant landlord. It simply read, *Call me.* Levi frowned and stuffed the note into his pocket. Perhaps the old guy had finally seen the light and was kicking her drunken ass out. He considered what would become of Bella then, picturing her on the leather couch of his apartment.

No fucking way.

He walked through the small, split-level house, scouting for repairs and any obvious hazards. He'd once found Bella passed out in a bed of broken glass—sleeping on a wine bottle she'd taken into her bed. Some days he figured it wouldn't be a bad way for her to go, but not today. Today, he had other shit to do.

Bella intercepted him on his way back through the living room. The kitchen was his last stop. After scoping the refrigerator for actual food, he was getting himself gone. "There's some soup on the stove. Take it with you. You look like crap."

His chest ached, a distant ache that reminded him she'd once cared enough to try to be his momma. "Thanks. What are you doing today?"

"What do you think I'm doing? It's all right for you in the city, throwing your cash around, partying and living it up. Did you stop to think about me? Do you ever stop to think about anyone other than yourself? If your daddy was alive, he'd..."

Her tone was acid, and just like that, the ache was gone, and a cold, dead weight settled over his heart. His daddy had been gone eight years, and with Levi at college in another state, she'd locked herself in the family home and run up huge debts playing online poker. The drink came next. By the time Levi dropped out of school to pay her debts, he barely recognized her. They'd loved each other once, he was sure of it, but these days, they'd forgotten how.

He left Bella to her gin and talk shows, shutting the door on her tirade. It was nothing he hadn't heard before. He pulled out his cell phone, punched in the number for Bella's landlord, and rummaged in the glove box of his car, searching for cigarettes. He didn't smoke much, only when he was pissed off and tired. Visiting with his momma typically left him with a whole lot of both.

"Hello?"

Levi paused in the action of lighting a Marlboro. He slammed the glove box shut and sat up, chuffing a lungful of smoke out of the open car window. "Mr. Draper? It's Levi Ramone. I got your note."

"My note? Oh, yes, I remember. I left that for you last month. I wasn't sure it'd reached you."

"Sorry, man." Levi rubbed a hand over his face. He picked up all the mail he could, but sometimes shit got lost. "I got it today. Everything okay? I don't owe you any rent, do I?"

"Oh, no, it's not that." There was a scratching sound at Mr. Draper's end, and the click of a closing door. "Actually, I've been meaning to catch up with you for a while. It's not about the rent, son. You've never been so much as a day late."

Levi took a drag on his smoke, enjoying it like the guilty pleasure it was. Savoring it. "So what is it? Is there something you want me to fix up? I haven't got a lot of time at the moment, but I'm sure I can work something out."

That was the other reason Mr. Draper was so tolerant of the abuse Bella inflicted on his property. They had an unwritten agreement that Levi would handle and cover the cost of any repairs. A promise he'd made good on more times than he cared to remember.

"Levi, I'm selling the house."

The pleasant warmth of the tobacco smoke in his mouth turned acrid and bitter. He choked on it, coughing it out of his lungs. "Wh-what? When?"

"Don't panic, son," Mr. Draper said. "I wanted to talk to you before I did anything. I don't want to kick your ma out, but Peggy's health isn't what it was. We're going to need the money tied up in that house to take care of ourselves. I know you do your best with your ma, son. I'm giving you six months to find her somewhere before I put the house up for sale."

Levi couldn't really complain. Mr. Draper and his wife were fast approaching their eighties. It wasn't unreasonable of them to want to release their assets into real cash. Besides, what other landlord would give six months' notice before the house was even put up for sale?

He thanked Mr. Draper and hung up, discarding his half-smoked cigarette. The image of Bella on his couch flashed into his mind again. He shuddered.

No fucking way.

CHAPTER FOUR

Levi leaned back on the wide, L-shaped couch, eyes closed and posture at ease. He was dressed in faded jeans—barefoot, no shirt, not even underwear. He felt relaxed. If he tilted his head back, he could pretend he was home and catch up on some much-needed sleep. Except, of course, he wasn't at home, and the smell of body oil and sex in the air reminded him exactly where he was.

He opened his eyes and glanced around the set, busy with crew setting up for the shoot. There weren't many of them—a couple of camera guys, light and sound and a photographer. Jon liked to keep filming low-key and intimate, and the scene in question was a casual affair—no cliché role-play or bullshit fantasies. Just some good old-fashioned fucking.

Speaking of fucking. On the back of the giant couch sat Kai, his partner in crime for the day. The guy was young, barely twenty-one, but he was kind of cute, all curly blond hair, long legs, and toothy smiles. Levi liked him, though he wasn't all that attracted to him. He considered Kai's slight frame. Levi had a big dick. It wasn't the monster Rex had, but it was long and thick. Kai was petite, with slim, narrow hips. Would he even fit?

"Levi? You ready, dude?"

"Huh?" He blinked, staring at Jon, who for his part looked vaguely amused.

"Get your head in the game, man. We're ready to go."

And so they were, and by the look on Jon's face, they'd been ready awhile. "Um, sure. I'm cool."

Jon ran through his final checks and held up his hand for quiet. The typical, strange silence fell over the studio. Levi took some deep and even breaths. He often felt he was on another planet in those brief few seconds before the cameras began rolling. The world faded away—street noise, the whir of the air-conditioning, even the thrum of his heart. Five seconds, five blissful seconds that were over far too soon.

"*Action!*"

"So this is, like, my second scene with Blue Boy. You're gonna go easy on me, right?" Kai turned to face him. His smile was soft and shy, innocent almost, and totally belied the context behind his question.

Levi stretched out his legs and folded his hands behind his head. He didn't like to talk much on-screen—and Jon seemed to think his brooding silence added an addictive, enigmatic air to him—but he never managed to dodge the prefuck banter. Jon was mad for that shit, and Levi knew how to play his role. "If that's what you want. You had Cam the first time, right?"

"Yeah. He was real nice to me."

That sounded about right. Cam was nice to everyone; all the new bottoms wanted to shoot with him first. "I can be nice."

Kai snickered. "Yeah, right. I've heard about you. You'll be nice until you get me where you want me. Then you'll break me."

"That so?" Levi was unimpressed with Kai's attempt at cockiness. The guy was so nervous he couldn't keep still. "Maybe I'll be gentle."

"Really? That's not your style." Kai slid a hand over Levi's thigh, palming his already half-erect cock. "I heard you like to pound guys into the ground with that big dick of yours."

"You shouldn't believe everything you hear."

"Oh, I don't," Kai said. "I watched all your movies to make sure."

"All of them?" Levi echoed. To his shame, he wasn't quite sure how many scenes he'd shot. There were so many—blowjobs, three-ways, groups, and locations shoots. Over the years he'd lost track.

"As many as I could download. My laptop's pretty crummy."

Levi smirked. "Is that why you're doing porn? To buy a new one?"

"Sort of." Kai shrugged. "But I've always wanted to do it. Guys like you are my ultimate fantasy."

It was classic bullshit, and they both knew it, but Levi didn't mind. It fit with the program and gave him the perfect hook to get the scene started.

"Well, I guess it's time to find out if I can make those fantasies real..."

Kai took his cue and leaned forward, his face inches away, but Levi turned at the last moment, and the kiss found air. He pounced before Kai could try again, tugged him down from the top of the couch, and deposited him flat on his face.

A tremor ran through Kai's slim body. Levi ignored it, pulling Kai's jeans down his lean legs in one swift, sure sweep of his arm. He stood briefly and stepped out of his own before flipping Kai again and throwing him down on his back.

They went through the motions—the obligatory foreplay, interspersed with posing for still camera shots. Levi was a veteran; sometimes he thought he could act out a porn scene with his eyes closed and still point his dick the right way, but

Kai's nerves betrayed him. A shaking hand. A mistimed gasp of air. A tiny whimper as Levi loomed over him, ready to roughly breach his tight, young body.

"A bottom is just a piece of ass to you, a hole to drill so you get paid. Have you ever stopped..."

He stopped. Took in Kai's wide eyes and heaving chest. For all his cockiness, the kid was scared to death. Scared to death of *him*. It wasn't something he'd thought of before, and he found he didn't like it. He didn't like it at all.

Damn you, Sonny Valentine. Fine, have it your way.

He took Kai's legs from over his shoulders and eased them back down. He bent and licked a slow, demonstrative trail up his chest as he considered his next move. Sonny was right in one respect. Pausing for thought wasn't his style at all, and he wasn't sure he even knew how to slow things down.

Kai bit his lip, confused at the sudden change in pace. Levi threw him a quick wink and made his decision. "I'm feelin' kinda lazy today," he drawled. "How 'bout you come over here and ride me, boy?"

He scooped Kai from the couch without waiting for an answer, spun round, and lowered himself down to lie on his back, propped up by the scattered cushions. Kai straddled him, aligning himself with his cock. Levi shifted, adjusting them both so the camera got the best money shot. It was an instinctive movement. Though Kai's body blocked his view of Jon, he needed no direction.

Kai bore down, taking Levi into him, and his eyes bugged out as Levi's dick slowly disappeared. "Fuck, you're so big."

Levi held still, supporting Kai's weight with his hands. "You like that, huh?"

"Fuck, yeah, I like big dicks." Kai's thighs touched Levi's balls. He could go no farther. He rolled his hips, playing up to the camera, and groaned. "You feel amazing."

Levi grunted and mirrored the movement. Kai was hot and tight. There was no denying it felt good. "Show me," he said gruffly. "Show me how good it feels."

Kai caught on, following Levi's subtle nudge and fucking himself on Levi's dick. He set a cautious pace, easing himself in, but as genuine pleasure began to creep over his features, his movements got faster, harder. He reached for his cock and cried out at the sensation of double-edged pleasure.

Levi was amused by the sight of Kai enjoying himself so brazenly. He leaned farther back on the couch and put his hand behind his head. Perhaps he'd been missing a trick all these years, and this *was* the right way to fuck.

Still, as relaxed as he was, he couldn't hold reality at bay forever. In his peripheral vision, Jon made the sign for a change in position. It was time to move on and pick up the pace.

He lifted Kai, turning his supple body so Kai could ride him facing the camera. It was a classic porn position, and one he often favored. Impersonal enough to maintain an illusion of detachment, and hot enough to get him where he needed to be.

He gripped Kai's hips and thrust up into him in long, gentle circles. "Damn, you're tight, boy."

Kai groaned, dropping his chin to his chest. "Harder."

"Like this?" Levi grunted and moved with more purpose.

Kai whimpered. "Just like that. Don't stop. Don't stop."

Levi obliged, increasing the pressure of his thrusts until a telltale tingling stirred in his belly, and Kai's slim thighs began to shake.

Through the haze of sweat and arousal, Jon gave the signal to wrap things up. Levi maneuvered Kai again, pushing him forward on the L-shaped couch and onto his knees. Kai gasped. Levi put a soothing hand on Kai's back and pressed his cock back inside him. He'd kept his word to quasi-Sonny and gone easy, but for this part he had to push a little harder. A shudder ran through him, and he allowed himself a wry smirk. He could stave off release for as long as was needed to suit a scene, but it was always reassuring to know it was there.

He leaned over Kai, positioning Kai's sweaty hands on the wide couch so he could support himself. "Hold on tight."

"Yeah? You gonna fuck me hard?"

Kai's voice was strained, laced with excitement and a touch of fear Levi wouldn't have noticed before Sonny invaded his brain. He reached around and took Kai's cock in his hand, using his other for leverage to push upright. "Hold on."

The temperature in the studio rose. Levi slammed his hips forward, fucking Kai as hard as he dared without awakening the Sonny-shaped demon on his shoulder. The effort of such control was hard work. Sweat ran down his back, and his breath came in stuttered, growled gasps. Beneath him, Kai writhed and groaned as Levi pounded him until Kai finally blew his load all over the squeaky leather couch.

Levi eased off, slowing the punishing roll of his hips until he withdrew entirely. Kai lay spent on his front, panting, exhausted. Levi gave him a moment, pulling off the condom and removing it from view. He took himself in hand, ready to jack off over Kai's back if necessary, but after a few seconds, Kai shifted, turned over, and slid from the couch. He dropped to his knees and batted Levi's hand away. "Let me do that for you."

"Yeah?"

"Yeah, I wanna see you come."

Levi wasn't going to argue with that. He leaned back on his elbows, jutting his hips forward as Kai took him in hand, tentatively at first, but then with more purpose as he responded to Levi's reactions.

"Fuck, yeah." Levi snarled, playing it up. Most of his scenes were loud and noisy, filled with guttural yells and grunts, but he didn't feel like that today. He let his eyes roll and groaned, feeling mellow as the faint, distant rush of release swept over him. Over the years, he'd perfected the art of separation, but an orgasm was an orgasm, and there was no denying the sweet pleasure as he came in Kai's hand.

Kai smirked a wicked smirk that seemed at odds with his young face, and licked the cooling cum from his hand. "You taste good."

"You like that, huh?" Inside, Levi cringed. He'd had his cum licked from his body a thousand times over, but it was still a fetish he didn't get.

Kai let out a breathy laugh. "Yeah, I like that. I liked all of it. Maybe we can do it again sometime."

"*Cut!*"

Levi showered alone. He wasn't entirely sure of Kai's whereabouts. Kai had disappeared shortly after sidling up to him, kissing his cheek, and pushing his number into Levi's palm.

"Thank you. I wasn't expecting to enjoy that, but I did. I really did. Call me."

That was a new one. Levi ran his hand over his head. He'd let AJ go at his hair with a pair of clippers the day before and now sported a short crew cut. His head felt lighter. Perhaps that was why his typical postshoot funk had failed to materialize. In fact, he didn't feel like he'd filmed a scene at all.

He washed up and left the wet room. Jon was waiting for him in the dressing area. That was unusual. The prep rooms were the models' domain. Staff and crew didn't venture back there much. Levi walked past Jon and dropped his towel on the bench. "Looking for me?"

"Maybe." Jon ventured into the dressing area and leaned against the wall. "So that scene was a little..."

He let the statement hang, trusting Levi to fill in the blanks.

Levi reached for his clothes. Jon had a way of getting under the skin of a man. It was part of the reason the studio was so successful; he knew what made people tick. Of course, it meant he noticed when even the slightest thing changed.

"You didn't like it?" Levi pulled on some of the free, brand-new designer underwear lying around the studio, something he didn't always bother with.

Jon held up his hands. "Dude, it's not that. The scene was great. The chicks love all that emo porn. I just wasn't expecting it from you. Gentle and sweet isn't your MO."

"Sweet?"

"You know what I mean. What's the deal? Is there something going on between you and Kai?"

Levi paused in the process of yanking his well-worn jeans up his legs. "What? Why would you think that? I only met him today."

"It didn't seem like it. Seemed like you actually gave a shit."

"And that's bad?"

"No, I'm saying, if that's the kind of scene you want to do, say so, and I can pair you up with the appropriate partner. That scene was great, but I've got requests coming out of my ears for that kid to get nailed. I kinda figured you were the guy for the job."

Levi swallowed. Kai's innocent gaze flashed into his mind, only to be replaced with Sonny's astute hazel eyes. Frustration washed over him. The last time he'd let that little prick get inside his head, he'd woken up on the couch with a boner and a raging hangover. A cold shower had calmed his dick. The hangover, not so much.

"What about the three-way? Have you decided about that?"

"Huh?" Somehow, though he hadn't thought of much else for weeks, the looming threat of getting topped by Rex the beast had slipped his mind. He stepped into his battered Converse and reached for his keys and cell phone. "Whatever. I'll do it. Just make sure your check don't bounce."

He left without waiting for Jon to reply. It was late, he was beat, and he was getting a motherfucking headache.

CHAPTER FIVE

Levi tossed his phone to the floor beside the couch and coughed into his elbow. Jon hadn't been impressed by him calling in sick and postponing an evening shoot, but when a bout of stomach flu had turned into real flu, he hadn't had much choice. With his bloodshot eyes and congested chest, he looked and sounded like a skanky coke fiend. Not a good look for porn.

He flopped back on the couch and put his arm over his scratchy eyes. He'd had a headache for days, and his whole body hurt. Add in the cough and raging fever, and he felt as bad as he looked. Still, though he was too sick for porn, he had a full day of work ahead of him at the garage. He'd cried off early the day before, but there was too much backed up for AJ to get through on his own. After snatching a restless nap, he hauled his ass off the couch and drove to the garage.

AJ looked up and whistled as Levi made his way into the stuffy, airless auto shop. "Man, look at you. Thought you still had your head in the can?"

"That was yesterday. I'm fine now."

"Yeah, you look it."

AJ's tone was dubious, but he said no more and returned to his work. Levi drifted over to the small office space and opened the diary. There were three bikes booked in. AJ was halfway into the first, and he'd left Levi the job they both hated— replacing defective pistons. With a full service and engine strip down, that shit was going to take all day.

Levi heaved a heavy sigh and dragged himself over to the waiting bike. He peeled off his shirt and stepped into his coveralls, lingering a moment by the stand-up fan and enjoying the weak, cool breeze on his overheated skin. The late-August weather had turned muggy, a sure sign that summer was coming to an end. He felt a flash of melancholy. He loved the summer. The bright, never-ending days seemed full of possibility, but with the weight of Bella's impending eviction hanging over him —a matter he'd yet to address—the prospect of autumn seemed ominous and foreboding.

Or maybe it was the headache.

The day passed in a haze of oil, gasoline, and wrestling with stubborn metal, but despite his pathetic state, he finished up before AJ and got the last job done too. After, he sat at the desk and caught up on neglected paperwork. The office space was by AJ's workstation. AJ was a reserved guy, content to work in companionable silence. Sometimes the quiet got under Levi's skin, but today he welcomed it.

Too bad AJ felt the need to be uncharacteristically chatty. "So how's life in the adult entertainment business?"

Levi glanced up from the account books. He'd been staring at them so long the figures were beginning to swim in his head. "Hmm? Oh, yeah, it's okay..." He coughed into his elbow. "I did some new promo shots the other day. Want to see?"

AJ snorted and flipped him off. He was no homophobe, but gay porn freaked him out. In fact, any porn freaked him out. For a badass biker, he was kind of conservative. He didn't often mention Levi's double life, and Levi got a kick out of making him squirm, but he was too tired. He just wanted to finish the books and crawl back onto his couch.

"Speaking of porn."

"Huh?" Levi glanced up again. He felt like hours had passed since the last time one of them had spoken, but it was clear by the amusement in AJ's eyes that he was being dopey. "What the fuck are you talking about now?"

AJ pointed across the street. Levi followed his gaze and spotted Cam, his one real friend from Blue Boy, heading his way. He shut the books with a relieved sigh. Cam lived in Venice Beach but sometimes dropped by the garage on his way to the gym. It had been a while, though. Levi had missed him.

Cam ditched his skateboard at the door, bumped fists with AJ, and made his way to the back of the garage. He flopped onto the tattered old couch and punched Levi's shoulder. "Whoa. So you really are sick. Man, you look like hell. Why aren't you at home in that big empty bed of yours?"

Levi rolled his eyes, and ruffled Cam's unruly hair. He should've figured his early-morning phone call to Jon wouldn't take long to reach Cam's ears. Maybe the rumors about their not-so-secret relationship were true. "Fuck you. I'm okay."

"You don't look it."

"Been saying that all damn day," AJ called from behind the bike he was working on. "Stubborn asshole just came in to bug me."

"Come here and say that." Levi scowled, but AJ shrugged and went back to his work. He'd known Levi too long to be intimidated by his trademark growl. Levi turned his attention to Cam, taking in his shaggy auburn hair and bright green eyes. The dude was hot and still looked twenty-one. "How's tricks?"

"Not bad, not bad." Cam leaned back, folding his hands behind his head. "Haven't seen you around the studio for a while."

"I was there on Thursday. You're the one who's never around."

That was the other reason he suspected the rumors about

Cam and Jon were true. He didn't pay much attention to such things, but he couldn't remember the last time Cam shot a hardcore scene.

Cam eyed him, as unfazed as AJ. "I've been around. I heard you were sick, but I thought you might be hiding out from Rex's monster cock."

"You heard about that?" Levi frowned. Jon had told him he was keeping the scene on the down low until it was shot. It was a big deal that one of Blue Boy's most exclusive tops was going to break his own rules, and it had to be managed right, though Levi suspected Jon wanted to be sure Levi would go through with it before he leaked any publicity.

AJ threw down his wrench and wiped his hands, cutting off Cam's reply. "On that note, I'm taking a lunch break."

It was midafternoon, but Levi wasn't about to point out that lunch had come and gone. Discussing the three-way in front of AJ didn't feel right. The dude was barely forty, but he was the closest Levi had to a father figure in his life. He waited for him to cross the street before he turned back to Cam and said, "I'm not hiding from anything."

"Wouldn't blame you if you were. I wouldn't want to be breaking myself in with Rex. What were you thinking? Are you fucking insane?"

Levi sighed. It was Cam all over to cut right to the chase. "Jon made me an offer I couldn't refuse."

"I'll bet."

Levi let the silence hang, waiting for Cam to confess that he was indeed sleeping with Jon, but no such confession came. He sighed again under his breath. It had been a few months since the rumors had started, but he'd never talked about it with Cam, and he found himself equal parts frustrated and relieved. Frustrated because, away from the madness of porn, he considered Cam a friend, and relieved because, well, he didn't get it. At thirty-eight, Jon was hot enough, and he'd always been good to

Levi, but really, who wanted a porn boss for a boyfriend? A man who spent all his time thinking about other dudes having sex?

"Earth to Levi?"

"Huh?"

Cam waved his hand in front of Levi's face. "Something on your mind?"

"Like what?"

"I don't know, maybe the fact that you're about to pop your ass cherry with some mutant-dicked giant? Seriously, dude. Why are you doing it?"

Levi reached for a bottle of water, opened it, and took a long swig. He had a vague memory of one beer-fueled night at Silver a few years ago when he might have told Cam more about his financial situation than he really wanted to. The night had ended at Cam's place with a bunch of other models, and besides the reaffirmed knowledge that he and Cam shared a respectful sexual chemistry, the only thing he remembered was that Cam gave *really* good head. "Why does anyone do porn?"

"You tell me," Cam said. "I got into porn to pay for college, and I still do it because I kinda love it. You, my friend, do not love it. You do it because you think you have to. I think you enjoy it sometimes, but that's the primal, animal side of you. Deep down, there's a big part of you that hates what we do."

"I knew that psychology degree of yours was gonna come back and bite me in the ass," Levi said. Cam was wrong. He didn't hate porn, and he wasn't ashamed of how he made a living. There was just something missing in his life right now, and he didn't know what.

Cam reached over and swiped Levi's water bottle. "I don't need academics to bite you in the ass. Been there, done that. If you've got an itch you want to scratch, there's better ways of—"

"You shot with Rex?"

"No." Cam twisted the cap back on the water bottle. "I've watched a couple of his scenes, though."

"And?"

"Put it this way. He's not gonna go easy on you, even if you ask him to. From what I've heard, that riles him up. The dude's got no respect."

Levi swallowed, remembering the fear in Kai's eyes a few days ago. Was that what people thought of him too? That he would actually fucking hurt them? "What about Sonny?"

Cam grinned. "Yeah, I've filmed with him. He's a damned good fuck, bendy as hell. We had a lot of fun."

Levi eyed Cam. Cam had never mentioned Sonny before, but the smirk on his face seemed familiar, like Levi was missing something obvious. "He seems like a whiny diva prick."

"Really?" Cam shook his head. "Nah, you've got that wrong. Sonny's a handful, but he's cool, and he's *all* fucking man. I told Jon I would've fucked him for free."

Levi snorted. Cam said that about pretty much every scene he shot. It was only the fact that he was as resolute about topping as Levi that kept them from fucking each other, just for fun, of course. "You say that all the time."

"Not true," Cam said. "Anyway, you'll find out for yourself soon enough. That's the plus side of getting nailed by Rex, right? You get to fuck Sonny. Trust me, you won't be disappointed."

Levi felt sick. He slumped and put his head on his arms. The prospect of fucking Sonny was intriguing but laced with apprehension. To fuck Sonny, he had to get fucked himself, and there was nothing exciting about that.

Cam reached over and laid a hand on his forehead. "Jeez, you're burning some fever there, man. Do you want me to drive you home?"

"You don't have a car." Levi shrugged him off. It was true, he did have a fever, but he knew the flush of his skin couldn't be completely attributed to being sick.

Damn you, Sonny Valentine.

Later that day, he left the garage and headed for home. He hadn't kept anything down for twenty-four hours, but he swung past the store all the same and picked up bread and ginger ale, hoping his churning stomach was a sign he was hungry.

He parked by his building and trudged inside, throwing the contents of his pockets on the coffee table. His cell phone beeped as it clattered against the glass tabletop. He picked it up and glanced at the message, expecting more well-meant ribbing from Cam.

Still sick? — S

Levi frowned. S? Who the hell was S? He fired back a message, threw the phone back on the coffee table, and retreated to the bathroom to shower away a day of oil and fevered sweat. After, he drifted back to the couch and flaked out in front of the TV. He was all but asleep when his cell phone roused him.

Sonny. Cam sed ure sick?

Sonny? What the fuck? Levi sat up and rubbed his eyes. His digits were known to quite a few models at Blue Boy, but he was pretty sure Sonny Valentine wasn't one of them. He wandered into the kitchen, tapping out a reply, and downed a generous shot of bourbon to clear the congestion in his chest.

Yea. B back soon.

Need anything?

Like what?

Drugs? Gatorade?

I'm good. Thx.

Levi paused after he sent the last reply, deliberating over another shot of hard liquor, before he sent another message.

Why?

Why what?

Why you askin?

There was a break in the quick-fire texts then. Levi took his cell phone into the bedroom and dropped it on the bed. He came back from brushing his teeth to find it still blank, and it remained so until it rang a little while later and woke him for a second time.

He fumbled for the phone, barely registering that the screen was lit up with Sonny's number, and pressed the Call button with his thumb.

"'Lo?"

"Did I wake you?"

"Yep."

"Sorry," Sonny said, though he didn't sound all that contrite.

Levi rolled over, scrubbed a hand over his face, and glanced at the clock. It was just after midnight, and he'd spent most of the evening asleep, but he still felt like death. Maybe the half-pint of bourbon wasn't such a good idea. "How did you get this number?"

"Cam gave it to me."

"Oh, yeah? Why did he do that?"

Sonny laughed softly. "Does it matter? Or would you rather know why I wanted it?"

There was a pause as Levi considered his answer. His apartment was quiet and still, but at Sonny's end, he could hear the distant sound of pounding dance music. He wondered if Sonny was dancing at Silver. "Why did you want it?"

"I saw your scene with Kai."

Oh. "And?"

"And...I don't know, man. Jon said you signed up for the three-way. I was kinda hoping you wouldn't."

"You woke me up to tell me that?"

Sonny was silent. Levi pushed himself up on one elbow and looked out of the window. The sky was dark and clear. A handful of stars glittered against the midnight backdrop. "Listen, this has been epic, but I feel like crap. I gotta sleep. Are we done?"

"Have you bottomed for someone like Rex before?"

Levi sighed. Clearly this wasn't over, but he wasn't about to admit that he'd never had *anything* bigger than a tongue up his ass before, let alone a monster cock like Rex's. "What do you care?"

"I'll take that as a no," Sonny said. "And I don't care, as such. I'm just trying to figure you out. I'm not like you. I like to know who's putting their dick in my ass."

"Porn star with a conscience?"

"Maybe. Or maybe I'm discerning. Ever tried it?"

And so it went on. Levi woke up the following morning with the keypad of his phone imprinted on the side of his face, and a vague memory of falling asleep with Sonny's soft accent still chattering in his ear.

Still, until Sonny appeared on his doorstep a week later, he was utterly convinced the whole conversation was the result of an alcohol-induced fever dream.

CHAPTER SIX

Levi yanked open his front door, fresh from the gym and dressed only in sweatpants. He did a double take at Sonny's lean, agile frame leaning on the opposite wall of the corridor. "What the hell are you doing here?"

Sonny smirked and pushed himself off the wall, eyeing his bare chest. "Nice. I told you I'd come by tonight and show you how to stretch for your big bottom scene."

"You did?"

"Duh, yeah." Sonny slipped under his arm and into the apartment. "What the hell? Were you drunk or something?"

"Or something," Levi said, unimpressed by the mere presence of Sonny in his home and the implications of something he had no memory of consenting to. He'd never bottomed, but he wasn't naive enough to believe that Sonny's version of stretching involved hamstrings and yoga poses.

Sonny dropped his bag on the floor and narrowed his eyes, his gaze appraising. "Feeling better?"

"Uh-huh." Levi eyed the bag. How long did the kid think he was staying?

"You sure look better than you sounded last week. Did you cut your hair?"

Levi sighed. "Do you ever quit asking questions?"

"Better than whining, right?" Sonny smiled, his rakish grin set off by a day's growth dusted over his jaw. It wasn't the thick, dark stubble Levi liked to wear, but it added something to Sonny, something he found far too intriguing.

"I guess. Tell me again why you're here?"

"You really don't remember?"

Levi shook his head, though in truth, now that Sonny was right in front of him, vague recollections of a rambling conversation he'd never dream of having while in his right mind began to drift back to him.

Sonny took advantage of Levi's silence and poked his head into the living room. "Nice place," he said. "Shoulda known you were a neat freak."

Levi bristled. It was an accusation he'd faced before. Cam figured his bordering-on-obsessive need for order in his home stemmed from his chaotic childhood, but Levi didn't much care. It wasn't like he spent all his free time lining up the cans in the cupboards. At least, not often. "You came all the way here for a home inspection?"

Sonny ventured farther into the living room with Levi trailing behind him. He spun in a slow circle to face him. "No I came over here to stop you from letting Rex rip your ass open. I thought we'd covered that?"

"What makes you think I need your help?"

"Okay, maybe you don't." Sonny migrated to the wall and peered at the one photograph Levi had of his parents. "What are you going to do instead? Bend over and hope for the best?"

Levi crossed the room in two strides, lashing out before he could stop himself. He yanked Sonny away from the photograph and pinned him to the wall with one arm. "What do you think? You think I'd let *anyone* bend me over?"

Sonny's eyes flashed, but he didn't fight Levi's hold on him.

"If you can't figure out how to control a three-way scene from the bottom, you'll have no choice."

"Why do you want to help me?" Levi ground out the words, his face inches from Sonny's. "I thought you were gonna enjoy every scream from my arrogant mouth?"

"I changed my mind."

Levi increased the pressure of his forearm across Sonny's chest. "Why?"

Sonny stared at him for a long moment. For the first time, Levi saw confliction flare in his cocksure gaze. "You need to prepare your body, or it's gonna tear you apart."

"Talking from experience?"

"I might be a 'whiny twink' in your eyes, but I was a stupid kid once, stupid and naive. You don't want to make that mistake, trust me. That kinda shit stays with you."

"Yeah?" Levi released his hold on Sonny, letting him regain his footing. "So what can you do to help me?"

"I can show you how I get ready for a scene."

Levi thought for a moment. He had a pretty good idea what getting ready for a bottoming scene entailed, though it wasn't something he'd ever envisioned himself doing. "You want me to watch you?"

"Might help."

"Nah." Levi shook his head, his mind made up. "I don't need to watch you. I can do it."

"Really?" Sonny raised an eyebrow. "You didn't seem so sure the other night."

Levi scowled. It was unnerving to barely remember a conversation about something so intimate. "Yeah, well, maybe *you* should watch *me*."

Sonny laughed and leaned back on the wall. "That's what I suggested in the first place. I said we could do it on Skype, but you mumbled some shit about being a technophobe."

Levi winced. That *did* kind of sound like him. He could

work a cell phone and his laptop for basic Internet browsing, but the world of social networking had passed him by. "Okay, how about I do it, and you tell me where you think I'm going wrong?"

Sonny shrugged. "Whatever you want."

The exchange should've been strange, or at the very least awkward, but it wasn't. Levi hadn't filmed with Sonny, but they shared the same lack of inhibition that came with the job. Though it was unchartered territory, agreeing to play with his own ass while a virtual stranger looked on felt perversely normal.

He reached for the waistband of his sweatpants, eager to get the ordeal over with. Sonny stopped him. "Really? In here? Don't you want to at least watch some dirty movie first? Get yourself in the mood?"

"In the mood? What the fuck? Are you a chick or something?"

"Dude, you don't want to go there for the first time without a good leadoff. Do you want me to suck you off?"

"What? No!"

"You're kinda coy for a hard-core porn star. It's cute."

"You're not touching me, Valentine."

Sonny laughed, but Levi frowned, disconcerted that it seemed to be obvious that he'd never touched himself that way before.

"Oh, please." Sonny pulled his shirt off and tossed it on the floor. "I don't need to touch you to make you hard."

Levi snickered, more intrigued than he cared to admit, even to himself—a sensation that made the irritation of Sonny cluttering up his neat and ordered home all too easy to ignore. "That a fact?"

"Uh-huh. With that body and the beard, you look like that dude from 300, all ripped and angry. If I close my eyes, I can pretend you're Gerard Butler and dance you up a storm. By the time I'm done, you'll be ready for anything."

Levi ran his gaze over Sonny's bare torso. Like his Blue Boy promo shots promised, he was compact, muscular, and subtly defined in all the right places. His tattooed skin was smooth and flawless, the kind of skin Levi dreamed about when he allowed his imagination to get away from him. He got the feeling he was playing right into Sonny's hands, but he didn't care. "Prove it."

"Where's your stereo?"

Levi pointed to a shelf an arm's length away. Sonny pressed Play on the CD player without looking to see what it contained. The opening chords of "Faded" filtered out of the speakers. Levi raised an eyebrow, pretty sure he knew where this was headed. "You're gonna go-go dance to Ben Harper?"

"No, I'm just gonna dance." Sonny backed him into the wall, caging him with his arms before he really knew what was happening. For a moment, Levi thought Sonny was going to kiss him, until he ducked his head and warm air rushed over his ear. "Stay still."

"Or what?"

"Do it, Ramone."

Levi leaned back against the wall. The music washed over him. He'd owned the album for over a decade. The deep, soulful baseline was already entrenched in his bones, but the sensation of Sonny's lithe, agile body dancing around him was new. Levi watched him through hooded eyes, taking in each sensual roll of his hips, feeling the warmth of his skin a hair's breadth away. He'd watched the dancers at the club before, seen them lose themselves in the rhythm of the beat and the charged heat of the club, but he'd never seen anyone dance like Sonny.

Never felt the way he felt as he watched Sonny dance only for him.

Sonny moved closer, ghosting his open mouth over Levi's chest. Levi felt his blood heat up and his heart thud against his rib cage. Sonny tugged at the waistband of Levi's sweatpants. They fell to the floor, revealing his already half-hard cock. Sonny smirked, and Levi shivered, anticipation teasing his skin.

"Commando?" Sonny tilted his head to one side. "You're such a porn star, Ramone."

Levi kicked the pants aside, leaving himself completely bare. "So?"

Sonny turned away without answer, spinning so his back faced Levi. Levi sucked in a breath, absorbing the spicy, musky scent of Sonny. His cock was an inch away from Sonny's denim-covered ass as Sonny continued his devilish dance in front of him. He watched his dick strain forward unbidden, desperate to feel the friction of the rough denim. It took all the control he possessed not to lunge forward and yank Sonny back into his arms.

He pictured what he would do as Sonny arched his back, tempting him with the smooth skin of his neck, all the while keeping himself just out of reach. Pictured himself undoing Sonny's jeans, sliding them over his hips, and bending him over the...

Sonny spun around, slamming his palms into the wall either side of Levi's head. "Well, look at that. Looks like I was right about you. Where's your bathroom?"

Levi took a deep and measured breath, the lust-filled haze dispersing a little and reminding him of the real purpose of Sonny's presence. "Second door on the right."

"Lead the way."

He did as he was told, leading Sonny to his bathroom. Sonny glanced around, dropping the bag he'd retrieved on the countertop. He ran his fingertip around the rim of the basin. "Your place sure is clean for a Neanderthal."

"What's wrong with clean?"

Sonny held up his hands. "Nothing. I like clean. Clean is good. Are you ready?"

Levi glanced down at his hard cock in answer. Sonny sighed. "You still don't get it, do you? This isn't about that. It's an act of faith, which is why you need to do it yourself first. This isn't like losing your virginity to someone you really love, someone you trust."

"All right, quit the preachin' already. Let's get this over with." Levi rolled his eyes. He didn't believe in any of those things—faith, love, trust. He must've once, but where had it got him? Naked in his bathroom taking lessons from a guy he couldn't stand on how to fuck himself in the ass. Yeah, life was good.

"Put your foot up on something."

Levi looked around, taken aback by Sonny's sharp order. There was a shelf beneath the sink. He placed the ball of his foot on the very edge. "Like this?"

"Legs wider."

He widened his legs. "Better?"

"You'll do," Sonny said. "Watching yourself in the mirror too? That's pretty hot."

Levi bit his tongue and resisted the urge to move away from the bathroom mirror. Staring at his own face wasn't something he'd considered, and he found the notion mildly horrifying. The feeling increased as Sonny reached for his bag and set out three different types of lube. Within the bag was an array of sex toys and dildos. Levi tensed, and not in a good way. Some of them looked *huge*.

"Don't worry, they're not all for you."

"I'm not worried." Levi reached for the first tube of lube without checking the label.

"Vanilla? Interesting choice, considering the context."

"Shut up." He picked up the lube and put it down again, feeling Sonny's eyes on him as he tried not to hyperventilate.

Get a grip, damn it. It's only your own fucking finger.

Sonny moved. Suddenly, he was behind Levi, reaching

around him for the lube. Though he left an inch between them, Levi could feel the warmth of him all over his bare skin. Sonny squeezed lube onto his own hand and applied it to Levi's fingers. He nudged Levi's legs farther apart with his knees. "Come on, I'll show you. Just say if you need to stop."

"I can do it," Levi murmured, as much to himself as to Sonny. He pulled his hand from Sonny's grasp and reached around, his slick fingers grazing his hip and leaving a trail of cool lube on his skin.

Sonny stepped away, heeding his unspoken request for some personal space. He hopped up onto the counter in a fluid movement that had Levi captivated before he returned to the task at hand.

Levi slid his hand over his ass and between the curves of muscle, letting the tip of his middle finger circle his entrance. He tensed, unused to the sensation. On occasion, whoever he was fucking would venture their hand back that way, led astray during a blowjob, but he always pulled them up before they got *that* far. He pressed, resisting the urge to jerk away from the pressure. The tip of his finger slipped inside. He gasped; he couldn't help it. It didn't hurt, but it felt too alien to bear.

"Keep going."

Sonny's voice was low, soothing almost. Levi closed his eyes and pushed his finger in as far as he could reach, sweeping it around. He moaned and dropped his head to his chest, feeling sweat seep out of his skin as the burning stretch spread through his body. It was an odd feeling. He lost himself to it for a time, consumed by the sensation, and jumped when Sonny spoke again.

"Add another."

"What?"

"Hey, hey, it's okay. Breathe out as you add the second finger. It will probably hurt a bit, but not for long. Hold still and breathe. It'll pass. It gets easier. I promise."

Sonny touched his shoulder, but Levi couldn't face looking up at him. He eased a second finger into his body, groaning again, but this time, less about feeling and more about pain. He clenched his teeth, panting for breath, struggling to get ahold of himself. "Damn." The oath was whispered.

Sonny touched his shoulder again. "Breathe. It'll feel good soon. I promise."

Levi bowed his head once more, letting his eyes fall closed. He'd had his fingers, his cock, and his tongue inside too many men to count, but it was startling to feel the smooth, tight heat of his own body clamped around his fingers. Despite Sonny's assurances, it didn't feel good, at least not yet, but after a time, it didn't feel *bad* anymore either. It felt...uncomfortable. He squirmed.

"Relax. The worst is over."

Yeah, for now. Levi's mind was full of the huge variety of sex toys Sonny had stashed in his bag. This time it was his own fingers, but next time, and the time after that, and Rex's...

Sonny slid off the countertop. A warm, strong hand closed around his wrist, moving the two fingers he had inside himself in a tentative, undulating circle. Levi grunted, gripping the counter with his free hand. Sonny steadied him, rubbing a soothing counterpoint into his back. "Stop thinking about it so much. Concentrate on your dick. It likes it, even if you don't."

Levi glanced down. He'd forgotten all about his cock, but sure enough, it was still hard, jutting out from his body and aching for some attention. Sonny scratched short, blunt nails down the length of Levi back. Gooseflesh covered him. He'd always had a thing for scratching. It drove him wild, sending wicked shivers down his spine. He craved the sensation of Sonny's perfect white teeth digging into his sensitive flesh.

What the hell? Where did that come from?

He swayed, his equilibrium rocked. He steadied himself on the counter. Sweat trickled down his chest, and steam misted the mirror. He was used to the vague physical attraction he had to the models he worked with, but he'd never felt anything like the deep-rooted yearning he had for Sonny in that moment. He'd never felt like that for any man, especially a man who'd barely laid a hand on him.

Sonny guided his fingers in a slow, pulsing rhythm. "Touch your dick."

"No." Levi shuddered, gritting his teeth. There was a part of him that longed to reach for his aching cock, but a bigger part of him was terrified, though of what, he wasn't quite sure.

Behind him, Sonny chuckled. "If you don't, I will. Go on. You know you want to."

Levi let go of the counter and gripped his cock. "Fucking sadist," he ground out. "You—" He cut off as Sonny matched the tentative strokes with the probing, sweeping rhythm of his fingers in his ass. He gasped, letting out a sound he hardly recognized as coming from him. "*Fuck!*"

"That's it," Sonny said. "Forget everything else. Let it happen."

Levi fought it; he fought it all—fought for breath, fought Sonny's invisible hold over him, fought the brutal, double-edged pleasure of his fingers and hand working together, fought the overheating rush of his impending orgasm.

Then it was too late. Sonny twisted his wrist, guiding Levi's fingers to brush the bundle of nerves deep inside him he'd often thought was a myth, and he released with a low and guttural cry.

He came back into himself, startled to find the sun had set while they'd been in the bathroom, and the full moon high in the sky had cast an eerie light over the apartment. Beneath the pounding of his blood in his ears, he could still hear the faint strains of Ben Harper coming from the living room. Despite himself, he laughed a weak and breathless laugh. "I'm gonna burn that CD."

Sonny guided Levi's fingers from his ass, relinquished his grip on Levi's wrist, and stepped away. "No, you won't."

Levi placed both hands on the countertop. Despite the residual heat of his dizzying orgasm, he felt chilled without the warmth of Sonny behind him. "Prove it."

Sonny laughed and scraped his nails down Levi's back one last time. "I think I've proved you wrong enough for one night."

CHAPTER SEVEN

Another late-summer evening, and another trip to the grocery store. Some days, it seemed to Levi that he did nothing but work, sleep, work some more, and take a detour on his way home to buy shit he'd run out of.

He wandered through the aisles, paying little attention to the boxes and packets he threw in his cart, until he came to the fresh-food section. Chicken, vegetables, fruit. Levi liked to eat well. It was cheaper, and though sugared breakfast cereals were his guilty pleasure, he knew he functioned better on good home cooking.

There was a line at the checkout. He bounced on the balls of his feet. It had been a long day, and he was tired, but he felt antsy, like there was something he'd forgotten to do.

The sensation was annoying, and it had been since it first appeared the morning after his loaded encounter with Sonny. He'd expected his ass to be sore, but it wasn't. In fact his body had borne no hangover from the night before at all. Instead it was his mind. He'd dreamed of Sonny that night and every night since, and in waking hours, the kid was on his mind any moment he wasn't distracted by work.

Like now. A shiver passed through him, and he let his mind

drift back to the most bizarre sexual experience of his whole life. It had been a week ago, but he was still reeling. The sensation of having something, *anything*, inside him that way blew his mind, but it wasn't the earth-shattering orgasm that lingered, the bone-shaking climax that left him weak at the knees. No. Instead, each time he closed his eyes, all he could feel was the hovering warmth of Sonny's body a heartbeat behind him and his nails... *fuck*, the scrape of his nails on Levi's skin.

He paid for his goods and began the short schlep back to his apartment. He was halfway home when he heard a chuckle behind him.

"Man, you are such a cliché."

Levi spun around. Sonny stood behind him, looking tired, slightly disheveled, and...gorgeous. "Cliché? How so?"

Sonny stepped closer and gestured for Levi to lower the stuffed paper bag in his arms. "Worked all day, hit the gym, and now home alone with what? Frozen burritos and beer?"

Levi rolled his eyes. "Guess again, dickhead," he drawled, though Sonny was right about the passage of his day and the beer. "Do I look like a guy that eats frozen burritos?"

"You don't want me to tell you what you look like." Sonny looked up from peering into the grocery bag, and Levi became aware of how close he was, of how he was leaning down, stretching his neck to get even closer.

Sonny licked his lips.

Levi swallowed and straightened, putting a respectable distance between them. "What are you doin' out here? Stalking me?"

"Dream on, Ramone. How've you been? Have you done any more prep?"

Levi glanced around and felt his face flush. He'd spent too much time thinking about their last meeting, but when privacy allowed, those thoughts ended with him taking himself in hand and scrupulously avoiding his ass. "A bit."

"Liar."

Sonny's tone was as hard to read as the rest of him. There was no accusation and for once no hint of mocking, but the single word felt loaded with heat.

Levi stared him down, shifting the grocery bag from one arm to the other, but Sonny was unfazed, like they met up like this all the time. Levi let out a growly whoosh of air. "Damn it. What the fuck do you *want*?"

Sonny raised an eyebrow. "Dude, I was saying hello. You're the one with a bug in his ass."

The pun made Sonny laugh, but Levi was less than amused. "All right, kid. You've made your point, okay? I'm beat. I'm going home."

He started to turn away, but Sonny caught his arm. "You can't ignore this. I told you before, it's gonna rip you up if you're not ready."

Levi waited for a couple of pedestrians to pass before he wrenched his arm from Sonny's grasp. "I'm not ignoring it. I just don't want to get into it on the fuckin' street."

Sonny shrugged, the gesture benign and casual. Then he moved like a snake, shoving Levi and catching him off balance. Levi stumbled backward and collided with the side of a building, and before he could recover, Sonny grabbed his hand and pulled him into a darkly shadowed alleyway.

Levi was taller than Sonny, and heavier. He could've put him down with a flick of his wrist, but for some reason he couldn't bring himself to fight back. He leaned on the bricks behind him and glared at Sonny. "You gonna make me fuck myself right here, right now?"

Sonny stood, relaxed and passive, his arms folded across his chest. "What if I did? Think you could do it? How do you think it would feel to ram dry fingers inside yourself? Think about it, Levi. Think about the burn and the sensation of being torn apart, 'cause that's how it's gonna feel if you don't hear what I'm saying."

Levi stared at him, his breathing hitched and his dick uncomfortably hard in his jeans. He heard Sonny loud and clear. How could he not? Sonny had been saying the same thing since they'd crossed paths in Jon's office. It was a warning, nothing more, so why the damned boner? Why did he want to punch Sonny in the face? And why did he want nothing more than to kiss the ever-loving shit out of him?

"Fine." The word came out as a growl. "Have it your fuckin' way. You wanna do this? Let's do it."

Sonny shrugged again, and a hint of a smirk ghosted over his features. "Lead the way."

Levi stomped home with Sonny in tow. Once inside his apartment, he dropped the grocery bag on the kitchen counter and pulled his shirt over his head. He left the rest of his clothes littering the hardwood floor and walked naked to the bathroom without looking to see if Sonny followed.

He opened the bathroom cabinet, searching for lube. Sonny appeared in the mirror behind him, shirtless and waving the same bottle they'd used before. "Not in here. Let's change it up."

Change it up. Those words would haunt Levi to an early grave. He shut the cabinet with a bang and twisted to face Sonny. "Where?"

"The couch. You should be comfortable, and this time I want you to look at me."

Sonny turned on his heel and walked away. Levi followed him back to the living room and saw his bag of tricks already spread out on the coffee table. "What, do you, like, carry that crap around with you?"

Sonny snorted and tossed the lube down. "Maybe, or maybe I was on my way here when you stepped out of the store looking all frustrated and shit."

"I'm not frustrated."

"We'll see. Sit."

Levi didn't move. His dick was still half-hard from whatever had passed between them in the alleyway, but there was still a part of him—a fading, mutinous part—that couldn't quite believe what he was doing. "What are *you* going to do?"

"What do you want me to do?"

"Get the fuck out."

"Nice try." Sonny pushed the coffee table back with his foot. "When this happens for real, there's going to be a room full of people staring at you, *including* me. Time to get used to it."

"Then you need to get naked." Levi eyed the out-of-place coffee table. It didn't feel right shoved up against the wall. It was crooked, and the angle was weird. "You'll be naked then, right?"

Sonny unbuttoned his jeans and shimmied them down his dancer's hips. "I'll lose the pants. I'll get naked next time. Maybe."

Next time? Levi swallowed a groan, tore his gaze from Sonny's muscular thighs, and moved to the couch. "Let's get this over with."

Sonny sat cross-legged on the floor, equidistant from the coffee table and the couch. He motioned for Levi to sit. "Lean back, and lift your leg. That's it. Like that."

Levi obeyed. He leaned back on the big couch and raised his right leg, letting it fall to the side. "Wanna pass me some lube?"

"Not yet. You're not even hard."

Levi rolled his eyes but took himself in hand anyway. He wanted to close his eyes, to let his mind wander as he worked himself up, but it occurred to him that there was little point. If he closed his eyes, he'd only see Sonny, and Sonny was right in front of him.

"What are you thinking about?"

Levi shifted, adjusting his hips as blood pumped into his

cock. "Why don't you tell me what to think about? You've told me everything else."

"You're a free man, Levi. I'm just here to help."

Free man. If only he knew. "Okay, give me some ideas, then. You think I'm a Neanderthal, right? Inspire me to be different."

Sonny hummed. "Inspire you, huh? I guess I need to figure out what you need the most first."

"You mean, apart from this?" Levi felt his heart quicken as he tightened his grip on his cock, and he began to relax into the natural rhythm of pleasuring himself.

"You'll get through it physically, Levi. Don't misunderstand what we're doing here."

Levi forced his eyes to stay open and quirked an eyebrow. "Thought you were trying to keep me whole?"

"I am."

Sonny uncrossed his legs and stretched them out in front of him. His foot came to rest millimeters away from Levi's, and Levi could feel the heat of him...could almost hear the blood pumping through his body. He let his gaze travel up Sonny's sinewy leg and to his tight underwear that did nothing to hide the bulge of his cock.

Levi swallowed. "Where will you be when I'm getting fucked?"

"Depends." Sonny reclaimed his legs and rose on his knees, leaning forward and scrutinizing as Levi passed his hand over his dick. "Close your eyes and picture it. Where do you want me to be?"

Levi closed his eyes, but he couldn't bring himself to picture Rex and his monster cock driving in and out of him. Instead, he pictured Sonny. Pictured Sonny straddling his chest and sliding his dick in and out of Levi's mouth...

Levi tapped his lips with the index finger of his free hand. "Here. I want you here."

He couldn't see Sonny's response, but he heard movement

and then felt the warmth of Sonny's body far closer than it had been before. The click of a lube bottle reached his ears, and he sucked in a breath as the cool liquid dripped onto his cock and became caught up in the sweeping strokes of his fist.

Damn. It wasn't vanilla this time; it was spiced with cinnamon and made his cock tingle in just the right way. He couldn't help it. He dropped his head to the back of the couch and moaned.

Sonny hummed too, and Levi could feel the heat of his body close to his face. He leaned forward, and his lips brushed over smooth skin. His chest? His neck? His arm? He couldn't tell, and when he opened his eyes, Sonny was gone—gone from his line of sight, at least.

Levi looked down. His rhythm had faltered while Sonny had been on the couch beside him, but he picked it up in earnest now, watching, oddly fascinated, as Sonny knelt between Levi's legs and held out his hand.

Sonny coated Levi's fingers with the tingly lube. "Close your eyes again. Close your eyes and remember how good it felt last time."

One finger, and then two. With Sonny guiding him, it felt even better than last time. Better, hotter, more intense. He rolled his hips to counter the warring sensations in his body—his dick pumping in and out of his lube-slicked fist, and his fingers stretching his ass. It felt right. It felt wrong. It felt fucking *amazing*.

Sweat beaded his chest. He trembled, let out a shaky breath, and his balls tightened, the first stirrings of orgasm already finding purchase deep in his belly. He couldn't take much of this.

Sonny nipped the inside of his quivering thigh. "Not yet, Ramone. Add another finger."

Levi's eyes flew open—despite his best efforts to resist Sonny's instructions, at some point, they'd drifted shut. Add another? Three fingers? No fucking way. He met Sonny's gaze, and Sonny grinned, but it wasn't his usual devious smirk. It was something else, something softer that made Levi's chest feel tight.

He slid a third finger into himself. It hurt. He bit down on his lip and thrashed his head from side to side. Too much, too much. He needed to grab something, anything, to hold himself down. "No...I..."

Sonny scrambled up the couch and stilled his head with gentle hands. "Shh." His voice was low, and his breath washed over Levi's ear. "I've got you."

He took Levi's hand from his cock, replacing it with his own and leaving Levi free to fling his arm over his head and grip the back of the couch.

Levi hid his face in his arm, his groan pained and strangled. "*Fuck*. Fuck, fuck, fuck."

"Shh," Sonny said again. "Focus on me."

Sonny bent his neck and enveloped Levi's dick in his mouth with a suction far gentler than any blowjob he'd ever received.

Levi closed his eyes and absorbed the languid, almost teasing sensations. He shuddered. His limbs grew soft, and his bones sank into the couch. Sonny nudged Levi's wrist with his free hand, and following the silent cue, Levi slowly rolled the three fingers he still held inside himself.

The effect was instant. He let his head fall back and jutted his hips forward, fucking himself in Sonny's mouth and then back onto his fingers. Heat roared through his veins. He felt hot, too hot, hotter than he'd ever been, and his mind swam. Sonny scraped his teeth slowly up Levi's shaft, and he was undone.

"Gonna come. Fuck."

He reached down to pull Sonny from him, but Sonny resisted. It was too late. Release hit him, and his whole world became nothing but a lightning bolt of pure, carnal pleasure. He cried out and came in Sonny's mouth.

CHAPTER EIGHT

It took a while for Levi to return to earth. He lay still, his arm hiding his face as he fought for breath. Until Sonny climbed up his body and straddled him, coaxing Levi gently to look at him. Levi opened his eyes, feeling Sonny's cotton-covered erection digging into his belly. He reached for it, but Sonny batted his hands away.

"Next time. You okay?"

"Think so." Levi nodded and cast his gaze around the room. Sonny's vast array of toys was still laid out on the coffee table. He wondered when they were going to use them, and the usual flicker of apprehension was strangely absent. "I'm fuckin' starved. Want some dinner?"

Sonny eyed him for a moment, then slid off him and reached for his jeans. "Depends. What have you got? Potpies or something?"

And like that, the spell was broken. Levi searched the room and found his discarded sweats in a heap by the door to the hall. He got up and pulled them on, feeling exhausted, exhilarated, and eerily calm all rolled into one.

He felt Sonny's gaze on him as he walked to the kitchen

area and called over his shoulder, "Stop with all this junk-food talk. Come sit yerself down and see what a real man cooks."

Sonny didn't follow right away. Levi heard water running and figured he was cleaning up. Levi washed his hands and set to work cooking the chicken he'd picked up at the store.

He was throwing the dish of enchiladas into the oven when Sonny reappeared a little while later. The evening had grown dark while they'd been steaming up the living room windows, and with the cabinet spotlights casting a warm glow over the kitchen, he looked tousled and beautiful.

Levi turned away and reached for some salad leaves. "You workin' at Silver tonight?"

Sonny slid onto a kitchen stool. "Maybe. There's a spot for me if I want it."

Levi glanced at the clock. It was after nine, but he knew some of the dancers didn't go onstage until after midnight. "You've got time to get some food in your belly, then. It won't be long."

Sonny chuckled. "Didn't know you cared."

"You don't know everything, kid."

Sonny made a noncommittal noise but said no more. Levi opened the fridge and passed a beer across the counter, but found he couldn't think of anything to say either. In the end, a companionable silence settled over them.

It wasn't as awkward as it could've been. Sonny usually ran his mouth like a damned chick, but he seemed tired, subdued almost—for Sonny, at least. Levi remembered his disheveled appearance when they'd crossed paths on the street. "Long day?"

Sonny glanced up, his surprise clear before he schooled his expression. "Not really. Too much to do, you know? Never seems to stop."

"I know that feeling." Levi retrieved the salad dressing from the cupboard and set it on the counter. "Maybe you should call it a day and hit the sack."

"Nah. The night is young. I might go out before I hit the club."

Levi let it go. He was familiar with the concept of working all day and partying all night, though it had been a while. Besides, if Sonny was tired, that was his problem. It wasn't like they were friends.

"Can I ask you something?"

Levi dumped some leftover corn bread on the counter. "As long as it's not about taking it up the ass. I've had enough of that shit for one night."

Sonny grinned, and the fatigue on his face faded like it hadn't been there at all. The effect was startling, and Levi found he had to look away.

"You're exclusive to Blue Boy, right?"

"I am these days." Levi swallowed a mouthful of beer. "Why do you ask?"

Sonny shrugged. "Some guy pulled me offstage a few nights ago. Said he was from Sizzler's and offered me some work. Has that happened to you?"

"Not for a while, but I'm getting on a bit now. Think they've figured out I'm not worth the hassle anymore." Levi put the last of the salad into the bowl and came to sit opposite Sonny. "You should tell Jon. He won't like it, but he'll be pissed if he thinks you're considering it behind his back."

It was true. Back in the day, Jon had been tolerant of Levi testing the waters with other studios—perhaps because he knew Levi didn't have the stomach for the cutthroat world of real hard-core porn—but things had changed. Like every other industry, adult entertainment was losing money, and Jon liked to keep his house in order.

"I told the guy no anyway. I like working at Blue Boy. It's hard-core, but it's got a depth to it, you know?"

Levi snorted. "If you say so."

"Why do you do porn?"

Levi paused. Though it was a question he'd heard before, it caught him off guard. "Same as you, I guess. I started off as a barman at Silver when Jon approached me to do some still shots. He offered me a bunch of cash to take things further, and at the time I needed the money. Still do."

"There's other ways to make money."

"So why do *you* do it?"

Sonny stretched his arm over his shoulder and scratched his back. "I started dancing because I love it, and the rest seemed to come naturally. I like it. It's interesting, and safer than picking up guys in clubs."

"A safe way of being promiscuous, huh?"

"If you like." Sonny didn't seem offended. In fact, his gaze turned shrewd and introspective. "I like reading between the lines too. Every scene has a story, Levi, even yours. Especially yours. You're this silent stoic dude until you start fucking someone. Then this haze comes over your eyes, like you're looking for relief or something."

"Relief from what?"

Sonny shrugged. "Only you know that, and that's my point. Most of us become someone else on-screen, even in the unscripted scenes, but you don't. You talk the talk, but the only person you're hiding from is yourself."

The oven timer beeped before Levi could respond. Bemused, he turned and pulled the sizzling dish from the oven, and when he set it down in front of Sonny, the light in the other man's eyes banished all thoughts of porn from his mind.

Levi was an old Southern mama at heart with his daddy's Puerto Rican blood, and he got a kick out of feeding folk real food. Even annoying folk like Sonny. He got a big-assed spoon and pushed a loaded plate Sonny's way. "Eat up."

Sonny raised an eyebrow and took a bite. "Wow. There really is more to you than your big dick."

Levi held his tongue. The comment was flippant and meant nothing, but it grated on him. Sometimes viewers—fans—came up to him on the street, and it was clear they thought there was nothing to him but porn either. It didn't usually bother him, but with Sonny, it kind of did. He took a bite of his own food and felt the pleasurable burn, not too dissimilar to the tingle of the lube, spread down his throat, and he chanced a glance at Sonny. "Not too spicy for you?"

Sonny coughed and took a long pull on his beer. A flush crept up his neck, and Levi grinned. Seemed the kid wasn't as tough as he liked to make out.

"Have some cucumber to cool it down. Have some other veg as well. It's good for you."

Sonny reached for the salad and rolled his eyes. "Man, you're worse than my mom."

Levi smiled, feeling content, and the sensation remained until Sonny cleared his plate and got up to leave.

He felt conflicted as he walked Sonny to the door. A sense of disappointment warred with relief that yet another bizarre encounter had come to an end.

Sonny opened the door and put his bag on his back. "So... thanks for dinner. Guess I should jump you on the street more often."

"Try it."

Sonny smirked and turned to go, but Levi's hand shot out before he could stop it.

He caught Sonny's sleeve and tugged him back. Their evening together had felt like a distorted date, turned upside down and shaken about for good measure. His mind and body felt out of whack, and it didn't seem strange to pull Sonny back and press his lips to the very center of Sonny's forehead.

"Good night, kid."

CHAPTER NINE

The plate hit the wall, fragmenting into tiny, jagged pieces. Levi dodged Bella's line of fire. "I'm not stealing your money, B. I put the cash in your account this morning. Just write the damn check."

"How do I know you're not after your father's life insurance again?" Bella looked around for another missile, her gaze clouded and bloodshot. "You'd bleed me dry if I let you."

"What life insurance?" His voice was low, patient almost, belying the fury simmering in his veins. "Dad's been dead eight years, and you squandered every cent he left before he was even cold."

Bella reached for her drink, stumbling over her own feet, knocking her frail shoulder against the kitchen door frame. Levi watched, his anger gone. This was his fault. He knew better than to visit her so late in the day.

"I'm sick of this." Bella took a long, deep drink of her precious gin, clutching it to her chest like it was her last prized possession. Perhaps it was. "You come in here whenever you damn feel like it and take my money. How am I supposed to live? Tell me that. How am I supposed to live like this?"

"You're not living, B. You're an old drunk."

Levi ventured away from the shelter of the kitchen cabinets, reaching again for Bella's much-abused checkbook. It was probably reckless to move so soon, but he'd lost the inclination to care. His cell phone vibrated in his pocket. He retrieved it, reading the message with half an eye on Bella, who seemed to have slipped into a daze.

Step 3 complete?—S

Levi bit his lip, picturing the small plug Sonny had left in his bathroom after their third...*date*. The plug was bigger than his fingers, wider, and the idea was that he jack off with it inside him, but it had been a week since he'd last seen Sonny, and he hadn't touched it. Couldn't. Didn't want to without Sonny to guide him, and perhaps even then, didn't want to slide it inside his body himself.

He'd pictured it a few times—standing, stretched and open with Sonny behind him, letting Sonny ease the plug inside him. He'd dreamed of it once too, before the dream morphed into something else, and he woke, sweating and desperate for a sensation he'd never dared imagine before.

And therein lay the problem. Though he was more terrified than he'd ever admit, his encounters with Sonny had left a huge part of him curious as to what it would feel like to have another man inside him.

Another man. Another man? Or Sonny? Each time Levi said good-bye to him and stumbled into the shower, he wasn't quite sure. He found Sonny insanely attractive—of that, there was no doubt—but he was... Well, he was still *Sonny*. Still annoying, precocious, and impossible to read.

After the scene, they'd probably go another few years without exchanging a word.

Fine by me, he thought to himself, but a separate, more realistic side of his brain protested. *Oh, yeah? So why the hell do you miss the little shit when he's not there?*

Damn.

His cell phone beeped again. He glanced down, happy to block out the irritating voice in his head. He'd never had another man on his mind the way Sonny seemed to occupy his thoughts.

Don't ignore me, Ramone. Get it done—S

He deleted both messages and shoved his phone in his pocket. Step three? Nope. The best he could do was go to sleep every night and dream about smooth, tattooed skin that was just out of reach.

Bella laughed. The sound was abrupt and harsh, startling him out of his sordid daydreams. "Why do you need my money, anyway? Are you in trouble?"

Levi sighed. "The payment on that loan you took out last year is due at the end of the week. I need to pay it."

"So pay it."

No chance. He'd made that mistake before—paying her bills from his own account. Six months later, a glitch in paperwork had led the debt collectors right to his door. It took him weeks to prove he hadn't accepted responsibility for Bella's debts. He slid the checkbook across the kitchen counter. "No, you need to do it. The money's there. Write the check."

Bella reached for the checkbook, closed her skeletal fingers around it, and tossed it away. "No. You're not having my money."

Levi retrieved the checkbook from the dirty kitchen floor, picked up a pen, and filled out the check. It crossed his mind to forge Bella's signature and be on his way, but he couldn't do it. He held out the book once more. "Just sign it, B. Please?"

For a brief, stupid moment, he thought he'd got through to her. Thought she was going to comply. But it wasn't to be. Bella lashed out, ignoring his outstretched hand and instead picking up the thin, glass work-top protector. Levi watched, frozen to his spot as she hurled it across the kitchen. It shattered on impact with his raised arm, chest, and abdomen.

"No! What happened to my boy, Levi? What have you done

with him? All you do is take from me. You were my sweet little boy, and now you're just fucking like him!"

Levi lowered his bleeding arm. Folded the check into a tiny square and shoved it into his back pocket. He looked down at his stomach. A small shard of glass protruded at a sickening angle. He pulled it out, watching with morbid fascination as a faint stream of blood oozed through his T-shirt.

He set the bloody glass shard on the countertop. Opened a cabinet, bent over, and reached for the dustpan. The picture frame caught him on the side of his head, a sharp, glancing blow that left him dizzy.

Dizzy and furious.

He flew across the room and backed Bella into the wall. Caged in his arms, she looked like a tiny, wizened old bird, but he knew better. He pried the small paring knife from her hands and dropped it to the floor. It wasn't the first time she'd come at him with a blade, so drunk she mistook him for his father one minute, an intruder the next.

Somehow, he always managed to convince himself it wasn't him she wanted to hurt.

"Stop it," he said.

Bella glared, her eyes still distant and somewhere else. "You're just like him."

"I am him. It's me, Levi."

The back door opened. Old Mr. Draper stepped in, his hands raised in a placating gesture and his eyes fixed on Bella. Levi wondered how much he'd heard before he'd made his move. The old man had put himself between them more times than Levi could count. "Everything all right in here, folks?"

Mr. Draper moved forward, maneuvering around the broken glass and shattered crockery. He reached Levi's side and put a hand on his arm. "Step away, son. You're bleeding. Your momma will be fine with me a minute."

Levi lowered his arms. Warmth trickled down the side of his

face. More blood. *Great.* He drifted to the sink and rinsed the gash in his forearm under the tap. Behind him, he could hear Mr. Draper murmuring to Bella in his soothing voice. The old dude could charm the birds from the trees, but it wasn't working today.

"No," Bella said, her voice rising again. "No, no, no. I don't care who he thinks he is, he's not having my money."

"He's not taking your money, Bella, darlin'. That's Levi, your boy. He's taking care of you."

Bella snorted in a way that belied her petite, feminine frame. "He takes care of no one but himself. All he cares about are his Nancy fairy boys, just like his dad."

Levi spun around, his wounds forgotten. "What did you say?"

"Levi..." Mr. Draper moved between them. "She doesn't know what she's saying. Leave it. Go home. I'll clean up here."

Levi stared hard at Bella. Often when she lost her mind, it was obvious in her face. Her eyes would become vacant, her voice distant. Even when she screamed in his face, he knew she couldn't really see him. She didn't look like that now. Though clouded by alcohol, her eyes were clear. Clear, evil, and fixed on him. "What did you say?" he repeated lowly. "You've been saying it all damn night. Finish what you started."

"What happened to you, Levi?" Bella shook her head. "You loved football and wrestling. Rock music and beer. You were my big, strong boy. What happened to you? He died, goddamn it, and yet he's all I can see."

"Like him? What? Fucking miserable? B, if that's what you want, you've succeeded, okay? Let it go."

"No. Don't give me that. You're not miserable. You're proud of what you are. I can see it in you. Don't think I can't. You're everything he wanted to be. I can even smell it. I can smell *him*, you dirty faggot bitch. I wish you'd never been born."

Levi felt like a semitruck had driven into his chest. He'd

never been sure Bella knew he was gay, but clearly she did. What the fuck was she trying to say? That his father had been gay too? That he'd killed himself rather than live with the shame? Killed himself rather than face her hate? He stepped forward, a rage long forgotten gripping him and surging through his veins.

Mr. Draper met him halfway, his old, wrinkled arms unyielding and strong. "Don't, son. You'll hate yourself in the morning. Go home. I'll take care of her."

Levi shook himself free. Took a step back. "Don't bother," he said, as much to himself as anyone else. "Leave her. Leave her to rot. I'm done."

"She hasn't banged you up this bad for a while. Why do you let her do it, man?"

Levi slid into AJ's truck with a heavy sigh, unsure of his answer. He could overpower Bella with one arm tied behind his back, yet somehow, she always managed to take a chunk out of him. Somehow, he didn't see it coming. Or perhaps he did, and he didn't care enough to move. Who knew? He didn't.

"Sorry for dragging you out of bed. They told me not to drive, and I left my cell phone there—"

AJ cut him off. "Dude, you've got six stitches in your arm, three in your head, and a mild concussion. I was always going to pick you up, no matter what. You shoulda called me from your momma's house. Don't worry about it."

Levi leaned back in his seat as AJ pulled the car onto the road. It was late—after midnight—but though he was exhausted, his mind was wide-awake. Bella's harsh, bitter voice echoed in his head.

"You're just like him. You dirty faggot bitch."

She'd said it before, but not for a long time. Was it really possible? He searched his memories—those faraway formative years in Texas, the chaotic childhood he'd spent on the wrong side of LA—searched for any clue that Bella's cruel ramblings could be true. But he found nothing. He'd loved his father like every son should, but in truth, he'd been a stranger. Ernesto Ramone had spent most of his time locked up in his backstreet chop shop, facilitating the gangs of car thieves and ringers from their neighborhood. Levi rarely saw him. It was only by chance that he'd inherited his trade and built it into something legitimate.

"You're everything he wanted to be."

Levi doubted that.

"Dude, wake up. You're home."

He opened his eyes and lifted his head from the window. AJ pulled the hand brake up and shifted in his seat. "You can crash at my place if you want. Sherri won't mind."

"Nah, it's okay. I'm pretty beat. I'll be out like a light."

AJ grinned. "That's what I'm worried about. That hot nurse said to keep an eye on you."

"What hot nurse?"

"The chick with the big... Oh, fuck it. Never mind. Even after all these years I forget you don't see that shit."

Levi had to smile at that. "Still? Really?"

"Hey, you know I'm cool with everything. I forget, is all. You're, well, you're you, you know? So I forget we don't see the world the same way."

"That don't make no sense."

AJ shrugged. "You know what I mean."

He didn't, he had no idea, but it didn't matter. AJ was the coolest motherfucker in town, and he'd had his back for years. "Thanks for picking me up, man. See you in the morning."

"Hey." AJ reached out and caught his arm. "What are you

gonna do? About your mom, I mean. This shit can't go on. It's going to kill you one way or another."

Levi looked down at his bandaged arm and felt the pulsing sting in his temple. AJ was right, of that there was no doubt, but the solution was less clear. There was every chance Bella's drunken ramblings were just that—ramblings—and their encounter today was no worse than many they'd had before. He'd driven away from her so sure he would never go back, but really, what had changed?

"Ask me tomorrow."

He got out of the car. His phone vibrated in his pocket. He pulled it out as AJ's taillights disappeared into the night.

Have it your way. 3 weeks, tough guy. Make them count—S

CHAPTER TEN

"So, how's tricks, man?"

Levi leaned back on the bar, absorbing the familiar, intoxicating atmosphere of Silver, enjoying the sight of the densely packed dance floor. Pounding music pulsated through his veins, the baseline so deep his bones buzzed with every beat. The club was dark and heady, lit only by scattered blue spotlights, and the air thick with the scent of sweat and sex. Cam was right. He did need to get out more.

He tipped back the last of his beer, nodded at the bare-chested barman for another. "Same old, same old."

It was mostly true. He didn't feel like explaining the costly broken bike ramp at the garage, or his healing wounds. Or that he hadn't checked on Bella for the best part of two weeks.

Cam raised an eyebrow, his sparkling green eyes bright with mischief. "Oh, yeah? Looking forward to your big orgy this weekend?"

"Thought you were worried about my mental well-being," Levi retorted drily. "You went all Dr. Phil on me last time I saw you."

Cam shifted on his bar stool and shrugged. "I was worried,

but you've had weeks to back out, so I figure you must actually want to do it. Am I right?"

Levi leaned over and swiped Cam's bourbon chaser, chugging it before Cam could protest. He didn't want to talk about the impending three-way. It was Thursday night. The shoot was scheduled for Saturday afternoon, leaving him less than forty-eight hours to get his game face on. The very thought made his eyes water. Despite Sonny's best efforts to persuade him, he hadn't managed to venture beyond having three fingers inside him, and even then, he suspected the unrivaled thrill he got from it had more to do with the heat of the body behind him than the sensation of his own fingers crammed in his ass. Besides, he hadn't seen Sonny for a while—Sonny had been busy, apparently—and his one attempt at flying solo had been an epic fail.

What are you going to do instead? Bend over and hope for the best?"

Yep, looked that way.

"So? What's the deal? Are you psyched, or what?"

"Or what."

Levi raised his middle finger but was saved from Cam's patented in-depth analysis by a pair of arms sliding around his waist—slim, pale arms that belonged to Kai, the blond he'd filmed with a few weeks before. "You didn't call."

Levi grinned in greeting, taking in the sight of Kai dressed only in a pair of tiny designer briefs. He stared with muted interest. Despite the charged air of the club and the grind of Kai's crotch on his thigh, away from the cameras, Kai did little for him. "Hey there, doll. How've you been?"

"You'd know if you'd called me."

Kai pressed his lithe body farther into Levi for emphasis. Levi played along, holding out his arms so Kai could clamber up onto his lap. "Why would I need to call you? You're right here."

"You're just about hot enough to get away with a line that

cheap." Kai reached for the hem of Levi's shirt and pulled it up to reveal Levi's stomach. He paused, his eyes fixed on Levi's face, gauging his reaction, then pulled it over his head.

"Only just? And yet here you are. What are you doing here, anyway? Workin'?" Levi had Kai's slight body pegged for a dancer, and he could think of no other reason for him to be running around the club in his underwear. It was a little early for that, even for a club as risqué as Silver.

"Yeah, actually, I'm supposed to be backstage now, but I saw you and thought I'd try and get a good-luck kiss from you. How am I doing?"

Beside Levi, Cam spluttered into his drink. It was well-known within the studio's inner circle that Levi didn't kiss—not on-screen, and not during any of the casual hookups that happened off set. Kai was new and clearly out of the loop. He was also a damned sight braver than when Levi saw him last. "Not so well with the kissing thing, sugar. It ain't my scene. Besides, what do you need luck for? Don't you get up on that stage three nights a week like the other dancers?"

"Hey, you can't blame a guy for trying. I'm dancing with Sonny tonight, so I'll have to ogle him instead."

"Yeah?" Levi leaned forward, his interest piqued. "Maybe I'd like to watch that. Which stage are you on?"

"That one." Kai pointed to the small stage farthest away from the bar, kissed Levi's cheek, and slid off his lap all in one smooth motion. "I gotta run. It was nice to see you. You're much nicer than everyone says you are."

He scampered away. Levi watched him go, but his mild irritation was tempered by the nagging anticipation brewing in his belly. Levi had taken to ignoring Sonny's texts and calls, hoping to put off the inevitable discomfort of taking his scene preparations forward, but there was no denying he'd missed him. Despite his stubborn silence, Sonny sent him a message of sarcastic encouragement every day, sometimes two. In recent days, he'd found himself waiting on those damned messages, his heart skipping a beat when Sonny's name flashed up on his cell phone screen.

"You've got an admirer there," Cam said, eyeing Kai's rapidly disappearing bare back. "That kid was drooling."

Levi shoved him. "Shut up. He's just hot for the scene we did. He'll get over it."

Cam snickered. "Oh, yeah? Why'd he run off with your shirt, then?"

"What?" Levi looked down where his shirt had been draped on his lap. It was gone. Damn. Not that it mattered. There weren't many guys running around in their underwear, but there were plenty without shirts.

The lights in the club dimmed, signaling the dancers' impending arrival onstage. Cam slid Levi a fresh beer. "Want to go out back and raid Jon's liquor cabinet?"

Smoke began to mist over the four small stages set out on the dance floor. Levi's gaze zeroed in on the one farthest from the bar. "Nah, I'm good here."

Flashing lights wrapped the stage in an eerie glow. A deep, sensual beat filled the club, buzzing through the floor and into Levi's veins. The rest of the club, even Cam beside him, faded away, and he could see nothing but the outline of the lithe, elegant body that teased his dreams. He was twenty feet from the stage, but as Sonny stepped out of the darkness, opened his arms, and let the rhythm of the music seep under his skin, the distance was nothing...as though Sonny was dancing only for him.

The music flowed like water, and Sonny moved with it as one, eyes closed, arms raised, hips undulating and smooth. Levi was entranced. *Sonny.* His strong, muscular thighs, shaped calves, and perfectly arched feet. Sonny danced alone, like he was the only soul in the world, and Levi couldn't look away.

Thud, thud, thud.

Levi's blood rushed in time with every pulsating contraction of Sonny's sculpted torso. His form was perfect, as if it had been carved from ethereal marble and inscribed by seraphic spirits. In his mind, Sonny was so close he could almost taste him...could smell him and feel the potent heat of the smooth skin he'd never touched.

Kai slunk onto the stage. Sonny's eyes opened, and his gaze became provocative and laced with a fire that rushed through the club like a blast from a furnace. He beckoned Kai to him, and they moved together, spinning an intoxicating and sinuous dance that left Levi breathless. For a moment that stretched so long Levi felt his nerves would snap, the two young dancers looked as though they would kiss—as though their lips would come together and finish the sensual game they'd started—but they didn't. Sonny closed his eyes and danced away, leaving every soul in the club dizzy and gasping for air.

Levi watched Sonny and Kai move together with an ironic ache in his heart. *Kai* was the one he'd been with—the one he'd pushed his cock inside and made his own. In the heady dark of the club, he knew without doubt that his whole world was upside down.

Damn you, Sonny Valentine.

A little while later, Levi pushed open the fire escape door and stepped outside. The night was balmy and sticky, but compared to the sweaty haze of the club, the light breeze was cooling against his overheated skin. He leaned his bare back against the wall. At some point, he would have to search out Kai and his stolen shirt, but not yet. Hunting him down would mean running into Sonny, and he wasn't quite sure he could face that.

At least, not until the calming night air reached *every* part of his body.

He chanced a rueful glance down at the telltale bulge in his jeans, the bulge that had appeared a heartbeat after Sonny preceded Kai onto the stage. It was official—the dude was a demon, though after his performance in Levi's living room, he couldn't figure why he was surprised. Hell, nothing Sonny did surprised him anymore.

His own reactions? Next question.

Frustrated, he let his eyes fall closed. An image of Sonny and Kai's sensuous dance appeared behind his eyelids. He shook his head in an effort to disperse it, but the two beautiful young men stubbornly remained, and it was all too easy to give in and let them have their way.

He watched the scene replay in his head. Sonny and Kai had danced together for over an hour, but there was a song in particular that resonated and indelibly imprinted itself in Levi's mind. The hard house club track was over a decade old, but it was timeless—the kind of track that would still be playing out for decades to come.

It had been playing in the very first gay bar he ever set foot in. Nineteen and fresh from coming out to his fellow jock, freshman roommate, he'd thought he knew about being gay, about what it meant to admire, appreciate, and revel in another man's body. Turned out he didn't know much about anything. A go-go dancer had opened his eyes to the world that freezing Pennsylvania night all those years ago. Seven years on, it seemed nothing had really changed. Perhaps *he* hadn't really changed. He had, after all, been stuck in limbo for most of his adult life.

Damn. The healing stitches in his arm throbbed. He banged his head lightly against the bricks behind him, willing Sonny and Kai back to the forefront of his mind. They didn't take much persuading. He watched them move together for a while, enjoying them both, but he was drawn to Sonny. Kai had a certain presence, all floppy hair, pouty lips, and unending long legs, but he lacked Sonny's elegance, lacked his effortless grace. Sonny moved like the music was liquid silver in his veins.

Levi opened his eyes with a heavy sigh. It was like nothing he'd ever seen, but since when did he notice shit like that? Since when did he notice anything that wasn't a damned red-topped bill? He pushed himself off the wall, adjusting his now comfortable jeans, and headed back inside to find his shirt.

His search led him to the dancers' bathrooms. He picked up the abandoned shirt and retreated, stepping over the piles of personal belonging and stage props and making his way back toward the tightly packed club. It was his intention to dodge Cam and head for home.

Blunt nails scraped down his back. "Looking for someone?"

Levi turned midstep. Sonny stood behind him, fresh offstage in nothing but a sheen of sweat and a pair of tight designer underwear. Levi's breath caught. He'd been staring at Sonny for most of the night, but somehow, it hadn't occurred to him that they might cross paths. "I, uh, was getting my shirt."

Sonny glanced between him and the rumpled shirt. He opened his mouth to say something but stopped, narrowing his eyes. He stared hard at Levi, squinting in the murky light of the corridor and tilting his head to one side. "What the fuck happened to you?"

"What?"

Sonny reached out and traced a fingertip along his injured forearm, then touched the healing gash on his abdomen. "You're hurt. What happened?"

Levi shrugged, caught off guard by the question and sorely unprepared for the sensation of Sonny's light touch. He considered lying, telling Sonny he'd fallen off his bike, but he didn't. He didn't say anything.

Sonny's hand hovered. Levi was almost sure he saw a tremor run through it, but then Sonny dropped it back to his side. The other dancers began to filter offstage and into the narrow corridor. A couple shot Levi curious stares; a few waved. Levi grinned back. He knew some of them by name, but not all. He'd never taken enough notice to care.

Sonny said something. Levi missed it over the pounding beat of the music. He leaned forward, frowning. Sonny met him in the middle, bringing his lips so close to Levi's ear, his warm breath washed over Levi's neck. "Come with me."

He grabbed Levi's hand and turned, tugging him forward. Levi followed him without thinking, all the way back to the fire escape, but before they reached the exit, Sonny opened the door to the backstage storeroom and pulled him inside.

Levi cast his gaze around the shelves of props and disused office equipment. He drifted to Jon's old desk and hauled himself up to sit on it.

Sonny leaned against a battered filing cabinet, his gaze shrewd and appraising. "So?"

"So what?"

"So..." Sonny folded his arms across his chest. "It's been a while. How's the prep going?"

Levi shifted. Sonny had watched all his scenes, seen him jerk off with his fingers up his own ass, and yet he could still make him squirm with an arch of his goddamned eyebrow. "It's, uh, going fine."

"Yeah, right." Sonny snorted, his disbelief clear. "You've been ignoring me for days. What's up? Been too busy with Kai?"

"What?"

"Kai," Sonny repeated. "He's pretty sweet on you, and I saw you with him earlier..." He trailed off, averting his sharp gaze.

"Saw what? Some kid jumping all over my lap?"

"Some kid? You fucked that *kid* seven ways from Saturday a few weeks ago."

"What?" Levi was used to Sonny's pugnacious nature—used

to him shouting down everything he said—but not quite like this. He took in Sonny's jittery hands and dilated pupils. *What's up with that?* "Are you pissed that I didn't call you back? You said you were busy."

"I'm not pissed. I just..."

"What? You said you were busy. Somethin' wrong?"

"No." Sonny pushed himself from the filing cabinet and ran his restless hand through his damp hair. "I *was* busy. I was busy with school. I had midterms. You know there's more to life than porn, right?"

Levi ignored the veiled barb, ignored the strange sensation he felt at knowing Sonny had been watching him as much as he'd been watched himself. He wasn't in the mood to lock horns with him, not tonight. He'd had enough fighting in recent weeks. "You're a student? Thought you said you were twenty-two."

"I am," Sonny said shortly. "I started late. What's that look for? Something wrong with getting an education?"

"No, no." Levi held up his hands. "I went to school, for a bit, anyway."

"What happened?"

"Life."

His clipped answer seemed to make sense to Sonny. He nodded. "Did you go to school here in California?"

"Penn State."

"Bet you were a jock, though, right?"

"Nope. Mechanical engineering. Was nearly done with it too, before this shit got in the way."

His candor surprised even him, and Sonny's eyes widened. Levi noted a bloodshot tinge he'd never seen before. *Damn. Is he high?*

He found the notion horrifying. He'd seen drugs at Silver before. Hell, he'd seen them just about everywhere, but the idea of Sonny touching that crap made him feel sick inside. He had to be wrong; he had...

Sonny shivered, wrapping his arms around himself and reminding Levi that he was standing in the drafty storeroom in his underwear, his heated, sweat-sheened skin now chilled and cold.

Levi opened his arms on instinct. Sonny stepped into them with equal lack of thought. Levi wrapped his arms around Sonny's shoulders and rubbed his palms over the coiled, defined muscles of Sonny's biceps. "Do you want my shirt?"

Sonny chuckled. "It would look like a dress. You're, like, a foot taller than me."

"Don't do drag, huh?"

"Nope. Do you?"

"What do you think?"

Sonny shifted, wedging himself between Levi's legs and resting his forehead on Levi's chest. His sigh was soft against Levi's skin. "I think there's a lot you still don't know about yourself."

Levi bit back his flippant retort. Sonny liked to push his buttons and rattle his cage, but he seemed different tonight, like his wicked sense of humor was somewhere else. Without it, Sonny was dark and intense, and Levi could feel an undercurrent of something simmering beneath his smooth, tattooed skin. His skin... *God*, that skin. Levi closed his eyes.

Another tremor ran through Sonny. Levi looked down at the sight of his arms and legs wrapped tight around Sonny's body, consuming him, caging him close. In the same moment, Sonny opened his eyes and looked up. Levi drew him closer, reached out and cupped his face. Sonny sucked in a shaky breath. "We can't."

"Can't what?"

Sonny closed his fingers around Levi's wrists. "We can't do *this*, not yet, not now."

Levi leaned down, his face an inch from Sonny's. "Says who?"

"Says me." Sonny peeled Levi's hands from his face and dropped his head, taking Levi's nipple in his mouth. He sucked on it, drawing those damned short nails down his chest. Levi shuddered. Sonny brought him alive in ways he'd never imagined, but the sensation of his warm tongue teasing him was almost too much.

"Fuck."

Sonny released him with a wet hiss. "Yeah? And what about this?"

He moved his mouth over Levi's abdomen and chest, ghosting his sensitive skin in places, licking and nipping in others, until Levi couldn't stand it.

Levi groaned and shoved his fingers into Sonny's damp hair, yanking his head to one side and burying his face in Sonny's neck. He sank his teeth into the soft flesh he found there. Sonny gasped, arching his body, and his hard, constrained cock ground into Levi's groin. Levi tightened his grip on every part of Sonny he could reach, touching him, tasting him, breathing in the sweet scent of his silky hair and smooth skin. It was too much, and yet not enough. He wanted more.

In his arms, Sonny trembled, responding fiercely until he reared up and pushed him away. "No."

Levi came back into himself, panting. Took in the teeth marks on Sonny's neck. He looked down. There were red scratches on his own chest, and somehow, his jeans had found their way open, and his rock-hard cock was half-out. How the fuck had that happened? "I'm sorry, I—"

"No! You don't fucking get it. Don't you see? You need this..." Sonny gestured between them. "You need to want me the way you do now. You have to, or this scene is going to break you."

Levi opened his mouth and shut it again. Sonny's words hit

him like a wrecking ball, and Levi knew without a doubt Sonny was right. He couldn't face the three-way scene without Sonny. Hell, these days it seemed he couldn't face *anything* without Sonny. "I can do it."

"I know you can." Sonny closed his eyes, banging his head on Levi's chest. "It's going to be all right. Let Rex do his thing. Then you can have me, okay? You can have me any way you want me."

Levi was silent for a while, entertaining himself with Sonny's hair while he considered his words. *"You can have me any way you want me."* Did he really want to have Sonny that way? What about Sonny? What did he want? What did he need? And what did any of it even mean? He felt a connection to Sonny that he'd never felt for anyone before, sexual or otherwise, but their relationship was built on...on what? On nothing as far as Levi could see. It didn't make any sense, and yet he knew without doubt that it was real.

Eventually, he grew weary and sighed. "How did this happen?"

"What?"

"This—you, me," Levi said. "I don't even like you."

Sonny shrugged. "Yeah, well. The feeling's mutual. The way you make me feel pisses me off." He brushed his lips over Levi's chest one final time before he disentangled himself from the grip of his thighs. "I've always hated you. Do you know we've worked in the same studio, hung out at the same club for two years, and you've never even spoken to me? I live, like, three blocks from you, and you walk past me on the street like I don't exist."

"What?" Levi didn't believe that. It was true that he'd written him off as a bitchy twink, but he'd always, always looked twice. Sonny was too beautiful to ignore. There was no way he'd ever walked past him. "I saw you. I let you hustle me home and cooked you dinner. How is that ignoring you?"

Sonny scrubbed his hands over his face. He seemed rattled. "You wouldn't have chosen it that way. *I* saw *you* and jumped your ass. Listen, I gotta go, but I'll see you at the shoot, okay? Call me if you need help before then."

He backed away.

Levi stared at the door, transfixed by the gaping void Sonny had left behind. It felt strange to be alone again, like he was in limbo, waiting to realize something really fucking important.

His cell phone roused him. He fumbled for it, answering without checking the screen as he tucked his still-hard dick back in his jeans. "Yeah?"

"Levi?"

"Mr. Draper? What's wrong?"

"It's your momma, son. You need to come home."

CHAPTER ELEVEN

"Levi?" Mr. Draper touched Levi's shoulder with his gnarled, weathered hand. "Levi, son? The police want to talk to you."

"Can it wait?" His voice sounded hoarse and weak, like he hadn't used it in days. He cleared his throat. "Tell them to wait."

Mr. Draper left the room, his usual shuffling footsteps silent against the shiny hospital floor. The door closed with a quiet click behind him, leaving Levi alone again— alone with all that remained of his mother.

He took a deep breath. Closed his eyes. He never saw the body after his father had turned his shotgun on himself. It was a bright spring day. He'd gone to school as usual, and by the time he came home, the only thing left of his father was the blood-stained, plastic tarpaulin someone had forgotten to remove from the porch.

This was different—Bella wasn't dead, not yet. She was still alive—for now, at least. A young Asian doctor with a black head scarf and kind eyes had told him it wouldn't be long.

Levi opened his eyes and ran his gaze over her, squeezing her thin, fragile hand. On the surface she didn't look so bad—the hospital team had cleaned her up before he'd got there—but he could see the deformities in her shoulders and the strange indents in her chest. He was sure if he pulled the sheets back, he'd see the wheel marks of the pickup truck all over her broken body.

She didn't stand a chance. Mr. Draper said it was an accident, that she had milk from the all-night store in her purse, but Levi wasn't buying it. Bella didn't drink milk at three a.m. There was no reason for her to be walking the streets in her nightgown, no reason at all. One parent had taken the easy way out. Why not her? She let out a weak, shuddering whoosh of air. He held his breath, but after an unending moment, she began to breathe again.

Not yet. Not yet.

"Mr. Ramone?"

He jumped. Somehow he'd missed the door ghosting open again. It was a nurse this time. She stepped into the room, assessing Bella with an appraising glance. "Why don't you step outside for a few moments? We just need a few minutes. We'll find you if anything happens."

Levi stepped outside. He was bone weary, so tired his body ached with every step. It had been hours since Mr. Draper's call tore him from his Sonny-filled haze in the storeroom of the club. Somehow, though, he was wide-awake, so awake he felt like he'd never sleep again.

He sank down onto a hard plastic chair in the busy ER corridor. It didn't take long for the police to find him. They ushered him into a side room, leaving the door open for an officer to keep an eye on Bella's room. An overweight, middle-aged beat cop pulled up a chair opposite. "Sorry, son. We'll try and keep this quick. I take it you know what happened?"

Levi bristled. *Son?* He could take it from Mr. Draper, but not from the cops. His momma was clinging to life by a fast-eroding thread. He wasn't anyone's son anymore. "She got hit by a truck."

"Yes, I'm sorry. It appears that she was crossing quite a way down from the pedestrian crossing outside the general store. The area isn't well lit at the best of times, and the truck had a light out. Do you have any idea why she wasn't at home and asleep at that time of night?"

"No."

"Your mother's neighbor said you buy groceries and deliver them to her. When did you last see her?"

Guilt burned a path from Levi's chest to his stomach. He'd missed his weekly checkup with Bella. The first time in years. "Two weeks ago."

"How did she seem? Was she her usual self?"

He snorted; he couldn't help it. "Yeah, she was her usual self."

The officer nodded and made a note. "Your mother has high levels of alcohol in her system. Your neighbor says that's not unusual. Is that true?"

"Yes."

"Is she an alcoholic?"

"Yes."

There was silence as the officer turned over a page in his notebook. Levi looked around the room, taking in the shabby equipment and faded pictures on the walls. Trust Bella to wind up at the worst ER in LA.

The officer cleared his throat. Levi glanced back at him, feeling somewhat detached. He kept waiting for the gravity of the situation to feel real, but it hadn't happened yet. Maybe he was still drunk himself, though the buzz of his night at Silver seemed a lifetime ago.

"Mr. Ramone, do you believe it's possible your mother was trying to..."

Urgent movement in the corridor cut the officer off. A nurse appeared in the doorway. "You need to come with me."

Levi shoved his chair back and pushed past the officer at the door. He followed the nurse to Bella's room, bypassing her when she trailed to a stop. He reached Bella's bedside and took her hand. At first it seemed that nothing had changed, but then he heard it, the faltering stutter of her failing heartbeat. A doctor hurried in. The chick was young; she didn't look much older than him.

"It'll be quick now."

He nodded, his gaze fixed on Bella. Her eyes were closed, her face smooth. They'd been saying for hours that she was beyond feeling any pain, and he believed them. She hadn't felt much of anything in so long.

Transfixed, he squeezed her hand as her chest made a strange rattling sound, and he brushed her hair away from her face. Bella had been a beautiful Southern belle once, but now her features were ravaged by years of misery and alcohol abuse. Paper-thin skin and frail bones. He'd always known the booze would kill her, but he'd never imagined he would say good-bye to her like this.

She shuddered. He watched the tremor travel through her body. To him it seemed like an animal shedding its skin, like she was trying to wriggle out of her life and force her way into whatever came next. The thought almost made him smile; then he noticed her chest was no longer moving.

He watched her for a long while, though in reality, it might have only been moments. Sometime later, he felt the hand of a stranger on his shoulder, and he knew she was gone. His momma was dead, she was free, and for the first time in years, so was he.

He drove back to Bella's house in a daze. Her death had

been quick and painless—for her, at least—but the formalities that came next had gone on for hours. Death certificates, funeral homes, donating her only fully functioning organs—her eyes—to be used for medical research—the list was endless. It was early evening by the time he pushed open her unlocked front door.

The house was just as she'd lived—chaotic and loud. It struck him as morbidly ironic that her last moments had been so quiet and peaceful. He passed through the cluttered kitchen and into the living room. The TV was still playing one of the quiz shows she'd enjoyed so much. He crossed the room in two strides and shut it off, exasperated. Why couldn't she shut the damned thing off?

He turned in a slow circle, searching for a point of focus. His gaze fell on the bureau, half-hidden by the open door. It was beside the liquor cabinet. He swiped a bottle of bourbon from Bella's stash and opened the first drawer.

It took a while, but he eventually unearthed a pile of official-looking papers and envelopes. He carried them, the bourbon, and a glass into the disused dining room and sat down at the table. Though he'd spent more time than he cared to remember toiling through Bella's finances, the stack of paperwork seemed imposing. The first inch of hard liquor helped, but not much. Though he poured another, he knew he wouldn't drink it.

He reached for the closest thick envelope. It was weathered and dog-eared, like it had been opened again and again and stuffed back in its drawer. Inside, he expected to find bundled-up betting slips or evidence of hidden debts he knew nothing about, but instead, his fingers closed around banded stacks of photographs. Bewildered, he pulled them out and set them in front of him. There were dozens and dozens of them, arranged in chronological order and spanning decades and decades of Bella's life.

Levi shook his head. The tidy pile of memories didn't fit

with the Bella he knew, and he couldn't remember a time when it did. He flipped through the first stack. Some were dated, some not. Some of them were labeled with names and locations; some of them he had to guess. He came to an old photograph of a trailer park in Nevada and paused, staring hard at the faded image. They'd lived in the trailer for a while. Bella had hated it and spent her days screaming at Ernesto to get a better job, but Levi had loved it. To a six-year-old boy, the tiny tin box on wheels had seemed almost magical.

Bella's phone rang. Levi ignored it, setting the photo aside and reaching for another. The next image took him forward in time, back to LA and the home he'd spent most of his life in. The photo was of his father, posing outside his new workshop. Levi had been too young at the time to know what Ernesto's dreams had been. By the time he was old enough to understand, the reality of the gang-affiliated chop shop had become normal. He didn't know any different until his own dreams had lured him away from California.

Levi turned the picture over with a heavy sigh, shoving it and the rest of them back in the box. He was stalling, using the masochistic trip down memory lane to avoid the arduous task of trolling through Bella's papers. There were things to be done— burial arrangements, notifications for creditors and insurance companies, and bank accounts to close. He wasn't going to bother with her personal belongings. There was nothing in the house for him but bad memories, and with no siblings or surviving family, who really cared? Not him.

He spent much of the night pulling together the paperwork he needed and compiling a list of calls to make in the morning. The sun was beginning to rise when he came across a stray photograph he'd missed. The image of Bella cradling a swaddled infant in her arms was grainy and smudged, but the words, printed neatly in blue ink on the back, were legible.

Levi, 6/9/1985. My love, my life, my world.

He swallowed, blinking hard, but the words blurred away to nothing. The numbness evaporated, and the hard cast protecting his heart cracked open a wide fissure. He cast the photo aside, buried his face in his arms, and wept for the mother he'd lost more than a decade ago.

CHAPTER TWELVE

Mr. Draper woke him sometime later. Levi sat up and rubbed his face, taking in the tidied paperwork and photos on the table. Even the untouched bourbon had been cleared away.

"Doing okay, son?"

Was he? Levi wasn't quite sure. He stretched his arms over his head and shrugged. Mr. Draper nodded, understanding like he always had.

"There's a lot to do, eh? No need to do it all at once, though. Go home, get some real sleep. All this will still be here tomorrow."

The old man shuffled around the room, plumping dirty cushions and straightening dusty ornaments. Levi watched him for a while, still somewhat asleep and detached from reality. He knew he'd cried; he could feel the dried tears on his face and the alien tightness at the base of his skull, but somehow, the last twenty-four hours seemed like they'd happened to somebody else. He glanced around him and shivered. He felt like he was in the wrong place. He wasn't supposed to be here; he was supposed to be somewhere else, but where?

His head ached as he thought hard enough to burst a blood

vessel. Then Sonny's face flashed into his mind. "What time is it?"

Mr. Draper checked his watch. "Eleven thirty."

"Eleven thirty?" *Shit.* He shoved back his chair. "I gotta go."

An hour later, he pushed open the familiar, blacked-out glass doors to the studio. The chick on the desk was on the phone. Her eyes widened when she saw him. She put her hand over her mouthpiece and started to say something, but he didn't stop. He made his way straight to the bathrooms, stripped off, turned the water as hot as he dared, and stood under the shower until he felt cleansed of the sweat and grime of two hellish days away from home.

The scalding water left a heated flush over his tanned skin. He glared at it, scrubbing with a towel, but the pink blotches stayed put. Short of scouring his skin right off, there wasn't much he could do. He went to his locker, searched out a clean pair of jeans, and pulled them on. On the shelf above the locker, a crew member had left a stack of T-shirts to go with his trademark loose, scruffy jeans. They were all white. Irrational annoyance burned through him. He dropped the shirts on the bench and retrieved his own shirt from the floor. It was crumpled, and the faded black material showed up the damp patches on his skin, but he didn't care. He pulled it over his head, jammed the rest of his stuff into his locker, and slammed the door shut.

It swung back open. He slammed it again, and again, but to no avail. Damned thing wouldn't close. Furious, he drove his fist into the flimsy locker door. The hinges snapped, and it fell to the floor in a heap of battered, twisted metal. He stared at it, seeing nothing but Bella's shattered body. She'd been dead a little over twenty-four hours, but he could still feel her cold, lifeless hand in his, could still smell the stale odor of her favorite gin on his skin. Goddamn it! He clenched his fists, ready to punch out every locker in the row, ready to tear the whole fucking room apart, ready to...

"Hey."

He spun around, startled. Though the studio was often a hive of activity, the three-way was scheduled as a closed shoot—essential cast and crew only. Aside from the chick on the desk, he hadn't seen another soul. He hadn't even heard the dressing room door open.

Of course it was Sonny. Who else would it be?

He found his tongue. "What?"

Sonny stepped forward, letting the door swing shut behind him. He glanced between Levi and the broken locker. "What's wrong?"

"Nothin'." Levi averted his gaze and bent to pick up the mangled door. "Locker broke."

"Broke? Looks like someone beat the shit out of it."

"So?" Levi straightened up to find Sonny right in front of him. The urge to lash out and hurl him across the room warred with a deeper, more desperate need to pull him close and hide away in all that was Sonny—his bright eyes, sarcastic grin, and hypnotizing smell. "What do you care?"

Sonny raised an eyebrow, unfazed. "You're about to stick your dick in my ass. I'd rather you weren't thinking about killing someone at the same time."

His choice of words stung. Levi's breath caught in his throat, cutting off his defensive reply. Sonny frowned. "What is it? What's wrong?"

"I..." Levi broke off. He couldn't do it, couldn't find the words to explain how his whole world had tipped on its axis since the last time he'd seen him. He stumbled backward, colliding with the lockers.

Sonny reached out, alarmed. "Hey, hey. It's all right. You don't have to do this, Levi, okay? Go home. I'll tell them you're sick. I'll tell—"

The dressing room door opened, cutting him off. Jon stuck his head in without looking at either of them. "Good, you're both here. We're ready to start. Come on through when you're ready."

He let the door close without another word, but the brief interlude was enough to break the tenuous hold Sonny had over Levi.

Levi sidestepped him and headed for the door. The three-way had been the last thing he wanted to do for weeks, but now it was all he could seem to focus on. He had a job to do, and he was going to damn well do it.

"Levi, wait."

He stopped with his hand on the door. Sonny's voice was low, gravelly with an emotion he didn't understand. The fractured, weathered shield on his heart threatened to give way. *No.* He clamped down the feeling. If he fell into Sonny's arms now, he'd never get up.

"Come on," he said without turning round. "Let's get this bullshit over with."

The set was silent. Levi sat on the back of the perennial L-shaped couch with his eyes down, avoiding Sonny's wide-eyed concern to his left, Jon's sharp gaze in front of him, and Cam's appraising stare from right at the back of the room.

What the fuck is Cam even doing here?

He chanced a glance down at Rex slouched on the sofa between him and Sonny, with one heavy arm resting on each of them, and considered him. Rex was tall with wide, thick shoulders and sandy-brown hair, but though he was blandly attractive, he did nothing for Levi. Big musclemen weren't his thing.

Rex shifted and leaned back. His posture mirrored Levi's, relaxed and casual, though Levi suspected his demeanor was sincere. After all, what did he have to worry about? He had two dudes to fuck. He was gonna have the time of his life.

Sonny let out a soft sigh. It echoed in Levi's ears. *Sonny.* Damn it. He could feel his presence just a foot away, and a strange current crackled between them. Most days, he found Sonny's energy exhilarating...thrilling, but today it disturbed him, taunted him almost, like it was the one thing that could push him over the edge.

Jon clapped his hands, as though calling for quiet on the stony, silent set. "Okay, the general plan is to keep it short—fool around, get each other going, then finish up with some hard fucking. Nothing cute, please, guys. We've got a brief to work from, and this is a raw scene. Everyone clear on what they're doing?"

Levi met his gaze and nodded. A few days ago, there'd been a tiny rebellious part of him looking forward to the shoot, curious as to what it would really feel like to take another man inside him. Now, though, all he felt was a short, sharp shock of disgust. The warmth of Rex's arm on him felt wrong, all wrong, in a way that no shoot ever had before. He just wanted to get it done and go home.

Warm fingers slid over his. Sonny tugged on his hand, leaning over to whisper in his ear, "It'll be okay, I promise."

Levi kept his eyes down, hardening his heart as anger rumbled through him like simmering lava. How could Sonny say that? What the fuck did it even mean? *"It'll be okay."* What the hell was that? The stupid kid had forced his way into Levi's life and now thought he had the right to tell him that? What the fuck did he know?

Sonny squeezed his hand, his grip strong and sure, like a buffer to Levi's anger. He held firm, and the fury surging through Levi's veins evaporated, leaving him hollow. He felt the urge to laugh, *really* laugh, like he'd never fucking stop.

He didn't. Instead, he turned away, leaving their hands

entwined, and before he could reconcile himself with his whiplash-inducing mood, Jon raised his hand to give out his final instructions.

"When I call action, skip the preamble and get right into it. We can record some preshow banter later if we need it. Okay? Have a good fuck, guys. Let's get to it."

Five, four, three, two, one...

"Action!"

For a moment, nobody moved. It happened at the beginning of every scene, even if all parties were eager and ready—that awkward, split-second pause. Levi was usually the one to break it, the one to reach out and pull a nervous bottom toward him, but not today. Today he couldn't bring himself to care.

Sonny slid off the back of the couch like a snake, inserting himself into Rex's reaching arms. In a flash he had Rex's shirt pulled over his head. Rex responded greedily. He grabbed Sonny and yanked him close, biting at his neck. Levi watched in a daze, until he glanced up and caught Jon's eye. The inflection in Jon's raised eyebrow was clear—*get your head in the game, Ramone.*

He released his death grip on the back of the couch and reached for the hem of Sonny's shirt. Sonny jumped, then raised his arms to let Levi pull the shirt over his head.

Levi sat back and stared. The skin of Sonny's bare back was as smooth and flawless as the rest of him, and Levi found himself transfixed by the sight of his slender, defined muscles rippling as he moved down Rex's body to undress him.

A flicker of tension ran through Sonny. It was subtle; Levi was sure no one else would've noticed it, but he felt it—a shot of apprehension he didn't understand. He looked up, following Sonny's line of sight to where Rex stood naked. Levi stared at his cock. Thick, long, and uncut, it was the biggest dick he'd ever seen, bigger than he'd imagined.

Holy hell.

His heart beat faster. The events of the last twenty-four hours had left him numb and separated from the world around him, but there was no denying the nerves that swept through him now.

He stilled his hands on Sonny's back. Sonny glanced over his shoulder, his eyes wide. He leaned back toward Levi but stopped halfway, perhaps uncertain of his reaction. Rex took advantage of the pause and undid Sonny's jeans. He yanked on them, knocking Sonny off balance, and it was enough to rouse Levi from his detached daze. He moved to steady Sonny, grasping his shoulders and pulling him close, letting his hands roam over Sonny's chest and belly and shivering despite the warmth of Sonny's skin.

Sonny arched and pressed his lips to Levi's throat. The kiss was soothing and sweet, belying the charged air around them. Levi buried his face in Sonny's neck and breathed deeply, losing himself. Bella's death loomed dark and sinister in the back of his mind, but a part of him was in the present, in the moment, and totally consumed by the lithe, young body in his arms.

I could stay here forever.

Sonny squirmed. Levi raised his head and loosened his grip. Sonny turned and shoved at his T-shirt. "You're wearing too many clothes."

"Oh, yeah?" Levi absorbed the sensation of looking Sonny in the eye for the first time since he'd walked out of the storeroom at the club two nights ago. Took in his light, sardonic grin and all-seeing hazel gaze. The cameras, the lights, and all the watching eyes faded away, and he felt lighter, like Sonny was all he'd ever needed to see. He tilted his head. "Watcha gonna do about it?"

Undress him with his teeth, it seemed, while Rex entertained himself.

Levi shuddered beneath Sonny's wicked mouth. In the weeks leading up to the shoot, he'd fretted that his dick would let him down. Needlessly, as it turned out. Sonny took Levi's nipple in his mouth, but instead of teasing Levi the way he had in the storeroom, he bit down, and the surge of exhilarating pleasure went straight to Levi's cock.

Levi kicked his jeans away and jumped off the couch, taking Sonny with him in one smooth, agile movement. Rex moved to stand behind him, but Levi ignored him for now, distracted by Sonny and the sight of him without a stitch of clothing. He'd never seen him naked before.

Wow. Levi's tongue stuck to the roof of his mouth. It seemed Sonny had tattoos everywhere. Levi leaned forward, straining to see the ink at the base of his cock. What was it? A cross? A heart?

His staring didn't go unnoticed. Sonny ran his tongue over his lips. "See something you like?"

Hell, yeah. "Maybe," Levi said. "Come here."

Levi led him back to the couch and sat down, pulling him over to straddle his chest. He stared at Sonny's dick. The tattoo was a tiny star with the words *no fear* running through it. Levi raised a curious eyebrow, but it wasn't the time for talking. He looked up and met Sonny's eyes again, then, without warning, took him deep into his mouth.

Sonny jolted and let out a surprised groan. "Fuck!"

Levi grinned around Sonny's dick. A rush of victory teased his gut. He had the upper hand. Finally, he'd caught Sonny off guard. He opened his throat and let Sonny in. His scene partners were often surprised he gave them head, like they expected him to sit back and be worshipped, but in truth it was something he enjoyed, something he knew he was good at. With the right dude it was exciting and fun.

With Sonny?

It was incredible.

Sonny gripped the back of the couch with one hand. The other found its way to Levi's face, rubbing Levi's cheek in time with Levi's tongue on his cock. "Fuck, yeah. Suck that dick."

The words were classic porn, but his tone gave Levi pause. He slowed his mouth and looked up in the same moment Sonny glanced down. Their eyes met, and what passed between them was so quietly profound Levi almost didn't notice Rex's dark silhouette appearing behind Sonny.

Almost.

Rex buried his face in Sonny's ass. Sonny cringed and rolled his eyes. Levi hid his smirk in Sonny's balls. He'd been the victim of overenthusiastic rimming himself. It wasn't the nicest thing in the world, but it was harmless. He took pity on Sonny and tried to make up for it by going to town on his cock.

For a while, the only sounds in the room were the squeak of the couch and the low, throaty rumble of Sonny's moans. Levi gripped his hips, holding him firm, and reveled in the feel of sweat dripping down Sonny's torso and onto his hands. Whatever was going on behind him, with Sonny's dick in his mouth, it was all too easy to ignore what Rex was doing to him. All too easy to forget Rex was there at all and pretend it was just the two of them, the way Levi knew it should've been all along.

The stinging sound of a hard slap pierced the air. Sonny cried out, staggering on his knees. Rex struck him again and shoved his other hand forward. Levi couldn't see where it went, but he could guess.

Sonny cringed, the discomfort in his face clear. He dug his fingers into the couch, ducked his head, and hid in the crook of Levi's shoulder. Levi pulled his mouth from Sonny's cock with a wet pop. He found Rex's eyes and shook his head. "Easy."

Rex grabbed Sonny by the back of the neck and yanked him away from Levi. "Nah, he likes it, don't ya? You're gonna love it when I tear you up, bitch. I can't wait to nail this tight little ass. Levi's gonna love it too. I know what he likes."

He raised his hand to slap Sonny again. The leer on his face was nothing Levi hadn't seen before, but something inside him snapped. He was damned sick of being told what he liked, what he was. *Who* he was. Bella, Sonny, Rex. It didn't seem to matter. What the hell did they know? A red haze descended over his vision, and all the rage he'd repressed over the last few days, months...years, boiled over.

No. Fucking. Way.

He kicked out. His foot connected with Rex's abdomen and sent him flying. Sonny yelped in surprise, falling off the sofa in a heap. His labored breaths disturbed the stunned silence. Levi scrambled to his feet, hauled Sonny back onto the couch, and stood in front of him. "Enough."

His command was directed at Rex, who stood doubled over, his eyes wild, but Levi meant it for anyone who cared to listen. The scene was over, done.

No one was touching Sonny again.

Rex charged forward, his body colliding with Levi as they met in the middle of the set. Rex was a big guy—a big angry guy—but Levi was madder, incensed with a blinding rage that turned his whole world red. Over and over, his fist connected with Rex's face. He felt the warmth of blood seep through his fingers, but he didn't care. Rex had attacked the only man who'd made him smile in years. The only man with a hope of seeing past the bullshit that weighed him down. To his grief-stricken mind...his heart, there was no greater sin.

Rex grappled with him, attempting to flip them over. When it didn't work, he kicked out, catching Levi in the stomach and ribs.

It took five hits to knock the wind from Levi. He paused for breath, letting up his assault, and it was the lull the shouting voices and grasping hands needed. The next thing he knew, two heavy bodies restrained him, and Sonny was nowhere to be seen.

Jon slammed the office door, bracing himself against it and using his weight to propel Levi farther into the room. "Damn it, Levi. Calm the fuck down."

Levi wrestled himself out of his grasp and took a step back. Away from the set and Rex, his anger was fading fast, but he still didn't trust himself not to take a swing at Jon. He'd punched Rex on his ass twice before they'd been pulled apart. "Where's Sonny?"

Jon glared at him for a moment before he turned and yanked open a drawer behind him. He pulled out a pair of sweats and tossed them across the desk. "Is that what this is about? Something going on between you two?"

"What makes you say that?" Levi took the sweats and pulled them on. Somehow, in all the chaos, he'd forgotten he was naked. Blue Boy had that effect on him. He straightened up and winced. His ribs smarted from Rex's defensive blows.

Jon sighed and sat down, gesturing for Levi to do the same. He didn't seem surprised when Levi remained on his feet. "You've never had a problem with a scene before. I know you didn't want to bottom, and perhaps I took advantage of knowing how much you needed the cash to persuade you, but I didn't want this. You have to know that." He broke off for breath. In his own subtle way, he seemed as worked up as Levi. "I don't want to see you like this."

"Like what?"

The door opened. Cam slipped inside. "Okay in here?"

Jon spared him a brief glance. Levi didn't miss the intensity that passed between them. "Look, if this is about Sonny, then trust me, I get it. It's hard to see someone you care about with somebody else, but you can't lash out like this. If you can't deal with it, you can't be here."

"Then maybe I shouldn't be here."

Levi strode from the room before Jon could respond.

He drifted to the dressing room to retrieve his things. On his way, he encountered no one. The studio was silent and still, the only sign of the brawl some scattered sofa cushions and an upturned chair. Even the showers were deserted, though that was unsurprising. The three-way made up the whole schedule for the day, and had ended in violence long before anyone had worked up a sweat.

Still, Levi had no desire to linger. He grabbed his bag and left the studio without even stopping to pull on a shirt. He crossed the parking lot to his car, opened the door, and threw his bag in the back. In his peripheral vision, he saw a lone figure sitting at the bus stop across the street.

Sonny.

He felt a strange ache in his chest at the sight of him slumped on the bench with his head in his hands, a pull he couldn't ignore. He snagged a shirt from his bag and crossed the street. "Hey." Sonny didn't look up. Levi reached out and touched his shoulder. "Need a ride?"

Sonny raised his head and squinted through the bright afternoon sun. "From you?"

"Might as well. I'm going your way."

Sonny's only reply was a noncommittal grunt. Levi sighed and patted his pockets for his cell phone. It took him a minute to remember he'd left it on Bella's table. "Look, I'm sorry about today, okay? I wasn't in a good place, and it got out of hand. I'm sorry you got caught in the middle."

Sonny nodded. "That's why you did it? Why you went for Rex? Because you were having a bad day?"

"I guess."

Sonny let out a short, humorless snort of laughter. "Leave me alone."

"No." Levi folded his arms across his chest. "You've been all up in my shit for weeks. You don't get to decide."

"Yeah, well. Maybe I didn't even want to be. Maybe Cam told me to. Thought about that?"

"Cam?"

"Why do you think I came after you in the first place?"

"You said you wanted to know who was fucking you."

"Maybe I lied. What do you want from me, Levi?"

"I want to drive you home."

Sonny was as stubborn as Levi, maybe even more. Levi knew he was close to toppling the final invisible barrier between them, but he sensed that Sonny needed something from him. Something, anything, to convince him the crazy heat between them was real.

He stepped closer and took Sonny's hands. "Please?"

They drove to Sonny's apartment in silence. Levi welcomed it, though he was used to Sonny talking his ear off. His body ached, and his brain felt fried. He needed a few quiet moments to bring the shattered pieces of his mind back together.

He pulled up outside Sonny's apartment block and shut the engine off. Sonny tore his gaze from the window and let out a heavy sigh. "I don't get it. I know you didn't want to do the scene, but I had no idea you were so upset by it."

Levi retrieved his faithful pack of Marlboro Lights from the glove box. He lit up and blew smoke out of his open window. "I'm not upset."

Sonny plucked the cigarette from his mouth and took a deep drag of his own. "I don't believe you." His voice was tired. For the first time, Levi noticed the line of exhaustion in his young face, like he was the one who hadn't slept in days. "You're an asshole, but you're not a violent asshole."

"I put you up against the wall the first time you came to my house," Levi reminded him.

A ghost of a grin flickered across Sonny's features. "That was because you wanted me."

Levi let that go. He couldn't explain *any* of the reactions he had to Sonny, let alone that one. He turned away and stared through the windshield. A part of him wanted to tell Sonny about his momma, but he couldn't find the words. He'd dealt with Bella by himself for so long it seemed fitting that he dealt with her death on his own. He hadn't even told AJ.

"Well, as fun as this is, I'm beat." Sonny moved to get out of the car. He paused with his hand on the door. "My apartment is number twenty-four if you change your mind."

"About what?"

Sonny shook his head. "About letting go of whatever's tearing you up. You don't need to be on your own, Levi. I don't know why I give a shit, but I do. I'll be here if you change your mind."

He slid out of the car and walked away before Levi could formulate a response.

Levi drove home, tired beyond belief but unnervingly wired. His apartment was cool and quiet, something he loved, *craved*, when he was elsewhere and surrounded by heat and noise, but just then he found it suffocating. He felt restless and agitated.

After a long shower and some clean clothes, he opened the refrigerator and stared. Seeing nothing of interest, he let it swing shut, only to lower his standards and open it again. This time he reached for sandwich fixings and threw together the first plate of food he'd seen in days. It tasted like cardboard, but he forced half of it down before admitting defeat and dumping it in the trash.

The rest of the evening followed a similar pattern. It was Saturday night, and he had nothing to do until an appointment at the funeral home on Monday morning. He thought about calling Cam, or AJ, or even going down to the garage and finishing up some overdue jobs. But he didn't. Instead he sat on the sofa and stared at the blank screen of his TV.

He fell asleep sometime after midnight, his mind still in bits. His dreams were fragmented, flipping between alternating images of Bella's broken body and Sonny's beautifully weary face. Though some part of his unconscious mind knew he was asleep, that they weren't real, he felt powerless to stop the carnage when they merged, and it was Sonny who was battered beyond repair and dying in his arms. Sonny who was gone forever.

"I'll be here if you change your mind..."

He woke with a strangled gasp, rolling off the couch. The wooden floor was hard against his knees, but he didn't feel the jarring impact. He stumbled to his feet and to the front door, taking the stairs two at a time until he burst out into the fresh air of the street.

The three-block jog to Sonny's apartment passed in a blur, and he found himself, shirtless and barefoot, outside the right door before he knew what he was doing. He knocked. Sonny opened the door, rubbing his eyes. Levi cast his hand aside, grabbed his face, and kissed him.

Sonny let out a grunt of surprise, but he responded without resistance, opening his mouth for Levi's tongue and pulling him inside.

Levi kicked the door shut. The loud slam echoed in the dark silence of Sonny's apartment, but he paid it no heed. He backed Sonny into the opposite wall, kissing him like a man possessed. Though he'd had more sexual encounters this year alone than he could remember, he couldn't remember the last time he'd kissed a man. It had been *years*.

He let his hands roam Sonny's body. Like him, Sonny was shirtless, dressed only in a well-worn pair of sleep pants. Smooth, warm skin met Levi's curious touch. He'd started this on set all those hours ago. Now he wanted to finish it, explore every inch of Sonny he could reach.

Sonny pulled away, his eyes wild. "What do you want from me?"

"I want you to fuck me." The words tumbled out before he could stop them, before he could stop to reconcile what he was asking for, but he meant them. He wanted Sonny more than he'd ever wanted anyone, wanted to feel him, to be consumed by him.

Sonny stared at him, panting, then held out his hand. "Come to bed with me."

Levi took his hand without hesitation and let Sonny lead him through his cluttered apartment to his bedroom. The room mirrored the rest of his apartment—clean but messy, like a whirlwind regularly passed through. Books and clothes littered the dresser and floors. Beyond the bed, a well-loved guitar took pride of place on the window ledge. Levi scanned the textbook titles, all of them related to psychology. *No wonder he gets along with Cam.* It seemed Levi was doomed to spend his time with some kind of wannabe shrink.

Sonny sank his teeth into Levi's bare back. "Come here."

He tugged Levi to the bed without waiting for an answer and pushed him down. Levi sat on the edge and leaned back on his elbows. The sheets were still warm where Sonny had been sleeping before Levi had woken him, and a sliver of moonlight peeked through the closed blinds. He wanted to feel bad for disturbing Sonny, but he didn't.

Sonny eyed him like he wanted to say something. Levi beckoned him forward and pulled Sonny down on top of him. He didn't want to talk, least of all about this. It seemed that *this* was something they'd talked about enough, albeit in a totally different context.

He kissed Sonny, holding him tight by the back of his head. Sonny's skin was intoxicating, and Levi made the most of it, so soft and warm beneath his fingertips and against his chest. He shifted his weight, eager to get Sonny out of his sleep pants. Easy enough, but his own jeans were more problematic.

Sonny growled, frustrated. Levi felt Sonny's dick, hard against his still-clothed thigh, felt him tremble in his arms, and a slow fire began to smolder in his belly. He lifted his hips. Sonny ripped his jeans down his legs and tossed them over his shoulder before he could blink. In some distant part of his mind he'd expected some resistance from Sonny, perhaps even feared rejection, but there was none, and he'd never felt so wanted.

They kissed again. Levi's lips felt swollen and bruised, his skin felt rubbed raw by the addictive stubble on Sonny's jaw, but he couldn't get enough. He flipped Sonny over, his palms falling either side of Sonny's head, and sucked at the juncture between his neck and shoulder, hard enough to leave a mark.

Sonny writhed beneath him, groaning and raking his nails down Levi's back. "Thought you wanted me to fuck you? Keep going like that, and it'll be the other way round.

He had a point. Levi wanted to fuck him, badly, but not as much as he craved the unknown feeling of having Sonny inside him. He rolled over again, letting Sonny take the lead. Sonny kissed him hard before he pulled back, his chest heaving. "Get in the bed. I want to do this properly."

Levi chuckled, amused, but Sonny's expression was earnest, so he did as he was told and folded his body into the bed to lie on his side, his head propped up on one arm. Sonny slipped in beside him and turned to face him. "I don't want this to be like anything you've ever done before."

"Nothing you do to me is like anything I've ever done before."

Sonny smiled and reached over him to the nightstand. He tossed a bottle of lube and some condoms on the pillow between them. Levi eyed the lube warily as Sonny squeezed some onto his fingers. Sonny caught Levi's face in his clean hand. "I'm not going to hurt you."

Sonny stared for a moment, then let go and trailed his hand down Levi's body. Levi shivered, goose bumps covering his skin as Sonny's devilish fingers grazed his abdomen, trailing lower and lower until he took hold of his cock.

Levi looked down, fascinated by the sight of Sonny working him over, and by the sight of Sonny's cock, rock hard and leaking. He longed to take Sonny in his mouth again, but he knew he couldn't, not now. He was at Sonny's mercy, the way he somehow knew he always had been.

Sonny lifted Levi's leg and slipped a slick finger into him. Levi's breath caught. Sonny's fingers were slimmer than his, but they were sure of their path. One finger quickly became two, and then three, stretching him so gently that instead of squirming in pain, he burned—burned with a pleasure so hot he wanted to scream.

He arched his back, pulling Sonny to him and crashing their lips together in a desperate, bruising kiss. Sonny groaned and pushed hard against his chest, forcing him onto his back. He broke away, panting. "Are you ready?"

Levi couldn't see his face in the faint light, but he was sure of his answer, so fucking sure. "Do it."

The tear of the condom wrapper punctuated the eerie quiet of the night. Levi reached out and took it, rolling it onto Sonny with steady hands. Sonny let out a shaky breath and lifted Levi's legs, opening them—opening *him*. He positioned his cock somewhere Levi couldn't see and paused, staring at him, like he was waiting for a last-minute rejection. Then the moment passed, and all Levi could see were blinding white lights as Sonny pushed into him.

It hurt. There was no denying it, but it was the best kind of pain, the kind of pain that inspired and exhilarated a man. Levi let out a long, low moan. "*Fuck.*"

Sonny rubbed a soothing hand over his clenched muscles, smoothing them out one by one. "Breathe. It'll fade, I promise."

Levi shook his head. He didn't want it to fade, didn't want it to ebb away into nothing. He liked the pain, needed it. "I want to feel you."

Somehow, Sonny knew what he meant, knew what he needed. He brought his hands up to the headboard and braced himself, rolling his hips in a long, slow circle. Sweat glistened on his beautiful skin as he lowered his lips to Levi's ear. "Feel that, Levi? Feel it all. This is what it's supposed to be. This is what's real."

Levi closed his eyes, giving himself over as Sonny moved inside him, steady and sure, like the beat of a drum, then faster, deeper and harder, until the tattoo of stampeding pleasure became too much to bear. Or so he thought, until Sonny lithely folded his body in two and took Levi's cock in his mouth.

Levi's eyes flew open, and he gasped in a harsh breath. *Sucking and fucking? Is he kidding me?*

Levi was done. He arched his back and yelled out, pounding his fist into the mattress. His climax ripped through him, roaring through his body, leaving no nerve untouched. Sonny swallowed around him, teasing him with his tongue until he was utterly spent and could take no more.

Sonny released him, dropping his head to Levi's chest. "Oh God, oh God."

Levi dug his fingers into Sonny's shoulders and wrapped his legs tight around him. "Keep fucking me," he said hoarsely. "I wanna see you come."

It didn't take much. Levi gritted his teeth through the aftershocks as Sonny picked up the pace again. Dirty grunts became groans, then desperate moans as he chased his own orgasm. Levi moaned too, clawing at Sonny, the bed, the headboard above him, desperate for anything to brace against the rapid thrust of Sonny's hips.

A violent shudder ran through Sonny, and he stilled. Levi held him close, felt the jolts of energy run through him, felt the pulse of his cock as he filled the condom. Levi felt everything, and the residual pleasure was so intense he could've wept.

Maybe he did.

Sonny rolled to the side, taking Levi with him and wrapping him in a tight embrace. Levi opened his mouth to speak, though to say what, he wasn't quite sure, and nothing but a strangled moan came out.

"Shh." Sonny pressed his lips to the side of Levi's face. "It's okay. Let it go."

Sometime later, Levi woke to find Sonny staring at him, tracing the healed cuts and fresh bruises on Levi's body with the pad of his finger. Something in Sonny's face bothered him. He forced his scratchy eyes open. "What's up?"

Sonny shrugged and made to look away.

Levi caught Sonny's face in his hand, forcing him to stay put. "Tell me."

"I feel like I'm missing something, something huge." Sonny tapped the side of Levi's head, his expression pensive. "Something's wrong. I know it is, but you make me kinda crazy, like I can't help myself."

Levi rolled onto his back and stared at the ceiling. An odd, dull pain throbbed at the base of his spine, but he found it comforting—grounding, almost—like it was just enough to remind him this was real. He opened his mouth. Shut it again.

Sonny sat up and scratched at Levi's chest. "What is it? Tell me."

"My mom died."

There, he'd said it. Sonny's nails faltered on his chest. "When?"

Levi's brain failed him for a moment. He glanced at the clock. It was Sunday morning, four a.m. "Friday."

"How? Was she sick?"

"Kinda..." Levi stopped and took in a shaky breath. "She was an alcoholic. She walked in front of a truck on Thursday night."

"Oh, God. Levi, that's awful. Why did you come to the shoot?"

Now there was a question. Most of Bella's debts had died with her. His porn career was over if he wanted it to be. Levi shrugged. The room was dark, but he knew Sonny could see him. "I don't know. Maybe, on some level, I thought I needed to do it. I...I don't know."

He was at a loss to explain. His daddy's death had left him with an ingrained sense of responsibility, a need to honor every promise he'd ever made. Perhaps it was that.

Or perhaps it was the need to be with the man in his arms. For weeks, he'd found himself torn between a real fear of what was to come next and an unbelievable desire for Sonny. Now, despite the shadow hanging over him, and despite the fact that there was so much more to say, with Sonny in his arms he felt at peace. He could tell him the rest later. Or not.

Sonny was silent for a while, the persistent light scratch of his nails the only sign he was even awake. Then he shifted and roused Levi from the light doze he'd fallen into.

"You know I wasn't going to let it get that far, don't you? With Rex?"

"Huh?" Levi opened his eyes drowsily. "What do you mean?"

Sonny finally stilled his fingertips, sat up, and put his chin on Levi's chest. "I knew you weren't ready...in any sense. I could see it in your eyes. I was going to jump you before he could, then let him take his revenge on me after."

"You'd take that bullet for me?"

"Yes."

"Why?"

Sonny groaned and ducked his head. "Oh, God. I don't know. I told you. You make me crazy. I couldn't see you get hurt like that."

Levi pulled him up and kissed him. "Trust me, darlin', I get it. Why do you think I kicked that douche bag across the room?"

Sonny shivered. "Man, you and that accent. Gets me every time."

Levi grinned, but though he was at ease in Sonny's bed, the nagging question of what came next was eating away at him. The sky was beginning to lighten, and with the dawn came reality and the looming prospect of going home to an empty apartment.

He opened his eyes. Somehow they'd fallen closed again without him noticing. Sonny was watching him. Levi reached out and touched his cheek. "Can I make you breakfast?"

Sonny smiled, his hazel gaze gleaming in the dim room. "Sure, and after that, you can take me to your bed and let me teach *you* how to fuck *me*."

Levi let out a startled snort of laughter, but in answer, he pulled Sonny to him and kissed him like he'd never kissed him before. He'd signed his life away more times than he cared to remember, but for once, he'd struck a deal he couldn't wait to see through.

VOLUME 2 — BONES

CHAPTER ONE

Cam fought the silk ties restraining his wrists. The knots were loose, and his arms were strong. With enough effort he could be free in moments. Free to roll over and demand what he wanted. Free to do anything and be anywhere but here.

A soft puff of air washed over his spine, belying the firm hands on his hips. "Still."

The effect of the command was instant, calming Cam from the inside out. His heart beat like a racing freight train, but the desire to defy his binds evaporated.

He sucked in a shaky breath. Away from Jon Kellar, his lover of sorts, he resisted the submissive role he'd accidentally fallen into, but when they were together, it was easy to give in to the dark temptation of Jon's bed. Easy to fall back into a place where time stood still and there was nothing in the world but the carnal pleasure of someone else calling the shots.

"Spread your legs."

Cam obeyed and arched his back with a groan, craving the sensation of Jon's cock pressing inside him, even though he knew Jon would keep him hanging for hours yet.

At least, it often felt like hours. Jon Kellar was a master

manipulator, and Cam knew he wouldn't give up his game of teasing temptation until Cam was begging...screaming for more.

Warm breath rushed over Cam's skin, and then the light brush of the feather Jon liked to skim over his cock. Cam shuddered, feeling the first strands of desperation deep in his belly.

Jon rubbed his hand over Cam's sweat-slicked back, kneading until he came to the curved muscle of Cam's ass. He slapped Cam with enough force to leave a pleasurable burn. "What do you want? Want me to fuck you?"

Cam moaned. It was too soon for him to lose his head, but *damn*, this shit felt good. Too good.

Jon chuckled and slapped Cam again, soothing the heated sting with the palm of his hand. "Maybe I'll rim you first. Would you like that?"

"Fuck yeah."

"Quiet."

The silence was long and excruciating. Cam trembled, and his thighs quivered with a need only Jon had ever provoked. Christ, Jon was the only man he'd ever bottomed for at all, let alone given over control of his body.

What the hell are you doing?

Some days, he didn't know, and others, he knew Jon had caught him at a weak time in his life and shown him how to lose himself in desire and sex until the rest of the world faded away. And then some days...fuck. Some days all he knew was a craving so deep his bones felt like they could combust into smoke and ash.

Jon trailed the tip of the feather down the crease of Cam's ass and moved lower, ghosting over his balls. On fire, Cam gritted his teeth and forced himself to stay still until he was finally rewarded by the sweeping touch of Jon's tongue.

He dropped his head to the mattress and widened his legs. He'd never been into rimming before he'd answered the ad in the back of the LGBT newsletter in his senior year at college.

Fast-forward four years and he was a veteran porn star, and he couldn't get enough. Especially with Jon. Everything was better with Jon, in the bedroom at least.

Jon teased him with the tip of his tongue, alternating between light, gentle licks and toe-curling, stabbing thrusts. He kept his hands busy on Cam's body too, manipulating his tense, twitching muscles and rubbing his back. He grazed Cam's balls with his nails and pinched the insides of Cam's thighs.

He was everywhere, except where Cam wanted him most.

Cam jerked and tugged again at his binds, watching his aching cock drip on the smooth cotton sheets below him. "Jon..."

Jon chuckled and bit Cam's ass cheek. "Something you want?"

"You know what I want." Cam ground the words out through clenched teeth. They played this game all the time—the one where he ducked his head and begged...said please like a good boy—but Cam always fought it. Always gave Jon a reason to push him harder.

"Do I?" Jon took his hands from Cam's body. The rustling sheets and sudden gust of cool air told Cam he'd moved away. "Maybe I need reminding."

The click of the lube bottle opening drowned out the crackle of a condom wrapper. Cam tensed, knowing the blunt intrusion of Jon's cock wasn't too far away. "Fuck me."

"I can't hear you, Cam."

"*Fuck me*," Cam said louder. "Goddamn it."

"Hmm." Jon drizzled warming lube on Cam's ass and massaged it in with his thumb. "Maybe I should make you wait a little longer."

The tingle of the lube stung a moment before it seeped into Cam's skin and warmed him from the inside out. He squirmed, knowing exactly what Jon wanted, and hating himself for giving it up. "Please."

Jon stilled his devilish thumb. "I can't hear you."

Cam sucked in deep breaths, trying to calm the tremors rocking his body. His senses dulled and narrowed his perspective, leaving only anticipation and the aching throb of his cock. Somewhere in the back of his mind, he laughed. How did Jon do this? Narrow his universe to just the heady brew of desire?

"Focus." Jon slid a single finger into Cam, stretching him with practiced motions. The snap of latex pierced the air. "Say it again."

A low moan escaped Cam. "*Please.*"

Jon's finger disappeared, replaced by his condom-covered cock. Cam arched against the intrusion, feeling the dizzying burn of being filled sweep over him.

Jon steadied him, his hands almost soothing on Cam's overheated skin. "Relax. Don't fight what you need."

In Cam's mind, he tore the silk ties apart, ripped free, and pushed himself back onto Jon, chasing the bittersweet slam of their bodies, but in reality he held stone still, ready for whatever Jon would give him.

Jon slid into him, hard and fast. Cam gasped and for a moment longed for Jon to hold him closer to wrap his arms around Cam's waist and cover his body, but the feeling faded as the punishing beat of Jon's hips overcame coherent thought.

Cam gritted his teeth as Jon fucked him and took him to the brink of something mind-blowing, over and over, only to ease off each time before the punch line. Frustrated, Cam moaned and shuddered, making sounds only Jon had ever heard. The need to come became the only thing in his world. Sweat dripped from his body. His hair hung low in his face, and his cock throbbed so hard it *hurt*.

He groaned, long and loud, clenching his bound fists, desperate to grab on to something, anything. Even his own hair. *So good. So good.* "More..."

On cue, Jon slowed his thrusts to a dull roar and reached around, closing his fingers around Cam's dick. "Like this?"

The light touch was like a thunderbolt. Cam jerked, bucked, and growled, low and deep. "Shit, yeah."

Jon moved his hand in counterpoint with his hips. Once. Twice. Three times. "Come."

The command lit the fuse and triggered the climax Cam had held back for so long. He came hard, yelling his release and fighting the silk ties that bound him to the bed. "Fuck, fuck, *fuck*."

Behind him, Jon grunted and pulled out, the only sign of his own climax the sudden, warm spurt on Cam's back, before he untied Cam and rolled away.

Cam fell forward, exhausted, and collapsed into the sticky mess on the bed, watching in his peripheral vision as Jon got up and left the room. The bathroom door closed. The shower turned on, and he knew that was his cue to move too.

He slid off the bed, gathered the sheets, and dumped them into the hamper. His clothes littered the floor. He picked them up, feeling the way he always did after sex with Jon—sated, satisfied, and empty.

A little while later, Cam took his turn in the shower and drifted into Jon's minimalist living space to find him already seated behind his computer.

Jon didn't look up as he entered the room. That was typical too. Their evenings together followed a predictable routine— dinner, frustrating foreplay, mind-blowing sex, and then...nothing. Recently, the prefuck dinner had become an optional extra, though there was always a plentiful supply of Jon's expensive liquor.

Cam suppressed a sigh. They weren't dating, and he wasn't

naive enough to believe he was the only Blue Boy model getting off in Jon's bed, but the silence stung.

He approached Jon from behind and put his hands on Jon's shoulders, squeezing the wiry muscle he found there. Jon was fast approaching forty but still had the body of a much younger man. "What are you doing?"

"The schedule for next month."

Cam peered at the screen. "What am I doing?"

"Breaking in some newbies."

Cam let the sigh he'd been holding escape. Really? More massages and dull-as-rocks blowjobs from skittish rookies? That was another thing about fooling around with Jon. Jon still paid him the same, but it had been *months* since he'd shot a full sex scene. Months since he'd done anything more than lie back and get sucked off on-screen. "Can't I do something else?"

"Like what?"

"I don't know." Cam stared at the faces of his colleagues rolling across the screen. Kai, Jimmy, Sonny. The fresh face of a model he'd broken in six months ago flashed up. "What about Jack?"

"Jack's a top."

"So?"

Jon looked at Cam for the first time since making him come like a train, and his icy blue gaze hardened. "You want to bottom on-screen?"

"Sure. Why not?"

Jon shook his head. "It doesn't fit your brand."

"My brand?"

"You're the top everyone loves. The top that looks after his bottoms and gives them a good ride. Getting fucked will undermine that."

Cam raised an incredulous eyebrow. Jon had always been difficult to read, but his porn philosophy was goddamned bizarre. How could he brand Cam a top when he hadn't assigned Cam a hard-core scene in months? "You didn't say that about Levi. You all but forced him into it."

"And look what happened there. The scene was a bust, and I lost a lucrative model."

Cam knew there was far more to Levi's departure from Blue Boy, but he held his tongue. There was no love lost between his friend and his warped kind-of lover, and the less said about each of them in the other's company, the better. "You sound like you're losing your nerve."

"And you sound like you've got too much time on your hands. Trust me, when I get requests for you, it's not from people who want to see you get nailed. Stick to what you're good at."

Jon turned back to his work, the discussion closed. Cam took his dismissal and left.

Pop. Slam. Skid.

Cam maneuvered his skateboard along the sketchy park railing and popped out a lackadaisical laser flip. The landing wasn't great, but he stayed upright. Not bad for seven a.m. Though there was no one around, he grinned and gave the air a punch. Levi said Cam was too old to be boarding to work, that he should hang it up and get a car like the rest of the world. Cam called bullshit every damned time. He was twenty-five, not fifty, and even then they'd have to pry his board from his cold, dead hands.

It was a long skate to work, though. Forty-five minutes when the weather was good. An hour if he had to pick up and walk. Lucky for him, part of his journey took him along the deserted, early morning beachfront—his favorite place on earth. The sun in his eyes, the ocean breeze in his face, he'd yet to find a better way to start his day.

He skidded to a stop outside Beat Shak, the music store that made up his day job, just before eight. He was the first there, but that was typical. Early shifts suited him, and there weren't often any other takers. Good job too, as he doubted anyone else would be awake enough to deal with the washed-up visitor waiting on the bench outside.

Sonny.

Cam greeted him with open arms. Sonny walked right into them and placed a firm, platonic kiss on Cam's lips, tangling his fingers in Cam's riot of auburn hair.

"You're late today. I've been waiting ages."

Cam glanced at his watch. "It's not that late, Son. What time did you leave the club?"

"Dunno, dunno." Sonny bounced on the balls of his feet, still wired from his night, dancing on the podiums at Silver, the hippest gay club in town. "Just wanted to see your freakish morning smile."

Cam rewarded him with a wide grin, knowing his cheerful early morning habits bemused the hell out of night-owl Sonny. "Have you got classes today?"

Sonny danced into the shop behind him and took a seat at the digital-services counter that doubled as a juice bar. "At ten. No point going home."

Cam rolled his eyes. He didn't dig Sonny's habit of staying awake for days at a time, but who was he to judge? He'd said his piece once, and that was enough. He was Sonny's friend, not his mother, and it wasn't like Sonny was banging coke up his nose, though in some ways, Cam could've dealt with that...understood it, even if he wouldn't like it.

He threw an extra breakfast burrito in the microwave. Didn't want the hottest dancer in LA to starve, and though Cam could tell Levi had been feeding Sonny up, Sonny was pretty crappy at feeding himself. "Good night?"

Sonny hummed, still grooving to his own tune. "Yeah. The tips were good. Some dude tried to shove a twenty up my ass, though. I'm down for a lot of shit, but that wasn't cool. Security chucked him out."

"Was Jon there?"

"I didn't see him." Sonny shot him a waspish stare.

Cam averted his gaze. "How does Levi feel about you dancing up a storm for other dudes?"

"Never asked him."

"That's dangerous."

"Not really." Sonny rubbed his eyes. He looked weary, despite his incorrigible spirit. "He knew what he was getting into. Besides, he'd be the one fucking the whole studio if his mom hadn't died. He didn't give up porn for me."

Cam absorbed that. "Can't be easy, though. Sharing you. Has he ever asked you to cut back on your hard-core scenes?"

"No, and I don't think he ever would. What's with all the questions? You know Levi's cool. Something on your mind?"

Cam rummaged in the under-counter fridge for soda. "Just curious. You know how it is."

Sonny grinned. Their shared fascination with psychology was what had brought them together in the first place. Working for Jon was a devilish and fortuitous coincidence.

"Look at it this way," Sonny said. "Levi and I do shit together we don't do with anyone else. Have never done with anyone else. Maybe you should do that too. Find someone to share something special with. Separate your real sex life from the studio."

Cam opened the cash register. He'd be lying if he said he'd never wondered about Sonny and Levi's sex life. Sonny was kind of toppy for a bottom—demanding and dominant—and Levi liked to be in control. It was an interesting mix and one Cam had pondered a lot.

But Sonny's choice of words distracted him from any X-rated musings, and not in a good way. Sonny was always talking about *real* sex, like there was another world out there away from porn, a world Cam had forgotten about. "I wasn't talking about me."

"Because of Jon?"

Cam didn't answer. Sonny knew something had happened between him and Jon a few months ago, but Cam had yet to admit it was still going on. He wondered what Sonny would say if he knew how Cam submitted to Jon and how readily he let another man take control of his body.

You know exactly what he'd say.

The microwave pinged. Cam slid a nasty, boxed burrito Sonny's way. Sonny wrinkled his nose. Cam laughed, glad of the distraction. "You're spending way too much time with Momma Levi."

Sonny shrugged, unashamed. "The dude cooks and puts out. The perfect man, when he's not a grouch bag."

"Levi's always a grouch bag. It's part of his charm."

"I know." Sonny smiled, though Cam got the distinct impression it wasn't for him and instead for the private moment between Sonny and whatever image was floating through his kooky brain.

Cam didn't mind. He hadn't seen much of Levi since he'd severed his contract with Blue Boy, and he knew that was because Levi figured Cam was too close to Jon, but he saw Sonny all the time and could tell something special was building between him and Levi. Something Cam had never foreseen, even when his own flippant remark to Jon had pushed them together...

"Levi and Sonny? Interesting." Jon beckoned Sonny over and put the idea to him.

Sonny rolled his eyes. Most models treated Jon with a kind of reverence, but not Sonny. "No fucking way. I don't do jocks with cocks."

Cam spluttered into his drink. "Are you kidding? Dude, Levi's not like that. He's the warmest guy you'll ever meet. And he's smart too, smarter than all of us. Don't put him down."

Jon raised an eyebrow, but Cam ignored him. He was the

wrong side of drunk to filter his words, and it annoyed the crap out of him when folk assumed big, brawny, huge-hearted Levi was as thick as his vital statistics.

Sonny stared at him with curious eyes. "Warm? He walks around like he's dead inside."

Cam sighed and tipped the last of his drink into his mouth. "If he ends up that way, it won't be his fault. That dude needs to be loved. Fuck, he deserves to be loved."

Cam had never expected Sonny to take his drunken rant so literally.

"Are you on the filming schedule tomorrow?"

Cam nodded through a bite of cheap, pasty burrito. "First up."

"Another handjob scene?" Sonny raised an eyebrow and picked at his breakfast. "You should just quit if that's all you're going to do. I'll see you right a few times a week. Levi wouldn't mind."

There was mirth in Sonny's words, but they struck a little close to home for Cam's liking. He finished his breakfast in silence and busied himself with his preopening checklist, hoping Sonny would get the hint.

Sonny didn't. "Why don't you come in on my scene with Luke? I can handle you both. It'll be fun, like old times."

A shiver of yearning ran through Cam. He used to shoot with Sonny all the time, more often than not carrying on long after they left the studio. He'd had Sonny every way he could think of, and it had always been fun. There were no romantic feelings between them, but their sexual chemistry was hot as hell when the context worked out.

His mind flashed unbidden to the last time he'd fucked Sonny, bent over the couch in his apartment. He pictured Sonny's perfect body writhing beneath him, shining with sweat and streaked with leftover body paint from a wild night at Silver.

Damn. The image in his head wasn't even Sonny. It was every guy he'd ever fucked. What the hell did that mean? Maybe Sonny was right and he *did* need to put himself out there again.

"Earth to Cam?"

"Huh?"

"Never mind." Sonny slid from his stool and came around the counter. He wrapped his arms around Cam's neck and pulled him down for another chaste kiss. "I might see you tomorrow if you're still at the studio. If not, call me, okay? Levi misses you, and you know he won't pick up the phone. He only calls me for the fuck-awesome phone sex."

Sonny spun away from Cam with a graceful twirl that belied his dirty wink. Cam said good-bye with an absent wave. He missed Levi too, and he knew better than to wait for the stubborn brute to come and find him. "Hey, Son?"

"Yeah?"

"Go home after class, okay? Get some sleep."

The rest of the day passed in a predictable haze. The store was a pleasant mix of the past and the ever-changing present, and Cam spent most of his day sorting stone-age vinyl on one side of the shop and helping the technologically inept get to grips with digital music on the other.

At lunchtime, he threw another plastic-wrapped roll of junk into the microwave on the juice bar.

"You're not going to eat that, are you?"

Cam glanced over his shoulder and met a set of the warmest brown eyes he'd ever seen. Darker brown than Sonny's hazel, they were flecked with gold and made the blond guy's grin like the early fall sun. "That's the plan."

The guy cast his gaze around the juice bar. "All this vitamin C and you choose that crap? Shame on you, man."

Cam shrugged. He'd heard it all before from his mom, when she was still around to notice, Levi, and just about every other weirdo who liked to pick their way through the grocery store, squeezing melons and prodding tomatoes. "It'll do me. Can I help you with something?"

"Aren't you on a break?" The guy gestured to the rotating microwave. "I can ask someone else."

"Nah." Cam came around the counter and held out his hand for the battered vinyl sleeve the guy was holding. "It'll keep. What do you need?"

The guy relinquished the sleeve. "I'm looking for this for my mom. She's had it since the seventies, but the record got broke when me and my bro were moving our bike shit around in the garage. I figure she won't be as pissed if I get a replacement before we tell her."

"Bike shit? Motorcycles?" Cam studied the record sleeve. The guy was starting to look familiar. Perhaps he knew Levi.

"BMX."

Something clicked in Cam's head. "Do you work at Tate's Bikes a few blocks away? I get board parts from there sometimes."

"That's my store." Hot Guy held out his hand. "Sasha Tate."

That explained the grungy board shorts, tanned forearms, and surfer-style hair. "Cam. Nice to meet you. I haven't been in for a while, but your place is pretty rad."

"Thanks. You should come by sometime after work. A bunch of us usually go hang at the Basin until sundown."

The Basin was the colloquial name for the only park in Venice Beach where skateboarders and BMXers rode together in harmony. Every other park in town was strictly one or the other, and *no one* liked the bladers. Cam hadn't been down there in a while, though. Most days life seemed to get in the way. "Sounds good. I'll check it out."

Sasha's grin widened, and for a moment, Cam forgot all about the record sleeve in his hand.

"So do you think you can help me with that? Do I have to order it or something?"

"Hmm? Oh, I don't know. Let me look on the system. We get heaps of this old crap in all the time. We might have it here."

"It's not crap, dude. It's a classic."

Cam rolled his eyes and took the old Beatles record to the computer on the vinyl side of the shop and tapped in his pass code. Sasha followed and stood beside him, close enough so Cam could smell the scents of bike oil and ocean breeze on him.

Nice.

The vinyl record came up on the computer screen. Bingo. They had it in stock. Cam logged off and pointed to a shelf loaded with vinyl records. "The system says it's somewhere up there. Might take me a while to find it. Do you need to get back to work?"

"I do, actually. Can I come by later and pick it up?"

"Works for me. If you're not back before three, I'll leave it behind the counter for you."

Sasha flashed another breathtaking grin, and this time Cam took note of the dimple in his left cheek. "That's awesome. Thanks, man. Check you later."

He punched Cam's shoulder and ambled to the door, leaving Cam to rub his tingling arm and spend the rest of his shift pondering just how much of Sasha's skin was touched by his deep, golden tan.

Later that evening, Cam's daydreaming got the better of him, and he came back to reality to find his father and older sister bickering over his head. About him, apparently, and his nonexistent plans for the future.

"Leave the boy alone, Kay. He came for his dinner, not an inquisition."

Cam shot his father a grateful look. His sister was the best, but she was like a dog with a damned bone when she had her mind set on something. Jesus. That would teach him for stopping by on a weekday evening. He was prepared for this shit on a Sunday.

Kay huffed. "Let me talk, Dad." She ruffled Cam's hair, and her expression softened. "I'm just saying, you graduated college three years ago. If you're not going to do anything with that degree, you should probably do something else. Find a nice man. Settle down, and give Dad some grandbabies. I was reading about surrogacy in—"

"Kay, stop." Cam groaned and laid his head on the kitchen counter. This was the con of having an open-minded family who knew and accepted every facet of his life—they had an opinion on everything too. "I'm not seeing anyone right now, and even if I was, I wouldn't be hustling them down the sperm bank."

He was saved by the oven timer. Kay turned away to deal with the bubbling lasagna, and by the time Cam sat down to a rowdy family dinner with his dad, Kay, and his younger twin brothers, the subject had been left by the wayside.

After dinner, he cleaned up with his dad. "Thanks for the save with Kay. She's been on my case about that for weeks."

"The school thing?" Wade dried a chipped plate. Mom had taken all the good ones. "Don't worry about that. She just worries about you. She wants to see you settled."

"I am settled."

"Settled doing nothin'." Wade raised his hand. "And don't tell me making those adult art films makes you happy, because Lord knows, I don't think it does."

"Dad, just call it porn."

"Humor me."

Cam grinned. There were elements of Blue Boy that were considered artistic—the location scenes, and the scripts Jon sometimes wrote, but he figured his pop's idea of porn involved rubber police uniforms and bad mustaches. "What pearl of wisdom are you trying to get out?"

"None, today at least. I think you've had enough of that from your sister. I'm just saying you've been working at the store awhile now, and doing your...filming. Maybe it's time to branch out."

Wade said no more, but that was typical of him. He liked to drop a bomb of astute philosophy on the table and let it fester. He'd come back to it in six months' time and expect Cam to have an answer.

Still, it could've been worse, a lot worse. Cam's family had fragmented in two, but what remained was strong and real. Not like the broken mess of Levi's childhood or the hotbed of rejection that had driven Sonny all the way to LA. Cam couldn't imagine a world without his family. His parents had been married thirty years, and they hadn't made it through, but the love that remained was the most important love of all.

They finished the dishes in companionable silence, and after, Wade shuffled off to watch his fishing show, leaving Cam to contemplate what to do with the rest of his evening. With the next day's shoot looming, he felt keyed up and restless, like he wanted to stay up all night, hanging out, playing pool, or shooting the breeze with someone who just...got him.

On cue, his phone vibrated in his pocket. A message from Jon.

Midnight. My place.

Cam stared at the text with a strange sensation in the pit of his belly. He craved companionship and warmth, but somehow, even though his night was sure to end connected to the body of another, he'd never felt more alone.

CHAPTER THREE

"Are you ready?"

Cam met Jon's gaze with a scowl. "Ready for what? All I'm doing is lying on a fucking couch."

"Are you going to be like this all day?"

"Like what?"

Jon fixed him with a steady glare. "Forget it. Just be on set in five. Matthew's ready."

Cam stared after Jon's retreating back, frustrated. He knew he was being a brat, but he couldn't help it. Jon brought out the worst in him when they were at odds, and even sometimes when they weren't. Bitter and bitchy—that's how he felt, and he didn't like it. He didn't like it at all.

A sleepless night didn't help. He'd answered Jon's midnight summons, only to be sidelined by a phone call that just couldn't wait. Jon never came back to bed, and Cam gave up waiting at two a.m. and walked home to glare at his own bedroom ceiling and wonder when he'd become such a fucking loser.

Cam got to his feet with a heavy sigh, feeling the burn in his legs from a frustration-driven predawn gym session. It hadn't always been like this. He remembered the first time Jon coaxed him into bed...that balmy summer evening his dad had sat him down and told him his mom was leaving for good. Distraught, Cam had found himself drunk and alone at Silver, nursing his eleventieth shot of bourbon. Jon had taken him home and fucked him. Lit some candles and made him feel special...safe. Like the world as he knew it wasn't imploding. The storm passed, but sometimes he felt like he'd been chasing that relief ever since.

He stomped his way to the set. A few of the crew shot him curious glances, letting him know his rare bad mood was more than a little obvious. Jon ignored him entirely, and to distract himself, Cam cast his gaze around, looking for his partner in crime for the day. He didn't have to look far. On the couch at the back of the set sat Matthew, another dancer from Silver who'd made the transition to Blue Boy model.

Cam crossed the set and flopped down beside Matthew. His own frame was slim and athletic, but Matthew was petite and Cam dwarfed him. "'S'up."

Matthew returned his fist bump. "Hey, man. How's it going?"

"Same old, same old." Cam wasn't about to pour his heart out. "You all set for today? Got any questions? Limits? Shit you don't like?"

"Nope, I'm good." Matthew grinned, showing Cam a set of perfect white teeth. With inky hair and green eyes too similar to Cam's own to hold any intrigue, he wasn't Cam's type at all. "I told Jon I was ready to dive right in, but he said I had to shoot a foreplay scene first."

"Really?" Dampening down eagerness wasn't Jon's usual MO. Cam filed the information away for later. "Well, it might be foreplay, but we can make it good. Sure there's nothing you don't want to do?"

Matthew shook his head. "I'm game for anything."

Cam rolled his eyes, wondering if the kid knew no one was listening, though it was possible he meant every word. Some models *didn't* care what happened to their bodies on set. In fact, some of them craved the pounding some of the tops liked to give out. Still, though Jon would've covered all bases, Cam always made a point of asking, even when he filmed with a model he knew well. Shit like that could change in a heartbeat, and he didn't want to be the bastard who gave a guy nightmares.

"How's the dancing going? You gonna keep it up now you've moved over here?"

Matthew stretched out his legs. "Probably. Sonny and Kai do both, right? And Sonny's in college too, so it can't be that hard."

Give it time. "See how you feel. You might find the extra cash isn't worth the effort."

"Maybe." Matthew shrugged. "Someone told me you're a dancer too, but I haven't seen you around."

"I don't dance anymore. I used to, back in the day, but I gave it up. It wasn't really my scene."

Like porn, Cam had fallen into dancing on podiums in the clubs by accident. It was fun and a cheap way to party. He didn't have half the moves the headhunted dancers at Silver did, but he could work a pole well enough.

"You're too big to be a dancer anyway. Most of us are tiny, except Sonny, and he's still pretty compact."

Cam snickered. "Trust me. Sonny ain't *that* small."

Matthew grinned and the conversation moved on, but an odd sensation crept into Cam's belly. He felt strange, like he could climb out of his own skin.

"Everybody ready?"

Cam nodded without meeting Jon's gaze, his mind already on autopilot. He counted down in his head. *Five. Four. Three. Two. One...*

"Action!"

Matthew slid into Cam's lap like a snake, and his lips were

on Cam's without preamble, negating any need for staged banter.

Cam went with the flow, like he did most scenes, relaxing into the kiss and letting his hands roam Matthew's supple body, getting a feel for him and searching for the common ground that would bring them together.

Matthew worked his lips down Cam's neck and tugged at his T-shirt. Cam pulled it over his head and returned the gesture, taking in the bold and bright tattoos stamped on Matthew's torso. They were like badges, or robots, maybe...Cam couldn't tell.

Cam frowned on the inside. Most of the smaller models were inked up these days, but Sonny aside, tattoos didn't do it for him. He much preferred naked skin, those swathes of flesh where he could see the true shape of a man—the curves of muscle and bone...

Matthew bit down on Cam's nipple. Cam shuddered, and his dick hardened, slow and sure. He liked teeth—grazing and nipping. He moaned to let Matthew know he was on the right track. Matthew bit him again, moving lower and lower until he came to Cam's waistband.

Cam raised his hips in response. "Fuck, yeah."

The scene continued, following a loose but predictable routine. Clothes disappeared, the leather couch squeaked, and before long Cam found himself on his back, his dick in Matthew's mouth, and Matthew's dick and ass hovering over his face.

He blew Matthew for a while, enjoying his thighs quivering and tensing around his shoulders. What Matthew lacked in on-screen experience, he made up for in enthusiasm. He was good with his mouth and hands, and Cam let himself be carried away by the hot, wet heat of another man's tongue on his cock.

A distant pleasure began to coil in the pit of Cam's stomach.

He pulled his mouth off Matthew's dick with wet *pop* and thrust his own hips up. "Yeah, like that, like that."

Matthew worked him harder. Cam closed his eyes and let it wash over him while he took a second to consider his options. Matthew had a nice ass, and he'd said he was up for anything...

Cam slid his index finger into his mouth and opened his eyes to find Jon watching him from behind the main camera. Was it his imagination, or did the man seem pissed?

What the fuck is his problem?

Cam deliberated a moment, then cut Jon out of his mind and pressed his spit-slick finger into Matthew, gauging his reaction to every twist and flick. Of all the facets of porn, this was probably what Cam, enjoyed the most—observing, fascinated, as each partner responded differently to his touch.

Sometimes he got carried away and found himself pondering the possible correlations between events in a man's real life and his behavior on the set, but not today. Today he was still squirming from his unsatisfactory encounter the night before, and he needed to fucking come.

For a moment he considered rearranging the whole scene and pushing his cock inside Matthew's tight body. It had been so long since he'd topped, the image in his head sent a shiver of energy through his overheated body. He looked around for condoms and lube. On set, such things were never far away.

Jon caught his eye, read his intentions, and shook his head. The message was clear. *Not today.*

Anger surged through Cam, but Matthew chose that moment to grind down on Cam's fingers, blocking Jon from view. "I'm gonna come."

Cam focused and wrapped his free hand around Matthew's dick. He wasn't even close, but that was easily fixed once Matthew shot his load. Cam twisted his fingers, finding the bundle of nerves inside Matthew and tickled it in time with each pass of his thumb over the head of Matthew's cock.

It didn't take long. Matthew yelped and spilled on Cam's chest, shivering like he'd never felt such a thing before. Maybe he hadn't. Cam watched him shudder with a wry smile. The number of bottoms he'd come across who'd never had their prostate touched often bemused him. How the hell did they live?

"Your turn."

Cam shifted on the couch, making his dick more accessible. Matthew took him in his mouth and set a fast pace that should've made Cam come with little trouble. But it didn't happen, and for a while release kept itself out of reach, teasing Cam with its nearness.

Impatient and feeling Jon's eyes on him, Cam gave Matthew a hand, literally, and relief swept over him when he came with a quiet cry. The last jolts of orgasm eased, and after, he lay still and stared at the ceiling, ignoring the bustle of the cleanup crew. He'd been craving this for days, but instead of satiation, he felt edgy and unfulfilled, and his balls felt heavy, like he'd only blown half his load. The logical part of his brain knew such a thing was impossible. Coming was coming, right? So why did he feel so damned unsatisfied?

Friday
Act(s)—Kissing, blowjobs, handjobs. Ass play (not mine)
Partner(s)—Matthew
???? I don't know. I used to feel upbeat after every scene. Energized, like I could take on the world. Today I feel like some fucker turned me inside out without ever laying a finger on me. It's not Matthew's fault, or even Jon's. I'm just in a weird place right now, and I don't know why. I feel strange. Like my skin's not my own.

It's been like this for a while now. After every shoot I feel more and more like I've only done half a job...like I've missed out on something or forgotten to do something really fucking important. Lol. Or maybe I need to rearrange those words. Maybe fucking has become too important to me.

Does this mean I should quit porn? Who knows? Maybe Levi. I'd ask him if the dude ever picked up his phone.

Cam sat back and squinted at the scrawl in his journal. The entry was shorter than his usual ramblings, but he had nothing else to say. He'd left the studio without watching the rest of the scenes unfold, and hit the gym again, hoping to dispel the discontent lingering in his veins, but it hadn't worked. Instead he'd found himself more restless than ever and unable to decipher his mood.

He set down his pen with a sigh. Perhaps that was the point. He'd been keeping a diary since he'd confessed his fledgling porn career to a fellow psych student a few years back. The chick had asked him to record his thoughts and feelings for a month or so, so she could analyze them for her thesis. He'd agreed, and three years later, it was a habit he'd yet to crack. The thick, spiral-bound notebook cataloged every scene or encounter he'd ever been paid to perform.

On occasion, he flipped through the scribbled accounts, trying to track his state of mind from month to month, year to year, but it had been a while, and today he was a little scared of what he might find. Had he really become such a fiend that he was only happy if he was banging the world?

Man, he hoped not. Porn star he may've been, but there was more to life than sex. There had to be, 'cause Lord knew he wasn't getting any. At least not the kind that mattered.

Quasi Sonny popped into his mind. *"Real sex—the kind where someone looks at you like you're their whole world. You don't get that in porn, Cam."*

CHAPTER FOUR

"Long time, no see."

Cam glanced up as a BMX skidded to a stop beside him.

Sasha, the hot Beatles fan, greeted him with a wide grin. "Hey."

Cam smiled back. It was early, as always, and he was kneeling outside the Beat Shak, cleaning the A-Board sign. Sasha's smiling face was a welcome surprise. Cam had missed his return trip to the store last week. "Hey yourself."

"Whatcha doing?"

"Cleaning, dude. What does it look like?"

Sasha made a face that set a spark somewhere deep inside Cam. A spark that made him giddy.

Huh.

"It's too early for cleaning, man." Sasha looked up at the sky. "Come for a ride."

Cam stood and took in the sight of Sasha astride his bike. With his broad shoulders and sun-lightened hair, it was quite a picture. "No can do. I'm the only one here, *and* I don't think my board would keep up with you."

"True. How about later? I'll lend you a bike, if you're game enough to ride with me."

Sasha was definitely gay. Cam knew even before the subtle flirtation lacing the challenge hit him full force. "What time?"

"Anytime after four. I'm the boss. I can do what I like."

Sasha stood up on his pedals and rolled off the sidewalk, zipping away before Cam found his tongue.

Cam wondered into the store in a daze. Did that really just happen? Despite the distraction of the studio, he'd thought of Sasha a lot since they'd met the week before. The guy was hot, and he had a grin that lit up Cam's world, where genuine grins, untainted by lights and cameras, were in short supply.

He'd kind of figured he'd never see Sasha again, though. After all, Sasha's BMX store had been in business a few years, and Cam had *never* set eyes on him before. He would've remembered.

Still, Sasha's rugged allure aside, the idea of a ride was tempting. Cam hadn't hit a BMX ramp for ages, and the thrill was something he couldn't deny.

At least, that's what he told himself when he clocked off shift at four thirty p.m. and skated the two short blocks to Tate's Bikes.

Sasha met him with that damned grin and thrust a bike at him with little preamble. "Race you to the Basin."

It took a while for Cam to find his rhythm. Boarding came to him like breathing, but the bike was a different animal. His muscles burned, and the speed blew his mind. It was terrifying, and he loved it.

And it wasn't long before he caught up with Sasha.

Cam followed him along the seafront until he veered off back inland to the local skate park. Cam pulled up as Sasha hit the ramps, watching as Sasha nailed a few tricks. The guy was good, though Cam reckoned he could match him any day on his skateboard.

When Cam had caught his bearings, he rolled his borrowed

BMX through the tube a few times, paying heed to Sasha's shouted instructions in the vain hope he wouldn't fall on his ass.

It worked, for a while, until he took a jump too fast and skidded into Sasha, sending them both clattering into the railing at the top of the concrete ramp.

Sasha took it with good humor, though the surprise on his face made Cam laugh so hard his eyes watered. The guy was graceful, given his size, and he looked funny as hell beneath an upside-down bike.

"Dick." Sasha gave Cam a playful shove. "Good thing we just met, or I'd put you on your ass."

Sasha's choice of words calmed Cam's laughter. He was so at ease with Sasha it felt like he'd known him for years, and for some reason it unnerved him a little.

Cam gave himself an internal shake. What was up with that? So what if they clicked? It wasn't a crime. The opposite, in fact. "Try it."

"Maybe later." Sasha set his bike down and sat on the edge of the ramp. "How long have you worked at Beat Shak?"

"A few years." Cam sat and mirrored Sasha's posture, dangling his legs down the ramp. "I got the job straight out of college. Never figured out what to do next."

"Me either. That's why I set up the store, to earn some cash while I fucked around with bikes."

Cam tilted his face to the sky, absorbing the late afternoon sun. "Worked out all right though, didn't it? Your place is rammed on the weekends."

"We do okay. Keeps me outta trouble, anyway."

"You don't look like trouble."

"Tell that to my mom. She blames me for every gray hair she's ever had."

Cam laughed, though he sounded hollow to his ears. He loved his mom, but the bitterness he felt for her desertion just wouldn't quit. He hadn't spoken to her since she'd packed up half their family home and jumped ship to "find" herself. "Bet she wouldn't have you any other way."

"Most days. You want to get something to eat?"

Cam checked his watch. He had a dinner date with Sonny, if Sonny remembered to show up this time. Maybe they could go to Levi's and hustle some real food out of the big man.

"Do you need to get to work?"

"Hmm?" Cam leaned away, startled. He hadn't noticed himself drifting closer to Sasha. "No, I'm done for the day."

"I didn't mean that." Sasha fiddled with his bike wheel. "I meant your, er, other job."

Cam frowned, glad Sasha seemed distracted and couldn't see the uncharacteristic flush heating his face. He made no secret of his unconventional occupation, but the words felt weird coming from Sasha. Somehow, he'd detached the best afternoon he'd had in months from his reality. "I didn't know you recognized me."

Sasha turned back with a shrug, though his grin seemed different, muted somehow. "Every gay man in LA knows who you are."

That wasn't news to Cam. He'd become accustomed to the attention he got in Silver, or any other club he ever ventured to. He'd even grown used to the stares in the grocery store and the whispers when fans discovered him working at Beat Shak and spent all afternoon peering through the windows at him. The scrutiny had never bothered him, but for some reason Sasha's fading grin felt like the end of the world. "I'm not *that* well-known."

"I reckon you are. I knew you were here long before we crossed paths."

"Yeah? How long?"

Sasha shrugged. "I heard a rumor a few years ago. Rode past here a few times, but I wasn't sure until I saw you up close in the store."

Cam tried to ignore the strange resentment brewing in his belly. He'd never cared if anyone knew he was in porn before. He'd told his own father without breaking a sweat, and his reaction to Sasha knowing confused him. Big-time. He wasn't ashamed of what he did, far from it. So why was this different? Why did he feel that the harder Sasha stared at him, the more unworthy Cam became of his attention? Cam had no idea, and the more he tried to decipher the whirlwind taking hold in his mind, the less he understood it. All he knew was something felt wrong...really wrong, with Sasha looking at him and seeing a goddamned porn star.

"Earth to Cam?" Sasha waved his hand in front of Cam's face. "You okay?"

Cam refocused. Tried to ignore the gentle warmth in Sasha's gaze. Ten minutes ago, he'd basked in it. Now he couldn't stand it. He retrieved his bike, stood up on the pedals, and pointed back the way they'd come. "You ready to go? I've gotta bounce."

He let his bike roll down the ramp without waiting for Sasha's response.

Thnx for the ride. C.

Cam set his phone on the kitchen counter. He'd exchanged numbers with Sasha after the porn bombshell, but for some reason it had taken him two days to compose a simple message, and almost as long to hit Send.

And now he couldn't keep still. There was something about Sasha, something more than his sunny smile and friendly eyes. More than his infectious laugh and easy ways. Something that Cam couldn't deny or stop thinking about.

He picked up his phone. Stared at the blank screen. Put it

down again. He'd gotten over the fact that Sasha knew about his alter ego, or at least put it to the back of his mind, but thinking about Sasha still made him antsy, and he couldn't figure out if he saw Sasha as a pot of gold or an unexploded bomb.

What the fuck? You just met the dude.

Cam calmed his seldom-indulged inner drama queen and opened the refrigerator, looking for supper. Sonny had rearranged their dinner from a few days before, but he'd canceled the rescheduled date at the last minute, blaming a forgotten exam. Cam could believe it, knowing Sonny as well as he did, but he figured it more likely Sonny had crawled into Levi's bed and decided to stay there.

And that wasn't necessarily a bad thing, 'cause Lord knew, Sonny needed the rest.

The contents of the fridge were uninspiring. Beer, cheese slices, and a dubious jar of pickles. Cam let the door swing shut and reached for his phone. Orange chicken and egg rolls would hit the spot. He ordered enough food to last until he next went home to his dad's. This cooking shit was for schmucks.

His phone vibrated as he tossed it on the countertop. He picked it up again, feeling his heart skip a beat as Sasha's Facebook photo lit up the screen. What was it about that guy with the sun behind him?

Fucking magic, that's what it was.

Cam opened the message.

UR welcome. Might feed you next time.

Next time? Cam drummed his fingers on the countertop and tapped out a message. *What would you feed me?*

A message pinged right back. *Anything not from a packet.*

Cam tapped the image of Sasha's smiling face and waited for the call to connect. He didn't have to wait long.

"'Lo?"

"Still judging me by that burrito, huh?"

Sasha laughed. "Hell, yeah. That shit was nasty."

"Nah. That was lunch. I had a cheeseburger for dinner."

Sasha made a noise that sounded a little too like Levi for Cam's liking. "What did you have for dinner tonight?"

"Nothing yet." Cam glanced at the clock. "It's only eight o'clock."

"And you're about to order pizza, right?"

"Chinese, actually."

"I gotta better idea. You got any other plans tonight, besides poisoning yourself with MSG?"

"That was about it." Cam opened the fridge again and grabbed a bottle of beer. "What have you got in mind?"

"Meet me by Beat Shak in an hour, and I'll show you."

Cam didn't need telling twice. He took the quickest shower known to man, canceled his food delivery, and jogged all the way to meet Sasha and his smug grin. Though he didn't discover the source of Sasha's amusement until they'd walked a few streets and Sasha pointed at a funky, glass-fronted restaurant.

"Sushi?"

Sasha's grin widened. "Yep. Don't tell me you're one of those freaks who live by the ocean and don't eat seafood."

Cam eyed the sushi bar with suspicion. "Hey, I eat fish. I just like it cooked."

"Don't knock it till you've tried it." Sasha held open the door to the restaurant. "And if you really can't handle it, some of the fish *is* cooked."

"I can handle it." Fuck. If he could handle a face full of spunk, he could handle a lump of raw fish.

Like his first ever blowjob, sushi turned out to be not that bad. Not that bad and kind of fun. Or maybe it was the company. Sasha laughed a lot and smiled even more. His good humor was irrepressible, and Cam found the antsy feeling he'd carried since the scene with Matthew at the studio faded away. Conversation was light and easy, and time passed in the blink of an eye.

At least until the elephant in the room made itself known.

"Sorry about dropping that porn shit on you last time."

Cam swallowed and set his water glass down. He'd been dreading this, the moment when his occupation tainted whatever was simmering between them. He measured his words with care. "I didn't know you knew."

"I didn't, at first. I wasn't sure. I had to check."

"How did you do that?"

"How do you think?"

Cam smirked; he couldn't help it. "Google?"

Sasha had the good grace to smirk right back. "I didn't have to look quite that far."

"You had me on your hard drive, huh?" Cam pushed his plate away, leaving only some weird floppy seaweed he couldn't quite stomach.

"Nothing recent. The scenes I have are a few years old."

"What happened? Did you grow out of your porn habit?"

Sasha put his elbows on the table. Despite the uncharacteristic nerves flickering in Cam's belly, Sasha seemed at ease, like this was a conversation he had every day. "My ex had a thing for Levi Ramone. Think he crushed on him more than he ever did me."

"Everyone's gotta thing for Levi."

"He is pretty hot, if you like 'em big and brawny."

"You don't?"

Sasha shrugged. "I don't know about porn stars, but I like a man with a brain."

Cam bristled like he had so many times before. "Levi's got more brains than all of us. Just never had a chance to use them."

"Shame. It's never too late though, right?" Sasha shifted. His leg brushed Cam's. "It's nice that you're friends. I've seen you around with that tattooed kid too. What's his name?"

"Sonny?"

"Yeah, that's him. I thought he was your boyfriend."

"We're just friends."

Sasha snorted, amused. "With benefits? Hassle-free hookups gotta be a perk of the job."

Cam couldn't deny it, and he didn't want to. Sasha seemed a laid-back kind of guy, and what was the point in lying to him? Friendships...relationships based on bullshit always went wrong. "I've hooked up with Sonny, but we've never dated. He's with someone."

"What about you? Are you seeing anyone?"

Yeah. My boss, but you really don't want to know. "Not really."

"Sounds complicated."

Cam shrugged. He didn't want to talk about Jon, but Sasha's sympathetic gaze persuaded him. "Kind of. It's more... unhealthy, you know? We're not good for each other. There are no feelings there."

"Just sex, huh? We've all been there, dude, but if it's not good for your soul, sometimes, you gotta walk away." Sasha checked his watch. "Look at that. We've been talking about porn for like, fifteen minutes already."

"Sorry."

"Don't be. I brought it up. I didn't want you to think it bothers me, 'cause it doesn't. I might be a bit out of touch, but there's more to you than porn, right?"

Cam leaned forward, taking in Sasha's relaxed posture and knowing the guy was telling the truth. "You don't watch it anymore at all?"

"Not often. I kinda went off sex for a while. It's a long story."

For the first time since they met, Sasha's eyes flickered with something other than humor and warmth. Curiosity burned on the tip of Cam's tongue, but a waitress interrupted, and when she'd gone, the moment had passed.

Sasha slipped a credit card into the bill folder. "Wanna ditch this place and get ice cream?"

"Ice cream? After all the bullshit you gave me about frozen burritos?"

"Course." Sasha winked, and the faint sadness in his eyes was all but gone. "I'm only human, Cam. Same as any other man."

CHAPTER FIVE

Survive the sushi?
Just about. Thnx for dinner. C.
I had fun :)
Me 2. Do I get to pick next time? C.
Depends...
On? C.
On what u got in mind.
Wht u like doin? C.
Same as u, probly.
Like 2 prty? C.
Course I do.
Then come out to play, C.

It took a few more unofficial dinner dates, sunset bike rides, and *a lot* more texts before Sasha agreed to meet up with Cam at Silver, and by then Cam knew that if he wanted to explore whatever was brewing between them, there was something else he had to do first, especially if they were going to party at Silver.

Jon had seen Cam with other guys before and paid little heed, and Cam had seen him disappear down the stairs to his office enough times, but this was different. This was *Sasha*. They'd become firm friends, but Cam wanted more.

God, did he more. When they were apart, he thought of little else. Except for the unfinished business that led him to Jon's office door a few weeks after popping his sushi cherry.

The office was empty. Cam found Jon in the storeroom, rooting through old props. "Hey."

Jon glanced over his shoulder, his gaze curious. Cam didn't often seek him out of his own volition. It wasn't how they rolled. "Hey. Need something?"

"Are you busy?"

"I'm always busy, Cam. What's on your mind?"

Cam checked the corridor and shut the door, steeling himself, though for what, he wasn't quite sure. "I might come to the club on Friday."

"And?"

"And..." Cam measured his words. He'd come to the studio full of purpose, but without a foolproof plan in mind, and as ever, Jon had gotten under his skin with just a flick of his eyebrow. "I won't be alone."

Jon shoved a box back onto a shelving unit. Cam couldn't see his face, but he could picture the disinterest well enough. Even if Jon cared, it wasn't his way to let it show. "I'm going to chuck all this crap out." Jon held up a leather harness. "We don't shoot shit like this anymore. Times are changing. Folk want more than fucking these days. Roma-porn, that's what we're making here."

"Roma-porn? What the fuck is that? That ain't a thing."

Jon snorted. "Not yet. Maybe I could become a pioneer. I got a request for a scene following George and Zac on a date. A motherfucking date. Can you believe that shit? What happened to good old down and dirty?"

"That comes after, right?"

"Right." Jon dusted his hands on his jeans. "So what are you trying to say? Are you seeing someone?"

Cam shrugged, perversely caught off guard by a conversation he'd instigated in the first place. "Maybe."

Jon closed the distance between them and put his hands on either side of Cam's head on the storeroom door, caging him. Cam swallowed, feeling his body betray him and respond to Jon's closeness. He wondered if Jon was the deciding factor, or if his senses were so conditioned by porn that any hot guy could make him hard.

Neither theory felt right. He wanted Sasha, damn it, not Jon.

Jon leaned closer. Cam could feel the heat from his skin. "What do you want me to say?"

"Nothing."

Jon stared at him, and for the first time since they'd come together last summer, Cam felt uncomfortable in his presence, like the buzzing current between them was something to be feared, not desired. An addiction that had run its course.

I don't want this.

The spell broke. Jon stepped back, and the intensity in his eyes faded, almost like he'd turned it off. Perhaps he had. "Cam, it's fine. You think you're the only one I tie to my bed?"

No. Cam had never thought that. Deep down he'd always known he was nothing more to Jon than a passing amusement, but something in Jon's demeanor bothered him. He hadn't expected Jon to profess his undying love, but the conversation had been easy...too easy. Jon didn't like to lose. Beneath the cool exterior, he was the ultimate alpha male.

"So we're cool? I mean, it's cool if I bring someone to the club, right?"

"Yeah, Cam. We're cool."

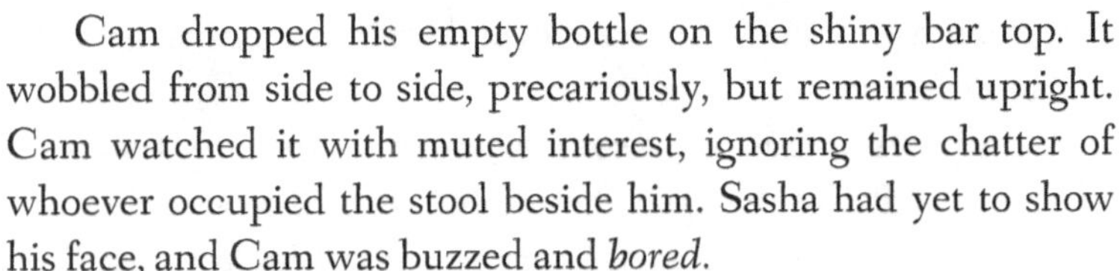

Cam dropped his empty bottle on the shiny bar top. It wobbled from side to side, precariously, but remained upright. Cam watched it with muted interest, ignoring the chatter of whoever occupied the stool beside him. Sasha had yet to show his face, and Cam was buzzed and *bored*.

He cast his gaze around the teeming club. The writhing bodies on the packed dance floor. The cluster of hard-core Blue Boy fans gathered around the podiums. And beyond, in the darker corners of Silver, the smattering of couples, no doubt bound for the private rooms at the back of the club.

Cam smirked and ordered another drink. He'd had some fun in those rooms over the years, but it had been a while. Outside of the studio, he'd been with no one but Jon for months.

But that's over now.

His fourth beer slid down like a dream. The pounding music ratcheted up a notch, and despite keeping his gaze trained on the door, Cam began to unwind, losing himself in the heady thrum that made Silver the hottest gay club in town. The dark dubstep bass line vibrated through his feet and shook his soul, teasing the long dormant part of him that used to dance the night away in this very club and others. The part of him that reveled in the sensation of a body gyrating against him, restrained only by a thin layer of cloth and the crowds of people around them.

Damn it. Drinking on an empty stomach always made Cam reflective...reflective and horny, and shit like that got him in trouble. Got him an apartment full of sweaty bodies he couldn't resist and a hangover that kicked his ass, though it had been a while since he'd hosted an impromptu Blue Boy party at his place.

Jon again...

But despite the sultry air of Silver working its magic, as Cam gazed out over the club, he didn't miss the hedonistic nights he'd enjoyed in the past. Something had changed in him over the past year, and though he craved the touch of another man, he wanted more.

A warm arm draped over his shoulders. "Drinking alone?"

Sasha slid into the space beside him like he'd been there all along. Cam grinned like an idiot, giddy and so happy to see him he felt like his face would split in half. "Thought you'd bailed on me."

"Nah, just had to wait for Chris to get his drunk on enough to come with me."

Sasha jerked his head somewhere behind them, blond hair gleaming under the club's lights. Cam looked around and saw Sasha wasn't alone. With him was a burly guy whose wide eyes told Cam he was straight as a goddamned arrow. "How drunk was that? He doesn't look so happy."

"He's fine. It's not the first time he's come over to the dark side. He likes it, really."

"What about you?"

"Me?" Sasha let his arm drop from Cam and signaled the nearest bartender. "I like *you*. That's enough for me."

Cam felt warm from the inside out. Sasha had that effect on him, even without saying shit like that. He chugged his beer, hoping Sasha wouldn't see the heat in his face in the murky light of the club. Sasha passed him another, and it was a pattern that continued for the rest of the evening. Sasha's friend Chris joined them for a while, but his tolerance for half-naked men squeezing his butt ran thin, and he cried off sometime around midnight.

Sasha didn't seem to notice him go. He leaned close to Cam and tucked his wayward auburn curls behind his ears. "Do you come here a lot?"

Cam shivered. Sasha was a well-built guy, tall and strong,

but his touch was light, teasing. "I kinda have to. Hanging here is part of my contract. I don't mind, though. The DJ's good, and I get cheap drinks."

Sasha glanced around. They hadn't moved from their spot since he'd arrived, but the scenery around them had changed as the night wore on. It was Cam's habit to hang by the far end of the bar, close to the podiums and DJ booth. Most of the Blue Boy models gravitated that way too, and though Sasha claimed he didn't watch much porn, he was bound to recognize some of the faces close by.

The other models had certainly noticed him, and who wouldn't? Sasha was gorgeous, and only amusement kept Cam from decking the parade of guys who'd approached them throughout the night.

Amusement and the fact that Sasha dismissed each one without tearing his gaze from Cam.

Cam reached for his drink. His arm brushed Sasha's. Sasha caught his eye and grinned, letting Cam know he felt the spark between them too. Cam's beer bottle was empty, and the current in the air had him suddenly restless.

Cam grabbed Sasha's hand, leaned close, and held his lips over Sasha's ear. "Wanna split?"

In answer, Sasha squeezed his hand and inclined his head toward the exit. "Lead the way."

It took a while to weave through the throng of sweaty, writhing bodies. Cam was stopped from time to time, asked to sign skin and pose for photos, and forced to dodge the advances of smitten fans. Most settled for a kiss on the cheek, but others were harder to shake off. Sasha took it all in his stride, or at least he seemed to until he found a gap in the crowd and pushed Cam against the wall.

"Okay, enough of this bullshit. When do *I* get to kiss you?"

Cam swallowed, enjoying the sensation of Sasha's bigger frame surrounding him. "You can kiss me."

"Oh yeah?" Sasha took Cam's face in his hands. Despite the heat of the club, his palms were dry as a bone. "What about if I kiss you like this?"

Sasha kissed Cam, slow and deep, a brush of lips at first, and then a gentle sweep of his tongue that turned Cam's limbs liquid.

Cam fell slack against the wall. They kissed over and over, hands grasping, clothes hitched. Sasha broke away for air, but Cam pulled him back and shoved his fingers into Sasha's silky hair.

The club faded away. Sasha, the smell of him, the feel of him, became Cam's whole world. He slid his hands under Sasha's shirt, found the smooth skin of his strong chest and rippled abdomen, and felt the solid outline of his cock, hard against his leg. Cam's own dick throbbed in his jeans. Silver was a den of shameless Epicureanism, and they could've fucked right there on the edge of the dance floor and not drawn much attention to themselves, but Cam didn't want that, not with Sasha. He wanted to take Sasha home, lay him out on his bed, and explore every inch of him until he eased himself down on Sasha's thick cock...

Huh. I want to bottom for this guy.

The thought didn't feel strange or frightening. It felt right, so fucking right. Cam tugged on Sasha's hips, grinding them together, before he slipped a hand between them and squeezed Sasha's dick. Sasha moaned into Cam's mouth and nipped his bottom lip. Encouraged, Cam moved his hand lower and lower until he grazed Sasha's balls.

Sasha froze. The air shifted. An abrupt change of atmosphere that hit Cam in the chest. Sasha pulled away like he'd been burned, his eyes wide and stricken.

Cam frowned, feeling the heat between them evaporate. What the fuck? Had he pushed too hard, hurt Sasha in some way? He reached out, his hands open in a placating gesture.

Sasha hesitated, and the mist in his gaze seemed to clear, but before they could regroup, someone else called Cam's name.

Irritated, Cam looked beyond Sasha for the first time since they'd embraced. His ire increased when he spotted Jon heading his way. Jon didn't often venture out of the back-room areas, and Cam had hoped to avoid him entirely.

Jon appeared at his side. "Where's Sonny?"

"What?"

"Don't give me that." Jon leaned into Cam's personal space, ignoring Sasha, who took the hint and backed away before Cam could stop him. "Where the fuck is your little boy toy? He was due onstage a half hour ago, and that's the third time he's skipped out on me this month."

Cam flinched; he couldn't help it. He wasn't scared of Jon, but the raw aggression in his tone was unnerving. Cam could tell he'd been hitting the scotch. "I don't know where Sonny is."

"Bullshit." Jon tossed a glance over his shoulder. "I know you're tight with that kid. Does your new trick know you'll be screwing Sonny on the side?"

"Fuck you." Cam twisted away, but Jon caught his arm. "Get off me."

Jon released him with a smirk, casting his gaze again over Sasha. "Have it your way. Shame, 'cause he's got a look I like. Bring him by my place if you change your mind. I know you like to share."

Cam shoved past Jon without looking back. His skin crawled. Jon could be a hard-ass, but Cam had never seen him so overbearing and possessive. Or had he? Was that what had been going on all this time? Had Jon controlled him in more ways than he'd ever known?

Cam reached Sasha and realized he didn't care. All that mattered was Sasha, and it was clear by the other man's face he'd heard every word of Jon's bizarre rant. "Sorry about that."

Sasha opened his mouth and shut it again, his expression torn. He gestured for Cam to follow him to the exit.

Clear air hit Cam, cooling his skin and dispersing the booze-fueled haze from his mind. He took a deep breath and waited for Sasha to face him.

He felt sick when he saw the resignation in Sasha's eyes.

"That's the guy you've been seeing, isn't it?" Sasha's tone was flat and defeated but held no malice or accusation.

Cam winced. It wasn't his nature to lie, and he couldn't deny it. "I'm not seeing him anymore. We broke it off a few days ago."

"Does he know that? 'Cause he was looking at me like I raped his momma."

"He knows. He's cool."

"It didn't look cool, Cam. It looked like unfinished business."

Cam was silent. What more could he say? He'd been honest with Jon and taken him at his word that there were no hard feelings between them. They'd hardly shared an epic love affair. Cam wanted to punch Jon, but he knew the blame lay with him for bringing Sasha into Jon's turf. For bringing Sasha into the melting pot of his alter ego's lifestyle.

"Listen." Sasha touched Cam's arm, then let his hand fall away. "Maybe we should cool it a little."

"What? No, don't say that. I'm sorry, okay? I shouldn't have brought you here. This place is intense."

"I don't care about all this shit. There's more to you than porn. I can see that. I just can't get involved with a guy who's still tied to someone else. I like you, Cam, I really like you, but I can't get hurt like that."

Cam felt his heart sink slowly into the pit of his stomach. "What are you saying?"

"I'm saying, I think we should just be friends."

"Friends?"

"Yeah, friends. Maybe you need one you don't fuck." The words stung, but before Cam could retaliate, Sasha shook his head and groaned. "Shit. I didn't mean that."

Cam snorted. "So what did you mean? That I'm a freakin' man whore?"

Guilt colored Sasha's features before he caught it and schooled his expression, but Cam saw it like a goddamned billboard sign. Sasha didn't want to fuck a dirty, used porn star.

"Cam, I didn't mean—"

"Save it." Cam held up his hand. "It's cool, okay? What do you think I'm gonna do? Force you?"

Sasha said nothing for a long moment; then he sighed, and the defeat in his long-drawn-out breath washed over Cam like a cold wave on a cloudy day. "I'm going home, Cam. I'll see you around."

CHAPTER SIX

Cam threw his phone across the living room. It landed on the couch, bouncing along the cushions until it came to an anticlimactic stop. He glared at it, perhaps in the hope its spontaneous flight would stimulate it into life, but nothing happened. The screen remained as blank as it had been for the two long weeks since Sasha had left him hanging outside Silver.

Though he'd done nothing to break it, the silence had driven Cam kind of crazy, and it wasn't just Sasha who hadn't called. Jon hadn't sent through his monthly schedule, and Sonny was proving elusive too. Cam was too pissed to care about Jon—he'd show his face soon enough—but Sonny's absence worried him. Sonny had issues, and Cam would've bet his right arm that Levi knew nothing about them. Sonny was a spiky ray of light to those lucky enough to be close to him, but life had taught him to play his cards close to his chest.

With a heavy sigh, Cam stomped into his battered sneakers and retrieved his phone. Despite his black mood, it hadn't been entirely silent. His dad had checked in, calling him home for Sunday dinner, and however deep the funk he was in, it was a call he couldn't ignore. Sunday was the day he tried to put his crazy life aside, when scheduling allowed, and went back to his old life...the life before porn. He wasn't in the mood to flick meatballs at his siblings, but perhaps he needed to do just that.

He took a cab to his old family home with the situation with Sasha still heavy on his mind. Wade took one look at him and folded him into the kind of embrace most fathers didn't bother to give out, especially to their adult sons, but Wade was different. Always had been.

"Come and help me with dinner, Son. I could use the company."

Cam gave his brothers quick high fives and followed Wade into the kitchen. The smell of pot roast hit him with a wave of nostalgia. In the old days, slow-roasted beef in gravy was the only thing Wade ever cooked. Man, how times had changed. Without a wife, the old dude had learned fast. Chicken sticks, pizza rolls, grilled cheese. The world was his oyster now.

"Peel some carrots. Your brothers need some vitamins."

Wade ambled to the stove, leaving Cam with a pile of vegetables and a heavy heart. Sasha was always saying shit like that. The guy had a junk-food phobia, and his attempts to wean Cam from his diet of takeout and beer was a running joke between them. Sushi, super salads, raw foods. Over the past month, Cam had tried them all.

"Are you going to tell your old dad what has your bottom lip stuck out so far?"

"Hmm?" Cam dumped a pile of sliced carrots in a pot, carrots he knew only Kay would touch. "I'm fine, Pops. Just tired."

Wade didn't answer immediately. He pottered around, getting plates from the cupboards and setting them out on a thick oak table that was older than Cam. The sight of it reminded Cam just how long his parents had been together before his mom grew tired of family life.

"Your sister's going to be late. She's got a yoga class or something."

"On Sunday?"

Wade rolled his eyes and stirred the mashed potatoes. "She's committed. Sometimes I think she's as bat-shit crazy as you are."

Cam took the ribbing with good grace. In many ways, Wade was his best friend. "Least the downward dog doesn't make her damaged goods."

"Trouble with your love life, Son?"

Cam followed Wade to the table and flopped into a chair. "Something like that."

"How so?" Wade slid a glass of lemonade across the table. "I thought you weren't looking for anyone while you had this other...job."

"When did I say that?"

"When I gave you a ride home from the airport a few months back, remember? When you went to New York?"

Cam snorted. The Blue Boy trip to New York had happened just after the infamous scene between Levi and Rex. Both models had severed their contracts, and to stave off gossip, Jon had taken a group of his most popular models to New York to hook up with another studio. A distraction of the best kind. Cam hadn't performed much in front of the ever-present cameras, but a private party in Jon's hotel room had gone on for days. It was still going when he left early to return to his job at Beat Shak, and he'd been up for thirty-six hours by the time his dad picked him up from LAX. "I probably said a lot of things then."

"Not really." Wade sliced some bread and pushed the board to the middle of the table. "And you've been out of sorts ever since. What happened? Did you meet someone?"

Cam glanced toward the den, but his brothers were engrossed in computer games and paying the kitchen no heed. "Kinda, but not then, and he's not from the studio. I met him at Beat Shak. He's got a BMX store a few blocks away."

"What's his name?"

"Sasha." Cam smiled. It felt good to say his name aloud, even if his absence was an open wound. "He's real nice, Pops. Laid-back, cool. You'd like him."

"I like all your friends, Son. Even the one that talks my ear off."

Sonny. Everyone loved Sonny. "Sasha likes the same music as you. All that sixties crap."

"Even better. So why the long face?"

"He wants to be *friends*."

Wade took a seat and leaned back on his chair. "What's wrong with that? Friends is good, right?"

"I guess." Cam put his head on his arms. "I just... For a while, it seemed like he wanted more, you know?"

"Did something happen?"

Cam shrugged. Wade was the best dad in the world, but Cam couldn't tell him about Jon. His father was an old hippie at heart, and he'd never understand the hold Jon had over Cam, or why Cam found it so hard to break.

Wade nodded, like the gap in the tale made perfect sense to him. "If you really believe there's something between you, I guess you gotta figure out what spooked him. If he's as chill as you say he is, something besides the, er, movies must have scared him off."

Cam ignored the bizarreness that was his father describing anything as *chill* and considered his theory. Something clicked in his mind. Wade was right. The fear had been in Sasha's eyes before Jon barged between them. But why? What did Sasha have to be afraid of? Him? Porn? Commitment? It didn't make any sense. Cam had asked nothing of him, and he'd seen no hesitation in Sasha until that fuck-hot kiss against the wall.

Wade sighed and clapped his shoulder. "Maybe it's time you looked beyond this place that's got you tied up so tight.

Money ain't everything. Fix what you can. Don't wait for other folk to do it for you."

Cam split soon after dinner, his father's sage advice ringing in his ears. With that in mind, he stopped at Sonny's place on his way home, but there was no one there. His cell went straight to voice mail, and his call to Levi didn't even connect.

Worry tickled again at Cam's belly. Sonny was a big boy, figuratively, at least, and capable of looking after himself, but sometimes he just...didn't. Perhaps it was time Cam grew a pair and stopped by Levi's motorcycle garage and touched base. It had been a while.

Resolved, Cam headed for home with a mind to bite the bullet and call Sasha too. Friends. He could do that, right? It was, after all, exactly what they'd been doing, just without the kissing. Or any prospect of kissing. Huh. Perhaps Wade was right and Cam *did* need to expand his life outside the studio. Porn used to be fun, a way of exploring his sexual identity and having a good time, but these days it seemed like a vise around his soul.

He missed Sasha. Sonny was his friend, Levi too, but though it had never seemed to matter before, Cam knew those friendships were colored by sex. His friendship with Sasha was real, like nothing he'd ever known, and without it, he felt lost. He'd seen other models lose relationships because of porn, but he never thought it would happen to him.

So do something about it.

Cam let himself into his apartment with his phone tucked between his chin and his shoulder. The call rang and rang until Sasha's voice mail kicked in. Cam's heart skipped a beat, jarred by Sasha's deep voice rumbling down the line. He considered hanging up, calling again and again until Sasha picked up or threw his phone at a damned wall, but he didn't.

"Hey, it's Cam. I'm sorry about the other night. Maybe you're right about being friends. I've gotta spare board if you'd dig a skate sometime this week. You can show me those tricks you think I can't do. Call me."

He hung up the phone and let out the breath he'd been holding. Putting the ball in Sasha's court felt good, like he'd taken a vital step forward, but his body felt tense and stiff. He needed a hot shower and an early night.

The jets of water worked their magic on his sore neck and shoulder muscles. Cam lingered under the spray. Sasha remained on his mind, but he tried to ignore the butterflies in his belly. Instead, he closed his eyes and soaped his body lazily, paying little attention as he passed his hands over his chest, abdomen, and lower. His cock hung limp between his legs, as uninspired as the rest of him, but he lingered a moment on his balls. He kept them shaved for porn—*manscaped* was the technical term—and the lack of body hair meant their outlined shape was fairly clear. Clear and *familiar*, so why did they feel different?

Perturbed, Cam pulled himself from his Sasha-filled daydreams, shut off the shower, and climbed out, wiping the steam from the mirror with the back of his hand. He turned this way and that, scrutinizing himself from every angle. His left ball had always hung lower and appeared larger, but in the misty bathroom mirror, the difference seemed disproportionate.

He cupped them in his hand, rolling them, squeezing them with gentle fingers. His balls were often sensitive, just a lick or a scratch from the right partner drove him wild, but there was nothing erotic about the sweat dripping down his back now. He focused on his left side, tracing the shape and texture. Was it his imagination, or did it feel too hard? Like a smooth rock had become lodged in his sac?

A rush of nausea swept over Cam. Dizzy, he stumbled back. He'd been on edge for days, and now the sensation of an intruder in his body was fusing with the sickening dread, merging the two emotions together and boiling over like angry, molten lava.

He sat down on the closed toilet, his heart beating like a drum in his ears. He was mistaken. He had to be, because the alternative was something he couldn't begin to imagine.

CHAPTER SEVEN

"I'm sorry, what?"

The doctor glanced up from his notes for the first time since he'd uttered a sentence Cam couldn't comprehend. "The lump in your testicle appears to be a tumor," the doctor repeated. "Combined with your blood work, I'd say it's a germ cell seminoma, but we need to run some more tests to be sure."

"Tests?" The word fell from Cam's lips with no conscious thought. He'd been at the doctor's office for less than an hour, and they were talking about fucking tumors? Screw this shit. He had to be freakin' tripping.

"Ultrasound, CT, chest X-ray. We'll take some more blood too."

"What for?"

"To ascertain for sure what we're dealing with, what stage it is, how far it's spread, and the sooner we do that, the better. Cancers like this are highly treatable, if we catch them early."

Cam blinked. "Cancer?"

The doctor sighed and tapped his pen on the table. Cam didn't like him. He preferred the other guy, the doctor he'd seen at the start of the week...the one who told him he had nothing to worry about.

"It's most likely a cyst. We'll take some blood, but it's probably nothing."

"Yes, Mr. Shaw. It's highly probable you have testicular cancer."

Mr. Shaw. The rare use of his legal name startled him, like it always did, and it took a moment for the implication of the doctor's words to hit him. "Probable? You don't know for sure?"

"Not yet, but I'll get the tests we need set up right away, and we should know within a few days."

A few days. Cam felt sick and dizzy, like his brain was about to explode. How the fuck could he sit on this for *days* without knowing for sure what he was dealing with?

The doctor passed him a plastic cup of water. "It's a lot to take in, I know, but you have time on your side. Given your profession, it's likely the lump hasn't been there that long. I'd imagine you, or a...colleague would've noticed it."

Cam nodded. The doctor's slip didn't go unnoticed, but he couldn't bring himself to care. Porn and the extensive health benefits that came with a contract at Blue Boy was the only reason he was flipping his shit in a plush private clinic rather than cooling his heels at the county hospital. And the doctor wasn't wrong. He'd been heavily intimate with a bunch of guys in the last month. Someone would've noticed.

Jon would've noticed, right?

Even as Cam shook the doctor's hand and left the office, he knew he couldn't be sure. Sex with Jon had deteriorated to the point where neither of them seemed to care who the other was. Cam knew he wasn't Jon's only lover, and *he* was a damned porn star.

A porn star with testicular cancer.

The following morning, Cam returned to the clinic and let the medical staff put him through a barrage of tests. Most of them involved being exposed in the most intimate way possible, but being naked in front of a bunch of strangers didn't bother him. Why would it?

Cam let his mind wander as they poked and prodded him, thinking back to last night and the evening he'd spent alone, brooding his fate. Though he hadn't touched a drop, he felt like he'd gone three rounds with a bottle of Jack.

Perhaps his pseudo-drunk state had been to blame for the text message he'd sent Jon, and the exchange that followed.

I want to fuck in my next scene.

Schedule is done for this month.

Change it.

What's going on?

What do you care?

There had been a long pause between the last two messages, and Jon hadn't bothered to reply. Cam wondered what he'd have done, even if Jon had. Would he have called Jon up and told him everything? Told him *this*? Guess he'd never know.

"Cameron Shaw?"

Cam glanced up. He was sitting in an empty room, waiting to see the specialist who'd tell him the collective result of every weird machine he'd been through. He'd sat down feeling like thirty minutes would seem like a year, but somehow, it had flown by.

He followed the nurse's directions into yet another bland office and sat down. A new doctor greeted him with a grim smile, the kind of smile that pulled Cam firmly out of his daydreams and into a harsh, uncompromising reality.

"The lump is a tumor," the doctor said without preamble. "Your preliminary diagnosis was almost certainly correct, and it looks like a classic germ cell seminoma. We've cautiously classified it as a T1 tumor."

"T1?"

"Stage one. From your test results, it doesn't appear to have spread."

"But it's still cancer, right?"

"Yes." The doctor turned his computer screen and pointed to an unintelligible, dark mass. "The tumor is here, on the left side. It's easily accessible and a common type for men your age. The best course of action is to remove it, and the surrounding tissue, and blast you with a course of radiotherapy. If that's successful, we may be able to avoid chemotherapy."

Tumors. Chemo. Cam's blood rushed in his ears. Someone was yanking his chain. They had to be. "How would you remove it?"

"We'd take the whole testicle."

"What? You wanna cut my balls off? Fuck, no!" Cam's heart thudded to a standstill. He stood. His chair tipped back and clattered to the floor.

The doctor raised his hand. The gesture was calm and placating, like the scene was a replay of something he'd seen a thousand times over. "It's not quite as brutal as that. The surgery is called an orchiectomy, and the diseased testicle is removed through an incision in the abdomen."

"No." Cam backed away from the doctor's desk. "There's nothing wrong with me. I feel just fine."

"And there's every chance you'll stay that way if you have the surgery and have it soon. As far as cancer diagnoses go, this is good news, Mr. Shaw. Very good news."

Cam stood very still. He'd known for the past week that this was at least a possibility, but that didn't make the images in his head any easier to bear. "What about..." He stopped. *What about my dick? Will it still work?* Was he really about to say that? Or was he going to say nothing and wait until he next dropped his pants on set and let the world know there was nothing there.

Fuck, what did you even call a man with no balls? Was he even still a man?

The doctor retrieved a card from a drawer and wrote something on it. "I'm sure you have a lot of questions, so I'm going to schedule an appointment with our psychotherapist. She's very experienced in this field, and a lot of my patients find her invaluable. She has a clinic this afternoon in the oncology wing. I'll give her a call and let her know you're coming."

Cam accepted the card and righted his chair in silence. The doctor made his calls, then produced a bunch of literature and proceeded to explain in excruciating detail how life as Cam knew it was about to implode.

After, he drifted out into the corridor, numb and almost detached from the chaos inside his own head. His phone vibrated in his pocket. He pulled it out and read the message from Jon.

Kai. Saturday 2 p.m.

Apathy swept over Cam. He walked three yards along the corridor and dropped his phone in the trash can.

It didn't take long to find the oncology wing. The building was neutral enough, but inside the scent of illness and death was strong, to Cam, at least. He made the mistake of looking up just once and, after that, kept his eyes on the shiny floor as he made his way to his eleventieth clinic of the day. He gave his name to another receptionist, who directed him to yet another hard, plastic chair.

He sat down and put his head in his shaking hands. The doctor had been encouraging...positive, almost. The surgery and subsequent biopsy would give a final, definitive diagnosis, but if his test results were accurate, his type of cancer had a 95 percent survival rate—survival and complete recovery.

He was lucky, he knew he was, but the roiling pit of dread in his belly wouldn't quit. Up until his lazy discovery, he hadn't felt the tumor at all, but now it was *all* he could feel...feel it eating him up from the inside out like the destructive intruder it was.

The doctor said he wasn't going to die, that he probably wouldn't even get that sick, but he felt sick now. Sick and tired. It had been a long day, and all he wanted was the solitary comfort of his bed. A sure sign that something wasn't right. He rarely craved his own company.

"Hey."

"Huh?" Cam raised his head, startled. He'd neither felt nor seen someone sitting in the chair beside him. He blinked, and his vision cleared to reveal a set of deep brown eyes he felt like he knew.

The brown eyes crinkled up at the sides as the tanned face they belonged to eased into a tentative smile. "Cam? It *is* you, right?"

Cam stared. Sasha's face was indelibly imprinted in his brain, but he'd thought of little beyond his own balls since the beginning of the week. He opened his mouth and shut it again. Words failed him.

Sasha frowned and touched his arm. "You okay?"

No. "What are you doing here?"

Sasha stole his warm gaze from Cam and took a glance around. "I might ask you the same thing. This *is* the clinic for young men with testicular cancer."

"You have cancer?"

"Not anymore. I just got my all clear. This is my last session with Dr. King."

"That's good. That's really good." Cam put his elbows on his knees. "You're not sick? You're okay?"

"I'm fine, Cam. Do you want some water?"

Cam waved the bottle away. "I'm good."

Sasha was silent a moment; then he put his hand on Cam's arm, squeezing when Cam didn't respond. "What are you doing here? Are you sick?"

"Apparently."

The single word was choked and hoarse, but it was enough for Sasha to change his posture...to move his chair closer to Cam and shift his hand up to Cam's shoulder.

Cam closed his eyes. It felt good, really good, like he could drift away to another world.

"Cam?"

Or not. Cam opened his eyes and realized Sasha was waiting for him to elaborate. "Germ cell seminoma. They want to cut it off."

Sasha nodded like the two clipped sentences spoke a thousand words. "When were you diagnosed?"

"Um." Cam checked his watch. "An hour ago?"

"And you're here by yourself?" Sasha raised an eyebrow, making his face seem wiser than his boyish features. "Where's your folks?"

"Haven't told them yet. The quack at the...fuck, I don't even know where. He told me to come here."

"To counseling? Makes sense. I didn't see Dr. King until after my surgery. Wish I'd manned up and come a lot sooner."

Cam took a shallow breath. With Sasha's warm, familiar presence beside him, the spinning room was coming back into focus. "Why are you here now, if you're not sick anymore?"

"Tying up loose ends. It's ironic, but the good news threw me for a loop. I didn't know what to do without a badass shadow on my shoulder. That's why I haven't called you. I've been kinda lost in my own head."

In spite of himself, Cam felt his natural, ingrained curiosity spike. "Do you know now? What to do, I mean?"

"Maybe. Ask me in a few weeks."

The receptionist called Cam's name. Dazed, he rose to follow her directions. Sasha caught his arm. "Wait. Call me later. Let me know you're all right."

Cam choked out a humorless bark of laughter. "I don't have a phone."

Sasha conjured a pen from nowhere and took hold of Cam's arm. "Don't wash this off, okay? Write it down and give me a call...anytime, dude. Just pick up the phone."

CHAPTER EIGHT

"Action!"

The command went over Cam's head. He hadn't seen Kai in a while, and his petite, flaxen-haired friend had been all over him the moment he'd stretched out on the bed beside him. It seemed they were starting their scene long before Jon saw fit to begin, and that suited Cam just fine. His head was fucked, and he needed this...needed the distraction of Kai and his smooth, pliant body. Kai was a little petite for his tastes, but he had a great smile and a subtle undertone of aggression that hadn't been there the last time they'd shot a scene together. The last time Cam had seen Kai get fucked on-screen was with Levi, and *no one* showed that side of themselves to Levi. Rex had tried and gotten his ass kicked across the set.

Cam rolled over, kissed Kai hard, and shoved his hand into Kai's curly blond hair. He tugged, enjoying the wide-eyed gasp Kai gave him in return.

Kai nipped at Cam's neck. "Hey. You're supposed to be the nice one."

"Who told you that?" Cam rose up and stripped his shirt.

Kai licked his lips and moved his hands straight to Cam's chest. "You did, when I first started dancing at the club."

Yep, that sounded like the kind of shit Cam spouted at the increasingly younger boys Jon recruited into his ranks. "What else did I say?"

"That you'd show me a good time. I've been waiting on this for months."

Makes two of us. Though, it wasn't Kai Cam had been waiting on. He'd just been...waiting.

He pulled Kai down the bed, undoing his fly with one hand. Kai was bare beneath his shorts and already hard. He bucked up into Cam's hand and let out a breathy gasp that went straight to Cam's own half-hard dick.

Half-hard. Huh. That was new. Cam's cock was usually the first to the party, on set or anywhere else sex was on the table.

Kai reached for Cam's waistband. Cam rolled away, deflecting him for now. Blue Boy fans didn't go for flaccid cocks. They probably didn't appreciate condemned balls either, but Cam had checked himself from every angle, and though the tumor was all *he* could see, the camera wouldn't pick it up, and neither would anyone else.

He took Kai in his mouth, hoping the sensation of a warm, pulsating dick would stir his own. He loved giving head, on and offscreen, but it had been a while since he'd had the pleasure without a camera watching his every move. Jon didn't seem to enjoy it, or anything else Cam wanted to do to him. No. That heady street of torture was all one-way.

Damn it. Why was Cam thinking about Jon? Before the tumor, he'd shut that shit down.

Kai shuddered. "Fuck!"

Cam smiled to himself, knowing he'd put Kai right on the edge with just the tip of his tongue. He was damned good at head; even Levi, Mr. Stoic himself, said so. It took a little longer to get his own dick to play ball, but Kai had come a long way in the months since he'd shot his first scene at Blue Boy, and he'd learned a lot.

And once Cam was naked and hard and presented with Kai's willing, open body, his mind went blank.

He drove his fingers into Kai, twisting and stretching him, testing the preparations Kai had no doubt done before he'd come on set. It was something Cam always did, even if he knew the other model was more than ready. He had to feel it for himself, had to *know* whatever came next would be a pleasure for everyone involved.

He found no resistance in Kai, just heated, clenching flesh. Kai countered his hand, pressing himself ever closer. He wrapped his arms around Cam's neck and kissed him sweetly on the cheek. "Feels so good, baby."

Cam smiled and pushed Kai's fast-dampening hair out of his face. He was good at these scenes—the ones the recent influx of female fans requested all the time. Jon set them up to be almost like two lovers, boyfriends, having their own private moment, and the more emotional viewers lapped them up, imagining real-life relationships that didn't exist, and barraging Jon with requests for more.

Usually, it was kind of humorous—a running joke that bonded the cast and crew of Blue Boy together—but not today. For Cam, today wasn't about emotions, good or bad. This was about getting off, raw and empty, and chasing the burn of pleasure that would leave his mind devoid of all else.

The scene snowballed, and the routine of hands, mouth and tongue passed Cam by. A condom appeared on his dick, by his hand or Kai's, he wasn't quite sure. A haze descended over his vision. He rolled Kai onto his belly, squeezed his ass, and slammed into him. Kai took the impact and gripped the metal frame of the bed, the one with the deliberately loosened bolts.

On cue, the bed squeaked and groaned, entwining with the brutal snap of Cam's hips, Kai's gasps, and resonating around the set. Cam breathed it all in, grinding out a rhythm that grew in intensity with every thrust. Hard and fast. Sharp and sure, belying the forty-eight hours of insomnia he'd lived through to get to this point. His muscles burned with the effort, tense and sore, but his body responded to the tight heat of Kai clamped around him, wanting...craving more with each slam of his hips.

Kai whimpered. Cam faltered, and Kai's tight face came back into focus, his discomfort clear.

What the hell am I doing?

Cam dropped Kai and reared back, horrified. Kai was his friend, and Cam wasn't that kind of top...wasn't that guy who pounded the men beneath him into submission. His stomach rolled, and the queasy sensation he'd had in the pit of his stomach for days returned full force.

I need to get out of here.

Kai sat up and caught Cam's shoulders. He pushed him back on the bed and climbed over him. "Yeah, let me ride you."

He lowered himself onto Cam's cock before Cam could protest.

Startled, Cam arched his back and winced. Something felt off. It wasn't pain, but the weight on his groin felt all wrong. Kai pressed down on him over and over, but the feeling increased until Cam couldn't breathe through the pressure in his gut.

Kai dropped to his chest, his thin arms shielding Cam from the camera. "Are you okay?"

Fuck no. Cam met Kai's gaze, his response silent and still but loud enough to reach Kai's young ears all the same.

Kai circled his hips, watching Cam's face, gauging his reaction. He kept his movements slow and gentle at first, only upping the pace when Cam got a tenuous hold on himself and nodded.

Let's get this shit done.

Cam clenched his eyes shut and focused on Kai—his lips and teeth on his neck. His ragged gasps and quivering thighs. The smooth heat of him wrapped around Cam's cock.

I can do this.

Cam sucked in a breath and opened his eyes. Kai studied him a moment, then leaned back, revealing Cam to the cameras again, and took him deeper into his body.

The angle change felt better…good, even. Some of the anxiety gripping Cam's chest faded. He wondered if his brief slip had been caught on-screen. One look at Jon's face would tell him, but he knew better than to search him out. Jon got real pissed when a shot caught models looking anywhere off set.

Kai pinched Cam's thighs. A faint hum of pleasure bloomed in Cam's belly. Encouraged, he widened his legs and took over the pace. Kai relaxed and threw back his head, groaning and pulling his own hair.

"Fuck, more."

Cam fucked him harder. Heat spread from his cock and into his veins. The black mist returned. Yes. He wanted this. He craved this. He pounded Kai faster, twisting his hips, and watched for the eye roll that told him he'd found the right spot.

Kai cried out and reached for his own dick. He fell forward, steadying himself on Cam's chest, and pumped himself at a brutal pace. "Gonna come."

Cam felt relieved. His mind was relinquishing control to the dizzying pleasure of being inside Kai, but his body was tired, and all at once, everything ached—like they'd been fucking for hours rather than minutes.

Kai came with a high-pitched gasp. His warm, sticky release hit Cam's chest. Cam watched his face contort, felt him shudder, and absorbed the sensation. He fucked him a few moments longer, then pulled out to finish himself off by hand.

For a minute that seemed to last a lifetime, his climax teased him, hovering just out of reach. Frustrated, he chased it down. Goddamn it. It was the only reason he'd showed his face at the studio at all. The only reason he'd left the pity party he'd created for himself on his couch.

He worked himself at a frenzied pace. Sweat beaded his

chest, and heat flushed his face. He growled, squeezing himself a little too hard, but it was enough. Just. He came with no sound, an anticlimax in every sense of the word.

"Cut!"

Cam stood with his hands flat on the tiled wall, letting the hot water pummel his neck. He soaped up and washed away the sweat and grime of the scene. His arms felt weighted and tired, but the lump of death in his balls felt heavier, dragging him down, like he could sink through the floor at any moment.

"Sorry if I jumped on you a little too hard."

Cam glanced at Kai. He'd half forgotten he was there. "Huh?"

"That bit where your eyes watered. Sorry if I caught you in the balls. I've done that before. Sonny keeps telling me to keep my pointy knees to myself."

He thinks that was his fault? "Don't worry about it. I'm not..." Cam stopped and gathered his words. "It wasn't you, man. Don't sweat it. I'm not with it today. Thanks for covering for me. Most guys wouldn't have noticed."

Kai shrugged and shut off his shower. "Sonny told me I had to watch every guy I filmed with. Look them in the eye, you know? Even if it's just a fucking handjob. He said no one comes to the studio without bringing a slice of their day with them. Guess you're having a bad day, huh?"

Fucking Sonny. He's too young to be so wise. "Yeah, I guess."

Kai kissed his cheek and left him alone, disappearing into the depths of the studio. Cam was grateful for the peace. Kai was a good friend, sweet and caring, and though they'd never hooked up offscreen, Cam had often let Kai sleep in his bed with him after a long night at Silver. He'd always gotten the feeling Kai didn't want to go home, and he wasn't about to argue with that. How could he? No one knew where Kai went when he wasn't at the club, the studio, or curled up like a lost puppy on someone's couch.

Cam finished up in the shower and got dressed, hoping to make a quick escape, but Jon caught him and pointed to his open office door. A summons, if ever Cam saw one.

"Lock the door."

Cam obeyed and leaned with his back against it, wondering what Jon had in mind. The ugly scene at the club seemed a lifetime ago, and they hadn't spoken since, but Cam recognized the gleam in his eye. "Do you need me for something?"

Jon pointed at his computer monitor. "Check this out."

Cam pushed off the door and rounded the desk to be greeted by a screenshot of himself, naked and jacking off over Kai's trembling form. Surprise coursed through him, though he wasn't sure why. It had been his reality twenty minutes ago. "You like it?"

"Hell, yeah." Jon pulled Cam into an embrace that would've appeared affectionate from anyone else. An embrace Cam couldn't bring himself to dodge. "I like watching you get off. I should get you to jack for me more often."

Cam rolled his eyes. Jon had a thing for watching him fly solo. "Was the scene good?"

"Mmm." Jon ground himself into Cam's back. "Very good. Did you enjoy it?"

No. "Yeah." Cam relaxed a little into Jon. The last few days had been lonely, and though he knew it wasn't meant as such, and however much Jon's arms weren't the arms he craved, being held felt comforting. "Kai's a good bottom."

"That he is." Jon's voice was distant and thoughtful as he popped the button on Cam's board shorts and slipped his hand inside. Cam hardened, despite his recent release. *Damn it, Jon.*

Their emotional connection was nonexistent, but the sexual energy between them was undeniable.

"I've never fucked you in here." Jon pumped Cam slowly. "Would you like it if I fucked you right here over my desk."

"Probably."

Jon tightened his grip on Cam's cock, asserting the dominant authority Cam had grown unhealthily addicted to. "Pardon?"

"Yes." Cam fell forward, his hands flat on the desk, rolling his hips in time with Jon's languid rhythm.

Jon chuckled and opened a drawer. "You'd have to be quiet, Cam. Silent. Do you think you could do that?"

"Ye—*Shit*." Cam jolted, feeling cool lube drizzle into his ass. Yeah. He could do that. Clench his eyes shut, jam his fist in his mouth, and get fucked.

Jon's fingers brushed Cam's balls. Cam froze. Reality slammed back into perspective, and he pulled away. He didn't want this. Not now, not ever. He twisted out of Jon's grasp and shoved his cock back in his shorts.

Jon raised a silent, questioning eyebrow, unfazed by Cam's abrupt rejection. Almost like he'd expected it. "Problem?"

Cam caught his breath and shrugged. "I'm tired. I'm gonna split."

"That's all you have to say?"

"What do you want me to say? I'm not your fucking sex toy."

"Okay." Jon folded his arms across his chest. "If you don't want to do *this*"—Jon gestured between them—"that's fine. But you need to at least tell me what's up with the rest of your work."

"Excuse me?"

Jon beckoned him back to the computer and clicked a few buttons, bringing up the viewer comments posted under the various scenes on the Blue Boy site. "Look at this, and this, and this. What do you have to say about that?"

Cam squinted at the computer screen. The comments were small, but there were reams of them, all saying the same thing. *What's up with Cam? Where's Cam's big smile gone? Why is Cam so sad? What's up with Cam? What's up with Cam? What's up with Cam?*

Cam frowned, looking at the dates. They went back months. He couldn't even blame the cancer diagnosis for most of them. There was only one correlation that made any sense. The breakdown of his parents' marriage and the shoulder he'd found to cry on.

Sudden, white-hot anger surged through him. He shoved the computer monitor away, tipping it onto its side, enjoying the crash and the shock in Jon's face. *"That's* how you gauge my well-being? You have me tied up in your bed, and some faceless Internet geek jerking off has to tell you I'm not fucking happy? Fuck you!"

"Cam..."

Cam dodged Jon's outstretched hands and started for the door. He heard Jon behind him as he fumbled the lock, but when the door swung open, he knew Jon wouldn't follow.

CHAPTER NINE

Cam breathed deeply, letting the salty air fill his lungs and the morning sun warm his face. The sea breeze refreshed him, and his board felt good beneath his feet. The squeak of BMX brakes sounded beside him. He opened his eyes and grinned. Sasha winked and tore off ahead of him, riding like a demon until he slowed to slide along a deserted bench.

The grind trick was a little rusty, but it made Cam smile. He'd had a long week. Doctors' appointments, filling out insurance forms. Trying to figure out who to tell first. Getting sick was a ball ache. Literally. By Friday morning he'd had enough, and the evening had found him searching his pockets for the scrap of paper he'd scrawled Sasha's number on and trudging to the store to buy a prepaid phone.

And here they were, careering along the dawn-lit seafront the very next morning. They'd exchanged few words, but it didn't seem to matter. Sasha was calm and warm...and he *knew*. Knew the dark secret Cam had yet to share with another soul.

Cam put his foot to the ground. The scenery whizzed by until he caught up with Sasha a few feet away from the bench. He jumped it, skidding along the seat, and came to a sharp stop by Sasha's front tire.

Sasha eyed him. "You're pretty fast on that thing. Thought I'd be waiting on you all morning."

"Bite me." Cam showed Sasha his middle finger. "How far do you want to go?"

"As far as it takes."

Cam tilted his head to one side. "For what?"

"For you to tell me what you need."

Sasha shot off again without elaborating. Cam followed him, pondering his answer. Sasha had asked him on the phone if he wanted to talk. He'd said yes, but now he wasn't quite so sure. His misguided day at the studio had been a mistake, of that he was certain, but could he find the words to explain that to Sasha? Probably not.

He met Sasha by a food cart, ignored Sasha's proffered water bottle, and bought an icy blue drink that stained his tongue.

Sasha rolled his eyes. "You need to take better care of yourself than that."

"Why? Doesn't matter if my balls turn blue, does it?" Cam kicked his board into his hands and drifted to a nearby bench.

Sasha followed, pedaling with lazy legs. He dismounted and leaned his bike against the back of the bench. "I know you're smarter than that."

"Do you?"

"Hell, yeah. Radiotherapy's gonna kick your ass. It's not like chemo, but it ain't no joke. You need to be ready."

It was the first time either man had overtly mentioned the elephant hanging over them. Cam remembered Sasha's words in the hospital. *"...a badass shadow on my shoulder."*

Yeah, or in my freakin' boxers.

"Something funny?"

Cam crunched the ice in his drink. "Nope. Just being a dick."

"You're allowed for the time being, at least until after your surgery. Did you get a date?"

"Wednesday."

Cam threw his half-full cup in a nearby trash can. Sasha was easy to be around, but Cam didn't want to talk about this, even to someone who knew exactly how he felt. Talking about it made it real. Fuck that. He had four days left to pretend, and he was going to make them count.

"How are your folks taking it? Mine freaked. Think my mom took it worse than me."

"Um..." Cam averted his gaze, but Sasha interpreted his silence with widened eyes.

"You haven't told them? Cam, you can't do this on your own. What about your friends?"

"Nope."

"Why not?"

Cam shrugged. "Haven't found the right time. My parents divorced this year. It's been rough, on my dad and my kid brothers. I don't want to put them through any more shit."

Sasha leaned back on the bench and stretched out his legs. Cam watched his calf muscles strain and relax. The dude had hot legs. Tanned and covered in fine, fair hair. The kind of legs Cam liked to bite and knead, given the right context.

"Dude, they'll be more upset if they find out after the fact. You're close to your folks, right? You've mentioned your dad a few times. You should tell them, and soon. Rip off that bandage."

Cam sighed. He felt more relaxed with Sasha, a virtual stranger, than he had in days...no, weeks, but no amount of eye fucking him could change his reality. "My sister's gonna lose her shit."

"That's what sisters are for." Sasha nudged his arm. "And maybe you need that. Denial only lasts so long."

Cam snorted. "I'm not in denial."

"Yeah? How do you feel right now?

It was a trick question, and the psychologist in Cam knew the answer on the tip of his tongue was exactly what Sasha expected him to say.

He said it anyway. "I feel fine. Don't feel sick at all."

"And that's the problem." Sasha fired his empty water bottle into the trash can and retrieved his bike. "You only know you're sick because some quack told you so—"

"Three quacks."

Sasha grinned; then his face fell serious again. "I know it's the worst bit, in the beginning, at least. Eventually, radiation and chemo make you feel like hell, but even that doesn't last. Most of the time, you only know you're sick 'cause dudes in white coats keep telling you."

"You had chemo?"

"Twice." Sasha mounted his bike and checked his watch. "Come over to my place tomorrow. I'll cook you some real food and tell you all about it."

Cam climbed out of the cab and stared around him in disbelief. He took in the sweeping driveway and landscaped lawns and shook his head. This couldn't be right. He squinted at the crumpled scrap of paper in his hand, deciphering his own scrawl, and gazed again at the lavish surroundings, but nothing changed. If he was in the right place, Sasha Tate was a freakin' millionaire.

The taxi rolled away. Cam started up the driveway, feeling out of place with every step. Some people in porn flashed a lot of cash, but not like this. Sculpted gardens, security cameras, and electric gates? This was *real* money. Cam half expected a cop car to pull up beside him and arrest him for trespass.

"You found it, then?"

Cam spun around. Sasha stood behind him, perched on his ever-present BMX, his grin lazy, like he'd just woken up. Perhaps he had. Cam knew he had a penchant for afternoon naps. The thought was a balm to his churning insides. "Hard to miss. What are you, a prince or something?"

Sasha rolled his eyes and scratched his belly, revealing a sliver of his taut, tanned abdomen. "This is my parents' place. I rent the pool house. Come on, this way."

Cam followed Sasha up the driveway and around the back of the biggest house he'd ever seen up close. Tennis courts, plush outbuildings Sasha said were a gym and his father's sports car garage, and finally, a large, heated pool.

"This is me." Sasha pointed to a redbrick bungalow that opened out onto the poolside. "I'll show you."

The inside of the bungalow was sleek and stylish, furnished with modern decor and appliances, but it was lived in, with little touches of Sasha everywhere—bike parts, tools, weathered sneakers, and a stack of CDs on the coffee table. Cam liked it. "Nice place."

"Thanks." Sasha pointed to a stool at the breakfast counter, directing Cam to sit. "I moved back here when I got sick. Made things easier for my mom. She worried less, you know? I should probably get a place of my own again sometime, but my folks spend most of the year on the East Coast these days, so I'm here by myself a lot."

"Because you're better."

It wasn't a question, and Cam uttered the words to himself as much as Sasha, but Sasha nodded anyway. "Yeah, I'm better, Cam. Want a beer?"

"Hmm? No, thanks. I'm fine." Cam's gaze fell on a bubbling pot on the stove. "What are you cooking?"

Sasha placed a bottle of water on the countertop. "Chicken stew. Dumplings. Figured you could use some comfort food."

Cam absorbed the scent of chicken and herbs with muted interest. He hadn't been hungry in days. "Thought you'd make me eat some wheatgrass shit or something."

"Maybe next time."

Sasha messed around in the kitchen a little while longer. Cam watched him, enjoying the natural way he moved. He'd missed this—the easy banter and warmth—and it was almost enough to blot out the real reason Sasha had asked him to come. To forget that he was here for no other reason than Sasha felt sorry for him.

Cam cast his gaze around the bungalow's living space, searching for signs of Sasha's illness, though what he thought he'd find, he wasn't quite sure. His balls in a jar on a shelf, maybe?

Stop it.

Sasha's hand landed, firm and warm, on his shoulder. "Earth to Cam? Come on, dude. Let's eat."

Cam jolted back to reality. Somehow he'd missed Sasha loading bowls with food and carrying them past him to the coffee table. He followed Sasha to the big, squishy couch and sat, accepting the bowl Sasha shoved his way.

"Eat," Sasha said again, "then we'll talk. I promise."

Cam ate. The stew was good, though he lost interest long before he had the nerve to put his bowl down. Sasha watched him the whole time, his gaze shrewd. When he was done with his own food, he took both bowls to the kitchen and returned with two mugs of coffee.

Cam raised an eyebrow. "Thought you didn't do caffeine?"

"It's decaf, and I'm not a saint, you know. Or one of those nuts you see dressed in burlap at the health food store. I got into eating better when I was having chemo. I felt like crap for the best part of a year, and the little things helped."

"My doctor reckons I might not need chemo."

"That's good." Sasha took a sip from his mug and set it

down. "That's really good. They musta caught it early. Mine was stage three by the time I started treatment."

Cam sat up, his curiosity roused despite the urge to stick his head in the sand. "Was your tumor really small?"

"No. I just didn't have the, um, balls to do anything about it. I knew it was there three months before I went to my doctor."

"Three months? Fuck. Did you know what it was?"

"I had a vague fear in the back of my mind, but mostly I was too embarrassed to walk into my doctor's office and drop my pants."

Cam chewed the inside of his mouth. Sasha's inhibitions seemed logical, in theory, but getting his cock out in front of people was second nature to Cam and, of this whole mess, was the least of his worries. "I couldn't stand it. I had to know. I went to my doctor the day after I found it."

"You did the right thing." Sasha nudged Cam with his elbow, reminding Cam he was just a heartbeat away from him on the couch. "I know it's scary as hell, but this could all be over in a few months."

"What happened after your diagnosis? Did you have surgery? What do your balls look like now?"

Sasha blinked at the sudden influx of questions, then raised the corner of his mouth in an ironic smile. "What if I told you I had none?"

"What?" Cam's stomach lurched, and he spluttered into his drink.

Sasha grinned. "I'm kidding, Cam. Calm the fuck down. I had my right one removed four years ago."

Cam glared, but weighed down with a bucketload of shameful relief, the effort was halfhearted. "What's it like? Does it look weird?"

"Not really." Sasha paused, his face thoughtful. "But it's different for me. I don't pay my bills with my junk. To be honest, I don't notice it much anymore. I'm only conscious of it in certain situations."

A click sounded in Cam's brain. His mind flashed briefly to the scene in the club, the kiss, the wandering hands. He figured he'd found the answer to Sasha's subtle shutdown, but something else caught his attention. "I don't pay my bills with porn, either. I have a regular job for that."

"So why do you do it?"

"At first, to pay for college, but I liked it, so I carried on. I give my dad some money from time to time, but I mostly leave the extra cash in the bank."

"What for? Saving up for something?"

"Not really." Cam swallowed a mouthful of tepid coffee. "It's just...there. Hey, can I ask you something?"

"Fire away."

"Were you scared?"

"Terrified," Sasha said without hesitation. "I heard the word 'cancer' and assumed I was gonna die. Then, when they told me it had spread, I figured it would be sooner rather than later."

"It spread?" Cam felt his heart slow to a sickening thud. The thought of a world without Sasha was unthinkable. "What happened next?"

"After my first surgery, they went back and took some lymph nodes from my belly. Then they blasted me with chemo until I felt pretty much dead anyway. Looked it too."

Cam stared, trying to imagine Sasha anything but the strong, tanned picture of health he was now. Couldn't do it. "When was this?"

"Three years ago. I was twenty-two when I was first diagnosed, but I've been cancer free for more than a year now. They think I'm done."

"That's good." Cam sank back on the couch, letting out a rush of air that made him feel somehow lighter. He knew there was far more to Sasha's story than he'd revealed so far, but the ending was clear—he was okay. He was alive. "What about your dick? Does it still work?"

Sasha rolled his eyes. "Dude, you're obsessed, but, yes, it works just fine. Don't think I'm all that fertile, but I guess that doesn't really matter."

They talked a little while longer, about cancer and beyond. Sasha's easy vibe had always made Cam feel good, and curled up on his couch, surrounded by all that was him, Cam couldn't help the wave of fatigue that washed over him. He hadn't slept well over the last few days...weeks, and the combination of a full belly and Sasha's comforting presence felt like he'd swallowed a sleeping pill. The light touches, the guiding hand on his arm. A friendship laced with a casual flirtation that didn't come at a price.

Cam's eyes drooped. Dazed, he considered going home, but Sasha's soft laugh and something heavy on his legs convinced him to stay.

It was dark when he woke up. Sasha was still beside him, but somehow in his sleep Cam had shifted closer than ever, slumping down with his head on Sasha's belly.

Sasha played with Cam's hair, watching him wake with amused eyes. "Okay?"

"Um, yeah. Shit. Sorry." Cam sat up, rubbing his face, and found himself inches from Sasha's lips. "Guess I was tired."

"Guess so." Sasha didn't move. He stared at Cam like it was the most normal thing in the world for them to be so entangled on his couch.

Cam's pulse quickened. Images of their first kiss filled his brain, but that wasn't what he wanted right now. Wasn't what he needed and craved. Sasha's breath was warm on his face, and he wanted to taste it, lose himself in it, and touch Sasha's lips with a kiss that felt like a gentle ocean breeze.

Their lips met, and it was everything he needed in that moment. The kiss was slow and soft and pulled Cam into a haze so sweet, he found his hands in Sasha's soft hair and his leg hooked over Sasha's hips before he knew he'd moved.

Sasha cupped Cam's face in his rough, work-hardened hands and kissed Cam back, grounding him and holding him close.

Then he inhaled and pulled away, his face torn until his lips thinned to a determined line. He rolled off the couch and stepped back, putting a distance between them that felt like a fissuring chasm. "This can't happen."

Cam felt like he'd been punched in the gut. He'd taken Sasha's rejection before, but that didn't dull the burn of humiliation. "Sorry. Guess I just can't stop myself jumping on you."

"Don't be like that."

"Like what?" Cam forced himself up from the couch. "It's not like we haven't done this before. Where the fuck are my sneakers?"

"Cam..."

Cam dodged Sasha's outstretched arm. Somehow, he'd lost his shoes and the snapback ball cap he'd worn to keep his wayward hair in check. He spied the hat behind a sofa cushion and jammed it on his head. A wider sweep of the room found his sneakers by the back door.

He stomped over to them, but Sasha beat him to it, blocking his path.

"It's not what you think, okay? I don't want... Shit..." Sasha lost his words.

Cam laughed; he couldn't help it. "Dude, I get it. You don't want me. It's not that hard to understand."

"*That's* what you think this is? Me not wanting you? Goddamn it, Cam..." Sasha stopped again. His hands hovered, like he wanted to grab Cam and shake him. "This isn't about me. You might not know it, but you're not yourself at the moment. You don't *know* yourself, let alone what you really want."

Cam shook his head. He was tired and confused, but simmering beneath all that he was angry, real fucking angry. "Don't turn this around on me. I know what I want."

"Yeah? And what's that? You wanna bend me over the couch and fuck me until you can't remember what's tearing you up? Use your dick to make you feel better? 'Cause let me tell you, man, it won't work. Five minutes later, you'll be more miserable than when you fucking started."

Miserable. Cam turned the word over in his mind. It fit, so he kept it...held onto it and tried to smother it over the disproportionate fury choking him.

It didn't work. He couldn't breathe. He tried to open the door, desperate for fresh air.

Sasha blocked him again. "Cam, please—"

"Damn it, Sasha. Move!" Cam lashed out and drove his fist into the glass. It didn't break, but a crack formed and spread out, slow and creeping, like the icy dread Cam could feel in his bones. He hung his head and closed his eyes. "Just let me go, please?"

Silence, and then the dragging slide of the glass door as Sasha granted his wish. Cam opened his eyes and stepped out into the sunlight.

He walked away from Sasha without ever looking to see if the muffled sob he'd imagined was real.

CHAPTER TEN

Act(s)—kissing, blowing, fucking.

Partner(s)—Kai

Sick.

Lost.

Two words I can't shake. I've never felt like this before, like sex was so dirty and wrong. It wasn't Kai's fault, or even Jon and his cameras. It was mine. I shouldn't have been there. Porn suited me while I was drifting, not tied to anyone, not even myself. But not now. I'm different now, and it doesn't feel right. I feel like the porn gave me the cancer, like I brought it on myself, but I know that's not right either. Before...Jon, I loved it. It made me feel free.

Now, I feel like it's poisoned me from the inside out.

Cam stopped and put his pen down. His hand shook. He usually wrote more, but he'd been wrestling with his emotions for weeks, and seeing his darkest thoughts spelled out on paper scared him. His time with Sasha had calmed his sheer panic, but it seemed the effect was temporary. Or perhaps only existed in Sasha's presence. Alone in his apartment, Cam felt real, cold fear creep over him again. The kind of fear that made his chest hurt and his heart race.

The kind of fear that overcame even the disquiet from his fight with Sasha and the lingering embarrassment of rejection.

Cam shivered and glanced at the open bedroom window. It was Monday evening, two days before his scheduled surgery, and he hadn't heard from Sasha since he'd bolted from his cozy poolside bungalow the night before. And he wasn't sure he wanted to. After all, what else was left to say? Sasha had pulled away from him...twice, and after a long sleepless night, Cam figured he understood the message loud and clear.

I don't want you.

And he'd given up wondering why. Cancer, porn, and unfinished business with a possessive ex-lover, the specifics didn't matter. Put together, he wasn't exactly a catch.

Cam took a deep breath and stared hard at the ceiling. He'd been lying alone on his bed since he'd finished work at Beat Shak four hours ago. His day had been long and dull, concluding with a meeting with his boss to explain the leave of absence he needed to take for the surgery and subsequent treatment. The meeting was the first time he'd talked about the cancer with anyone who wasn't a doctor or Sasha. The short conversation had exhausted him, but despite that, he felt restless and keyed up, like he could climb out of his skin and claw his own eyes out. Sasha and the impending surgery kept him awake, but more than that, he couldn't stop thinking about porn, and the limitations he hadn't noticed it imposing on his life. His apartment was cold and lonely, *he* was lonely, and why? Because there was no one outside the studio he could call and confide in. Sonny was his friend, but he'd been MIA for weeks, and Cam couldn't face Levi's voice mail again.

But he couldn't spend another minute kicking around his apartment. The doctors had told him to rest up before surgery, take it easy and relax, but instead, Cam was driving himself crazy. He wasn't used to spending so much time by himself. This time last year, he'd had a place full of people, drinks flowing, temperatures rising, and perhaps that was part of the problem. Perhaps he'd been alone all along.

Cam rolled from his bed, giving himself a slight head rush, and moved to his closet. He'd ditched his Beat Shak T-shirt as soon as he'd come home, knowing he wouldn't need it for a while, and he'd been shirtless since then, intent on crashing out in bed and hiding under his duvet until the day of his surgery dawned. But it wasn't going to happen. There was something he needed to do, and he needed to do it *now*.

Thirty minutes later, he strolled past security at Silver as if he didn't have a care in the world. He bypassed the dance floor and made his way to the crowded bar. Silver was kicking, even on a Monday night, but Bull, Silver's resident manager, saw him and pointed to the backlit refrigerators. As a resident model, Cam had the right to help himself.

He took a cold bottle of beer and chugged half of it down in one long gulp. The rest slid down just as easy, *too* easy. He took another and continued on his way, downstairs to the staff-only basement of the club.

Jon's office was empty when he punched in the code to open the door. Cam wasn't surprised. Jon checked in at Silver every evening, but never before midnight. Cam glanced around, looking for a suitable medium for his leave of absence notice. A pen and paper didn't seem to cut it.

He rounded the desk and flicked on the computer. It usually took a few minutes to boot up, so Cam was surprised when the screen flashed to life almost instantly, and shocked when the image on-screen registered with his convoluted consciousness.

What the fuck?

Cam froze. He'd seen himself on-screen more times than he cared to remember. Watched his own scenes for pleasure. But he'd never seen himself depicted the way he was now. Tied up and begging. Head down, ass raised. Jon's to do with whatever he pleased. Cam leaned closer, clicked a few buttons. More images of his private moments with Jon lit up the screen. Jon's bedroom, Jon's couch. The wide, flat coffee table. Even the harsh words they'd exchanged at the studio after the scene with Kai were saved as an MP4.

Cam clicked on the thumbnail, turned the sound up, and watched himself let Jon back him into a corner, shove his hand down Cam's pants, and almost talk him into getting fucked right over the desk. Performing for a camera he hadn't known existed.

Ironic nausea rolled in Cam's belly. He opened the liquor cabinet and reached for a bottle. He took a robotic swig. Expensive whiskey burned his throat but did nothing to calm the horror building in his gut. Having sex with an audience was second nature, something he enjoyed when his life wasn't imploding, but this? Cam read the titles, and his tongue stuck to the roof of his mouth. He opened a document and read the eleven words that described the project for which he'd become an unwitting star.

Bound and Begging. Cam Carter as you've never seen him before...

Cam clicked on a few more links and files. He didn't know much about distribution, but the electronic paper trail was clear. Every sexual encounter Cam and Jon had ever had was edited to remove any identifying sign of Jon, polished, and ready to be loaded to the Blue Boy website.

Numb, Cam made a grab for the desk phone and jammed his finger on the Zero button, knowing it dialed Jon's personal cell. The cell he never turned off, even in bed...in bed with Cam.

Jon answered on the third ring. "Who's in my office?"

"Who do you think?"

Silence. Then, "Cam?"

"Had to think about that, didn't you? How many people know the code?"

"That's why you're calling?" Jon's condescending amusement washed over Cam like acid. "I know you can think of a better reason to be in my office than that."

"How about getting a preview of your new project? *Bound and Begging*. Sounds like pretty interesting viewing."

The pause at the other end of the line was barely detectable, but to Cam, it was deafening.

"Do I want to know why you're going through my personal files?"

"Personal?" Red-hot anger flushed Cam's face. He felt like he was burning for all the wrong reasons. "There's nothing *personal* about putting this shit online."

"Says who? You've never had a problem with it before. Something you want to tell me?"

"Like what? Like I didn't consent to having my private sex life sold to line your pockets? Fuck you, Jon."

Jon sighed. "Really, Cam? You're going to play coy with me now? Nothing we do at Blue Boy is private. It's business...art, and I know you love it. Admit it. Being with me showed you a side of yourself you didn't know was there. Self-discovery. That's what you're all about, isn't it?"

Cam swallowed bile. Part of him wanted to argue, but the devil on his shoulder knew Jon's words were laced with truth. Bottoming, submitting, giving up control. He *had* loved it. He thought of Sasha, his big hands, strong arms, and muscled legs. Would love it again. Just not with Jon. Not anymore.

"It's not art if both parties don't consent, you sick fuck. It's just you being a motherfucking pervert."

Cam slammed the phone down without waiting for Jon's reply. With shaking hands, he returned to the computer and clicked through to the control panel. He wiped the hard drive, swallowing several more mouthfuls of fiery whiskey while he waited for the process to complete.

Then he unplugged the machine and pulled it apart with his bare hands for good measure. He poured what remained of the whiskey bottle over the twisted mass of metal and wire. Considered lighting the whole damned lot on fire.

The pounding bass of the dance floor above brought him to his senses.

Horrified, Cam lurched away from the desk. His breath caught in his chest. He needed to get out. *Now.*

He stumbled to the door and slipped out into the murky corridor. Silver was packed, hot and heady. Around him, half-naked bodies stood pressed up against the walls, kissing, clutching, squeezing. More. Cam pushed past them, ignoring the voices that shouted his name. Dodging the hands that reached for him.

Jesus. Was this what he'd become? A commodity? Nothing more than a product of the Blue Boy brand? Nothing more than a pawn in Jon's game?

Cam made it into the main area of the club. The crowds closed in around him. Beyond the dance floor he could see the exit. It was twenty feet away, but the distance felt like a mile. His blood roared in his ears. Sweat dripped down his back. The lights, the noise. The bellyful of liquor on an empty stomach. His vision narrowed, and it all came crashing down, closing in on him until he could no longer breathe. Couldn't see. Couldn't think.

He stumbled again, bumping shoulders with someone hard enough to leave a bruise. He closed his eyes, waiting for the impact of the hard, sticky floor.

It never came. Strong hands caught him. Cam opened his eyes to meet a familiar hazel gaze he'd missed more than he'd dared to admit.

Sonny held Cam's face, his eyes wide. "Cam? What's wrong?"

CHAPTER ELEVEN

Sonny kicked open the fire doors and pulled Cam outside. Cam blinked. He hadn't thought of that. A little way down the street, away from the buzz of the club, Sonny sat him on the curb. "I need to get my stuff. Stay here."

Cam sat. Despite his anxiety to escape the club, he'd run out of energy. It seemed like no time at all before Sonny was back. Sonny hauled Cam to his feet. He was half the size of Cam but looks were deceptive; Sonny was strong. Cam stumbled. Sonny caught him and steadied him with his arms around Cam's waist. "Whoa. You're wasted, dude. What's the occasion?"

Cam laughed, the sound so dark and bitter it surprised even him. "I'm not celebrating."

Sonny eyed Cam a moment, looking up at him, still holding him by the waist. From a distance, they probably looked like lovers. "You look lost."

"Maybe I am."

"You're definitely drunk." Sonny stretched up and kissed his cheek. "Come on; let's walk home."

Cam let himself be tugged toward Sonny's part of town with little complaint. He was tired, and it wouldn't be the first time he'd crawled back to Sonny's place after a wild night at Silver. "What time is it?"

"Just after twelve. I haven't even gone onstage yet. Jon's gonna fire my ass."

"No, he won't." It was true. Like Cam, Sonny was a commodity, but it would take more than a few missed shows for Jon to fire Sonny. Sonny was the hottest dancer in the city. Jon wouldn't let another club snap him up, and a few no-shows was probably good publicity, fueling a buzz with the crowds of fans who flocked to Silver to see the Blue Boy models up close.

Still, it was early, for Sonny, at least. "You don't have to come with me. I should go home."

"And miss you falling over your own feet?" Sonny squeezed Cam's hand—the hand he'd yet to release—and bumped his shoulder. "No chance. You're coming home with me. We haven't seen you for ages."

"We? Is Levi at your place?" Cam came to an abrupt stop, fulfilling Sonny's prophecy and tripping over his feet.

Sonny kept walking, yanking on Cam until he complied. "No. He doesn't like my place, he spends all his time tidying up, but I have a key to his apartment. Plus, I gotta bottle of back-shelf vodka in my bag, and I know the best way to wake him up."

Cam wasn't so sure. For a porn star—*ex*-porn star—Levi was pretty tame. Even back in his day, he hadn't partied much, preferring to duck out early and hit the sack. Besides, if he'd read the glint in Sonny's eyes right, the kind of awakening he had in mind was best done by himself. It had been a long time since Cam had last fooled around with Levi. He wasn't sure how the big man would react if Sonny jumped on his bed with Cam in tow.

But it turned out not to matter. Levi was awake when Sonny let himself into his apartment, lounging on the couch, beer bottle in hand, and he seemed pretty pleased to see Sonny.

Cam hovered in the doorway. Levi caught his gaze over Sonny's shoulder, his expression inscrutable, and Cam felt himself withdraw into the troubled darkness he'd come out to escape. Levi's place was familiar. He'd spent many nights here, taking advantage of Levi's skill in the kitchen and putting the world to rights over a crate of beer, but without Levi's usual warm welcome, it felt all wrong.

Levi appeared in front of him. Cam hadn't noticed him move, nor Sonny disappear. Levi put his hands on Cam's shoulders. "What's up?"

Cam shrugged. His mind was weighed down by a plethora of bullshit. He couldn't find the words to begin explaining it.

Levi pulled him into a light, platonic hug. "It's good to see you, man."

The embrace felt good. Safe. Cam pressed his face into Levi's shoulder. His anger-laced whiskey buzz was beginning to wear off. "It's good to see you too. I've been calling you."

"Really?" Levi released him with a clap on the back. "I changed my cell. Did Sonny give you my new number?"

"Aw, shit, I forgot." Sonny jumped over the back of the couch, dressed in nothing but the shiny underwear he was supposed to have danced in. "I figured we could just call you, but your cell keeps going to voice mail."

"I, uh, lost it." Cam averted his gaze. He'd yet to contact the phone company and tell them he'd "misplaced" his phone. Maybe he'd do it after the surgery.

"Lost it?" Sonny poured three shots of vodka over ice and beckoned Cam and Levi to the couch. "Not trying to avoid someone, are you?"

Cam trailed Levi to the big leather sofa, waiting for him to slouch down beside Sonny before he took his place at the opposite end of the couch. It felt a little strange to see Levi and Sonny so comfortable together. He'd worked, partied, and fooled around with them both, but somehow never at the same time. Having them all in one place felt weird. Good but weird. "Who would I be hiding from?"

"Jon?" Sonny's gaze was steady, but despite his constant chatter, his eyes were pink and tired, like he hadn't slept much over the weekend, though Cam imagined his own face looked much the same. "I saw you come out of the office at the club like a bat out of hell."

Cam snagged a shot of vodka and chugged it down. "I'm not seeing Jon anymore."

Sasha aside, it was the first time he admitted there was something between him and Jon to anyone, but Levi's expression didn't change at all, and Sonny's only reaction was to dump his feet in Cam's lap. Cam rubbed his thumbs on Sonny's muscled calves. The gesture was absent...natural, until he remembered Levi. He chanced a glance at Levi now, wondering if he'd react. He didn't.

"Is that what's been bothering you?" Sonny said. "How serious was it? I can't imagine you with someone like him."

Cam considered his answer. He'd never perceived his encounters with Jon as anything more than some crazily intense sex, but his throat still burned from his discovery in Jon's office. He didn't feel hurt; he felt...sick. "Don't imagine it. You won't like it."

"Then tell me...us. Talk about it, Cam. Putting shit in boxes doesn't work for you. Don't let it eat you up."

Sonny knew him well, and combined with his instinctive understanding of how his mind worked, Cam knew he couldn't hide from him. And perhaps he didn't want to anymore. "You won't like it."

The repetition caught Levi's attention. He shifted on the couch, not seeming to notice Sonny crawl into Cam's lap. "What the hell did he do to you?"

Cam swallowed, hiding his face in Sonny's neck for a moment. Could he do it? Could he really tell them that his own stupidity had allowed Jon to take advantage of him? That he'd become so distracted by sex he hadn't even noticed? With Sonny playing with his hair, maybe he could.

Sonny and Levi listened in silence as Cam made his confession. He told them everything, from the submissive sex games to the hidden cameras.

Levi's frown grew with every word. When Cam was done, he swallowed a shot of vodka, the last of the bottle. Somehow, they'd polished it off while Cam had been talking.

"I don't get it," Levi said. "That some kinda BDSM shit? I didn't know you were into that."

Cam shrugged. "Neither did I. It was good, though, for a while, at least."

"When did you start seeing Jon?"

"Summer sometime." Cam thought back. "I went to his Fourth of July party."

Cam let the sentence hang. Sonny shifted and pressed a soft kiss to his neck. "I get it. You were freaking out about your mom, so letting Jon make decisions for you comforted you. Submission is like that sometimes, an escape."

"You think I discovered a new kink and used it as an avoidance tactic?"

"Maybe."

It was an interesting theory, but Cam was past caring, and part of him was resigned to the fact that he'd probably never understand what had driven him into his warped relationship with Jon. Admitting his stupidity to his friends was more embarrassing than traumatic. Secret cameras aside, it wasn't like Jon had ever forced him into anything. He'd enjoyed the sex. It was the rest of it that left a bad taste in his mouth.

Levi's frown deepened. "I don't get it. What happened to your mom?"

"She left."

"Huh? Left? As in, broke up with your dad?"

Sonny raised his head and slanted a glance at Levi. Cam couldn't see his expression. "Didn't you know?"

"Nope. I had no fucking idea. When did this happen?"

Cam let out an ironic chuckle. "July third."

"Why didn't you tell me?" Levi shook his head. He could be hard to read, but Cam could tell he was shocked.

Cam shrugged. "It seemed tame compared to what your momma was putting you through."

"So? Doesn't mean I don't give a shit."

Cam sighed. "I know you do; it's just this mess with Jon. I knew you didn't like him, even before...Rex, and I kinda found myself caught up with him before I knew what I was doing, you know? And by then, I couldn't seem to tell anyone."

"You told me about your mom, but you never said a word about Jon," Sonny said. His tone was contemplative, though he didn't seem pissed.

Cam looked down at the patterns Sonny was tracing on his chest through the thin cotton of his T-shirt. "You didn't ask."

"Bullshit. I asked you about Jon last time I saw you. You blew me off."

Cam smirked at Sonny's choice of words. The extra vodka was seeping into his bones and making his head swim. "You've never complained before."

But his grin died when Sonny scowled. "See? That's what you've been doing ever since Jon got his hooks into you. Being all evasive and shit. We used to talk about everything. Now you don't talk to anyone."

Cam's humor sobered as he considered Sonny's theory. And his stomach dropped as he realized Sonny was right. Ever since his mom had decided raising a family was too much for her, he'd spent most of his time working, partying, or fucking. Or all three combined. But as he'd come to realize over the last few weeks, those pursuits had left him pretty damned lonely. The only exception was Sasha.

Cam's chest ached.

"Hey." Levi's hand was warm on his shoulder. "You wiped the hard drive, right? That mess with Jon is over now. Don't think on it no more."

Cam nodded and closed his eyes. Levi was closer than he thought, and combined with Sonny wriggling on his lap, the warmth from Levi's solid body felt reassuring.

Sonny let out a mellow laugh. "Give him a kiss, Levi. That'll cheer him up."

Cam peeled an eye open. "Levi doesn't kiss."

Sonny's grin was smug. "He kisses me."

"Really?" Cam eyed Levi, who looked amused. "Thought kissing was for schmucks?"

"What can I say?" Levi shrugged, unruffled. "Sonny broke me."

Sonny hissed through his teeth. "You didn't take much persuading."

Cam absorbed the smoldering glance Levi sent Sonny's way with conflicting emotions. The obvious affection between his friends warmed his heart, but beneath it all, he was jealous. He wanted it for himself, not from them, but from Sasha. And worse, he knew it had been his for the taking before Jon Kellar and his porn empire got in the way. "I was seeing someone else for a while."

"The hot blond you brought to the club?"

Cam cut his eyes at Levi. "How the hell do *you* know about that?"

Levi pointed at Sonny.

Sonny shot Cam a look that made him squirm. "Kai told me. Did you really think you could take him to Silver and keep it quiet?"

Cam had no answer, because Sonny was right. Taking Sasha to Silver had been fucking ridiculous, doomed from the start. The scene with Jon had just been the icing on the cake.

"Doesn't matter now. He wants to be *friends*."

Cam's sigh was heavy, but Sonny smirked and gripped the hem of Cam's T-shirt. "Aw, don't look so sad. Friends can be good."

Despite his heavy mood, the gleam in Sonny's eye was tempting. Cam met Levi's gaze as Sonny relieved him of his shirt. "Are we cool?"

Levi's grin was soft and blurred by the empty bottle of vodka on the coffee table. "We're cool, man. Just don't leave me out."

Cam's reply was muffled by Sonny's lips on his. Cam's body responded to the kiss like an old friend. Used to Sonny's dominant inclination, Cam fell pliant beneath him and let himself be pushed and pulled until his back collided with Levi's bare chest.

Levi wrapped his arms around him, wove his fingers into Cam's hair, and tugged his head aside to expose his neck. He nipped the soft flesh. Cam shivered. They'd played this game before, more times than he cared to admit, but on Levi's couch with Sonny kissing a path down his belly, somehow it felt more...intimate? Cam was too drunk to find the right word.

Cam lay back and let his eyes fall closed. Let his strained muscles relax, one by one. Despite Levi's words it was clear they'd somehow decided between them that Cam was the center of their affections. Not that Cam was complaining. A Levi-Sonny sandwich?

Yeah. He could lose himself in that.

Clothes disappeared like they'd never been there at all. Cam didn't have to look to see Sonny's back arch and his graceful neck flare. To see Levi's strong arms ripple and pop. Cam writhed and shuddered. Absorbed it. Drank it all in through his tired bones. He felt Sonny's dick on his thigh, and Levi's hard at his back, and wondered idly how things were going to go down. He'd fucked Sonny many times over, and it was always good, but the thought of Levi inside him was thrilling. Levi was *big*. Perhaps bending over for him would make him forget...

Sonny blew warm air over Cam's balls. Cam jumped. For the first time in days, the poisonous intruder in his body had been the last thing on his mind.

He sat up, feeling Levi follow him, still molded to his back, and watched his dick disappear into Sonny's mouth. Even from the safety of Levi's arms, he could see the tumor bulging to the left of Sonny's stubbled jaw. Bold and crass. *Huge.* How could Sonny not see it?

Sonny flicked his tongue over the tip of Cam's cock. Cam moaned. Distracting pleasure surged through him, and he dug his teeth into Levi's forearm.

Levi rumbled in Cam's ear. "You like that?"

Cam arched his neck and searched out Levi's earlobe, sucking it into his mouth, enjoying Levi's low growl. "Fuck, yeah."

Sonny hummed, staring up at them and watching them interact as he swallowed Cam whole. Cam gasped. He'd taught Sonny the art of deep throating himself, and he'd taught him well. He broke away from Levi with a breathy grunt and fought to keep himself on the couch. Sonny's attention felt good, almost too good, like a guilty pleasure of the best kind.

The first, faint flickers of release tickled Cam's belly. He was a sucker for good head, and it had been a while since anyone with real skills had gone to town on him. And Sonny didn't hold back. His rhythm was sure and steady, and when Cam began to lock up and shake, Sonny let his fingers wander, tracing Cam's oversensitive balls and lower, brushing over Cam's ass like a ghost.

Frustrated, Cam ground himself down onto Sonny's fingers, chasing friction and the addictive burn of being breached.

Sonny released Cam's dick from his mouth, his gaze telling Cam he knew exactly what he wanted. "You sure?"

"Do it." Cam squirmed, unable to keep still. "Do it hard."

Sonny ignored him and sucked his index finger into his mouth, putting on a show that made Cam's toes curl.

Levi chuckled in Cam's ear, low and deep. "Don't watch him do that. He knows it drives me fucking crazy."

Cam tried to smile, but he was too far gone, lost in the haze of vodka-fueled lust. He moaned and opened his legs, licking his dry lips. Sonny took the hint and eased his finger into Cam's ass.

The burn was light and sweet. Cam craved something deeper, but his subconscious pleaded with him to relax and trust Sonny to guide him. He tried to listen and was rewarded with the devilish twist of Sonny's single finger and a blunt nail scraping the bundle of nerves hidden inside him.

Sonny took Cam into his mouth again, sucking him hard, countering the gentle sweep of his finger. The sensation was immediate and overwhelming. Cam's body clamped down on Sonny, and he came with a throaty cry.

His mind went blank. His head spun, and he thought he might faint. The blackness felt fucking amazing, but brief. Too brief.

A noise escaped him, a desperate, plaintive sound.

Levi stroked his damp hair away from his face, soothing him like he had a fever. "Easy now."

Cam fought for breath and focused on Sonny, watching him as he climbed over Cam's body for a kiss before stretching up to find Levi. Cam listened to them kiss, absorbing their growing moans and tiny gasps of air, but he didn't look up. Though Levi still held him tight and Sonny held his hand over Cam's thudding heart, watching them *kiss* felt wrong, like he was intruding on a private moment. Instead he let the rush of his fading orgasm carry him until his stomach lurched in protest of a night on the booze with no food to sustain it.

Cam wriggled from the couch and excused himself to the bathroom. Levi and Sonny didn't seem to notice him go, but when he came back a little while later, his belly purged of beer and hard liquor, Sonny was dressed in sleep pants and chucking pillows on the opened-out sofa bed. Aside from the smell of sweat and sex in the air, there was no sign of the sweetly frenzied three-way.

"Levi's too sober for an orgy," Sonny said by way of explanation. "He thinks we should have a slumber party instead."

Levi snorted and punched his arm, still in the boxers he'd never gotten around to shucking. "Shut your mouth. I could watch Cam fuck you all night, but it's not what he needs." Levi turned his shrewd gaze on Cam. "Don't look for answers in sex. They ain't there for you no more."

"Or at least call your mystery dude up and invite him," Sonny quipped, though his crazy energy seemed to have faded while Cam had been blowing chunks in the bathroom.

Cam sat on the arm of the couch, watching Levi lunge for Sonny and pin him to the bed with one arm. In his heart, he knew Levi was right, and the underlying message caught him off guard. He'd sought comfort from Jon in the worst way, and where had it got him?

Playing third wheel to his two best friends.

Sonny tugged on his arm. "Wanna be Levi's little spoon? He'll keep you warm."

Cam hesitated, wondering if he should just go home. Then Levi held out his hand. "Come on, dude. There's plenty of room."

Cam let himself be pulled from the arm of the sofa. He landed in a clumsy heap by Levi. Sonny laughed and set about arranging them all the way he saw fit—Cam with his back to Levi, and his face buried in Sonny's chest. Cam didn't fight it or even protest. He knew he was in the wrong place, but knowing his friends were wrapped around him, hands clasped and sharing quiet, loving kisses, somehow, he fell asleep.

CHAPTER TWELVE

Cam woke at dawn. His head was on Levi's chest. He looked for Sonny and found they'd scooted around in the night. At some point, Sonny had climbed over him and sandwiched Levi between them, both of them using the big man as a pillow, protected by his strong arms.

Tiny Kai aside, it had been a long time since Cam had woken up with someone. Dribbling on Sasha didn't count. When he spent the night with Sonny, they usually partied all night, fooling around and murdering songs on Sonny's beat-up guitar, and he'd never slept with Jon.

He peeled his cheek from Levi's chest and found Levi awake, watching him a wry grin.

Cam took a moment to focus. "Hey."

"Hey." Levi lifted his arm so Cam could move. "Sleep all right?"

Cam stretched, noting he was the only one still naked. "Yeah."

It was mostly true. He'd woken a few times, convinced he could hear Sonny and Levi fucking, but when he opened his eyes in the darkness he'd seen Levi on his back with his legs wrapped around Sonny, and he knew that couldn't be right.

Levi maneuvered himself from beneath a sound-asleep Sonny, covered him with a blanket, and pointed at the kitchen. "Go get cleaned up. I'll make breakfast."

Cam wasn't hungry, but he needed a shower. He accepted the sweatpants Levi tossed his way, and drifted to the bathroom. The shower cleared his head. It felt good to tuck his damp, wayward hair behind his ears, and the smell of whatever Levi was cooking made him feel even better.

Cam dropped onto a kitchen stool and slumped on the breakfast bar, poking idly at his crappy prepay phone. The phone that never fucking rang.

Levi slid him a glass of orange juice. "Expecting a call?"

"No." Cam pocketed the phone.

Levi grinned and punched his shoulder. "Bet you're glad we didn't have a fuckin' orgy last night now, huh?"

Cam looked up at Levi, took in his broad bare chest and gentle grin. "Yes and no. You were right, but…"

Levi nudged him again. "If we were meant to roll in the hay together, it'll happen. Get the rest of your life in order first."

Levi dropped his words of wisdom and returned to his spicy skillet. Cam watched him cook for a while. Onions, peppers, mushrooms. Eggs, potatoes, and cheese. If Cam put all that in a pan, he'd end up with a hot mess. Not Levi. Everything he cooked tasted like magic.

"Sonny still asleep?"

"Hmm?" Levi glanced over his shoulder, and his smiled faded. It was subtle, but Cam saw it all the same. "Think he's been up all damned weekend. I wonder how he functions sometimes."

That sounded like Sonny. "You know how he functions though, right?"

A shadow passed over Levi's face. "I've got an idea, but enough about Sonny. When are you gonna tell me all the shit you left out last night?"

"Meaning?"

Levi flipped spicy hash onto three plates. He covered the third and set it aside. "Listen, I know I'm not a fucking psych expert like the rest of you, but I'm not as dumb as you think."

"I don't think you're dumb."

"That's sweet." Levi slid a plate across the countertop. "But I still don't get it. Jon did a number on you, but there's more to this than him. Dude, you're like...inside out. What's done that to you?"

Levi was smiling, but his words hit home. The bullshit with Jon, the booze, fooling around with his friends. None of it was anything more than a distraction, and in the hungover haze of the early morning, Cam lost the will to hide. He stood, walked around the breakfast bar, and pushed his borrowed sweatpants over his hips.

Levi raised an eyebrow. "Hey, now. I thought we understood each other."

Cam ignored him and lifted his flaccid cock away from his balls. "What can you see?"

"Huh?"

"Give me your hand." Cam grabbed Levi's wrist. "Can you feel that?"

Levi stared at him like he'd grown two heads, but didn't resist as Cam guided his hand to the left side of his sac. For a long moment, Levi's expression remained the same, but Cam saw his eyes widen when he felt the hard, misshapen intruder.

"What the fuck is that?"

Cam stepped back, heat flushing his face, and tucked himself back into Levi's sweatpants. "A seminoma."

"A what?"

"A tumor." Cam dropped back into his seat, his appetite and tentative resolve gone.

Levi opened his mouth. Shut it again. "Is it..."

"Cancer? Yeah, they think so. They'll know for sure when they take it off, but they seem pretty certain."

Levi swallowed, then turned his back on Cam, washed his hands, and reached for the kettle. The silence seemed endless, punctuated only by the hiss and swoosh of water as Levi poured it into two mugs.

Cam slumped forward again and put his head on his arms. He let his eyes droop. Levi's hand on his shoulder startled him.

"What happens now?"

"They cut it off, analyze it, and decide if I need chemo. The way it stands now, they reckon I might get away with a blast of radiation."

"Cut it off?" Levi looked a little green.

"Yep, they're gonna take the whole thing, ball and all. I'm gonna be lopsided for the rest of my life."

"But the tumor will be gone." Levi let his hand drop from Cam's shoulder. He seemed to have forgotten it was there. "And that's good about the chemo, right? If you don't need it?"

"I guess. They don't know that for sure, though." Cam reached for one of the mugs Levi had dumped on the counter. It looked like tea, in a weird, gray sort of way. He took a sip and cringed. "What the hell kind of tea is that?"

Levi shook his head. "I have no idea. You kinda threw me a curveball. I was trying to be nice."

"Sorry."

"What?" Levi looked startled. "Aw, hell no, Cam. I'm the one who should be sorry. You've been going through all this shit, and I never fuckin' noticed. And for what it's worth, I *am* sorry. You've always been there for me. I shoulda been there for you."

Cam let it go. He was as guilty as Levi for letting the drama at the studio get between them, but he didn't feel like arguing.

"Does Jon know?"

Cam shook his head. "No. Apart from my boss at Beat Shak, you're the first person I've told." *And Sasha.*

"Not easy, is it? Telling people the bad stuff." Levi's gaze clouded, and Cam remembered his face when he'd let slip about his momma's death. Flat, distant, empty, but beneath the forced apathy, the pain had glittered like a snake in the grass. "When's your surgery?"

Cam blinked. *Fuck.* "Tomorrow."

"Tomo—what? Why so soon?"

Cam shrugged. "This kind of tumor grows real fast, and it's not that soon. I've known about it for a week or so."

"Are you ready?"

Am I? Cam considered the question, and reality crashed into him. He wasn't ready...not even halfway there. He hadn't told his dad, his sister...Sonny. "I need to go."

Levi caught him as he rolled off his stool. "Easy. Eat your breakfast first."

Cam shook his head. He needed to go, now, or he'd lose his nerve. "I need to see my dad."

"Cam." Levi stared at him like he wanted to say so much more. Then he reached for his keys. "Come on. I'll drive you."

The ride to his dad's place was silent. Levi wasn't much of a talker at the best of times, and Cam knew he'd shocked him. Cam stared out of the window, watching the familiar scenery fly by. He felt odd...detached somehow from his mind. When Wade's house appeared in his line of sight, it seemed almost surreal.

Levi shook him. "You awake?"

Cam stared at him. Of course he was fucking awake. Did Levi think he could sleep with his freakin' eyes open? "I'm cool."

He made no move to get out of Levi's truck. It was seven a.m. on a Tuesday morning. Wade would be stomping around, throwing paper-wrapped lunches and backpacks at his brothers before he set off for a long day at the truck yard. Did Cam really want to drop this on him now?

Levi read his mind. "You're out of time, dude. Just tell him. He's your family. He'll understand."

How Levi knew that, Cam would never know. Levi was all alone in the world, and he had been long before his crazy momma took a walk in front of a truck. "What about Sonny? I need to tell him."

"Don't worry about Sonny. I got him."

Levi's tone gave Cam pause. He stopped with his hand on the truck door and looked back. Something flashed in Levi's eyes. Betrayal? No. Cam couldn't have that. Sonny's secret was precious, and one Cam had discovered by accident, but he couldn't let Levi believe that Sonny was anything less than the brilliant young man he was.

"It's not what you think."

Levi's gaze hardened. Despite the cryptic overtone, he knew exactly what Cam was talking about. "I ain't judging him, but I can't watch him destroy himself. I can't go through that again."

"It's not his fault."

"Isn't it?" Levi looked away.

Cam grasped Levi's arm, forcing him to look back. "It's *not*. He's not a coke whore, Levi. It's fucking Ritalin. He's been on it since he was twelve."

Levi stared at him, his dark gaze flickering with unanswered questions, but it was the wrong time. Cam loved Sonny and Levi probably more than he should've, but Levi was right. He'd run out of time to worry about anyone but himself.

"It's okay, Cam." Levi reached across him and shoved open the passenger door. "Everything's gonna be okay. You take care of this, and I'll take care of Sonny."

Cam paced his hospital room, his socked feet making no

sound on the shiny white floor. Wade watched him from the chair at the side of the bed, his shrewd gaze tracking Cam's every move.

"Sit down, Son. You'll wear yourself out before they've even got started."

Cam ignored him. Wade's presence was comforting, but with just a few minutes to go until they came to shoot who knew what into the IV in his hand, his nerves were getting the better of him. He stopped at the window and stared out over the hospital grounds. Wade's reaction to the cancer had been predictable—a horrified silence and then a bone-crushing hug that stole the breath from Cam's lungs. A day on the couch, a hot meal, and a good night sleep in his childhood bed had followed, but even the comfort of home and what remained of his family wasn't enough to quell the fast-rising panic in his belly.

This was it. There was no going back. In a few short hours he'd wake up literally half the man he used to be.

"Are you sure you don't want me to call your mom?"

Cam considered the question, anything to keep his mind from his condemned anatomy. He hadn't spoken to his mom for so long he couldn't recall if her presence had ever made him feel better. And what about Wade? He'd taken his wife's departure with dignity and grace, but Cam remembered the pain in his eyes as she'd driven away into the sunset, leaving her four kids and the only life they'd ever known far behind.

Screw her. "I'm fine, Dad. I don't need her."

Wade's sigh was soft, but Cam heard it like a supersonic boom. Felt it like the sledgehammer of a text message Sonny had sent him long before dawn that morning.

Get better. We love you — S

Five little words, words that meant everything and nothing, because despite it all, Cam still felt totally and utterly alone. His room had been a revolving door of doctors and nurses, waving forms for him to sign, poking him with needles, and jamming things into his ears and mouth, but the sense that someone was missing lingered, and the only thing Cam knew for sure was it wasn't his damned mother.

"Mr. Shaw?" Cam looked around. A nurse stood in the doorway, flanked by an orderly with a wheelchair. "It's time to take you to the OR."

Nausea rolled in the pit of Cam's stomach. He stared at the wheelchair and willed himself to man up and step forward, but he couldn't do it. "I don't need a wheelchair."

"It's either that or we wheel you down on a gurney."

"I can walk."

The nurse looked irritated, as though she'd had the conversation a thousand times that day already. "It's procedure."

"Let the boy walk," Wade said. "Can't do no harm."

The nurse relented and let Cam shuffle past her in his hospital gown and socks, but the orderly followed close behind, brandishing the wheelchair like a gun.

Cam drifted along the corridor in a daze, his legs like lead. His chest hurt. It took him a few steps to realize he'd stopped breathing. He sucked in a harsh breath. A choked noise escaped him. Wade touched his arm.

"Easy, Son."

The gesture, and the appearance of the imposing double door to the operating room, reminded Cam that they were moments away from being separated. Terror bubbled up in his throat. He opened his mouth to call for his dad, but the words never came.

"Cam! Cam, wait."

Cam looked over his shoulder. The hospital corridor moved in slow motion, and Sasha appeared in front of him like a dream, his hair crazy and windswept, his eyes wild.

Cam stared at him. "What are you doing here?"

Sasha took his hands and squeezed them in a grip so tight it should've hurt. "I... Fuck. I had to see you before you went in. I'm so sorry, Cam."

Cam stared. Somewhere in the back of his mind he knew they were surrounded by nurses and orderlies...even his own father, but the rest of the world faded away. "What are you sorry for?"

Sasha kissed him, lightly at first, but then harder...kissed him until Cam swayed on his feet. "For everything. I'm sorry I made you feel like shit, and I'm sorry I pushed you away so many times. Get through this, and I promise, I'll never push you away again."

Cam opened his eyes. It seemed like no time at all had passed since a white-masked doctor had instructed him to count backward from one hundred, but if the brutal pain in his belly was anything to go by, he'd made it through the surgery.

He swallowed, trying to make sense of the stretched tension in his groin and the numbness down his left side. His back felt stiff. He shifted to relieve the pressure and cringed. Bad move. *Fuck*, that hurt.

Someone called his name. He peeled his eyes open again and found his father's steady gaze.

"Okay, Son?" Wade squeezed his hand. "The nurse put a pain pump in your hand. Press the button if you're uncomfortable."

The instructions rang a bell. Cam vaguely remembered the surgeon explaining the self-administering morphine pump to him. At the time, he'd figured he wouldn't need it. How bad could it be?

Pretty fucking bad, as it turned out. Cam pressed the button.

His faculties returned to him one by one. Beyond the pain,

he felt sleepy and sick, but the feeling faded as the fog clouding his brain lifted. "Dad?"

Wade rubbed his shoulder. "I'm here, Son. Everything's okay. The procedure went well."

Cam frowned. The words were reassuring, but it wasn't what he wanted to hear. There was a gap in his mind. Something...someone was missing, but who? Cam peeled his tongue from the roof of his mouth and tried to articulate the nameless face in his mind. "Sash?"

Nearly. It would have to do, and when Sasha appeared in his sight line, he didn't seem to mind the slurred, shortened version of his name. He squeezed Cam's other hand. "I'm here."

Cam smiled. He could feel the effects of whatever was in the pump beginning to seep into his body, and it felt *good*. Seeing Sasha grinning at Wade, like they'd known each other years rather than just a few hours, felt good too. "Where's your bike?"

"At home." Sasha chuckled and touched his cheek. "Sleep it off, dude. I'll be here when you wake up."

Cam stared at the area between his legs reflected in the mirror. "Are you sure it doesn't look weird?"

Levi sighed. He'd been Cam's first visitor that morning, with a subdued Sonny in tow, and he already looked fed up. "Stop staring at your dick. It doesn't even look that different."

"What about up close? What if you were blowing me?"

Sonny snorted from his perch on the window ledge, the first sound he'd made since he'd drifted into the room behind Levi, red-eyed and disheveled. He'd sat behind Cam on the bed for a while, combing his fingers through Cam's hair, but he'd retreated when a doctor had checked in, and he'd yet to return. "When did *Levi* last blow *you?*"

It was true. Giving Levi head was way too much fun to let him reciprocate all that often. The big man loved a good blowjob, and it was always fun to watch him unravel. "Okay, fine. Can *you* look then?" Sonny hesitated. Cam held out his hand and beckoned him forward. "Please? For me? You're the only one I can trust to tell me the truth."

"Hey." Levi looked put out.

Cam rolled his eyes. "Come on. Are you seriously telling me you weren't going to tell me everything is just fine and dandy?"

"It is. I wouldn't lie to you."

Cam wasn't convinced. Despite his enduring rep on the porn scene, Levi was a nice guy. Too nice. Sonny would give it to him straight.

Sonny slid off the window ledge. He took Cam's hand and kissed his cheek. Cam nudged him with his shoulder. Sonny was a firecracker, but he didn't seem himself today. Cam wondered if something had gone down between him and Levi. Then he wondered if Sonny was pissed at him for telling Levi about the Ritalin. But he didn't look pissed, he looked...sad. Which wasn't like Sonny at all. Sonny was vibrant and exuberant, a free spirit in every sense of the word. It bothered Cam to see him so down.

Sonny kissed Cam again and averted his gaze to Cam's groin. "Does it hurt?"

Cam glanced down. A dressing covered the three-inch incision in his groin. It hurt when he moved or stretched too far, but otherwise, the pain pills the nurses were feeding him at regular intervals were doing their job. "Just aches a bit."

"You look better than I thought you would."

Cam drummed his fingers on the mattress. He *felt* better than he'd thought he would, but he didn't give a shit about that.

He wanted to know what Sonny thought of his lopsided balls. "I'm *fine*."

Sonny took the hint and stooped to take a proper look. He kept his distance at first, hesitant for reasons only he knew. Cam got impatient, grabbed the back of Sonny's head, and shoved him closer.

"Okay, okay. I'm looking." Sonny laughed and wriggled out of Cam's grip. "Hey, that doesn't look so bad. I thought you'd look mutilated."

"Not helping, Son."

Sonny huffed. Cam felt his breath on his thigh. "I'm being positive. It looks fine, Cam. I mean, I can tell something's missing, but it doesn't look weird."

"Even up close?"

"I'd blow you."

Cam swiveled his gaze to Levi. "What about you?"

Levi rolled his eyes. "I would as it is now."

Sonny glanced over his shoulder. "What's that supposed to mean?"

Cam reached behind him and snagged the plastic implant he'd shown Levi while Sonny had been in the bathroom. Cam had opted not to have it inserted immediately, and judging by Levi and Sonny's collective reaction, he'd made the right decision.

"A fake nut?" Sonny batted the bouncy rubber away. "Fuck that. You don't need that. Levi, come see. He doesn't need a fake one, right?"

"That's what I just said." Levi grumbled but dropped down beside Sonny all the same. "It doesn't even look like something's missing. It just looks...smaller."

"Smaller?" Cam let his dick go so it hung over his balls. "What about now?"

Sonny and Levi both looked closer. Of course Sasha chose that moment to open the door. "Cam? Oh. Shit. Sorry."

Cam met Sasha's liquid gaze and forgot all about his friends at his knees. "Hey."

"Hey, yourself." Sasha ventured farther into the room. "Is this a private party, or can anyone play?"

"Depends," Sonny quipped from the floor. "Do you have lopsided balls? We're doing an in-depth analysis here."

Cam shot Sonny a look. He hadn't told anyone about Sasha's history. Sasha had been by his side since he'd come around from the surgery two days ago, flanked by Wade, but they'd yet to talk about anything other than Cam's immediate state of health. Cam had been too groggy and distracted by the line of painful stitches in his belly.

But he felt better today, bright and alert. Alert enough to worry about scaring Sasha away before they'd had a chance to reconnect. Cam stared at Sasha and felt his stress levels rise. He didn't have it in him to watch Sasha walk away again.

Sasha held his gaze for a long moment; then he undid his fly and dropped his jeans. "See for yourself."

Cam's mouth fell open.

Sasha shrugged, unfazed. "What? You think I don't like getting naked?"

Cam had no answer, both shocked and caught in a haze of intense curiosity. "Come closer."

Sasha took a few steps forward and lifted his T-shirt so Cam could see what remained of his balls. "See? Looks just fine, right?"

Cam stared, transfixed. Below Sasha's taut, tanned abdomen lay an image of what his own body would look like when the scars and swollen flesh had faded away.

Sonny held out his hand and helped Cam down from the bed. "Stand together. Let me look properly."

Cam wondered if now was the best time to introduce them all, but he was distracted by Sasha's cock. Though soft and limp, it was thick and long, the kind of cock every porn star wished they had.

Sonny stooped again and whistled. "Who needs balls, huh? You both look good enough to eat."

Levi rolled his eyes. "Okay, now we all know that, it's time we weren't here. Sonny, come on. I gotta get to the garage."

For a moment, nobody moved. Then Sasha pulled his jeans up, fastened them, and held out his hand to Sonny. "Hey. I'm Sasha."

Sonny took Sasha's hand and grinned. "I kinda figured. Levi told me how hot you were."

Cam let his hospital gown drop and cut his gaze to Levi. "How did you know Sasha was hot?"

"We met yesterday. I was on my way out as Sasha was coming in."

"You were here yesterday?" Cam frowned. He didn't remember much of the day before. He'd spent most of it asleep. He remembered Kay talking his ear off about some meditation class he just *had* to take, and Sasha... Cam could remember the low rumble of his voice, but Levi? Nope. Cam couldn't recall seeing him at all.

Levi said nothing, but his eyes glittered, betraying his mirth over something Cam didn't understand.

Sonny came to Cam and kissed his cheek. "I'll come by tomorrow. Feel better, okay?"

Cam swallowed a lump in his throat. Sonny looked so sad he couldn't stand it, but Sonny ducked out of the room before he could speak.

Levi started to follow, but Cam grabbed his arm. "What's going on with you two?"

Levi sighed and steadied Cam. "We're going to spend some time apart...I think. Maybe. It's complicated."

"What?" Cam felt his stomach turn over. "I didn't tell you his private shit so you could ditch him. Come on, man."

"I'm not ditching him. I would never do that. I love..." Levi cast a glance at Sasha, who was pretending not to listen. "Fuck. Look, Sonny needs to figure out what he wants. I can't *make* him better. He's got to want it, Cam, and I don't know if he does."

Levi was wrong. Sonny did want to get better; he just didn't know how. No one did. Sonny had been popping Ritalin since he was a kid, and that was only the start of it. Manic highs and crippling lows, Sonny was probably sicker than Cam was, and he needed help Cam couldn't give him. "Levi, help him."

"I will." Levi drew Cam into a hug and pressed his face into Cam's neck. "But he's got to want it."

Levi departed, leaving Cam alone with Sasha. Sasha was silent as Cam hoisted himself back onto the bed. Cam eyed him, wondering how he felt seeing Cam so casually tactile with his friends. Levi didn't seem to mind the closeness Cam and Sonny shared, but it was different for him. Porn had changed his perception of relationships. Sasha had never had that, and though they'd yet to define their relationship, Cam knew they had much to talk about.

Sasha eased himself carefully between Cam's legs. "Close your mouth, Cam. You look like you're catching flies."

"Huh?"

"You look shell-shocked. What's up?"

There were so many answers to that question. Cam went with the least painful. "How come you showed Sonny your balls, but you didn't show me?"

Sasha's eyes widened, and then he laughed a real, deep belly laugh that filled the room and overpowered some of Cam's worries. "I never meant to, it just kinda happened, but you should know, I'm not quite the prude I've made myself out to be."

Cam raised an eyebrow, intrigued despite the pain in his groin. "What do you mean?"

Sasha sighed. "I don't want to get into the whole sex thing right now. That'll come for us, if it's meant to, but I don't want you to ever think what happened to you...to both of us, is something to be embarrassed about."

"I don't think that."

"Yeah, you do, and I reckon I haven't done much to help you with that." Sasha fiddled with Cam's hospital gown. "I was embarrassed... Fuck, I was mortified when you touched me that time in the club, and then I was so pissed off when I realized it was going to happen to you."

Sasha stopped. Cam wanted to say something...anything to comfort him, but he somehow knew Sasha had more to say.

"I'd just about gotten over it when you came to my place. I figured we'd talk and find a way to make it right, for both of us, but then I saw you... Fuck, Cam, I knew you were losing it. If we'd hooked up that day, you'd have wound up hating me for it, or at least regretted it. I couldn't bear that."

Cam shook his head. His heart ached, but he didn't believe it, not for a second. "I could never hate you."

Sasha smiled. "That's sweet, but don't underestimate what this demon can do to you. We'll talk about us, I promise, but for now, just know I'm not going anywhere, okay? I'm here, in whatever capacity you want me, for as long as you'll have me."

"And we'll talk about the sex? Soon, yeah?" Damn it. Cam wanted to say something profound, but it seemed his narcotic-addled brain had other ideas.

Sasha laughed and kissed Cam's forehead. "Soon. I promise. Now forget about it for a while, okay? Did the doctor come by yet?"

"What?" Cam felt himself return to earth with a clunk. "Oh, yeah. He came before Levi and Sonny. He said I can go home later today."

"What else did he say?"

Cam heard the question Sasha didn't ask. He wanted to

know the results of the path tests on the tumor. "Same thing he said before the surgery. It's cancer."

Cam said the words with little emotion. The confirmation of his initial diagnosis didn't mean much to him, because he hadn't expected anything else. The plan was the same as it had always been. Cut the bastard out and nuke his body with radiation. What else was there to say?

Sasha rubbed Cam's shoulder and combed his fingers through Cam's hair with his other hand. Cam closed his eyes. Two days in bed had left his hair a mess—tangled and wild. Sonny had picked his way through some of it, but somehow Sasha found a few errant knots.

Cam sighed and felt himself relax. Sasha's touch felt good. *Too* good. Cam knew it would be all too easy to float away on it and ignore the nagging sensation in his brain that he had no right to enjoy Sasha's easy affection, the affection that, ever since he'd come around from the surgery, had slipped into his life like it had always been there. He opened his eyes and caught Sasha's wandering hands. "I need to tell you something."

Sasha regarded him with his warm, open gaze. "Okay. Let's hear it."

Cam chewed the inside of his mouth, unsure of where to start. "You know who Levi and Sonny are, right? You know I work with them?"

Sasha nodded. "I've, um, seen them around."

"Well, I kinda...the other night..." Cam lost his words. How did he explain what had gone down between the three of them? How did he explain how much he'd needed the warmth and love of his friends without sounding like a needy whore?

Sasha's chuckle caught him off guard. "You're not gonna tell me all about Sonny's fuck-hot blowjob again, are you?"

"Huh?"

Sasha smirked. "Cam, you told me about Levi and Sonny

two days ago. Yes, I know you fooled around with them and, no, I don't think you're a whore."

"What? When...what, exactly, did I tell you?"

Cam was officially lost. The last few days were a little fuzzy, but he'd remember something like that, right?

Apparently not, much to Sasha's obvious amusement. "You were babbling about it when you came out of surgery. Think it was the drugs they gave you."

"What did I say?"

"Not much. Just that you'd had some kinda three-way, and that you were thinking of me the whole time."

Cam winced. "Did I really say that?"

Sasha held his gaze for a moment, then broke out a grin that made Cam feel twenty pounds lighter. "Guess you'll never know, huh?"

Cam laughed, but then he sobered. "I wasn't rambling, you know. It's true. Levi and Sonny are my friends, but things sometimes get..."

Damn it. Cam lost his train of thought again, but it didn't seem to matter.

Sasha squeezed his hands. "I get it, okay? At least, I think I do. I'm not gonna lie. I've slept with, like, four people, and I'm not friends with anyone the way you're friends with them, but I *know* you don't look at them the same way you do me."

"You do?"

"Yeah. Listen, I don't know how dealing with this..." Sasha gestured around the hospital room. "How any of it is going to affect you, but for me, confronting my mortality taught me to look beyond the obvious. I forgot that for a while when we first met, but I'm back on it now."

Cam rubbed his face as a wave of postsurgical fatigue washed over him. "I love them. They're my best friends."

Sasha eased Cam into a careful hug. "I know, and I can see how much they love each other too. I'd be mad if I thought that was wrong. Besides, you were right about Levi. He's pretty sharp, huh?"

Cam had almost forgotten the long-ago conversation at the sushi bar. "Yeah, he is. He's good for Sonny. Sonny's a little…"

"Wild?"

Cam hummed his agreement. It was hard to concentrate with Sasha kneading the back of his neck.

"Cam, you still with me?"

"Just about." Cam raised his head.

Sasha smiled back at him a moment before he fell serious again. "I don't want you to worry about the porn thing. If I had a problem with it, I wouldn't be here. I'm not saying I want to have a gang bang with your friends, but I know who you are, and I like it. I like *you*, okay?"

"Sonny thinks I look for answers in sex."

"Then use this as a clean slate. Take the bones of who you are and make it better."

"You don't hate me?"

"For what? Seeking comfort from your friends when I pushed you away? No, of course I don't. I know you come from a different way of life, and I'm glad they were there for you."

Cam couldn't quite believe it was as simple as that, but for now, he let it go. He was tired, but he felt antsy and wanted more than anything to escape the sterile, white walls of the hospital.

"So…" Sasha let the word hang. "Now we've figured out we're both on the same page, I want to ask you something too."

Cam raised an eyebrow, curious. "Oh, yeah?"

"Yeah. I was talking to your dad, and he said he's gotta work a lot next week. With your kid brothers and all, I reckon he's going to have his hands full."

Cam nodded. That was nothing new. Kay helped out where she could, but Wade spent most of his time running in circles between sports clubs and the grocery store. "So?"

"So how would you feel about staying with me for a few days? You can have my bed, and I can take care of you while you recuperate."

"Recuperate?"

Sasha flicked his arm. "Yeah. Cam, you just had surgery. You need to rest and take it easy."

Cam considered Sasha's offer. He didn't want Wade running around after him, and the thought of going home to his empty apartment was depressing, but he had one issue with Sasha's offer. He used his legs to hook Sasha closer and wrapped his arms around Sasha's waist. "Dude, the only way I'm sleeping in your bed is if you're right there next to me. What do you say?"

Sasha grinned and kissed Cam's forehead. "I say...hell, yeah."

CHAPTER FOURTEEN

Cam took his place at the end of the on-set couch. Sonny dropped down beside him and curled into his side.

Sonny trembled. The shudder was subtle, but Cam felt it ripple through him. He put his arm around Sonny and kissed the top of his head. Sonny's answering sigh was shaky and soft, but he sat up again before Cam could press him. "This feels weird. Something's up."

Cam glanced around the studio and was inclined to agree. He and Sonny were on-set at Blue Boy, like they'd been so many times before, but the scene that surrounded them wasn't anything like the usual preparations for a shoot. There were no cameras or specialist lights, just every staff member Blue Boy employed, cast and crew, sitting around and waiting...but for what? Cam had no idea. All he knew was Sherry, the studio's receptionist, had left a message on his voice mail requesting his presence for a full staff meeting, and though porn was the last thing on Cam's mind, the prospect of a studio full of witnesses seemed the ideal time to face Jon for the first time since Cam had trashed his computer. All he needed now was for Jon to drag his sorry ass out of his office.

Sonny nudged him. "How are you feeling?"

Cam shrugged. No one was supposed to know about the surgery, but a few models had noticed he wasn't quite himself. "I feel good, man. Can't even feel it anymore."

"Really?"

"Really." Cam understood Sonny's skepticism, but it was true. It had been a month or so since the surgery, and all things considered, he felt pretty good. His planned short stay at Sasha's poolside bungalow had turned into an extended vacation, and aside from some irritating numbness in his lower belly, he felt healthier than he had in years.

Perhaps it was the lack of beer and the freakishly healthy diet Sasha was feeding him. Who cared? Not him. He felt great, and that was enough for him.

Sasha. Cam grinned as his mind got away from him. Despite the inconvenience of having surgery, the past few months had been...enlightening. Getting to know Sasha was a lot of fun, and the tentative affection they'd begun in the hospital had become something more. Cam couldn't imagine his life without Sasha now. Didn't want to. The hours they'd spent talking, kissing, and just being together were branded on him in a way he'd never imagined. The only thing missing was...

Jon's office door opened. Cam tensed, and all thoughts of finally getting Sasha naked evaporated. He squared his shoulders and prepared to do battle, but his words died in his throat when he realized he was glaring not at Jon, but at a total stranger. A freakin' *huge* stranger.

The tall, bear-shaped man was followed out of the office by another man, smaller in stature but with a similar build. Both in their late thirties, at first glance, the men looked like brothers, though looking closer and absorbing the heated stare that passed between them, Cam could tell they were lovers. *Real* lovers.

The men crossed the studio and came to a stop where most of the cast and crew had gathered in a loose semicircle. A hush fell over the group, and the taller man smiled, showing a set of perfect white teeth and a grin that rivaled Sasha's in warmth. "Afternoon, folks. Thanks for joining us at such short notice. We'll keep this brief. I'm sure you've got lives to get back to."

The smaller man stepped forward. "I'm Jude Regan. This is my partner, Mac, and we are the new owners and directors of Blue Boy Enterprises. As of last night, the studio, and all businesses attached to it belong to us."

There was a collective, stunned silence. Cam felt the numbness in his belly spread throughout his body. Jon had sold Blue Boy? That didn't make any sense. The studio was his life's work, his passion. *His obsession.* Why would he sell it?

"What about Silver?" Sonny called out. He looked relieved, and Cam could understand that. Levi hated Jon. Sonny's life would be much easier without him on the scene.

"Yep. Silver too." Jude nodded to Mac, who held up a stack of paperwork. "Over the next few days we will be meeting with each of you individually and reviewing your contracts. Dancers, models, back-room staff, we'll be talking to you all."

An anxious hum rippled through the studio. Jude signaled for quiet. "Easy, folks. No one's getting fired. We just feel this is a good time for all of us to take stock and figure out what direction we're going, to move forward. You have a strong base here, but we believe we can make it better. Move beyond the commercial markets and create something special."

"In the same vein," Mac said, "this is also a chance for you to renegotiate contracts you're not happy with, or sever them completely if you feel you've outgrown the industry. It happens, and we're not here to fuck anyone over."

"What about outstanding payments?"

Cam glanced at Caleb and rolled his eyes. That dude was all about the money.

Jude said, "All payments outstanding will be honored. Silver will continue to operate as normal, but for the next few weeks Blue Boy Studio will be temporarily shut down while we figure things out behind the scenes. I know you all probably have questions, but rather than keeping you all here for hours, save them for your one-on-ones."

It seemed to be a dismissal, but nobody moved. Cam took a deep breath. Jon's disappearance was a weight off his mind, but he couldn't imagine Blue Boy without him. The guy was a douche, but he hadn't always been that way. In the beginning, he'd taught Cam how to survive in a brutal industry.

Sonny squeezed his thigh. "You okay?"

"Hmm?"

"You're not upset about Jon leaving, are you?"

Cam frowned. Was he? No, that wasn't it. "I don't think so."

Sonny raised an eyebrow, considering him, and Cam knew he was running through the bank of psychology theory he had stacked up in his big-ass brain. "Ah, I get it. It's fucked up your plan. You were going to quit, weren't you? Now you're not sure if you want to."

Cam sighed. Sonny might've been on to something, but before they could hash it out, Jude called Cam's name. It seemed they'd decided that Cam was at the top of their list.

"I'm on tomorrow's list," Sonny said. "Do you want me to wait for you?"

Cam got to his feet. Sonny had been miserable for weeks, and Levi didn't seem to be faring much better. Cam had tried to get them to talk about whatever had gone wrong between them, but it was like banging his head against a brick wall. They'd both been frequent visitors at Sasha's place, but never together, and that made Cam's heart ache. He didn't know what Levi was hoping to achieve, but he knew for sure it wasn't doing Sonny any good at all. "Nah. I got this. Go home and get some sleep. I'll call you later, okay?"

He left Sonny on the couch and made his way to the office. He hadn't set foot in there since Jon had tried to fuck him over the desk, but when he got inside, he saw that overnight, the office had been stripped of anything that reminded him of Jon. It was like a different world.

"Have a seat." Mac shut the door and leaned against the wall.

Cam eyed them both and dropped into the nearest chair. He felt like he recognized Jude, though he couldn't say where from. "Any reason you hauled me in first?"

"Not really." Jude pulled what Cam assumed was his contract from a desk drawer. "You are one of the longest-serving models, though. You seemed a good place to start." Jude flipped through the paperwork. "You've not been around much the last few months. Thinking about moving on?"

Cam shrugged. "Maybe, but that's not why I haven't been around."

Jude gestured for him to elaborate. Cam analyzed him a moment, then thought, fuck it. What did he have to lose? He had nothing to hide, and keeping secrets had proved a toxic game. "There's a few reasons I haven't been around lately," he said. "And they're all pretty fucked up."

"Go on," Mac said from his position by the door. "We heard a rumor you and Jon were together. What happened? Did you break up?"

"Something like that. We've been on bad terms for a while. He made some videos of me without my consent."

Jude exchanged an inscrutable look with Mac. "That's not cool, but you should know Jon's gone for good. Last we heard he was headed East Coast way to start fresh. That's not it, though, is it? What else is bugging you?"

Cam wondered when he'd become so easy to read. "I was diagnosed with testicular cancer a few months ago. I've had surgery, but I've got a course of treatment coming up. I'm going to be out of action for a while, if I come back at all."

There. He'd said it, and it felt...refreshing.

Jude made a note in his file. "That's rough, and we're sorry to hear that. I want you to know your contract and all its benefits will remain valid until you say otherwise, whether you work for us again or not."

"Thanks. I appreciate that." Cam would be lying if he said he hadn't worried about how leaving Blue Boy would affect his insurance status. He'd even considered filming a few scenes between treatments to keep his contract intact.

At least he had until Sasha.

Sasha, Sasha, Sasha...

Mac said something. Cam blinked. "Huh?"

Jude grinned. "He said, we've just bought a new house in Venice Beach. When we're settled you should come over for dinner, bring your guy."

"How do you know I have a guy?"

"Because I know that look." Jude shot another loaded glance at Mac. "Seems like you've got a lot of figuring out to do, but whatever happens, even if you don't feel up to filming again, there's probably a role for you behind the scenes. You've been here a long time. New models need someone like you to guide them. Someone who's not signing their paychecks."

"It's something to think on, Cam," Mac said. "You're a popular model, and we want you to stay, but we understand that's not a decision you can make right now. Take as much time as you need, and come and see us again when you're ready."

Cam nodded and took it as his dismissal, but he didn't get up. For some reason, he couldn't stop staring at Jude.

Jude cocked his head to the side and gave him a boyish grin. "Something else you want to talk about?"

"Where are you from? I feel like I've seen you before."

Mac snorted. Jude rolled his eyes and opened a desk drawer. "Maybe you have."

He tossed a DVD case on the table. Cam picked it up, studied the cover, and staring back at him he found a younger version of Jude, tied up in leather and chains. Wow. The dude was *hot*, and Cam recognized the name—Rocco Vain. Fuck, Jude was a living legend, in the porn world, at least. "You were a model?"

"For a long time. I've been out of the game for a while; we both have." Jude glanced at Mac. "But we're back now, and we're going to do it right, Cam. Whatever happens, we'll take care of you."

Cam walked out of the studio feeling twenty pounds lighter, and in a good way. Jude and Mac seemed like decent guys. He'd felt comfortable spilling his guts to them, and the idea of putting off a decision about porn was appealing. His head was all over the place, and he wasn't entirely convinced by Sasha's claim that he was cool with dating a porn star.

He climbed into Sasha's truck and drove back to the bungalow. Sasha was tinkering with his BMX on a plastic table by the pool, his hands smeared with oil. He was a sight for sore eyes, but Cam blurted out the events of the meeting before he had a chance to brood on it.

Sasha showed no emotion at the news of Blue Boy's management transition, and Cam wasn't surprised. Sasha didn't know all the gory details, but he'd made his views on Jon clear.

"*I don't want to know anything about that manipulative asshole,*" he'd said. "*There's some shit I'm better off not knowing.*"

"What are you going to do?" Sasha wiped his hands on his T-shirt. "Do you want to go back?"

"I don't know. I need to get through my treatment first. I haven't thought much beyond that."

"But?"

Cam shrugged. "I *like* porn. To me, it doesn't feel dirty or wrong, and it's something I'm good at. Even if I don't film again, I can't imagine not having it in my life. Does that sound weird?"

"No." Sasha paused, and Cam could tell he was choosing his words with care. "And I don't think you should worry about what it sounds like. The people who matter have your back."

Cam thought of his family, his friends, and the man who was fast becoming the love of his life. "I know that."

"So don't worry about it. Get better, and after, if you want to go back and finish what you started, you can fret over it then."

"I'm not fretting."

"Oh, yeah?" Sasha pulled Cam close and rubbed the pad of his thumb on Cam's forehead. "Stop frowning then. Makes you look old."

Cam's retort was swallowed by a fuck-hot kiss, the kind of kiss that went on and on, until he forgot the rest of the world existed. The kind of kiss that should've led to more but didn't because Sasha pulled away.

"We need to talk about something else." Sasha looked pensive. "I think we've got some shit we need to work out."

Cam steeled himself. He'd noticed Sasha had been quiet the past few days, and for once, he figured he knew why. Sex. It had to be. They'd been sleeping side by side for weeks but hadn't ventured beyond hours and hours of kissing like teenagers. It had been the longest Cam had been without sex in years, and though he'd fast learned there was more to life than fucking, he knew they'd also reached a tipping point. Something had to give, and he'd made up his mind long ago that it was going to be him. "I know what you're going to say."

Sasha raised an eyebrow. "Do you?"

Cam let his arms drop from around Sasha's waist and pointed to the swinging chair. "I reckon so. Come sit with me?"

Sasha let Cam tug him to the seat. They sat close together, not touching, but close enough that Cam could feel the intoxicating warmth of Sasha's solid body. "It's about the logistics, right?"

"Logistics?" Sasha looked puzzled before he caught on. "Um, yeah. Something like that. Cam, I've *seen* you. I know you don't bottom."

Do you? "So what were you thinking when you came looking for me in the hospital? That we just wouldn't have sex?"

Sasha averted his gaze. He was an open kind of guy, but talking about sex didn't come as easy to him as it did to Cam. "I guess I figured I'd...well, I decided I'd bottom...for you, if that's what you wanted."

"For me?"

"Yeah. I kinda woke up that morning and knew I'd do *anything* for you."

Cam swallowed, feeling the heated sting of tears in his eyes. "What if I said you didn't have to? That there was another way?"

"Like what?"

"Just because you've never seen me bottom on-screen doesn't mean I don't do it. You said it yourself: there's more to me than porn."

"I knew *that*, Cam, but, man, really? You really bottom?"

Sasha couldn't hide the cautious excitement in his face, and it warmed Cam's heart. "Yeah, really. I haven't done it a lot, and I'm pretty sure I've never done it right, but I want to do it with you. When I picture us together, it's what I see."

"Wow." Sasha seemed stunned. "I never thought of that. I mean, I did, but I figured it was just a fantasy."

Cam grinned. "Yeah, well. Sometimes fantasies come true."

"Oh, God." Sasha groaned. "Don't say shit like that to me. I'll be dragging you inside before you can blink."

Cam pulled off his shirt in a swift, practiced motion. "What are you waiting for?"

CHAPTER FIFTEEN

Cam let Sasha push him onto the bed. He was a little surprised they'd made it that far. Turned out Sasha knew what he wanted and wasn't afraid to take it. He was careful of the healed incision on Cam's belly, but that aside, all bets were off.

Clothes littered the hardwood floor of the bungalow. Cam's lips burned with the heat of Sasha's bruising kiss. His heart was beating out of his chest, and lower...*lower* his cock throbbed with an aching need he'd feared was gone forever.

He pushed at the waistband of Sasha's shorts. He'd felt the outline of Sasha's dick and seen it soft and limp in the hospital, but he'd imagined the sight of Sasha naked and hard over and over.

He couldn't wait any longer.

Sasha helped Cam tug his shorts over his hips. Cam kicked them away. Sasha's cock stood out, long and proud, and Cam was captivated. He had mixed feelings about the loss of his own nut, but with Sasha... Man, there was *nothing* missing there. He licked his dry lips and gripped Sasha's muscled thighs, savoring the strong legs he'd spent so long dreaming about. Whatever was going down between them, one thing wasn't in doubt. He needed Sasha's cock in his mouth.

He lay on his back, and Sasha straddled his chest. He took Sasha in his mouth, and there was something magical about Sasha's reaction as Cam opened his throat for him. Sasha gasped. His chest reddened, and sweat beaded his brow. Cam swallowed. Sasha's legs quivered, and he dug his fingers into Cam's chest.

Cam went to town on Sasha, guiding him with his hands on his hips, letting his tongue explore every inch of the man who'd become his rock. He let his hands wander, tracing Sasha's ball and trailing lower. He rubbed the rough patch of skin behind Sasha's sac and wondered...

He pulled off Sasha for air. "Have you ever?"

The question was vague and unfinished, but Sasha interpreted the meaning. He looked down at Cam with his trademark steady gaze. "Nope. I don't mind a finger or two, but never a dick. Never found the right one."

Cam tapped Sasha's entrance with the pad of his finger. Part of him wanted to plunge inside, show Sasha what he was missing, but a louder part of him knew it wasn't the right time for that. They both needed something...something safe and warm, and nothing was going to come between them.

Not today.

He swallowed Sasha whole again. Sasha moaned and shivered, and Cam drank it all in, absorbing it and filing it away in the huge cavern Sasha had carved out for himself in Cam's heart. The noises he made rattled Cam's bones, and before long, Cam was reaching for his own cock, needy and desperate.

Sasha caught the movement and batted Cam's hand away. "Uh-uh. That's mine."

Cam grinned and released Sasha's cock from his mouth. He'd put Sasha right on the edge, and knew he could make him come with a flick of his tongue, but as appealing as that was, he needed something more.

Sasha bent and kissed him before he moved down the bed, pausing to kiss Cam's surgical scar.

Cam watched, enthralled, as Sasha played his own game with Cam's dick, teasing, licking, blowing, but never taking it into his mouth. Cam writhed, enjoying the torture in a masochistic kind of way. In his mind, willing it to be over, but pleading out loud for Sasha to never, ever stop.

"Lift your leg."

Cam thrashed his head from side to side and raised his leg, expecting the probe of Sasha's fingers or the sweep of his tongue. He was sorely unprepared for the sensation of his remaining ball being sucked into Sasha's mouth. He arched his back and shuddered, twisting the sheets in his clenched fists. "Fuck!"

Sasha hummed low in his throat and then released Cam. He kissed his way up Cam's body until they were face-to-face again. "They never told you that, huh? That what you've got left is sensitive as fuck?"

Cam panted, squirming as heat rushed through his veins. "*You* coulda told me."

"I know." Sasha placed his hands either side of Cam's head and nipped his bottom lip. "But where's the fun in that?"

Sasha ground his hips in a slow circle. His thick cock dug into Cam. Cam raised his other leg and relaxed his pelvis, straining for friction where he needed it most. Sasha's body felt so good pressed against him. Better than good. Better than he'd ever dared imagine.

He wound his arms around Sasha's neck and pulled him down for a kiss, grinding them together, desperate for more. Sasha picked up the pace and thrust against Cam with a force that made them both groan.

Sasha reached over to the nightstand and retrieved condoms and lube. Cam's pulse quickened, and his muscles clenched.

Anticipation rushed through him. This was really happening, and he couldn't fucking wait.

"How do you want me?" Sasha waved the lube in Cam's face. "You said you've seen this in your head. What did you see?"

Cam wriggled out from beneath Sasha and rolled over. They'd landed sideways on the bed, and he could see the shimmering surface of the pool. "I want you to fuck me like this."

Sasha made a sound Cam hoped was a grunt of approval. Either way, a shot of excitement ran through him as Sasha nudged Cam's legs farther apart with his knees. The click of the lube bottle pierced the air. Sasha slid one finger into Cam, then two, following the natural cues of his body.

Cam gasped and ground himself into the mattress. The pressure niggled the scar on his stomach, but the discomfort was worth the bright lightning bolts of pleasure brewing inside him. "Fuck, yeah."

Sasha twisted his fingers, searching out the gland that made Cam's toes curl, but he touched it only once before he withdrew, and Cam heard the rustle and tear of the condom wrapper.

The wait seemed endless, but then it seemed that no time at all had passed before Sasha was sliding his cock between the firm muscles of Cam's ass. He teased Cam a moment, circling his entrance but not applying much pressure.

Cam growled his frustration and raised his hips. "Goddamn you. Just do it."

Sasha laughed, but he cut off as the blunt head of his cock breached Cam's body.

The burn and stretch was incredible. Cam sucked in a breath, and his eyes watered. He'd done this many times over, but never sober, and Sasha was a bigger man than Jon, in *every* way. He bit down on his lip and let out a shaky moan.

Sasha stopped and rubbed the small of Cam's back. "Okay?"

"Yeah." Cam panted out some harsh breaths. "Keep going."

Sasha eased himself all the way inside Cam. When he could go no farther, he stilled, letting Cam adjust and absorb the sensation of being filled.

Cam's eyes rolled. The pressure seeped into him, and he felt heat flush his skin. He buried his face in his arms and raised his ass, circling his hips and pushing back on Sasha's cock. Sasha held still while he did it again, and again, until he found the angle and depth that made his vision blur and his limbs feel weak.

Sasha caught his cue. He moved with care, meeting Cam halfway until he found the rhythm and took over, rocking into Cam in a motion as smooth as the tantalizing skin on his back.

Cam groaned, long and low. "So fucking good."

"Yeah?" Sasha picked up the pace and leaned over Cam, wrapping his body around him like he'd never let go. "What about this?"

Sasha claimed Cam's mouth in a bruising kiss. The distraction allowed him to snake a hand between them and grasp Cam's dick. He jerked it slowly, contrasting with the punishing slam of his hips.

Coherent speech abandoned Cam. Sasha was playing him like they'd been lovers for years, and every nerve in his body tingled, laced with a dizzying pleasure he could hardly stand. He gripped the edge of the mattress, fighting to keep his body steady. "You know...you'd make a fuck-awesome porn star, right?"

Sasha responded by releasing Cam's cock and pressing his sweat-slick palm over Cam's mouth. "Yeah? Well, you just think on that. Think about me fucking you in front of a camera, with your friends watching us."

Cam's toes curled, and there was no denying the thrill that ran through him. Sasha wasn't serious, he couldn't be, but the thought alone was enough to make him cry out. The notion spread, from his lust-crazed mind to his heart, and in that moment, he knew that if he ever had sex on-screen again, it would be with Sasha. He shrugged away from Sasha's hand. "Tease."

Sasha chuckled, but then the vibe between them shifted. Deepened. Sasha slowed his brutal pace and wrapped his arms around Cam, holding him tight and keeping them both balanced as Cam faltered. The unmistakable scent of sex hung in the air, punctuated by the protesting slide of the bed on the hardwood floor. Cam felt liquid. He gave himself up to Sasha and let the slow grind of their bodies moving together take over his whole being. He hid his face in the crook of his arm again and took himself in hand, chasing the building pleasure he craved so much.

Sasha covered him with his whole body, murmured words of encouragement, and fused his lips to Cam's neck. Cam wanted to weep as he realized that this was what he'd been missing...searching for all along—the undeniable sensation of shaking in a man's arms, of being held like he was that man's whole world. Sasha's world.

Orgasm hit. Every part of his body tightened with painful pleasure, and he came with a guttural cry. Wet warmth spilled over his fingers. He fell slack in Sasha's arms and moaned again. Sasha's rhythm became stuttered and sharp, and with one last, stabbing thrust he stilled and groaned low and deep in Cam's ear. Heat pooled where they were joined. Cam whimpered. The sensation was almost too much. He convulsed, racked with whole-body shudders, and collapsed on himself as Sasha let him go.

Sasha lay over him, quiet and still, pressing soft kisses between Cam's shoulder blades until Cam felt able to raise his head and look around. Sasha met his gaze with a gentle grin. "Okay?"

Cam nodded. "Yeah. That was...fuck."

He had no other words. His tongue felt loose and swollen, and his mind too hazy to think. He felt inside out. Claimed, desired, and...loved. He felt whole.

Sasha kissed him once more before he rose, fetched a towel, and cleaned them both up. Then he pulled back the comforter and coaxed Cam into the bed. Cam felt boneless as he crawled under the covers and collapsed in a heap. Jon had pushed him physically in the bedroom, but he'd never felt connected to him. Something was always missing. Being with Sasha was beyond different. It was mind-blowing, and he felt *wrecked*.

Sasha stretched out beside him, pushed Cam's sweat-damp hair away from his face, and kissed his forehead. "Wow. I didn't think I'd ever see you like that."

Cam trembled; he couldn't help it. He felt like his body was not his own. "Like what?"

"So..." Sasha seemed to search for the right word. "Involved, maybe? On-screen, you all seem kinda cold. I guess I figured you'd done it all before."

Cam took a moment to gather himself. A phrase came to him, and he allowed himself a wry grin. "It's not the same. That's work, even if it's one of my friends. This is real sex."

"Real sex, huh?" Sasha shifted onto his back and pulled Cam against him. "I can live with that."

Cam closed his eyes and sank into the warmth of Sasha's chuckle and the comforting weight of his arms around him. He'd been afraid since the bright summer day his mom walked out of his life, but now, despite the looming prospect of treatment and the uncertainties that came with it, with Sasha he felt like he could take on the world.

Take on the world and win.

VOLUME 3 - BOLD

CHAPTER ONE

Kai slipped into Jack's arms like a rag doll. Jack spun him around in a choreographed move and took his place at Kai's back. The position felt natural, like it wasn't the first time they'd ever fucked.

Jack played Kai's body, probing and testing with his fingers. He found a sensitive spot, grazed it. Kai arched his back and fell forward. Jack was a little predictable, but he had some skills. Kai would give him that.

The snap of a condom pierced the air. Kai closed his eyes, bit his lip for the camera, and waited for the scene to play out. *His hand on my hip, his nails digging into my skin. The thick head of his cock pushing into me...*

Jack didn't disappoint. He pushed into Kai with a low groan. Kai absorbed the sound, let it travel through him. Jack was no Levi Ramone, but he had a deep voice and his rumbly moans were kind of hot. Kai relaxed and panted out a few quick breaths. Jack wasn't the biggest he'd ever had, but the sensation of being filled still took a few moments to feel good.

"You ready?"

Kai smirked. Tops always said that, like they thought he'd be the one coming apart at the seams.

Don't underestimate me.

Only two tops had ever gotten under Kai's skin enough to make him nervous. Levi Ramone, his first ever fuck on-screen, was one. Cam was another, but that was more because Cam had surprised him. An easy ride had turned into something loaded and intense, and Kai had hardly seen Cam since.

Get your head in the game.

A twisting thrust brought Kai back to the present. He let out a moan, making more of the light shock of pleasure in his belly. Jack followed the script, and Kai relaxed into the steady beat of Jack's cock in his ass. It felt good, like an early-morning stretch or a stroll in the park, but it wasn't quite enough to blow his mind. He needed more.

Kai flattened himself on the bed, pushed his ass up in the air. "Pull my hair."

Jack tugged on Kai's floppy blond curls. "Like that?"

"Harder."

Jack was unsure, Kai could tell, but Kai rammed his hips back and slammed himself down on Jack's cock for good measure. I can take it. I want it. Damn. Why did all the power tops have to move on? Life sure was boring without Levi Ramone riding his ass.

"Harder, goddamn it."

Jack yanked Kai's hair. The shock of pain went straight to Kai's dick. He moaned, long and loud. Clenched himself tight. Jack grunted and shuddered, and Kai grinned into the virginal white sheets of the bed.

Yeah. He likes that. Kai rewrote the loose scene plan in his head. Jude, his new boss, had told them to go with the flow, but what did that really mean? As Jude slid around the studio in socked feet, snapping stills with his ever-present camera, Kai played out some possibilities. Jack was sweet and hot, and fucking him like a champion, but Kai's mind began to wander all the same.

That had happened a lot in recent weeks. Jack gripped Kai's hips hard enough to leave bruises, but Kai hardly noticed. Instead, a strange sense of misplaced desire distracted him. Something was missing.

Jack pulled out. Kai rolled over on autopilot and raised his legs. He parted them as wide as they would go and absorbed the surprise in Jack's gaze.

Splits. Yeah. I'm your flexible friend.

The thought almost made Kai giggle. He covered it with an artful whimper and threw his head back. "Make me come."

Jack took the hint and picked up the pace. The exertion crept over his pale skin, a flush that made Kai's balls tighten. Though Jack's hair was too fair, Kai had a kink for pale skin. Liked to see the heated, rushing blood of a dude about to come like a train.

Kai clenched himself tight, clamping down on Jack's dick. Jack gasped, and Kai smirked an evil smirk. He was supposed to come first and then finish Jack off whichever way felt right, but he wondered how easy it would be to push Jack over the edge.

He scooted back on the bed, raised his arms over his head, and found the bed frame. The change in angle steadied him and gave Jack more resistance...more friction and burn. Jack's eyes rolled. Sweat dripped down his chest. Kai went for broke and drove his pelvis up from the bed, shortening the distance between them so every drive from Jack became a short, sharp, stabbing thrust.

Jack shot him a desperate look. He tried to slow down, but Kai chased his cock with every roll of his hips. Jack let out a garbled cry. "Shit, I'm gonna come."

He pulled out of Kai and tore the condom off. He pumped himself once and blew his load over Kai's belly. "Oh, my God. Fuck."

Kai watched Jack come, watched his orgasm take over, his eyes widen and his jaw go slack. He loved watching tops come, especially the ones who seemed so sure of themselves. He remembered Caleb, a notorious brute on the Blue Boy books. He'd tried to nail Kai, twice, but Kai had gotten to him first. Had him screaming.

Don't underestimate me.

Kai took himself in hand. He'd been stroking himself while Jack fucked him, leisurely and slow, but he moved with more purpose now, chasing the thrill of Jack's release.

Jack crawled onto the bed, his breath harsh and short. He lay down and pulled Kai over his chest. "Come in my mouth."

Another thrill ran through Kai. *Stand over you? Jerk off into your face?* Hell, yeah. Kai wasn't about to say no to that.

CHAPTER TWO

Kai showered with Jack. Sometimes it was nice to spend a few quiet moments with the guy he'd filmed with. He'd heard it didn't happen at other studios, but it was one of many elements he liked—loved—about Blue Boy. The studio had changed hugely since he'd joined a year ago, big names had come and gone, but some shit never changed, and luckily for Kai most of the good shit had stayed the same.

He left Jack in the wet room and padded nude through the dressing room. He caught sight of his hot water-pinked skin in the mirror. Jack's finger marks stood out, loud and proud. Kai twisted to look closer. The scene had gotten a little wild at the end, and he'd goaded Jack into biting down on him, drawing out his release in a haze of stinging pleasure.

Kai liked that from time to time. He wasn't into BDSM—some of the photos on Blue Boy's office wall scared the crap out of him—but he enjoyed the sensation of a man's teeth on his skin. It was a real shame the marks remained long after the afterglow.

Kai raided Sonny's locker for lotion. Sonny wouldn't mind. He smoothed it over his reddened skin, hoping Jack's finger marks would fade by the evening. He had a dancing slot at Silver that evening, and hickeys and bruises didn't go with his favorite sparkly underwear.

"Shit, did I do that? Sorry, man."

Kai glanced up. Jack stood in the doorway, dressed in a T-shirt that showed the damp patches on his skin. Jeez. Did no one dry themselves properly these days? "It's okay. I liked it."

"Really? You didn't seem that into it at the end."

Oops. Perhaps Kai had let his imagination get away from him. "Sorry. You know when something slips into your mind and you can't get rid of it?"

Jack looked offended, but a knock on the door cut off whatever he'd been about to say. Jude Regan, the main boss of the studio, grinned at both of them, but his gaze fell on Kai. "Got a minute?"

Kai bit his lip and nodded. Jude had been super nice since he and Mac had taken over the studio, but then no one had stepped out of line. Kai wondered if Jude had noticed his distraction on set, and his stomach turned over. The old boss, Jon, used to get real pissed about that.

Kai kissed Jack good-bye and slunk into Jude's office. The room was now home to an L-shaped couch, but Kai dropped into a chair. Lounging on the squishy leather wouldn't feel right if Jude was about to rip him a new one.

"What's up, Kai?"

Kai met Jude's dark gaze and swallowed hard. Jude was a big guy, all beard and muscles. Only his bear-like husband, Mac, was bigger. "Huh?"

Jude sat on the edge of his desk. "You look like you have a bug in your ass. Everything okay?"

"Everything's fine." Kai tried not to squirm. "What do you need?"

"Nothing, Kai. Is there anything you want to talk about?"

"Nope."

Jude rolled his eyes, making himself look far younger than the thirty-nine years he was rumored to be. "How about we touch base anyway? It's been a while. How are you getting on?"

"You tell me." Kai shrugged. "You're the boss."

"One of them," Jude corrected. "But that's neither here nor there. I know how I *think* you're getting on. I want to hear it from you."

Kai drummed his fingers on his knee. "I'm good."

"You seem frustrated." Jude eyed him a moment, but Mac stuck his head around the door before he could speak. Jude met his gaze and smiled. "Do you need me?"

"Always." Mac didn't venture any farther into the room. "I'm taking the car to meet my brother. Do *you* need anything before I go?"

Jude shook his head. "Can't think of anything. You'll be back tomorrow, right?"

"I'm heading out first thing. Be good while I'm gone."

No more words were exchanged, and Mac left, but the look that passed between him and Jude left Kai feeling like he'd intruded on a private moment. Mac and Jude were like that.

"So..."

Kai refocused on Jude. "So."

Jude let the word hang, waiting, like he'd figured out Kai wasn't happy, but it was up to Kai to figure out why.

"I don't know," Kai said in the end. "I liked the scene, and Jack's uber hot and all, but I felt like I'd done it a thousand times over, you know? I was..."

"Bored?"

Jude's interjection caught Kai off guard, but the word fit.

"Maybe." Kai wriggled some more in his seat.

"It's not a bad thing, Kai. I've gone over your scenes, and they're pretty formulaic. It's okay to want something more."

Kai sighed. Jude was right; he did want something more, but what? He'd done everything on his safe list, three-ways, four-ways and more. He wasn't into the nastier stuff—though he *loved* watching—so what else could he do?

Jude said nothing, and for the first time since Blue Boy's old boss had disappeared overnight, Kai found himself missing Jon Kellar. The guy had been kind of a creep in a real subtle way, but he'd been good with this stuff. He would've had the answer before Kai had even walked into his office.

"Cam's here today. Why don't you talk it over with him? He might help you work through some ideas."

"You don't have any?"

Jude shrugged. "I have plenty, but this isn't about me. We don't do that here anymore. I want you to create the scenes you want to shoot. No one can sell a fantasy better than the person it belongs to."

Kai absorbed the theory, along with the news that Cam was in the building. Cam was never at the studio anymore. Kai thought he'd quit, though there'd been rumors of him coming back as a mentor for newbie models.

Jude drummed his fingers on the desk. "What was the first full sex scene you ever shot?"

"Levi Ramone." Kai didn't need to think about it. "The end of last summer."

"I've watched that scene," Jude said. "I think it's one of your best. It's very honest."

"Honest?"

"Yeah. Natural. You were nervous, but you used that to your advantage and connected with Levi in a way that made him think. You should watch it back, and take note of how he looks at you. You might be surprised by what you find."

Kai glanced around the office. Gone were the days of utilitarian chairs and filing cabinets. Jude's office was more like a den. A couch, a dartboard. Photographs from Jude's own porn star career. Some of the pictures were more graphic than others, but Kai could tell he'd done it all—top, bottom, Dom, sub. He wondered what Jude looked like naked. Somehow, his cock was covered in every shot. "What was your first scene?"

"Me?" Jude's lips twitched with amusement, but he pushed himself off the desk and pulled a box down from a shelf. "Don't judge me by the tacky sets. It was the nineties."

Kai took the old VHS case, and his eyes widened. "Fuck. Is that Mac?"

Jude grinned. "The one and only. That's how we met."

"Wow." Kai was lost for words. He knew Jude used to be a big name in the business, but he'd had no idea Mac was a porn star too. "Did you meet on set and live happily ever after?"

"Not quite. That was my first scene, and his last. He left the industry to become a firefighter. It was ten years before I saw him again."

A porn star and a firefighter? Suddenly Mac, the boring accountant, had gotten a lot more interesting. Kai wanted to know more, but something in Jude's gaze told Kai there was an epic tale of love and loss behind the older man's sad smile. "You're happy now, though, aren't you?"

"Hell, yeah. Mac's my world, and I wouldn't have it any other way." Jude took the old video and tossed it back in the box. "Speaking of Mac, though, he's probably going to come looking for you when he gets back from Orange County. You're on his list."

"What list?"

"His list of waifs and strays. You didn't finish high school, right?"

"No." Kai felt the wariness he'd brought into the office return. High school had been a total bust. He'd skipped out when he was seventeen and never gone back. "What's that got to do with this?"

Jude's fond smile turned wry. "Porn is a tough game, Kai.

You're an amazing model, but at some point you'll want to do something else with your life. While you work for us, we'll give you every chance to make that happen, and that means getting your GED. Don't hide from Mac. He can help you."

CHAPTER THREE

Kai escaped Jude's office a little while later and made his way downstairs to find Cam. The idea of going back to school in any form was slightly terrifying, but he had other things on his mind. Jude was an intense character, but he was right about the porn. Something was missing, and if anyone could help him figure it out, it was Cam.

Cam greeted him with a hug. Kai cuddled into him and kissed his cheek. "Where've you been? I haven't seen you for ages."

"Oh, you know." Cam ruffled Kai's hair, making it flop into his face. "I've been around."

Kai reluctantly detached himself from Cam and fixed his hair. He eyed Cam, considering a revenge attack. Cam had the best hair, auburn and wild. He smelled good too, like the beach. "Are you back for good now? We missed you."

"Aw, you're sweet." Cam took a seat in an armchair on one of the dormant sets and gestured for Kai to do the same. His cell phone beeped. He read the message and grinned. "Jude says you've got something on your mind. What's up?"

Kai scowled. "Dunno. Jude thinks I'm bored."

"Are you?"

"Maybe." Kai gave Cam the same answer he'd given Jude. "I don't know what he wants me to do about it, though. It's not like I want to quit."

"Okay." Cam looked thoughtful. For a moment, he actually reminded Kai of Jude. "Let's talk about your scenes. They're all pretty similar, aren't they? Getting fucked by a big top?"

Kai shrugged. "I guess, but that's what I like. I did some rimming scenes with Sonny last month. I liked those too, but—" *But what?*

"I watched the scene with Jack," Cam said. "What's with the biting? You've never asked me to do that."

Kai shrugged. "I didn't need you to. What we were doing was enough." *Enough.* Maybe that was it. Maybe the slam of a man's dick in his ass just wasn't enough anymore.

Cam seemed inclined to agree. "I get the pain thing, but I like that shit when I'm pissed about something else. Anything you want to talk about?"

"No."

"Sure?"

"I already told Jude I'm fine, just bored is all."

"That fits." Cam leaned back in his chair. "If you're not into subbing, perhaps you're frustrated. When you perform the same role over and over, you can get kinda jaded, and that can fuck you up. Maybe you're ready to think outside the box Jon put you in."

"How the fuck would I do that?"

"Have you thought about topping?"

Kai snapped his gaze to Cam. He hadn't. Ever. "Topping? Who would I top?"

"Who would you want to top?"

"You?" Kai figured he'd try his luck. "We could think outside the box together."

Cam smirked. "You'd have to get past Sasha first. My ass is his."

Cam bottoms? Kai blinked, but Cam didn't seem to realize what he'd given away. "Um, so who? Zeb, or someone?"

"Maybe." Cam looked beyond the set to the photos on the walls. Blue Boy's wall of fame. "I can't see it, though. I'll ask Jude. He might have some ideas."

Kai scowled. "I did ask Jude. He said I have to figure it out on my own."

"Not completely on your own, or he wouldn't have sent you to me. I think it's more that he wants you to have a creative influence on your work."

Kai said nothing. Creativity was a word he'd often heard thrown around the studio, but he'd never seen much real evidence of it. Porn was porn. Get laid, get paid.

"The biting kink is kinda hot, though. Hang on. Let me grab someone." Cam got up and walked to the edge of their quiet corner. "Hey, Matthew. Come over here, would you?"

Matthew, a dancer turned model from Silver, appeared in Kai's eye line. Cam pointed to a nearby couch. "Have a seat. We're talking about trying some new things. Kai's thinking of topping, and you haven't shot a full scene yet, right? What do you think? Could be interesting."

"Um..." Matthew frowned and glanced at Kai. "Wouldn't that look weird? He's kinda small."

Kai bristled. "My bones are slender, asshat. There's nothing small about my dick."

"It's true," Cam said. "I've shot with Kai. He's hot as hell."

Kai flushed as the backhanded compliment hit home. Despite some weird moments in their last scene together, Cam was in his top three fucks for sure.

Matthew sat down. Cam prodded him with a few more questions, but Kai tuned them out and considered Matthew's physical attributes. *Fucking small. I bet he's got, like, five pounds on me.*

Size aside, though, Matthew was pretty easy on the eyes. He

had none of the bulk of Kai's usual crushes, but his black hair and tattooed pale skin were a killer combination. He'd had his lip pierced since Kai had last seen him too, a silver ring set to the left side of his mouth.

I could tug on that.

"What's this? Some kind of porn star powwow?" Sonny Valentine slid over the back of Cam's chair, stopping short before he landed in Cam's lap. "Seriously. You guys need a teepee and a fire. What's up?"

Kai grinned and bumped Sonny's fist. He figured Cam would answer the question, but he didn't. Instead, he took Sonny's chin and stared at him, and Sonny stared right back, like they were checking each other for cracks...cuts and bruises Kai couldn't see.

Oblivious, Matthew broke the silence. "Cam wants Kai to top me."

That got Sonny's attention. "That sounds cool. You've bottomed before, right? It's not your first time ever?"

"Fuck, no."

Matthew looked affronted, but Sonny ignored his scowl and turned his attention back to Kai. "What about you? You've never topped before. Are you sure you want to pop that cherry on-screen?"

Kai felt his cheeks heat up for the eleventieth time. "I haven't really thought about it. It was his idea."

Kai pointed at Cam, who seemed distracted by something on his phone.

"It's a suggestion," Cam said without looking up, "not an order. Jude might not go for it anyway. I just figured you could give it some thought."

Kai kicked Sonny's foot. "Jon asked you to top me a few months back. Why'd you say no?"

"It's taken you this long to ask?" Sonny quirked an eyebrow.

Kai shrugged. Jon had put the idea to him like it was a done deal. It had never occurred to Kai that Sonny would refuse, and he'd be lying if he said the rejection hadn't stung. Sonny seemed to be game for anything. Why not him?

Sonny kissed Cam's cheek and leaped lightly over the arm of the chair. He landed on his feet like a cat. Kai liked to think of himself as graceful, but he had nothing on Sonny.

"I didn't want to bring that side of me to the studio," Sonny said. "I've only topped for one guy in the past three years, and he's everything to me. It's personal, you know? You've got to keep something back for yourself, or you've got nothing to come home to."

Cam looked up from his phone. "Who've you been... Never mind." Cam stopped as his brain seemed to catch up with his tongue. He opened his mouth. Shut it again. "You never told me that."

Sonny shrugged. Kai got the feeling he was missing something obvious. And then it clicked. Levi. Fuck. Sonny fucked Levi? *Man, this day is getting weirder and weirder.* Kai felt heat flood his groin. He'd never given topping much thought, but he'd had the biggest crush on Levi for as long as he could remember. He'd top him in a heartbeat.

Cam said something. Kai missed it, too caught up in lustful fantasies, but whatever it was darkened Sonny's gaze. He stuck his middle finger up at Cam. "You call him, then."

Sonny walked off the set and disappeared into the depths of the studio. His departure was abrupt. Cam looked like he might go after him, but he didn't get up. Instead, he sighed and scrubbed his hand over his face. "He's gonna be the death of me."

Cam let out another long breath. Kai went to him and slunk onto the arm of his chair. Sonny had been strange recently, and Kai was fond of Cam. He didn't want him to feel bad. He put his head on Cam's shoulder. Cam smiled, but it looked like a lot of effort.

From the couch, Matthew drank it all in, eyes wide. Kai took pity on him too. For all Matthew's posturing, he'd only been with the studio a little while. He probably wasn't used to how intense things could get. "It's okay to be nervous if you haven't got much experience. We can figure this out."

"I have experience," Matthew said. "Just not here."

Kai sat up a little. "Did you work for another studio?"

"No, but I..." Matthew glanced at Cam. "You're with that Sasha guy now, right?"

Cam frowned. "So?"

"Um, so." Matthew swallowed. "You don't mind that I was seeing Jon before he left, do you?"

"Seeing?"

Kai looked between Matthew and Cam, and felt the air shift. He'd heard the rumors about Cam and Jon, it was the worst kept secret in LA, but then Jon left and Sasha had appeared on the scene, holding Cam's hand like he'd always been there, and Kai had forgotten about the heat he'd often seen between Cam and Jon.

"He told me not to tell you, but he's gone now..." Matthew's voice fell away.

Cam's eyes flashed. "Maybe that's why he limited you to jerk-offs and blowjobs. Jon likes to keep his toys in line."

Cam's tone wasn't harsh, but it felt odd to Kai. He glanced between Cam and Matthew again, sensing something he didn't understand. The hardness in Cam's gaze had been brief but undeniable.

Matthew shifted, uncomfortable. "So what's the plan? Do we set a date for this scene, or what?"

The clunky change of subject was awkward, but Kai felt Cam shake himself. Watched him force a grin back onto his face, a grin that gradually became genuine.

"Let's not get ahead of ourselves," Cam said. "You might not be compatible. Get to know each other first. See if you like each other. I'll talk to Jude, and if everyone's game, we'll figure something out."

They talked it out a little more. Kai was used to such candid discussions, but it took Matthew a while to warm up. The guy was laid-back and cool, but he didn't say much, and the little he did say gave Kai no clue as to what he was thinking.

That lip ring, though. Man, it was distracting.

When the conversation eventually dried up, Kai slid off the arm of Cam's chair and stretched out the kinks in his back. He needed to get home and get ready for his dancing slot that evening. He didn't usually hit Blue Boy and Silver on the same day, but Jude hadn't noticed the scheduling glitch and Kai was feeling restless. A spin on the pole would clear his mind, and give him some perspective on his clusterfuck of a day.

Matthew drifted away from the set. Kai started to follow. A heavy hand on his shoulder stopped him. He turned. Cam was right behind him, but he looked strange, vacant, like he wasn't there at all. Kai frowned. "Cam? What's up?"

"Dizzy." Cam blinked a few times, and sank to the ground before Kai could catch him.

CHAPTER FOUR

"Matthew!"

Kai's yell rang out across the studio as he dropped to the ground. Cam was crouched on the floor, supporting himself with one hand, but he looked unsteady. Kai put his arms around him, but he couldn't take Cam's weight and they both fell to the side.

"Cam? Are you okay?"

Cam didn't answer right away. He found Kai's hand, like he needed to feel someone close. "I'm fine. Stood up too quick."

Matthew crawled into the space between the couch and the chair. "What's wrong?"

"I don't know." Kai eyed Cam. He'd made no move to get up. "Cam? Are you okay?"

Cam's only response was to drop his head. Kai shot a worried glance at Matthew. "Get someone."

Matthew scrambled to his feet and darted across the studio. Shooting was done for the day, and most of the crew had gone home while Kai and Matthew had been talking with Cam, but Jude would still be here. He was always the last to leave.

It felt like Kai was alone with a barely conscious Cam for hours, but then Jude appeared like magic, solid and calm. He helped Cam from the floor and onto the couch. Upright and supported by Jude's strong arms, Cam seemed to come back into himself. Jude dispatched Kai to fetch some water. Cam was talking by the time he came back.

"Jude, I'm okay, man. You don't need to do that."

Jude rolled his eyes, his phone tucked between his cheek and his shoulder. "If I had the car, I'd take you myself. Sasha's not picking up. Is there anyone else who can give you a ride home?"

"Levi, maybe?"

Cam pressed a few buttons on his own phone, but his focus was off. Kai stepped in and found Levi's number. He hadn't seen Levi in months, but he didn't think twice about calling him now. He could tell by Jude's face that something was wrong.

Levi picked up on the third ring. Kai could hear the sound of his auto garage in the background. "'Lo?"

"Levi, it's Kai."

The revving engine cut off. "Kai? Why have you got Cam's phone?"

"Cam needs a ride home. He's at the studio."

"Is he okay?"

Kai glanced at Cam. He was responding to Jude, but he was pale, like he could puke or pass out at any moment. "I don't know. I think he fainted."

"Be there in ten."

Levi hung up. Kai drifted back to the couch; he'd stepped away while he'd been on the phone. He held out the phone to Cam. "Levi's on his way."

Cam nodded. "Thanks."

"Kai, you and Matthew can split now. I'll wait with Cam."

Jude kept his eyes on Cam, but Kai knew a dismissal when he heard one. He backed away, right into Matthew. Somehow, he'd forgotten he was there.

"Come on," Matthew said. "Let's grab our stuff and get out of here."

Kai followed Matthew on autopilot. Walking away from Cam felt all wrong. They were friends when things worked out that way, and seeing him so rattled was horrible.

Matthew touched his arm. "If we go out the back exit we can sit on the wall and watch the front door."

"Huh?"

"You're worried, right? If we sit on the wall across the street, you can see he gets his ride home."

It seemed as good a plan as any. They sneaked out the back fire exit and slipped around the front of the building. Kai hoisted himself up onto the wall just in time to see Levi Ramone's truck pull up. Levi got out and jogged straight inside. Kai didn't see his face, but his tanned, muscular back was as alluring as ever.

Sonny's a lucky guy.

Matthew seemed to think so too. "Damn. Levi Ramone is so freakin' hot."

The echo of his own thoughts made Kai grin. He took a cigarette from Matthew's proffered pack and lit up. He only smoked when he was too drunk to care how bad it was for his skin, but it had been a long day, and he still had to dance the night away yet. "Yeah, it's a real shame he quit, for us at least."

Matthew blew smoke into the bright California sky. "What do you mean?"

"Nothing, really." Kai thought back to Blue Boy as it had been when he'd first signed up. "He just never seemed happy. I don't think he liked it much."

Matthew started to answer but fell silent as the front door of the studio opened. Cam walked out of his own accord, grinning, and but for Jude hovering close behind, looked no worse for wear. Kai breathed a long sigh of relief that turned to a rueful grin as Levi opened Cam's door and gestured for him to get in the truck.

A gentleman too. Be still my beating heart.

Kai giggled. Matthew didn't appear to notice. They watched Levi shake Jude's hand before he got in the truck and drove away. Jude watched the truck too, then cast his gaze around. For a moment, Kai thought he'd spotted them skulking on the wall with their hoods up, but then he went back inside the studio and locked the door behind him.

Matthew jumped down from the wall. "So…"

He let the word hang. Kai jumped down too and pushed his hood back. "So?"

Matthew flicked his spent smoke away. "We should probably get together sometime, figure this shit out. I'm game for the scene if you are. It's not like I'd have to do much. Just lie there and take it, right?"

"Are you kidding?" Kai shook his head. "Who the hell told you that?"

"No one. It's obvious."

Kai snorted. He'd only met Matthew a few times before today, and he'd always struck him as cocky, but now he was beginning to realize that perhaps he was just misinformed. "You're right about one thing. We definitely need to meet up. There's no way I'm sticking my cock in you while you're spouting crap like that."

Matthew scoffed, dismissive and amused, but as they made arrangements to hook up after the weekend, Kai knew they both had a lot to learn before they set foot on a porn set together.

The weekend passed in a blur of dancing and vodka. Kai worked the podiums like a pro, and woke up Monday morning with a nice pile of tips and a raging hangover. He usually slept in on Mondays. His roommates spent all day at work, and he had the place to himself. Shame his phone had other ideas. A call woke him at nine a.m.

"Rise and shine, kiddo."

Kai grunted and peeled his face from his pillow. He'd crawled home from Silver sometime after four and passed out in his clothes. He felt disgusting. He hadn't even washed the body paint from his skin. "Who is this?"

His tormentor chuckled. "Mac. You awake, or what?"

"Or what." Kai sat up and took in the chaos of the small room he called home. There was shit everywhere—clothes, shoes, and DVDs. He could barely see the ugly beige carpet. "Was I supposed to be somewhere?"

"Nope, just thought I'd catch you unawares. You gave me the slip at the club on Friday."

Oops. Kai had noticed Mac heading his way and, heeding Jude's warning, he'd ducked into the dressing rooms and kept a low profile until it was time to go on stage. Mac and Jude didn't hang at the club much, and Kai had danced the late slot. Kai figured he'd dodged a bullet, but Mac clearly had other ideas.

"GED, Kai," he said without preamble. "I want you to get it, and I've got some information for you to look through. What are you doing today? I'll bring it to you."

Kai blinked, and tried to clear the vodka-laced fog in his mind. He'd partied with Sonny last night and things had gotten a little wild. "Bring it to me?"

"That's right. Just think, if you'd faced the music on Friday, this conversation wouldn't be happening. Come on, kid. Where are you at? I'll deliver it to you. Can't say fairer than that."

There was mirth in Mac's tone, but Kai scowled and hauled himself out of bed. His apartment was a dump. There was no way he could let Mac come here. "Can I meet you somewhere?"

Somewhere turned out to be a coffee shop a few blocks from Kai's building. He found Mac in a booth at the back, tapping on a laptop with an empty coffee beside him.

Kai skidded onto the leather bench seat. "Sorry. Am I late?"

Mac looked up from his work. He was wearing glasses. The steel frames added something to him. With his shaved head, full beard, and huge frame, Mac looked like an overgrown Spartan wrestler with a big-assed brain. "You're an hour late, but it's okay. I figured you would be, and I've got plenty to keep me occupied."

Kai craned his neck and peered at Mac's computer screen. "What are you doing?"

"Paying your wages." Mac spun his laptop around. "You and everyone else at Silver."

Kai frowned. It took him a moment to make sense of them, but then he saw the method behind the convoluted mass of numbers. "What's this line? The cleanup crew?"

"Yep, and right there is the bar staff, security, and the dancers."

"Wow. Good thing we charge so much, huh?"

Mac's grin was boyish, like he wasn't twenty years older than Kai. "Don't say that too loud. What do you want to drink?"

Kai shook his head. He'd made good tips at the weekend, but rent was due and his roommates didn't always pay their share on time.

"Don't be shy, kid. Go up and get what you want. My treat. Get me a black coffee while you're there, will you? Oh, and get something to eat. You look like crap."

Kai let the dig slide. He'd caught sight of himself as he'd run out of the apartment, haggard and hungover. He needed caffeine, and cake...definitely cake. He took a tray to the counter and loaded up with sweet treats, a frothy Frappuccino and a more masculine, plain coffee for Mac.

"Cake pops for lunch?"

"Breakfast, actually." Kai slid Mac's coffee across the table, careful to avoid the ominous stack of paperwork. "I got you some pie."

"Thanks, but you can take it home with you. I'm meeting Jude at the gym later. He can smell cinnamon from three blocks away."

"And that's bad?"

Mac smirked but didn't elaborate. "Stop trying to distract me. You know why you're here."

Busted. Kai sighed. "Do I really have to get my GED?"

"No. You don't have to do anything, but I want you to think about it. And beyond too. What are your interests outside the studio?"

"Huh?"

"Interests. Hobbies. What do you like doing when you're not filming and dancing?"

"Um..." Kai had to think hard, because working for Blue Boy took up most of his time. He danced three nights a week, worked the bar a couple more, and most of those nights spilled over into the next day. With filming on top of that, he didn't have time for much else.

"Okay. Let's try it another way." Mac reached for the folder Kai knew was bad news. "I've got some preparation packs. Here, have a look. Math, science, reading, and writing. Think you can handle it?"

Kai gulped a mouthful of syrupy coffee, hoping the caffeine-laced sugar fest would inspire a rush of articulate intelligence. It didn't. The first paragraph on the top sheet of paper was long, and printed in teeny tiny print. Kai couldn't figure out which sentence came first.

He pushed the papers back at Mac. "I don't want to."

Mac hummed, like Kai had played right into his hands. "I think you do, or you wouldn't have come. Look again, and tell me what's bugging you."

Jeez. Why does everyone keep asking me that?

"Can you read?"

Kai huffed. If only it was that simple. "I'm not stoopid, Mac. I can read, just not fast and not with you staring at me like that."

"Okay." Mac took a slow sip of coffee. "What about numbers? The same? Worse?"

"Better, actually. I was good at math."

Mac said nothing for a moment or two, but the silence wasn't uncomfortable. Kai knew his limits, and he'd adapted his lifestyle to suit them. Given enough time, and some occasional help from his friends, he could make sense of anything that mattered.

He ate Mac's slice of pie while Mac opened up his laptop and clicked a few buttons. When he was done, he put his head on his arms and let his eyes drift closed, hoping Mac would get the hint and let the whole thing drop.

"Are you dyslexic, Kai?"

No such luck. Kai opened his eyes with a world weary sigh. "Maybe. They wanted to test me in high school, but I dropped out."

"I see." Mac clicked a few more buttons. "Well, the first thing we need to do is get you tested and diagnosed, then we can look at getting you some specialized help with the GED test. It says here you can take an audio test, no reading at all. How does that sound?"

Like hell. "Um, great?"

Mac chuckled. "That's good enough for me. Your legal name is Kai Whitlock, right?"

"Yep."

Mac shook his head. "What's with you kids using your real names for porn? Back in my day, half the fun was figuring out a cool as fuck alias."

"Sonny doesn't, and the rest of us don't use our full names.

Only Levi ever did that, and Cam said it was because he didn't give a shit."

It was true. Levi Ramone was Levi Ramone, and he didn't care who knew it, but the rest of them stuck to first names. Only Sonny used a real alias, and Kai had heard it was because his family was super religious. But then, he'd also heard it was because Sonny was on the run from the Albanian mafia, so hearsay meant nothing.

Kai considered Mac, picturing the faded VHS case Jude had shown him. He already knew Jude had performed as Rocco Vain, but Jude had never told him Mac's porn star name. "What was your cool as fuck alias?"

Mac winced. "I said we had fun figuring them out, not that we were successful. I was 'Gun' as in a loaded gun. Lame, huh?"

"Rocco and Gun?" Kai giggled. "It's, um, not that lame."

"You don't have to humor me, kid. Hindsight is a wonderful thing. Jude could work it, but I was just a dillweed with a big dick. Lucky for me, life moves on. We're about done here. Do you need a ride somewhere?"

Kai didn't. He was headed home to take a hot bath and catch up on his sleep before his noisy roommates got back, but he walked with Mac to his car anyway. He wanted to ask Mac about Cam. The incident at the studio had been on his mind. "Have you seen Cam lately?"

Mac nodded. "I saw him yesterday."

"Is he okay?"

"Far as I know. He's going to start helping Jude with production, so hopefully my man can tear himself away from the grindstone once in a while."

Kai had already figured Jude for a perfectionist. A workaholic too? Man, some people were weird. As much fun as porn could be, Kai didn't like being tied to anything. Except maybe a bed. He'd never tried...

"What's going on with this topping scene with Matthew?" Mac asked.

"Huh? Oh, nothing yet. I'm meeting up with him tomorrow."

"Yeah?" Mac eyed Kai with his gentle, curious gaze. "What are you going to do?"

Kai shrugged, because he didn't actually know. He'd arranged to meet Matthew at Matthew's apartment, but they hadn't gotten much further than that. "You were a porn star. What do you think we should do?"

"Take it slow." Mac unlocked his car. He seemed unfazed by Kai's bold question. "Go back to the start and be friends. Make it fun."

"Fun?"

"Yeah, fun. And who do you have the most fun with, huh? Your friends."

Kai thought of the wild nights at Silver, and the rimming scene he'd shot with Sonny when they'd laughed all day. Perhaps Mac was right. He jumped up and gave the big man a hug that seemed to surprise him, and made his way home with a lot to think about.

CHAPTER FIVE

"Fucking assholes!" Kai's exclamation stirred little reaction in Tag, his least annoying roommate, so Kai kicked the couch for good measure. "Did Bianca have people over last night?"

Tag flicked the ash from the end of his joint. "Who knows? I was at Lisa's. What's up?"

"Someone stole my laundry detergent."

"Why would anyone do that?"

It was a fair question, given that Kai was the only fucker who ever washed clothes, cleaned the bathroom, or did the dishes. Everyone else seemed happy to live in squalor. "Who did she have here? Was it that deadbeat Brian?"

"Dunno." Tag turned his vague attention back to his computer game and tuned out of the conversation.

Defeated, Kai shoved the last of his laundry in a bag and flounced out of the apartment. He walked three blocks to the Laundromat and set about wrangling with the coin-operated machines.

Kai's hands were small, and he had a lot of clothes. Some fell to the floor. His favorite spandex hotpants took pride of place, electric blue and impossible to miss. Kai scooped them up, but not in time to stop the butch guy beside him wrinkling his nose.

"Fuckin' fags taking over the goddamn world."

The guy stomped away. Kai glared after him and considered retaliating, but common sense told him to keep his retort internal. Bullshit like that was nothing new. A flashback of having his head shoved down the john in junior high barged into his mind. For a moment, the memory made itself at home, but Kai distracted himself by folding his less flamboyant underwear into perfectly symmetrical bundles. Away from the safety of the club and the studio, he sometimes forgot there were still some folk who abhorred who he was. Surrounded by his friends and Silver's burly security, he had little to fear, but it was different in the real world.

Kai escaped the Laundromat and lugged his clothes home. On the way, he imagined a house with a basement, with a washer and a real dryer, the kind that left towels fluffy and soft, and wondered how many scenes he'd have to shoot to make the dream a reality.

Too many. But the incident brought Kai's thoughts back to a more pleasant place. It was Wednesday and he was meeting Matthew that evening. Mac's sage advice had been playing on his mind, probably in an attempt to dodge the rest of their coffee meeting, but still... "Be friends. Make it fun." How hard could that be?

Kai came home to an empty apartment. Tag had decamped to his girlfriend's place, leaving behind a trail of mess and a heavy smog of stale bong smoke, and Bianca had yet to come home from whoever's bed she'd crawled into the night before.

Who's the whore?

Kai sighed. His roommates weren't the worst he'd ever had, just messy, and crappy at paying their share of the bills on time. But that was enough. Their contract was up in the spring, and Kai couldn't wait. Perhaps he'd ask Sonny if he wanted to room with him. He'd probably get even less sleep than he did already, and Sonny was crazy messy, but at least Kai wouldn't have to worry about his favorite hat getting used as an ashtray.

Kai made a halfhearted attempt to clear up, then dug his laptop out of the locked box under his bed and closed his bedroom door. He logged on to the Blue Boy website. It had changed a little since Jude and Mac had taken over—Jude had a thing for photography—but it didn't take Kai long to find Matthew. He brought up the list of Matthew's scenes, surprised to find only two—a solo audition scene, and a fuck-hot foreplay scene with Cam. Kai bypassed the solo scene and clicked on Cam's face. He'd been a Blue Boy fan long before he'd signed his own contract, and Cam had always been his not-so-guilty pleasure. In fact, Kai was surprised he hadn't watched the scene before, but as Matthew and Cam filled his screen, he knew there was no way he'd seen Matthew on-screen before.

Wow. There was no other word. Kai was used to the way Cam's easy on-screen presence seeped into him, but Matthew was something else. Cocky, aloof, and endearingly nervous, it was a killer combination. Kai watched the short movie unfold. It was billed as a simple foreplay scene, a newbie and a veteran, but it didn't play out as Kai expected.

Cam seemed distracted and detached, and for a while Matthew had the upper hand. Then Cam switched gears—Kai watched him come to life—and Matthew was done. The misplaced bravado faded away and instead he seemed awed by Cam and the sensations he'd provoked with just a sweep of his fingers. Matthew seemed lost for the rest of the scene, swept away, and Kai allowed himself a wry smirk. He remembered that feeling all too well, and his conversation with Jude a few weeks ago drifted into his mind.

"You need to act on instinct," Jude had said. "Your scene partner isn't always going to say or do what you expect. You need to be malleable, and adaptable, and more than that, you need to want to be."

Kai considered the scene he'd just watched. Matthew had started with a vision, and by the shocked haze in his eyes it was clear the endgame had turned him inside out in the best possible way. Kai could see Matthew had loved it, and the only thing marring the perfectly composed scene, were the subtle glances both performers sent to the man behind the camera.

Jon.

Huh. Kai didn't like the idea of either man looking to Jon Keller for approval, and he liked the idea of them in his bed even less. Jude and Mac were unknown entities, but Kai liked them more already than he ever had Jon. Especially Mac.

Kai considered the screen again. Matthew and Cam were both jacking Cam, their hands clasped around Cam's dick. Cam looked kind of bored, but Matthew? He looked fascinated, wide-eyed and hot as hell. Kai trailed his fingers over his own cock. His touch was light and teasing, and he wanted more, but something stopped him. Mac had told him to be friends with Matthew first, and friends didn't beat off over each other, right?

"Barbecue pizza? Ace. How did you know?"

Kai shrugged and passed the extra-large box to Matthew. "I didn't. I figured I'd eat it all if you didn't like it. That's why I brought dough balls too, and wings. Oh, and curly fries."

Matthew took the overstuffed paper bag and waved Kai into the foyer of his third-story apartment. "Dude, that's a lot of food, even for two."

Kai didn't think so. "I have hollow legs."

"Yeah?" Matthew inclined his head to his small kitchen. "Get some beer. Let's test that theory."

"Beer, really?" Kai wrinkled his nose. Beer tasted like bad ass. "What else have you got?"

"Vodka, apple juice, or soda. Help yourself."

Kai poured himself a generous inch of vodka and sweetened it with cherry coke. Matthew had wandered off with the food. Kai followed the smell to Matthew's warmly lit living room. With just a couch, a coffee table, and a TV unit, there wasn't much to it, but compared to Kai's chaotic apartment, the place was a comforting palace. The Iron Man poster was a nice touch too.

Kai took a seat on the couch. "Nice place."

"Thanks. Beats student digs."

Kai had a vague memory of Matthew telling the other dancers at Silver he was a student when he'd joined their crew. "What are you studying?"

"Virology."

"Virology? What the fuck is that?"

"A subfield of microbiology."

Kai snorted. "Dude, I didn't finish high school. You'll have to explain it in dumbfuck terms."

"Study of viruses...like their classification and evolution." At Kai's blank expression, Matthew pointed to a folder on the coffee table. "I'm writing a paper on the molecular structure of hepatitis C."

"C? Does that mean there's an A and a B?"

Matthew shook his head. "Don't get me started. Let's eat before I bore you to death."

Kai wasn't bored, far from it, and he was used to hanging out with clever motherfuckers. Sonny was one of the smartest people he'd ever met. He was hungry, though. Tag had found his stash of groceries hidden behind the cleaning products and cleared him out. He'd left a note, but still. They dug into the mountain of junk food. They shot the breeze while they ate, but inevitably, the conversation settled on their main common ground: Porn.

"I watched your scenes today," Kai said around a mouthful of curly fries. "You and Cam were hot together."

"Thanks. I watched yours too. Took me all afternoon."

Kai smirked. The idea of Matthew spending all afternoon watching him get off made him feel kind of buzzed, like he'd had four drinks instead of one. "Oh yeah? Which one did you like best?"

"Honestly?" Matthew chewed on a spicy chicken bone. "I thought I'd like the one with Levi best. I saved it till last 'cause, well, damn, he's smokin' hot, right?"

"Right..." Kai let the word hang, curious.

"But I reckon the rimming with Sonny is better. It was like you were playing tricks on each other, you know?"

Kai laughed. "That's pretty much what happened. We had a bet on who would come first. I lost."

"Not a bad way to lose, though."

Matthew had a point. Kai stole the last slice of pizza and pondered his next move. He'd been at Matthew's place for more than an hour, but though they'd talked nothing but porn, they'd yet to broach the purpose of their pizza-fueled summit. For a geeky nerd in disguise, Matthew was a lot of fun, and time had flown by.

"So how do you want to do this?"

"This?"

"The scene," Matthew said. "If we actually do it, I mean."

"You don't want to?" Kai felt his stomach churn with disappointment. Over the past year, he'd learned to take scene suggestions with a pinch of salt, but an afternoon spent ogling Matthew on the tiny screen of his netbook had gotten him psyched. The responsibility of topping still terrified him, but he wanted to try...with Matthew. Wanted to be the one Matthew looked at like a god.

No one had ever looked at Kai that way.

"Hell, I want to."

"You do?" Matthew's enthusiasm surprised Kai. Despite his reticence, he'd seemed less than convinced at the studio. "Thought you didn't want to get nailed by a little guy?"

Matthew coughed and covered his mouth. "I've watched your scenes, remember?"

Kai smirked. "Okay. So let's figure this out. I want to top, and you're down with that, right?"

"Right, but I've never done a full scene. Sonny reckons we should spend some time together first, and maybe, uh, practice."

"Practice? You want me to fuck you before we do the scene?"

Matthew shrugged. "Maybe. Couldn't hurt, right? Sonny told me he never does a scene with someone he hasn't seen up close and naked before the shoot."

Kai could believe that. Sonny was game for anything, but always, always on his own terms. No one told Sonny what to do. Kai picked up his drink and considered Matthew over the rim of his glass. They were mushed together on the small couch. Kai could feel the heat of Matthew's body. The warmth was alluring...tempting, but somehow, the idea of jumping him, fucking him over the coffee table, didn't feel right. Too much. Or maybe not enough. Kai didn't want to cram himself inside Matthew and move on to the next scene. He wanted to do something...more.

"Maybe we should take it slow."

Matthew smirked. "What, like, we're dating?"

"Dating?" Kai rolled his eyes. "I mean the sex, asshat. It might not be good if we jump right in. I've never done this before."

"Okay." Matthew appeared to give it some thought. "Maybe it should be like dating, then. Like, kissing, and second base and all that shit. I guess there's no point trying to fuck if we can't get the first part right."

"You don't think we're overthinking it? We could just fuck and be done with it."

Matthew shrugged. "Jude said we could do anything we wanted, but I'm swamped with schoolwork at the moment. I could use the distraction."

"So we're playing the long game?"

"Hell, yeah."

Matthew held out his fist. Kai bumped it absently, wondering what the hell he was getting into. Porn wasn't supposed to be this complicated. "I haven't been on a date since I was sixteen, and that was with a girl. Do we kiss now, or what?"

"I'd be down with the 'or what,' but we should probably make out some. You know, to make sure it's good."

It was the most uninspired proposition Kai had ever heard, and the excitement that bubbled out of his chest in the form of a giggle caught him off guard. Since Cam had put the idea of fucking Matthew into his head, he'd thought about it more than he cared to admit, but kissing? It wasn't something he ever gave much thought.

Matthew shifted on the couch. Kai's pulse quickened, and he felt seventeen again...like the night he got to put his lips on another boy for the first time was still ahead of him, not four years gone. Kai put his hand on Matthew's face. He brushed his silver lip ring with his thumb. The smooth metal felt warm, like Matthew's blood pulsed through it. Huh. Kai had expected it to be cold.

Get a grip.

Kai kissed Matthew, lightly at first, a tentative brush of lips, but then something changed. A switch flipped in Kai's brain. He shoved his hand into Matthew's inky dark hair and pulled, yanking Matthew's head to an angle that suited him better.

Matthew made a sound that traveled through Kai, from his scalp to the tips of his toes, and the kiss exploded into something that became slowly perfect. Kai's heart hammered, his skin tingled, and his lips burned.

Too soon, Matthew pulled away, panting and breathless. "For continuity purposes, if you're gonna kiss me like that, you gotta stop calling me an asshat."

Kai laughed. "Okay, but if we're working on continuity, we should probably make out some more."

Two days later, Kai found himself lost in a haze of reliving that fuck-hot night of kissing and a boner that just wouldn't quit. Matthew was on his mind twenty-four/seven, kissing him, touching him, making wicked plans for what he'd do to him when they finally moved on to second base. Kai, more than ever, had porn on the brain. Shame Mac had other ideas.

Damn you, Mac...

Kai sat in the waiting room of the psycho-education testing center with his head in his hands. Against his better judgment, he'd taken the stupid dyslexia test and it hadn't gone well. Now he was waiting for some dude with greasy hair to call him back in and give him the bad news. The reading aloud had been the most humiliating part, and Kai was glad Sonny had stood him up, and he'd come to the test center alone.

He squeezed his eyes shut and thought of Matthew. Forty-eight hours had passed since they'd spent half the night kissing on Matthew's couch, and until Kai had arrived at the freaky test center, he'd thought of little else.

Matthew was an amazing kisser. Or maybe it was Kai. Or both of them. Or maybe their chemistry was off the freakin' scale. Whatever. Kai didn't care. Kissing Matthew was the bomb, and he couldn't wait to do it again.

Kai's phone beeped. A message from Sonny.

Sorry. Got held up. Did it go OK?

Kai sighed and tapped out his response.

Waiting for results. But it was shitty. Happy now?

Sonny didn't reply, and Kai felt bad for being so snippy. It wasn't Sonny's fault Kai was a dumbfuck. On the other hand, though, it was Sonny's fault Kai had agreed to take the test in the first place. Sonny had seemed indifferent toward Blue Boy's burly new management, treating them with the same distant apathy he had Jon, but on this, he'd teamed up with Mac. Teamed up and pressganged Kai until he'd agreed to start studying for his GED. And that meant taking the bullshit dyslexia test.

"Kai Whitlock?"

Kai tore his gaze from the blank screen of his phone. Greasy Guy was waiting for him by his open office door.

Here goes nothing...

Kai followed the dude into the office and sat down. Greasy Guy clicked his computer mouse a few times and turned his screen so Kai could see it.

"Right, Mr. Whitlock, let's start with your literacy..."

Later that night, Kai found himself quite happily drunk off his ass. He was supposed to be working, but no one had noticed he was trashed yet. Probably wouldn't all night.

Kai sloshed another shot of tequila into the glass he'd hidden down the side of the cash register. It slid down like a dream. He grinned to himself. He loved the burn of hard liquor deep in his belly. It was almost as good as that wicked first dig of a big fat cock.

Almost.

Kai grinned some more and drifted to the back bar to replace the tequila bottle. *Where would I be without cock to distract me?*

Now there was a question. Kai's mirth faded. His fears about the dyslexia test had proven well founded. He'd scored high, which was bad, and Greasy Guy had classified him "on the severe end of the moderate scale." Whatever the hell that meant. Greasy Guy had been awful nice about it, but that hadn't stopped Kai coming away feeling like he'd failed first grade.

Where would I be if I couldn't spin on a pole? Flipping goddamned burgers?

Kai wasn't sure he wanted to know.

The night wore on. He served a few customers. Mixed drinks and fended off advances from the less respectful Blue Boy fans, but lucky for Kai, it was a quiet night in the club, as quiet as Silver ever got, at least.

The line at Kai's end of the bar eased up. He shut the cash register. *Fuck it. I want another shot.* He retrieved his precious glass and tripped over his own feet. Only the back bar saved him from a nasty tumble.

"Whoa. How many of those have you had?"

Kai spun around. Matthew was right behind him. He had his jacket on and a messenger bag slung over his chest. In the heady surroundings of the club he looked like a nerd—a smoking-hot nerd—and his lip ring was even sexier than Kai remembered. "I've had a few."

Matthew shook his head, though his green eyes danced with amusement. "Has Bull seen you?"

"Nope." Kai hiccupped and took a moment to place the tequila bottle back in the right place. "He's looking for Sonny, I think...or maybe that was yesterday."

Matthew laughed. "You're wasted. Hope he doesn't catch you."

Kai shrugged, indifferent. Bull was a pussycat. Matthew on the other hand...this was the first time they'd seen each other since that kiss. Somehow, Kai had forgotten how Matthew made his heart beat faster and his lips tingle. *Hmm, the tingling is new. Maybe I can get him to kiss me right now.* "Are you dancing tonight?"

"No. I came in to get my slots for next month. Mac said the e-mail system is down." That was news to Kai, but he'd done his best to avoid Mac when he'd arrived at the club and Mac had since gone home. "Anyway." Matthew started to turn away. "I'd better get going."

Kai caught his hand. "Don't go."

"Why not?"

"Um..." Kai lost his words. What was he supposed to say? *I'm a drunk-off-my-ass dumbfuck. Please stay and talk to me?*

Why not?

Kai hoisted himself over the bar and jumped down the other side. He yanked Matthew to a bar stool. He pushed him down and ignored Matthew's halfhearted protests. "We're supposed to be friends, right?" Matthew nodded. "Good. That means you get to listen to all my woes. Sit down. I've got lots to tell you."

I'll be home by eight. Bring your books!

Kai sighed and shoved his phone under his pillow. Dammit. His first ever topping scene and the hottest kisses ever had somehow descended into some warped kind of study hall. How did this shit happen to him?

Kai blamed Mac. And Sonny. And whatever genes had made him stupid. But the dyslexia test wasn't even the worst bit.

No. The worst bit had been hitting the back shelf on his bar shift at the club and telling Matthew all his troubles in a tequila-fueled haze of drunken rambling. Kai had little memory of talking Matthew's ear off, or getting home. In his head he liked to think he'd played it cool and pulled Matthew to him for a repeat of their first encounter...maybe more, but he'd woken up the next morning, alone, stinking of liquor, and the proud owner of a voice mail from Matthew offering to help him study.

Dammit. So much for dating. They'd seen each other every day since, and each meeting had followed the same formula—studying, junk food, more studying. They hadn't even kissed again, and man, Kai wanted to kiss Matthew again. So much. Some days, he thought of little else, especially when the dull-assed practice papers Mac had given him began to blur in front of his eyes. Shame Matthew took schoolwork, even Kai's pathetic GED shit, seriously. He even wore glasses...glasses that made Kai want to suck on his face. What was it with dudes in glasses these days? Topping be damned, Kai just wanted to make out.

Kai's phone vibrated beneath his pillow again. He pulled it out and saw the Blue Boy logo flash onto the screen. "Hello?"

"Morning, Kai. How's it going?"

Jude. Shit. "Um, fine?"

"You don't sound so sure. Not still hanging from Tuesday, are you? Don't think I don't know about you slamming shots behind the bar."

Kai winced, but took the fifth and waited for the ax to fall. Perhaps Jude had called him up to fire his ass.

Jude's deep chuckle took Kai by surprise. "Listen, kid, I'm gonna let it slide because we've put a lot on you the past few weeks, but don't do it again, got it?"

"Got it." Kai swung his legs over the side of his single bed. He'd been awake for a while, but with the sound of Bianca blowing her latest conquest filtering through his paper-thin bedroom wall, he'd had little motivation to get up. As a result, he needed to pee, bad. He padded across the room and opened his bedroom door. The coast looked clear. He started toward the bathroom, and then remembered Jude. "Did you need me for something else?"

"Nope. Just checking in. You're scheduled to film with Carl this weekend. Are you all set?"

Actually, the upcoming scene had slipped Kai's mind. "What day is that?"

"Saturday. I can get someone else, though, if you're not in the right place. Carl's easy."

Kai turned it over, but the ache in his bladder was distracting. He tiptoed into the bathroom, hoping Jude wouldn't know he was taking a leak.

Relieving himself cleared his mind. He pictured Carl—tall, dark and handsome, and a friend of Jude and Mac's who'd followed them from wherever they'd come from. The guy was pretty hot, and Kai had been holding out to work with him, but now the opportunity was there something didn't feel...right. "Would you be pissed of I didn't do it?"

"Not at all. That's why I called. I know you're working some stuff out. Tell you what, give me a call in a few days and let me know. Sonny's available, so he could probably fill in for you, and, hey, worst comes to it, I can do it my damned self."

Jude hung up before Kai could figure out if he was kidding.

***

That night, Kai headed over to Matthew's with his books and enough Chinese food to feed a small army. Matthew met him at the door with a grin.

"Thought you were getting fried chicken?"

Kai tipped his hood back and fixed his crazy hair. "It's raining. Moo Shoo's is closer."

Matthew snorted, and Kai stared. With his dark-framed geek glasses already in place, Matthew's smirk made him look like a young Johnny Depp.

Fuck my life.

Kai drifted to Matthew's living room without being asked. Over the past week or so, he'd become comfortable in Matthew's apartment, and it felt natural...normal to flop down on the cozy couch and put his feet up on the coffee table. He couldn't do that at home, there was always too much trash in the way.

Matthew brought out soda. "Food first?"

Kai rolled his eyes. Did he really have to ask? "Can you test me on social studies while we eat?"

"Sure." Matthew slid over the arm of 'his' side of the couch. "Did you try the reading I showed you yesterday?"

Kai made a face. "Some of it. I got Sonny to read me most of it, though. He tested me on science too."

"How did that go?"

"Okay, I guess."

Matthew laughed and flashed the subtle dimple in his left cheek, the dimple Kai had never noticed in all the months they'd danced at the same club. "You need to get better at guessing. You won't know the answer to every question, so you gotta learn to guess logically."

"Huh?"

Matthew rolled his eyes. "Don't play dumb. I know you're not."

"Oh, yeah? Then why did Mac give me a book called GED for Dummies?" Kai muffled his asinine retort with a mouthful of black bean chicken. They'd had this conversation a hundred times over. Matthew was as laid-back as he was freakishly smart, but Kai's ingrained habit of playing the dumb blond seemed to get on his nerves.

They ate their way through the mountain of food Kai had brought over while Matthew read Kai questions from the pile of practice papers that had become Kai's constant companion. Kai listened hard to the questions and each of the possible answers. The special tutor Mac had taken him to had told him to trust his instincts, that most of the multiple choice questions were common sense, but Kai had never considered himself to have much of either, and Matthew had an annoying habit of not telling him the correct answers until they'd gone through the whole test.

When they were done eating, Kai turned his attention to math, a copout of sorts as math was the one subject he could figure out all by himself. So much so that after a while, he became distracted and allowed his attention to drift.

He chanced a surreptitious glance at Matthew, who was typing on his laptop like a demon. Kai frowned at the reams of words Matthew had written since he'd last looked up, but even without the muddles of dyslexia, none of them made any sense.

Kai gave up and looked around the room instead. There wasn't much to Matthew's living space, just books and the occasional picture frame. Most of the photos seemed to have been taken on a beach, one of those amazing beaches with white sand and the deep blue sea. "Where was that picture taken?"

Matthew followed Kai's gaze. "Bondi Beach. My dad lives in Australia."

"Wow. What about your mom?"

"Boston."

Kai drummed his fingers on the arm of the couch. "Is that where you grew up?"

Matthew kept his gaze on his computer screen. "Hmm? Oh, yeah. I spent every summer in Sydney, though. That's why I'm doing porn. My dad lost his business last year, so he can't pay for my flights anymore. I want to go traveling next summer too, Bali and Thailand, maybe Indonesia. See the world before I have to get a real job."

Kai was sorry he'd asked. He'd never left LA, and to him, tending bars, getting fucked, and spinning on a pole was a real job, at least the only job he'd ever had.

Speaking of which...

CHAPTER SEVEN

Kai dumped his books and papers on the coffee table and pushed it away with his foot. "I'm done with this shit. When are we gonna work on our other project?"

Matthew grinned without looking away from his laptop screen. The smile was lazy and mellow, despite the intense concentration in his eyes. "Got something specific in mind?"

"Maybe." Kai chewed on his lip. "I was talking to Sonny about it and he said now we know we're hot together we need to figure out if we like the same stuff."

Matthew was silent a moment, then he shut his laptop with a snap. "We are hot together. Making out was fucking awesome. I've been thinking about it all week."

"I know, right?" Kai felt a giddy rush of relief. The kiss had been on his mind constantly, but he'd be lying if he said he hadn't worried Matthew hadn't felt the same...hadn't felt his heart hammer and the crazy heat burn through his veins. "We should definitely do that again."

"Yeah, but what else?"

There was a question. "What do you like?"

"As a bottom?"

Kai shrugged. "I guess. Do you top too?"

"Sometimes, not for a while, though. I haven't slept with anyone since Jon left."

Kai slanted his gaze to look Matthew in the eye, but Matthew's expression was unreadable. "Why not?"

"Time, I guess. I've been swamped with classes and stuff, so when I go to the club I just dance and go home, you know? And at the studio, Jon kept saying I wasn't ready to get fucked on-screen, and then he left."

It was on the tip of Kai's tongue to ask how Matthew had ended up in Jon's bed in the first place. He bit it back, then asked anyway.

Matthew hissed through his teeth. "I transferred to UCLA this summer. I got a job dancing at another club in the city, but I hated it. The other dancers were bitches. I did a private dance for Jon one night, and he offered me more money to come to Silver. When I said yes, he took me home and fucked me."

It seemed logical enough to Kai. Jon had personally installed every dancer at Silver. He'd recruited Kai from a rival gay bar, sneaked up on him in an alley one night after closing time. He hadn't offered to take Kai home, but he'd waved enough money to be sure Kai couldn't say no. "What do you like doing?"

"Doing? Oh, you mean, like, sexually?"

"Duh. Yeah, I like everything, but be careful with your nails. Some douche top scratched me a few months ago. Hurt like a bitch."

Matthew winced. "I can imagine, but shouldn't it be the other way around with us? You're topping, remember?"

Oh, yeah. Kai thought about all the scenes he'd done and tried to compare his role with that of the tops he'd been partnered with. "I like getting my dick sucked. We could do that."

Matthew nodded, thoughtful. "Yeah, and then you could rim me?"

Heat flooded Kai's veins. He loved rimming other guys, but

it had been ages since he'd last had the chance. "What else do you like? Kissing? Scratching? What's your favorite position?"

Matthew shifted on the couch. It didn't escape Kai's notice that he brought his leg up to hide his groin. "I don't know. Sonny said doing it on-screen isn't the same, and I might like different things when there's an audience watching me, but in private I guess I like getting fucked on my stomach."

"Is that a logical guess?"

"Very funny." Matthew slugged Kai hard enough to shove him into the arm of the couch. "What about you?"

"Riding," Kai said without hesitation. "I like being on top and watching the other guy lose it."

"That happen often?"

Kai snickered. "Depends how big his cock is. Sometimes I gotta try real hard not to bust too soon."

"Yeah, I wasn't worried about that until we made out. I figured I could control it. Jon taught me to...shit, never mind. Put it this way, now I'm freaking out about it."

"Don't freak out." Kai leaned closer to Matthew. "Jude's pretty cool. If you come too soon, he'll probably let us do it again."

"And that can't be a bad thing, right?"

"Right." Kai caught himself as he realized he was on the verge of climbing into Matthew's lap. A loaded beat of silence stretched on and on.

Kai swallowed hard. "Uh, what about kink? Got any freaky shit you like?"

Matthew blinked. Behind his glasses, his green eyes looked huge. "Nothing too freaky, but I like teeth and nails. You know when you bite a guy and his dick throbs in your hand? That's so hot."

Kai couldn't believe his luck. This got better and better. "Well, you can bite me anytime. I love it."

"Take your shirt off, then."

Kai didn't need telling twice. He pulled his T-shirt over his head and gestured for Matthew to do the same. Bare-chested, they both stared. They'd seen each other naked many times over, but always from afar in the club, in the crowded backstage dressing room, or on a computer screen. Kai touched one of Matthew's tattoos, the biggest one on his chest, and traced the bright lines of colorful ink. The design looked like a robot with a detachable head. "I like this one."

Matthew raised an eyebrow, cool and calm, but Kai was sure he felt him shudder. "Just that one?"

"Well, no. I like them all, but this one is my favorite." Kai took his opportunity and gave Matthew a gentle shove. He pushed him back on the couch and straddled his lap before he could protest. "Do I get to kiss you again before you bite me?"

Just saying the words had Kai's cock pulsing, but his dirty memories had nothing on the real thing. Matthew answered his question with a brush of his lips, a fleeting, barely-there kiss that sent shock waves down Kai's spine.

Matthew kissed him again, once, twice, three times. "Like that?"

Kai growled. "Don't tease me. I'm the top, remember? I can make you suffer."

"Yeah, but you won't." Matthew slid his hands up Kai's back. "You're gonna make me feel amazing."

I freakin' hope so. The heat of Matthew's body made Kai feel giddy, like the lightest touch would set him on fire, and he couldn't help pushing his ass down on Matthew's groin just a little bit. "So you say. I'm still waiting for you to bite me."

"Won't be any fun if you know it's coming."

Kai exhaled a shaky breath. "Distract me, then."

Easy enough. A deeper kiss was all it took. Kai fell into it face-first, and yeah, tugging on Matthew's lip ring was as much fun as he'd imagined.

Matthew responded with roaming hands, light scratches

and playful pinches. Kai writhed on top of him, until things boiled over and they tumbled to the floor.

Kai hit the carpet with a thump. His breath left his body, but Matthew was on him before he could recover. Kai fought back, laughing, and they rolled together until Kai got his way and took the unfamiliar position of lying on top of Matthew, grinding their cocks together.

They kissed again, a bruising kiss with tongues, and then Matthew made his move. He sank his teeth into the sensitive skin behind Kai's left ear and bit down.

Kai cried out. Every drop of his blood rushed to his dick. "Fuck, yeah. More."

Matthew dug his nails into Kai's back. For a moment, Kai was flying, surging toward the end of something they'd hardly started, then Matthew groaned from somewhere deep in his belly and released Kai's tender flesh. "Man, we gotta stop. I could come right now, but I need to build up some freakin' resilience."

Disappointment warred with the undeniable thrill of putting Matthew on the edge so soon. Kai didn't want to stop, but they should...right?

He laughed, breathless, his heart beating like a train. "Let me blow you. Test you. See how long you last."

Matthew groaned again. "That's not part of the plan. I'm supposed to blow you."

In answer, Kai wriggled down Matthew's body. From that vantage point, he could see the outline of Matthew's cock through his sweatpants. See the heaving rise and fall of his chest. Screw the plan. He was having some of that.

Matthew raised his hips and let Kai tug his sweatpants down. His cock sprang back and slapped his tattooed stomach. Yum. Kai pounced before Matthew could talk them both out of it. He took Matthew in his mouth and sucked him down, long and deep.

"Fuck."

Matthew jerked and let out a surprised gasp. Kai stilled him. He liked it when a guy wriggled beneath him, but he wanted Matthew to really feel him before he lost his shit.

He went to town on Matthew, pulling out all his best tricks. He reckoned he could make Matthew come in just a few minutes, but Matthew held out for a while, his clipped grunts and sweat-slicked skin the only sign of his inner fight for control.

Kai turned up the volume. Matthew moaned, and Kai hummed around his dick. Despite his innocent smile and dirty laugh, Matthew could be a cool customer, but Kai had learned his craft from the best—Cam, Sonny, Levi. These days, Kai liked to think they had nothing on him.

Matthew gave in to the inevitable. He raised his leg and draped it over Kai's shoulder, lifting his hips from the floor. Kai swallowed hard around Matthew's cock and gave his balls a light tug. It was his intention to suck his finger into his mouth and seek out Matthew's prostate, but then Matthew tensed and yanked Kai's hair.

"Oh, man, I'm gonna come already."

Smirking, Kai fought the hold Matthew had on his hair and kept his mouth on Matthew's cock. He wanted to see Matthew's cum face, but the time for that would come later, and despite his confidence, the ache in his own dick was distracting enough to persuade him to stay put.

Not that he needed much persuasion. The jolts and jerks of Matthew's body as he came hard in Kai's mouth felt fucking amazing.

Kai pulled his mouth from Matthew's cock with a messy, wet pop. He met Matthew's glassy gaze. "How's that for control?"

Matthew laughed, languid and lazy. "I'm so fucked."

"That's the plan." Kai crawled up Matthew's body and

dropped his hands either side of his head. "Maybe we should practice that bit again, though."

"You'll have to give me a minute. Take off your pants."

Kai wriggled out of his skinny jeans and underwear and reclaimed his position straddling Matthew's body. His cock lay hot and hard on Matthew's chest. Matthew eyed it. Kai wondered if he could feel it pulsing and thrumming. He took himself in hand and jacked himself slowly. He wanted to come, but though he enjoyed the dominance he'd discovered in himself in recent months, he wasn't quite sure what to do next.

Mathew pried his fingers loose and batted his hand away. "Let me."

Huh. Maybe he didn't have to do anything at all.

Kai rose up and fell back on his hands as Matthew jerked him off. Handjobs had a tendency to become a means to an end…boring, even, but Matthew's touch, hesitant and testing, made his eyes roll. "Yeah, like that."

Matthew grew in confidence with every stroke. He brought Kai to the edge with a gentle twist of his wrist and held him there, teasing him with a brief falter in rhythm. Then he dug his nails into the soft flesh at the top of Kai's thigh, and Kai was undone.

Kai came with a low moan and spilled onto Matthew's pale, heaving chest. He stared at the mess he'd made. He usually found himself on the receiving end of a cum shot, but there was something crazy-hot about seeing himself painted all over Matthew. "What now?"

"Um, kiss me?"

Why not? Kai leaned down and kissed Matthew, smooshing the stickiness and sweat between them. They kissed until they ran out of air, then Kai pulled away with a reluctant grin. "It's late. I should probably go."

He rose onto his knees. Matthew wriggled out from beneath him. "Hang on. I'll get a towel."

Matthew darted to the bathroom and came back with a damp towel. They both cleaned up, then Kai looked around for his clothes while Matthew pulled on his sweats.

Commando. I like it.

"Can I tell you something?"

Kai glanced up from shimmying into his jeans. Sweat-dampened skin made the task trickier than shucking them in a lust-filled haze had been. "Sure."

"Including Jon, I've only been with, like, four guys."

Kai shrugged. "So?"

Matthew chewed on his bottom lip. "So nothing. I just figured you might be wondering why I suck at being cool and keeping myself in check. Do you think it will show on-screen?"

Kai buttoned his jeans with undue care. He and Matthew were close in age, but Kai suddenly felt older...way older. Since when had he become the one with all the answers? "Porn viewers see what they want to see. You shouldn't worry about that."

"You don't think I'm a dork?"

"What? No. I've lost count of the guys I've been with. Do you think I'm a whore?"

"No." Matthew frowned. "Why would I think that?"

"Exactly." Kai pulled his shirt over his head. "Numbers don't mean anything unless you let them."

The answer Kai had stolen from Sonny seemed to reassure Matthew a little, and the soft kiss that followed finished the job.

Man, this guy is too cute.

"So, I guess I'll see you tomorrow sometime?"

Matthew shook his head. "Actually, no. I've got classes all day, and then I have a study session with my class group. I'll see you the day after, though? At the club?"

"At the club?" Kai was surprised. Though they both danced a pretty heavy schedule, they rarely crossed paths at Silver.

Matthew danced the early slots and didn't often linger to party, and Kai danced late and partied all night long.

"Yeah, I'm pulling the midnight slot on Friday. I have an evening seminar across town, so I can't get to the club till late. Who knows? Maybe we'll be on the same stage?"

I'm so fucked.

CHAPTER EIGHT

Yep. Definitely fucked. Kai stared at the podium schedule, half-thrilled, half-terrified. Friday nights usually found him writhing around a pole with Sonny or Zeb, and partying until the sun came up. But not tonight. No. Tonight Matthew's self-fulfilling prophecy had come true, and at the stroke of midnight they'd be dancing on the middle podium...together.

Kai wasn't sure how he felt about that. For the first time in two weeks, he'd spent twenty-four hours away from Matthew, and his regained perspective was starting to scare him. Topping? Studying? Lying awake at night, fantasizing about a guy not that much bigger than him? Damn. What the hell had happened to his die-hard crush on Levi Ramone? These days Kai couldn't close his eyes at night without seeing Matthew's flawless inked-up skin.

"You're early."

Kai jumped and spun around. Jude was behind him, peering at the screen of the cash register on the main bar. "It's not that early."

"It's seven o'clock, Kai. You're not due on stage for five hours."

Oh. Kai hadn't checked the time when he'd abandoned his

apartment to escape the growing stench in the living room. He'd never been much of a stoner, and he couldn't dance right with a weed-muggy head. Silver was safe, quiet, and warm...until the DJ got there, at least.

"Everything okay?"

"Uh-huh." Kai drifted closer to the bar and sat down in a stool. Belatedly, he wondered why Jude was even there. He and Mac didn't spend much time at Silver, preferring to leave managing of the club to Bull, the pint-sized manager. Of the two of them, Mac was there more, and he'd been the one running the club while Bull was on vacation. "Is Mac here?"

"Nope. He was feeling his age this morning, so I figured I'd give him a night off."

"How old is Mac?"

Jude glanced up from the screen, his dark blue gaze dancing with amusement. "Thirty-nine, but don't tell him I told you. He's been that age for a while."

That made sense. Mac and Jude both had short hair and salt-and-pepper beards, but each of them had a glow that came with a good life, and Kai reckoned they'd both age like fine wine.

Yikes. I don't even like wine.

Jude slid a bottle of soda across the bar. "How's the studying going?"

"Okay, I guess." Kai took a pull on the soda bottle. "The essay part's gonna suck, though."

"Maybe, but it's only one, right? After that, you never have to write an essay ever again."

Kai grumbled under his breath. He didn't see why he had to write one at all. Did it help him dance, or look good on camera? Fuck, no. It just gave him a cramp in his wrist for all the wrong reasons.

Jude fell silent for a while. Kai slumped on the bar and closed his eyes. Chances were, he'd be up all night, and his apartment building had been noisy all day. He was drifting into a Matthew-filled doze when Jude shook his shoulder.

"You can't sleep here, Kai. Go lie down in the office if you want."

"I'm not sleeping." Kai huffed and sat up, though he had to wonder if Jude knew how often Bull let him catch a nap in Silver's basement office.

"Have you spoken to Matthew today?"

"Nope."

Jude rolled his eyes. "Gonna be interesting to see you hit that stage together. If I get a chance, I might shoot some stills of you."

Kai nodded absently. He'd noticed Jude took more photographs than Jon ever had, but only a few made it through his scrupulous editing process. "Matthew's never danced the late slot. I think he might turn into a pumpkin."

Jude snorted. "Maybe, but his scheduling conflict did us a favor. Zeb's on vacation and James is sick. You'd get kinda lonely up there on your own."

It was true. Kai had danced alone in the cages at the back of the club before, but he didn't like them. He needed the heated flesh of another guy to really get going, and on a Friday night that flesh usually belonged to someone in particular. "What about Sonny?"

"He's taking the early slot."

"Huh?" What the fuck? Sonny was the hottest dancer in town. He never danced early. "Has he got exams or something?"

Jude didn't seem to hear the question. He studied something on the computer screen. "Damned freaky computer shit. How the fuck does Mac understand this crap?"

Kai leaned over the bar. "What are you trying to do?"

"Load the cash register. Any ideas?"

Kai slithered over the bar, peered over Jude's broad shoulder, and clicked a few buttons. He knew the club's system from his bar shifts, and he'd often watched Bull set up. "There you go."

"Well look at that." Jude still seemed bemused. "Photoshop and my cell phone are about my limit. Thanks, kid. Here you go. Get yourself some dinner before you start work."

Jude pulled a twenty out of his back pocket. Kai took it and folded it into tiny pieces. He'd be lying if he said he wasn't hungry, and he'd spent most of his tips on the best pair of underwear before he'd realized Tag hadn't paid the cable bill. "Do you want me to set up the rest of the bar first?"

"I'm good, thanks. Eat, then go make yourself pretty."

Kai hopped back over the bar. "I am pretty, Jude."

Later that night found Kai on stage way earlier than he'd planned. Sonny hadn't showed for his slot, and seeing as Kai was already there, filling in for him was a no-brainer. Kai danced into the dressing room at ten p.m. hot, sweaty, and in need of a shower before he hit the stage again in two hours' time.

He walked right into Sonny, who looked like he'd just arrived. "Hey. Thought you were a no-show."

Sonny grinned and dumped his bag on the counter. "Nope. I'm here, bright and early."

"You're two hours late."

"Early for me, then. Is Bull mad?"

Kai looked on as Sonny bounced on the balls of his feet and set his stuff out on the counter at a million miles an hour. He felt lazy just watching him. Sometimes, Sonny moved so fast Kai couldn't keep up. "Bull's not here, remember? Jude is."

"Jude?" Sonny winced. "Damn. He was already mad at me."

Sonny didn't seem worried, but then, he never did. Sonny

was like a unicorn...a mythical creature in his own graceful world. Even the glare Jude sent his way when he stuck his head around the door didn't faze him.

Jude narrowed his eyes. "What time do you call this?"

"Sorry," Sonny said, though he didn't seem contrite. "Stuck in traffic."

Jude eyed him a moment, and Kai fought the urge to hide behind the lockers. Jude had way more presence than Jon ever had. "Do you want to dance tonight, or not?"

"I'm here, aren't I?"

"Yeah? Doesn't look that way to me. Get yourself together, kid. Be ready in five, or go home."

Jude left. His warning had been firm but fair, and it worked. Sonny looked rattled, like he'd fallen out the wrong side of bed and hit the ground running.

Kai sidled over to him and gave him a hug. "I've got some orange chicken left. Do you want some?"

"No, thanks." Sonny returned Kai's embrace, but his expression changed to one Kai didn't quite understand. "Levi force-fed me quesadillas when I woke up."

"Aw. He's a big sweetie, really, huh?"

Sonny hummed an absent answer, stepped out of Kai's arms, and drifted to his locker. Kai felt suddenly sad, though he couldn't say why. Sonny had always been kind to him, and though Sonny had just an inch on him in height, Kai looked up to him, as a colleague and a friend. But something wasn't right. Sonny was changing, day by day, week by week. The light in his eyes was fading, and his boundless energy seemed forced, and rough around the edges.

Kai eyed the Jude-funded take-out box he'd left on the counter. "Are you sure you don't want any food?"

Sonny shut his locker with a bang. "I'm good, babe, honest. But can I borrow that glitter shit for my eyes? I look like a crack whore."

Crack whore or not, Sonny was beautiful, and with a little help from Kai's box of tricks, he bounded onto the biggest stage with his sparkle restored. Kai watched him dance for a while, watched him own the crowd like no other dancer ever could, but eventually tore himself away and went back to the dressing room to get ready for round two.

Matthew was waiting for him when he came back from the shower, fresh and clean. "Hey, Kai."

"Hi."

Matthew pulled his T-shirt over his head. Kai had seen his slim, tattooed torso in his dreams, but for some reason he had to look away. "How was your geek thing?"

"The seminar? It was as exciting as it sounds. How about you? Good day?"

Kai shrugged. His encounters with Matthew often started out this way, stilted and tense, like their fast-growing sexual attraction needed to be tempered somehow. "Sonny was late, so I danced the early slot. It's pretty kicking out there."

Matthew rubbed his face. "I better liven my ass up, then. Can you get me a Red Bull from the bar?"

Kai slipped out of the dressing room and grabbed Matthew's pick-me-up. Matthew was undressed by the time he got back, and standing in front of the mirror in a shiny pair of black underwear. Kai stripped his sweatpants and stood next to him in his own sparkly silver hotpants. With their contrasting hair and skin, they looked like night and day.

Jude put his head around the door. "Come on, kids. Let's go."

Matthew chugged some of his energy drink and wiped his mouth with the back of his hand. He didn't acknowledge Jude's brief presence, and his gaze never left Kai's in the mirror. "Nice," he said softly. "Are you ready?"

Kai took a deep breath. He'd danced at Silver more times

than he could count, but tonight, with Matthew, it felt like the first time all over again. "Let's go."

They made their way along the dark corridor to the stage. Matthew shivered. On instinct, Kai walked closer behind him and rubbed his arms. "Won't take long to warm up out there."

"Oh, I know."

Matthew threw a smirk over his shoulder, reached back and grabbed Kai's hand. A thrill ran through Kai. There was no one around to start the show early for. Matthew's gesture was all for Kai. Kai squeezed Matthew's hand. Matthew squeezed back, and it felt fucking amazing.

They passed Jude at the stage door. He flashed them a wink that belied the irritation—Sonny-induced, no doubt—in his gaze. "Knock 'em dead."

Matthew slowed a moment to fire his empty can into a nearby trash bin. Kai took the lead and started up the steps to the podium.

"Hey, Kai?"

Kai turned, one foot on the stage. Matthew grabbed him and kissed him. "I missed you yesterday."

He slipped by Kai without waiting for an answer and danced out onto the stage.

Smoke machines. Sweat. Deep, vibrating bass. Strobe lights. Neon paint. Kai spun around the pole and arched his body into his favorite 'dragon' pose. He held the position a moment, waiting for Matthew to dance past him; then he whirled around the pole and landed on the balls of his feet.

Matthew caught him. He pressed himself against Kai's back, grazed his lips along Kai's exposed neck, but all too soon, he danced away.

Kai followed with a rueful smirk. They'd been playing this

game since they'd come on stage. Matthew wasn't the best dancer at Silver, and his pole skills were basic, but he'd tied Kai in knots with a single kiss and now he was playing him...playing him hard, much to the delight of the baying crowd.

If only they knew.

Kai dug deep into his repertoire. His pole moves were self-taught, with a dash of Sonny's mastery, and he knew he was good. He caught up with Matthew and wound his arms around his waist. Bare but for their contrasting underwear, the heat of Matthew's skin sizzled against Kai. A few times, he'd caught himself looking down, sure he'd see smoking wounds where they'd touched, but instead he found sweat-slicked skin smeared in ultraviolet paint. Fingerprints and nail tracks.

He put his lips to the hollow behind Matthew's ear. His cock fit perfectly between the curved muscles of Matthew's ass, like it was meant to be there. Matthew raised his arms and found Kai's hair with his hands. He tugged, still moving in time with the music.

Heat shot through Kai and mingled with the sweetest pain. He let his hands roam over Matthew's chest until he reached his throat. He hesitated, and Matthew made his move first. Matthew sucked Kai's finger into his mouth and rolled his hips in a slow circle. Kai closed his eyes, letting the heavy baseline merge with the crazy-hot sensation of Matthew's tongue, and together they touched every part of him.

Without warning, Matthew wriggled from his arms and danced away. He shot Kai a wicked smirk...a smirk that did nothing to help the growing lack of space in Kai's underwear.

Kai moved back to the pole. He liked this side of Matthew, playful and hot. He was right there in front of Kai but somehow remained elusive. Kai put his hands on the pole, raised himself into an inverted Marchenko pose. It was an extreme position, and not one Kai could hold for long, but when he lowered himself, spun back around the pole, and met Matthew's wide-eyed gaze, he knew his work was done.

It's on, baby.

Kai beckoned Matthew to him and pushed him into the pole, his arm around his throat in a loose choke hold. He bared his teeth at Matthew's neck, felt his groan rumble through him over the wicked thrum of the music. For a moment the club faded away, and it was just the two of them, alone, but for the thick fog of attraction between them. For the first time, Kai felt a real, raw desire to slide inside Matthew and make him his own.

I want to fuck him.

Kai wondered what it would feel like, wondered if his dick would cope with Matthew's heat closing in around him, or if it would all prove too much and he would be the one busting out early.

He tightened his hold on Matthew. The crowd hooted and whistled their approval. Crumpled bills showered the stage. Something hit Kai from behind. Rolled-up bank notes, or perhaps a toy of some kind. Die-hard fans loved to throw dildos on stage, a convention Kai thoroughly enjoyed when they were brand-new and boxed.

The music eased down a notch. Kai released Matthew. Kissed his cheek, and stepped away. They stared at each other for a long moment. Beneath the flickering spotlights, Matthew's chest heaved, and his eyes blazed. There was a hunger in his gaze, a hunger Kai felt deep in his own bones.

He held out his hand. Matthew mirrored the gesture and stepped forward, but a shout caught their shared attention. Among the shouts and catcalls, something stood out. Kai looked over his shoulder. A bottle crashed into his head and sent him tumbling over the side of the stage.

CHAPTER NINE

Kai hit the sticky club floor with a sickening thud. His shoulder took the impact, but the jarring pain was obliterated by the stars blurring his vision. Black, white, gray. Most of Silver's interior was blue, and the lights were colorful and bright, but Kai saw nothing but the misty snow he remembered on his grandfather's archaic TV.

Then it changed. The lights of the club forced their way through and reality hit. A bottle had slammed into his head—beer, he could smell it—and he'd fallen six feet from the highest stage in the club.

Kai groaned. The left side of his body throbbed like a bitch and something warm and wet dripped from his chin. Blood. *Fuck. I'm gonna puke.* Kai had never been good with blood. He forced himself into a sitting position and glanced to his left. He'd landed in a dark corner, but already he could hear someone shouting his name and footsteps fast approaching. He worried they'd trample right over him. His good arm wobbled, but before he could slump back to the floor, strong hands scooped him up.

"Easy, kid. I've got you."

Jude.

Jude lifted Kai from the hard ground. The world spun. Kai heard the chaos of whatever was going down in the club, but it faded, slowly, along with the flashing lights, and before Kai could blink, he found himself on the couch of the basement office.

Jude held his face. "Kai? Come on, kid. You with me?"

Kai blinked a few times. His eyelids felt sticky with blood. "My face. Is my face okay? Did it cut my face?"

"Your face is fine." Jude put two fingers under Kai's chin. "The blood is coming from your head. Something hit you."

"It was a bottle, Jude. I can smell the fucking beer." Kai heard his voice rise an octave, and he shivered. The office held none of the heat of the club and...oh, God. Matthew. "Where's Matthew? Did it hit him too?"

Jude spoke quickly over his shoulder. Someone Kai couldn't see murmured an answer, before Jude turned back to him. "Take it easy. I saw you fall and grabbed you before you got mobbed. Last I saw Matthew was safe on stage, but we'll find him, okay?"

Kai nodded and shivered again. Damn, he was cold.

"You're gonna need stitches in your head, but what about the rest of you? You came down pretty hard. Do I need to call the paramedics?"

Kai tested his body. His head felt strangely numb, but his shoulder throbbed and seemed to be getting worse with every breath he took. "My shoulder hurts."

Jude coaxed him forward and touched his stinging skin with gentle fingers. "I probably shouldn't have moved you. Are you sure nothing else hurts?"

"I'm fine. Can I go home?"

"Hospital first. I'll drive you."

Jude's tone was firm and left no room for argument. He lifted Kai from the couch and cradled him against his broad chest.

Jude carried him through the dark corridors of the club and out onto the street. The cool November air hit Kai's bare skin, but he was wrapped in something warm and bundled into the front seat of a car before he could blink.

Then the world stopped. Kai could hear Jude's voice but couldn't make out any words. He slipped into a daze until Matthew wrenched the car door open.

"Kai! Oh my God, Kai. Are you okay?"

Kai stared. His vision was clouded by blood, but Matthew's face was sharp with lines of worry. "I cut my head."

Matthew's frown deepened. "I've got your clothes. Can you put them on?"

It took Kai a moment to comprehend what Matthew meant, but with a little help from Matthew he managed to pull a T-shirt over his head and slip one arm into its sleeve. Skinny jeans followed. Kai left them undone.

Matthew put his hands on Kai's shoulders and guided him back into the car. "The cops want to talk to me. Jude's going to take you to the hospital. Call me, okay? I'll find you."

Kai nodded. He felt more human with his clothes on, which was odd, because most days he didn't truly feel alive until he was prancing on a stage in his underwear. "Did you see Sonny? Is he okay?"

Jude slid into the driver seat. "Sonny split right after he came off stage. Mac's on his way to make sure everyone else gets home okay."

The car purred to life. Matthew hesitated, like he wanted to say so much more, but then someone called his name from behind and the moment passed. He shut the car door, and Jude drove away.

Kai curled against Jude's chest. Jude had carried him into the hospital and held him in his lap while they'd waited to be seen. Kai had left the safety of his arms for an examination, an X-ray, and a small row of stitches in his hairline, but he'd unashamedly crawled right back into them as soon as the nurse had left them with a pile of paperwork.

Jude's shirt was soaked in Kai's blood and tears, but he didn't seem to mind. He coached Kai through his insurance forms and then sat quietly while they waited for the doctor to come back and discharge him.

"Sorry I snot-cried on you."

Jude chuckled. "I'm cool with bodily fluids, kid. I'm just glad you weren't more badly hurt."

Kai made a noise of discontent. The doctor had said he'd been lucky to get away with bad bruising and a few stitches, but fuck, it hurt. He wasn't looking forward to schlepping all the way back to his apartment and crawling into his lumpy single bed.

"It was going pretty well until then, though, huh? You and Matthew looked great together, and you blew me away with those moves on the pole. I didn't know you were so strong."

Kai sat up a little. He'd forgotten it was probably the first time Jude had seen him perform, and he had pulled out his best moves. "I did Bikram yoga with Sonny all summer."

Jude smiled, and seemed far gentler than Kai had ever seen him. "So Sonny can commit to something, huh?"

Kai opened his mouth to respond, though to say what he wasn't quite sure. It was clear Jude had Sonny in his sights, and not in a good way. But he was saved by the bell, or rather the swish of the curtain being pulled back by a stern-faced doctor.

Discharge time.

The doctor was brisk and thorough. It was Friday night in the emergency room, and despite listening to Kai's story in patient silence, it was clear the doctor had classed his injuries as pretty much self-inflicted. Kai wondered just how brisk the dude would've been without Jude's hulking presence.

"The head wound is superficial. There's no swelling around the cut, but someone should keep an eye on you for a day or so. Do you live with someone?"

"Kind of..."

Kai let it hang. If his roommates were around at all, the chances of them noticing Kai had dropped dead were slim.

"We'll take care of him."

Kai glanced at Jude. "I'll be okay."

"Uh-huh."

The doctor ignored their exchange and peered at Kai's bruised shoulder. "That's going to ache for a while, and it will probably turn a nasty color. Ice it, and take ibuprofen for the pain."

And that, it seemed, was that. The doctor left, and it was time to go home. Apprehensive, Kai gazed down at the floor. Jude had carried him everywhere since he'd fallen from the stage, and he was tired now...bone tired, like he'd be dead on his feet the moment they hit the floor.

Jude appeared in front of him. He wrapped the blanket they'd brought from the club around Kai's shoulders and offered his arms. "Come on. We've made it this far."

Being carried through the hospital by Jude didn't feel weird, even as Kai's faculties returned to him. He felt safe and warm, and he almost cried again when Jude set him down in the waiting area.

"Stay put a moment. I'll bring the car around."

Kai gazed around. The ER was one of the better ones in the city, but it was still four a.m. at the start of the weekend. The waiting area was packed. Don't leave me. "Okay."

"Sure? We can—"

"Jude!" Large arms tackled Jude from the side. Mac. He

enveloped Jude in a fierce hug before he dropped down to Kai. "Aw, shit, kiddo. Let me take a look at you."

Mac tilted Kai's head to inspect the damage. Kai's bottom lip trembled. *Damn it. Stop fucking crying.*

"The cops are all over the club," Mac said, glancing up at Jude. "They took statements from everyone and the data from the surveillance cameras. They'll come after Kai in the morning, but they want to talk to you tonight."

"It is morning." Jude looked pissed. "And I didn't see jack. What about the others? Anyone see anything useful?"

Mac's gaze darkened. He took his hands from Kai and straightened up. "No one saw much before the bottle hit Kai, but some people heard..."

"Heard what? Don't be fucking coy with me now, Mac."

"Faggot. They called me a faggot."

Mac and Jude both cut their gazes to Kai in perfect synchrony. "Are you sure?" Jude asked. "Because if that's true, we're looking at something far more serious than some trashed jackass chucking bottles around."

Kai thought hard, and shook his head. "I'm not positive, but I heard something that bothered me just before the bottle hit me."

Mac growled. "Fucking hate crime in our own fucking club? Are you kidding me?"

Kai flinched, though he knew Mac's anger wasn't for him. "I don't know. I'm not sure. I'm sorry."

Jude reached out to calm both of them. "None of us know anything for sure. Mac, can you go to the drugstore and get Kai some Advil?"

Mac pursed his lips, clenched his fists at his sides. Kai felt the fury seeping out of him. He'd always been more intimidated by Jude, but angry Mac? Bearded and seething? Biceps bulging? Yeah, he was pretty fucking scary. Kai trembled and let out a sound that cut through the simmering tension. He slapped his hand over his mouth, but Mac's expression softened, and he dropped into the seat beside Kai and coaxed him into a careful, one-armed hug.

"Hey, kiddo. Come on. You're safe now, okay? I'm just freaking out 'cause you two look like the walking dead, all busted up and bloody."

Kai looked down at his stained shirt. Mac was right. Between him and Jude, they looked like a horror movie. "Oh, man. That's gross. I need to take this off."

Mac laughed. "Here, take mine. It'll drown you, but it should keep you warm."

Mac shucked his jacket and stripped off his T-shirt. His bare furred chest earned them some curious glances. Neither Mac nor Jude seemed to notice, but Kai hesitated and fingered the hem of his own ruined shirt. No fucker was going to heckle Mac, but...

Jude pointed to the restroom. "Go change in there. We'll watch the door."

Okay then. Kai put his feet to the test and shuffled off to the bathroom. It was empty—thank God—and once he'd swamped himself in Mac's huge shirt, he took a moment to look in the mirror and assess the carnage for himself.

He was a little underwhelmed. Despite the stomach-turning spilled blood, the cut on his head was tiny, an inch long, if that, and held together by four tiny stitches. The stark patch of shaved hair hurt more. What the hell am I supposed to do with that?

Kai wet a paper towel and made a halfhearted attempt at wiping the dried blood from his neck. A nurse had cleaned his face before they'd stitched him up, but the rest of him was a mess, and even without the gory blood, he looked like hell. His skin was pale and his eyes sunken and red. Kai gave up trying to make it better and left the solitude of the bathroom to return to the noisy waiting area.

He found Jude alone, guarding Kai's chair and the folded-up blanket. "Where's Mac?"

"Drugstore."

"Without his shirt?"

"Yep."

Kai sat down. His adventure to the restroom had worn him out. "Is he still mad?"

"He's just pissed he wasn't there."

"What about you?"

Jude looked down at Kai, and for the first time since he'd scooped him from the floor of the club, Kai saw real rage flicker in his gaze. "I'm spitting blood, Kai, but I've learned the hard way to keep my temper to myself. I'm not like Mac... I don't yell a bit, then calm myself down. I lash out, usually at the wrong people, so I've learned to rein myself in."

Kai absorbed that. He could tell there was something about Jude, something real fucking important, he didn't know. Beneath the caring warmth Kai had felt from him tonight, Jude carried a darkness...like Sonny...maybe. Kai shuddered. *Huh.* Maybe he was better off not knowing.

Jude touched his good shoulder. "Don't worry about anything but healing, okay? We'll take care of the rest."

Mac reappeared, still half-dressed, and tossed a paper bag Kai's way. "There's some security douche giving me the stink-eye. We'd better split before I get arrested."

Jude nodded. "Kai needs a place to stay. Gotta keep an eye on him."

"We've got room for a little one."

"You don't have to take me home with you." Kai wrapped his arms around himself. There was room enough for three of him in Mac's shirt. "I'm fine."

"We know that," Jude said. "We just want to be sure. The doctor said you shouldn't be on your own."

Kai noted how quickly Jude slipped into 'we' when Mac

was around. He liked that. It made the distant pain in Jude's eyes fade, like it had never been there at all.

Man, they really love each other.

Kai considered his options. Jude and Mac made him feel safer than he'd ever felt in his life, but did he want to spend the next twenty-four hours with them? Watching them remind him how he had fucking nobody to look at him the way they did at each other? Nobody who'd even notice he'd had his head caved in?

Mac sensed his mutiny. "Kai..."

"He can stay with me."

The voice came from somewhere behind them all. Kai spun around, and beyond Mac's hulking frame stood Matthew, Kai's bag in one hand, his cell phone in the other.

"Come home with me, Kai. I'll take care of you."

CHAPTER TEN

Morning came like a sledgehammer. Kai woke up in a strange bed, sore, stiff, and in desperate need of a piss. The only trouble was he couldn't quite bring himself to leave the soothing heat of the body he'd cuddled up to while he slept.

He opened his eyes. Matthew's bare back greeted him, and the pain coursing through his body faded from an inferno to a mild flicker. He cuddled closer and put his chin on Matthew's shoulder. He loved sharing a bed, sleeping curled up in the comforting warmth of someone else, but it had been ages since he'd had the chance. The last guy he'd slept with had been Sonny, but Sonny hadn't stayed in the bed. Kai had woken alone a few hours later and found Sonny dancing around his apartment in a world of his own.

Kai absorbed Matthew's by now familiar smell. Breathed him in. They hadn't talked much after Jude dropped them off. Instead Matthew had taken Kai into his bathroom, pulled off his borrowed shirt, and gently cleaned the blood from his skin. After that, it had seemed only natural to fall into Matthew's bed and hold each other until they both fell asleep.

And it still felt natural, apart from the agony of Kai's throbbing shoulder and head, and the persistent ache in his bladder.

With a reluctant sigh, Kai shifted away from Matthew and rolled awkwardly from the safety of the bed. He staggered to the bathroom and relieved himself. With that done, he used the toothbrush Jude had bought him on the way home and searched out his paper bag of pain pills. He palmed a handful and swallowed them down with a slug of water from the tap. The urge to stare at his ghoulish reflection in the mirror was strong, but he ignored it and drifted back to Matthew's bed.

In Kai's absence, Matthew had rolled onto his stomach and wrapped his arms around a pillow. He looked so peaceful. Beautiful. Kai bit his lip and considered leaving him, going home like he probably should've done all along, but he found himself crawling back under the covers before the thought gained any traction.

He lay on his good side and stared over Matthew's sleeping form, taking in Matthew's room with its calm, quiet order, punctuated only by geeky comic book posters. Matthew's neatness was a balm to Kai's soul, and the posters made him smile. *Hottest nerd I've ever seen.*

Kai shifted. A shot of pain made him wince. He closed his eyes, hoping sleep would distract him until the pills kicked in, but a cell phone—his—rang somewhere in the bed. Kai felt around for it, trying not to jostle Matthew in the process. He found it jammed between the mattress and the bed frame. Mac's number flashed up on the screen as Matthew's sleepy eyes flickered open.

Kai pressed the speaker button, put the phone on the pillow, and took Matthew's outstretched hands. "Hey, Mac."

"How you doing, kiddo?"

"I'm okay."

Mac chuckled. "How did I know you were going to say that? How's the head? Any dizziness or weird shit when you got up?"

"I didn't get up yet."

There was a rustling noise on Mac's end of the line, then Mac sighed. "I'm jealous. Some of us never got to bed."

"What about Jude?"

"Jude's at the club dealing with the cops," Mac said. "Someone sprayed a bunch of graffiti all over the back wall."

Kai studied Matthew's hands. In contrast to his groomed, toned body, his nails were bitten down to the quick. "What kind of graffiti?"

"Not the kind I want to talk about, but listen to me, Kai. Whatever went down last night wasn't just some jackass throwing a bottle. We need to take it seriously and do what we can to make sure it doesn't happen again."

Kai frowned, and chewed on his lip. Even with the dark bruise spreading down his shoulder, he'd somehow managed to put its origins to the back of his mind.

Hey, faggot.

Fuck. Suddenly, Kai hated Mac for invading his bubble of warmth.

Shame Mac didn't care. "The cops need your statement, Kai. I'm going to swing by Matthew's place this afternoon and take you down the precinct, okay?"

Kai made a face. Matthew's bed was way too comfortable to contemplate leaving, especially to face a station full of hard-faced cops.

Matthew rolled his eyes. "What time do you want him, boss?"

"I'll come by around four." Mac's tone was dry, like he'd expected Matthew to chime in all along.

Crap. He knows we're in bed together.

"He'll be ready." Matthew ended the call with a jab of his thumb. He put his hand on Kai's chest. "You okay? You're shaking."

"Am I?" Kai rolled onto his back. The pain pills had kicked in while he'd been distracted by Mac, but the gravity of what had happened scared the crap out of him. If they weren't safe from haters in Silver, where the fuck were they supposed to go? "Did you see who threw the bottle?"

Matthew shook his head. "I didn't see anything. I heard some dude shout, then the next thing I knew security grabbed me and hustled me back to the dressing room. I thought they'd taken you out the front. I didn't know you'd been hit until the cops turned up."

Kai let his eyes fall closed. The aftermath in the club was a bit of a blur. All he remembered was the crack of the bottle hitting his head and the sanctuary of Jude's chest. "I'm glad it didn't hit you too."

The bed sheets rustled. Matthew touched Kai's face and kissed his cheek. "Me too. Now go back to sleep."

A terrified scream woke Kai sometime later. He raised his head and followed the source of the noise to the TV. "The Walking Dead?"

Matthew glanced down from where he was sat up against the headboard. "You're awake."

"Just about." Kai wrestled himself upright and accepted Matthew's proffered bottle of Mountain Dew. "What time is it?"

"Noon. Do you want something to eat?"

"What have you got?"

"Doughnut holes." Matthew grabbed a box from his nightstand. "And Twinkies."

Kai bypassed the Twinkies and stuffed a doughnut hole into his mouth. His head had cleared while he'd slept, and he was starving. "Thanks."

"Have some more." Matthew pushed another piece of sweet

pastry into Kai's mouth and waved another threateningly. "Want some cereal too?"

Kai giggled and swallowed. "Are you trying to fatten me up?"

"Maybe." Matthew popped the brandished doughnut into his own mouth. "Jude called while you were asleep. He said to make sure you ate."

"Jude called?" Kai made a halfhearted attempt at brushing powdered sugar from the bed sheets. "I think I dreamed about him."

Matthew raised an eyebrow.

Kai scowled. "Not like that. What did he say?"

"Not much. He sounded pretty stressed, but he said to call him if you need anything."

Kai lay back down and eyed the TV screen. The Walking Dead was his favorite show, but he was way behind on season three, and by the looks of it, he'd missed a lot. "Merle's back with the group?"

"For now. You watch this show?"

"When I can, but I don't have a TiVo box anymore. My roommate spilled a beer bong on it. What episode is this? I think I've only watched up to five."

"This is eleven, but I have all the ones before. Want to watch it from the beginning?"

Hell yeah. Kai ran to the bathroom while Matthew set it up. When he got back, Matthew held up the comforter for him and Kai slotted right in and put his chin on Matthew's chest. He loved cuddling, and the ever-present heat between him and Matthew made it even better.

Matthew draped his arm around Kai. His hand found its way to Kai's head and the sensation of him running his fingers through Kai's hair was nearly enough to send Kai right back to sleep.

Nearly. His dick kept him awake.

They watched the show in companionable quiet for a while. Kai had never been into science fiction, but zombies got under his skin. He knew it was only makeup, but that didn't stop him cringing against Matthew every time one of them got too close to a human character. With a raging boner, it was an interesting combination.

They were on their third episode when Matthew broke the silence. "Rick is so hot."

"Really?" Kai wrinkled his nose. "I like Daryl, but they're all so dirty."

"So would you be if you hadn't showered for six months."

Matthew stretched his arms over his head and yawned. The motion jostled Kai's head, but he didn't mind. It was time he moved anyway. He sat up and touched the cut on his head with tentative fingertips. The wound itched and stung a bit, but otherwise, he could hardly feel it. His shoulder hurt more.

Matthew rolled out of the bed and came to stand in front of Kai. He took Kai's chin and peered at him. "What are you going to do with your hair?"

Kai tugged a curly lock straight and let it spring back. He'd considered shaving the whole lot off, but he was too pale and slender for that. People would think he was a dope fiend. "I don't know. Is it really noticeable?"

"Depends what side you're looking from." Matthew stood back and scrutinized Kai from different angles. "What about an undercut?"

"Really?"

Matthew nodded. "Shave it underneath but keep this side long so it covers your scar while the rest of it grows back."

Interesting. Kai went to the bathroom with Matthew in tow. He stared at himself in the mirror, parting his hair this way and that. "Do you have a shaver?"

"Uh-huh." Matthew opened a drawer in the bathroom counter. "Do you want me to do it?"

Kai hesitated only a moment. His hair was his baby, but he knew from the conversations they'd had over the past few weeks that Matthew cut his own hair, and Matthew's ink dark locks were just about perfect.

Kai stood stock still with his eyes closed as Matthew buzzed the shaver over his scalp. He felt like he heard every strand hit the tiled floor, but of course, he didn't, and it wasn't long before he heard the shaver shut off.

Matthew touched his bare back, right between his shoulder blades. "All done."

Kai opened one eye a fraction. Squinted through his lashes. He liked what he saw, kind of. Liked it enough to open both eyes. He touched the back of his head, feeling the short brush of fine stubble Matthew had left behind. With the longer hair on the top of his head flopped just so, the gash in his head was undetectable. "Ooh, I like that."

Matthew grinned. "Really?"

"Really." Kai considered his own reflection. "Can I borrow your glasses?"

Matthew shot him a quizzical look but left the bathroom without comment. He was back in a flash and handed Kai his dark-rimmed glasses. Kai slipped them on, and the effect was instant. Half-nude, bruised, and with his brand-new hair, he looked like a roughed-up, porn-star hipster.

Every cloud.

Behind him, Matthew coughed and swallowed hard, his voice tight and strained. "Dude, you need to come back to bed, like, now."

Kai didn't need telling twice. He held out his hand and let Matthew lead him back to the bedroom. They stopped at the foot of the bed and kissed. Kai swayed on his feet. Kissing Matthew was easy. Touching him. Smelling him. Breathing him in. Containing the heat that exploded between them was harder, and as they tumbled onto Matthew's bed, Kai let out a grunt of discomfort.

"Oops." Matthew rolled over and pulled Kai on top of him to relieve the pressure on his tender shoulder. His lips were on Kai again in a flash, and his hands were everywhere.

Kai arched under the nails raking down his back and fell headlong into everything that came with kissing Matthew. The thump of his heart. The heady rush of his blood in his ears. The sizzle of skin as their bare chests pressed together. Kai had slept in borrowed sweatpants that smelled of Matthew, and Matthew in thin sleep pants, and it didn't take long for them to shed their clothes and be totally naked together for the very first time. No half-assed stripping, sparkly underwear, or jeans tangled around their ankles.

Wow. The pain in Kai's shoulder faded away. He broke the kiss and gazed down at Matthew, at his neat, compact body, so perfectly formed. He traced his fingertips down Matthew's abdomen. Man, I love his abs.

Matthew shivered, like a live wire connected them. "This is crazy. I feel like I'm gonna explode."

Kai licked his lips. He felt the same, but if he was going to have any hope of keeping his composure, he couldn't let Matthew know how deeply he affected him. "How do you want me to fuck you? On camera, I mean."

Something flickered in Matthew's gaze, brief and dark, but it was gone before Kai found his tongue. Matthew shot him a devilish smirk and rolled over. "I told you. Like this."

Kai gulped. He loved getting fucked from behind, but it was...intense, and painful if the top was an inconsiderate douche bag. He crawled over Matthew and straddled his hips, touched his back, traced a pattern at the base of his spine. Somewhere in the back of his mind, he was glad Mathew had dropped down to lie on his stomach, passive and prone. Fucking Matthew on his hands and knees?

Yeah. Kai wasn't ready for that image.

"Fast or slow?"

Matthew rolled his hips, a slight motion that quickened Kai's pulse. "Both."

Kai licked his hand, rubbed it along his dick, and slid his cock between the firm muscles of Matthew's ass, mirroring the dance they'd performed in the club. They'd had protection then...from themselves, at least, the thin barrier of their underwear. Now they had nothing, and Kai's head spun. "That could work."

Matthew moaned and pulled a pillow over his head. Kai grinned. He loved the way Matthew veered between bold and bashful. It would've been enough to give Kai whiplash if he wasn't so lost in his own haze. He lay over Matthew and ground their bodies together. He nudged the pillow away. "Like this?"

"Yeah."

The single, breathed-out word was Kai's undoing. He sank his teeth into Matthew's back, sucked his wiry flesh into his mouth for a delicious, protracted moment, then rolled off with a frustrated groan. He wanted this, badly, but something wasn't right, not yet. His desire for Matthew was overwhelming, and they'd become firm friends, but Kai needed something...more, before he could ease inside Matthew's body, on or off camera.

Kai groaned again. Since when did he get all deep and shit over sex? "I can't do this. Maybe you should just fuck me."

Matthew said nothing. He reclaimed his pillow, stuffed it under his chin, and stared at Kai, silent and still, like they hadn't just climbed all over each other, naked and desperate. Kai held his gaze a moment, then gave up and glared at the ceiling.

"We don't have to do the scene, you know. Jude said it was cool if we didn't."

"Hmm?" Kai turned his head a fraction. "Oh, I know. It's not that. I just...I..."

I want it to be perfect.

Matthew reached out. He touched Kai's hand, and then his

wrist, his bicep, and traced the dark bruise on his shoulder with the tip of his nail. Then he moved like a snake and bit down on Kai's nipple. "Dude, stop fretting. We're gonna blow that shit apart."

CHAPTER ELEVEN

Kai knocked on the wide wooden door and paused with his hand on the brass knocker. Something on the other side of the door smelled good, really fucking good, like Taco Bell on steroids or some shit. Not the dry turkey, boxed mac and cheese, and cabbage his mom usually served up at Christmas. No. This smelled like heaven.

The door swung open. Mac fixed him with a megawatt grin. "Hey, kid. Merry Christmas Week."

"That's not a thing." Kai shuffled into the spotless hallway of Mac and Jude's home. "And Christmas is a week away. I thought this was just dinner?"

Mac shrugged, pausing a moment to examine Kai's head. "It is, but I get a bit dorky at Christmas. Makes up for Jude's grouchiness the rest of the year. Put your coat in the closet and go through to the lounge. The guys are all there."

Mac disappeared fast enough to belie his huge frame, leaving Kai to open a few doors until he found a closet and stashed his coat. Then he hovered in the entrance hall of the big house. The living room? Where the fuck was that? Kai peered through a few doors. A bathroom, a study, another closet. Jesus, how many doors did this house have? He stopped and took stock; then he heard voices, familiar voices, and followed the sound to a door behind the winding staircase.

Kai had never been one for noisy entrances. He slipped like a ghost through the door that led to a den, and neither Jude nor Sonny noticed him at first. Jude was by the window, his back to the glass, staring at Sonny with what looked like tested patience. And Sonny... Sonny was sprawled on a squishy couch, looking a little like a coiled snake, ready to strike, were it not for the oddly vacant haze in his eyes. Kai frowned. He'd seen that look before, usually the morning after a wild night, and it was never a good thing. Sonny scared him when he was like that, so quiet. It often seemed like Sonny had taken a break from the world—from his own brand of hectic—and there was no guarantee he'd come back.

Now, though, it seemed Jude had his attention. "Don't tell me you don't care who you shoot with. I know that's not your MO."

Sonny shrugged, listless, barely lifting one shoulder. "I don't care. Put me with whoever you like. What does it matter?"

"Is this about Levi?"

"What do you know about Levi?"

"Not much." Jude ventured away from the window and took a seat on the arm of a chair. "But I know you guys were together last time we had a conversation, and you were pretty fucking particular about the work you wanted to do. What's changed?"

For a moment, Kai didn't think Sonny would answer, that he'd deflect any notion of his and Levi's mysterious relationship like he always did. But then something changed in his eyes. Life and emotion...pain, flickered into them. "I'm not with anyone, so I don't care who I fuck."

Kai's heart sank. Jude raised an eyebrow. "If that's your state of mind, maybe you should take a step back."

"Firing me, Jude?"

"No, I'm saying perhaps you're not in the right place to make rash decisions. Maybe you should focus on school for a while."

"And pay my rent with what? Magic fucking beans?"

Kai winced. Sonny was his own unique force of nature, but talking to Jude like that was asking for trouble. A shadow kept Kai from seeing Jude's face, but he could imagine the flash of his eyes well enough. Jude was like that. Something simmered in him, just below the surface of his careful control.

But it seemed Kai's concerns were imagined. Jude did nothing but sigh, and then he looked Kai right in the eye, like he'd known he was there all along. "New hair?"

Kai instinctively touched his hair. It had been a week or so since Matthew had cut it for him, and he'd grown used to his new style. The healed gash itched, but he'd found scrutinizing it in the mirror an odd distraction from the stack of practice GED papers Mac had sent his way. "Matthew did it."

"Looks good." Jude glanced at Sonny. "What do you think, Sonny?"

Sonny ran his gaze over Kai. "I like it."

That was good enough for Kai. He hadn't been out much since the by now infamous night at the club, and even when he'd finally forced himself from the sanctuary of Matthew's apartment, his own roommates hadn't noticed he'd been MIA for three days, let alone his half-shorn head. In the cab on the way to Blue Boy's impromptu Christmas party, he'd worried the lack of hair on the left side of his head made him look too scrawny.

Jude cleared his throat. "Are you okay for your bar shift tomorrow?"

"Tomorrow?" Shit. Kai had forgotten about that.

"If you're ready to come back." Jude eyed Kai, like he could read the uncertainty fluttering in his belly. "There's no rush. Take a couple more days."

Kai breathed a silent sigh of relief. He remembered the ramped-up benefits structure from the new contract he'd signed when Jude and Mac took over Blue Boy, but at the time it had seemed too good to be true. Then Mac had given him two weeks' paid leave while he recovered from his tumble off the stage and Kai realized how wrong he'd been. "Did you get the graffiti cleaned off the club?"

"Yep. All gone." Jude grinned, but Kai saw the flash of anger in his gaze all the same. He hadn't seen the hate sprayed all over Silver, but Matthew had, and Kai knew it was bad... Real fucking bad.

"What about the cops?" Sonny said. "Do they have any leads?"

Jude shrugged. "If they have, they're not telling me, but they seem convinced it was an isolated incident. Some loner with an ax to grind. They're monitoring the situation. Sending squad cars by every few hours when we're open. Reckon they'll lose interest pretty quick, though."

Kai was inclined to agree. He'd given his statement to a hard-faced detective who'd made no effort to hide his disinterest in the whole sorry affair. He'd only taken pictures of Kai's injuries because Mac asked him to.

A quiet settled over the room, the kind of quiet Sonny filled with crazy talk and wild ideas, but he said nothing now, and the silence seemed to get under Jude's skin. He blew out a blustery breath and socked Kai's shoulder. "We'd better move this to the living room. Mac's gonna tan my hide if he finds us talking shop in here."

Jude led by example and left the room. Kai looked at Sonny. "Are you coming?"

"In a minute."

Sonny didn't meet Kai's gaze. Kai admitted defeat and left him to it, following the smell of hot spicy food to the huge living room he'd somehow missed the first time around. There, stretched out on the couches and sprawled out on the floor, he found almost every model still on Blue Boy's books congregated around the biggest bowl of chili Kai had ever seen. Only a few faces were missing. Shame they were Kai's favorite faces.

Big arms reached around him and dumped dishes of chips, shredded cheese, and guacamole on the table. "Dig in," Mac said. "There's heaps of food."

No one present needed telling twice. Kai took a seat on the floor beside Zeb and filled his bowl. The chili was good, spicy and rich, and it had been a long time since Kai had last eaten home-cooked food.

Mac hovered around them, refilling dishes like a mother hen, while Jude looked on, clearly amused by his fussing. Kai stuffed his face until he could take no more, then he sat back, rubbing his rounded belly, and took a proper look at his surroundings.

The house was big, and nice, but it wasn't quite what Kai had pictured when Mac had called him up and summoned him over to touch base and have dinner. *What the fuck did you expect? Life-size dirty pictures and giant cocks everywhere?* Maybe, but the reality couldn't have been more different. There were pictures...photographs on every available wall, but though some of the faded photos of a young firefighter Mac were all kinds of hot, there was nothing remotely pornographic about the images. Instead each frame documented the warm and happy life Mac and Jude shared away from the daily grind of running the Blue Boy network, the life where Mac looked at Jude like he was his whole world, and Jude stared right back like he couldn't believe his luck.

Kai felt a pang in his chest. For weeks, he'd spent every day at Matthew's apartment, sometimes studying by day and plotting out the scene by night, depending on their schedules, but it had been a few days since they'd seen each other. Matthew had been swamped at school, and Kai, well, he'd kind of figured he'd give Matthew some space. After all, they were colleagues, right? Friends? Matthew had given him refuge after the incident at the club, but he was just being nice, he had to be. What else could it mean?

Even as the thought crossed Kai's mind, he knew it was wrong, but the alternative had yet to come together in his brain. Matthew wasn't staying in LA, he'd made that clear. Come the summer, he'd be on the other side of the world, so what was the point in clinging to him like a freakin' limpet now?

"Kai." Kai glanced up. Mac rolled his eyes, amused, like he'd called Kai's name over and over. "Do you want a drink?"

"Vodka," Kai said absently, his mind still on Matthew. "Oh, and orange soda."

"You can have the soda, but you'll have to wait till later for the hard stuff. We don't keep booze in the house."

It was on the tip of Kai's tongue to ask why not, but a tap on his shoulder cut him off.

"Hey, Kai."

Cam! Kai scrambled to his feet. Matthew was still on his brain, but though the grinning face behind him wasn't his, it did belong to someone else who'd been on his mind. "Hey, stranger. How are you? Are you feeling better?"

Cam held his hands up to the barrage of questions. "I'm cool. Sorry about falling on you at the studio. Didn't take you down, did I?"

Kai looked Cam over. With his trademark easy grin and twinkling eyes, he seemed a world away from the pale, shaking mess he'd been the last time Kai had seen him. "No, not at all. You scared the crap out of me, though. What happened? Did you pass out or something?"

"Or something." Cam glanced over his shoulder. His gaze found Sasha who was helping Mac clear the table. "Take a walk with me?"

Taking a walk turned out to be finding a quiet spot in the

immaculate yard. Cam slung an arm around Kai's shoulders as they walked. "How's the head? Jude says you took a nasty hit."

Kai touched the healed gash on his scalp. "It's fine. It looked a lot worse than it was."

"Must've been scary, though. Jude said Matthew was pretty freaked out."

That got Kai's attention. Beyond concern for Kai's physical well-being, Matthew had seemed pretty chill. "It wasn't a big deal."

"Uh-huh." Cam didn't sound convinced. "Have it your way, man, but Jude thought it was...is a big deal. He's sacked the security team and hired a new company. From now on, you're gonna get escorts to and from the dressing room and there's going to be a cordon around the stage until further notice."

"Sounds like you talk to Jude a lot."

Cam smiled, faint and wry. "I do. He's a good guy."

Kai felt like he was missing something. "Are you ever going to tell me what's going on with you?"

Cam sat on a bench and looked down at his hands. "I've been having treatment for testicular cancer. I had surgery a few months ago, and radiotherapy. Now they're blasting me with chemo to be sure it's all gone."

The world stopped. No light, no sound, just the slowing thud of Kai's heart. "You have cancer?"

Cam chuckled. "No, and how's that for irony? It's complicated, but basically, I had a tumor. They took it out, and treated me with radiotherapy, but then they found some suspect cells. They're tiny, dude, like, the width of a human hair, but they need to nuke everything to be sure."

On instinct, Kai touched Cam's hair... Cam's wonderful, wild hair. "I'm so sorry."

"Don't be." Cam smiled, and Kai could tell it was genuine. "The treatment is a precaution, and I'm getting off easy. The dose of chemo is low, and I'm hardly getting any side effects. I'm just tired, man, and a little run-down."

"Run-down?"

"Yeah. I get to keep my hair, but I feel like I've been hit by a bus. It won't be for long, though. I'll be done by spring."

Spring felt a long way away, but Kai kept the thought to himself. "Is this what's been going on all winter? With you, and Sonny and Levi?"

Cam shrugged, but he let the question hang without verbalizing an answer. "Hey, you paint your nails sometimes, right?"

Kai blinked. *Random, much?* "Sometimes. Depends what I'm wearing. Why?"

Cam held out his hands. "The chemo nurse said I might lose my nails if they get too much sun. I don't feel like spending the next six months inside, so do you think you could paint them black for me?"

"Of course." A rush of affection swept over Kai. Cam was a skater boy. He loved the sun, and the wind in his face. Kai couldn't bear the thought of him being caged inside. He took Cam's hands and squeezed them. "Does it have to be black? I think you'd look better with a dark steel blue. Like Jude's eyes."

Cam snorted a laugh and moved to get up. "I'll ask and call you. Hey, what are you doing on Christmas Day? Some of the guys are coming to my dad's with me. Wanna come?"

Hell, no. Kai shook his head. It had been a year or so since his mom had last asked him home for the holidays. Thanksgiving had come and gone without so much as a phone call, and these days, she was too busy with her new family, and Kai had lost much of his desire to care. He'd grown used to partying the whole season away and forgetting his family had ever existed. "Thanks, but I'm working."

Cam used Kai's hands to haul himself up. He shot Kai one of those piercing looks that seemed to come from nowhere, but said no more.

They wandered back into the house. The chili detritus had been cleared away and replaced with the fixings for ice cream sundaes. Sonny had taken his place in the room too. He sat on the floor, strumming a guitar he must've found somewhere in the huge house. Cam flopped onto the couch behind him and kissed his neck, the way he always did. Sonny smiled, and glanced at Kai. He patted the space next to him, but Kai shook his head. Cam had thrown him a curveball and he felt antsy now, like he had bugs under his skin.

He perched on the arm of the chair Jude had poured his large frame into. "Does Mac cook a lot?"

"Yep." Jude grinned and shot Mac a fond look. "He likes it. He's got this mama bear mode he can't repress."

Zeb rolled over on his floor cushion and rubbed his full belly. "Don't knock it. My mom can't cook for shit. She's brought home the biggest turkey ever from the grocery store, but whatever she does it will still suck. She was stuffing it with some grey shit when I saw her today."

Kai wrinkled his nose. His mom's turkey was gross too, and the concept of sticking sausage up a big bird's ass ironically gave him the creeps. "Why do people do that?"

He didn't expect anyone to answer, but Cam opened his eyes from his lazy doze behind Sonny. "Symbolism. It's to show the abundance of nature, isn't it?"

Cam looked at Sonny, who shrugged, still picking out chords on the guitar. "At face value, maybe. Spiritually, food is stuffed to show the fullness of life."

Dang. Kai had forgotten Sonny was like the smartest dude ever.

Kai slid off the arm of the chair and pondered the table of sweet treats. He took a bowl and built his dessert. Caramel ice cream, hot fudge sauce, cherries, and sprinkles. He considered the nuts, lost in thought, until someone batted his hovering hand away.

"No nuts. They're gross."

Kai felt warm all over. Matthew. Finally. He'd told Kai on the phone he'd be late, but for some reason Kai had taken that to mean he wouldn't show at all. "You don't like nuts, huh?"

Matthew shook his head and stuck a spoon in Kai's bowl. "Devil food. Oooh, this is good."

Kai swallowed hard and resisted the urge to lick sauce right off Matthew's lips. He handed over the bowl. Matthew dug in like he hadn't eaten in a week. The sight was endearing.

"There's plenty of food in the kitchen," Mac called from the corner of the room where he was talking up a storm with Sasha. "Don't be shy. Help yourself."

Matthew grabbed Kai's hand and yanked him out of the room. Kai thought he heard Mac chuckle, but he couldn't be sure. "Kitchen's that way."

"I know." Matthew ditched the half-empty bowl on a nearby bureau. "Come with me."

It was easy to let Matthew drag him through the maze of doors until they came to a bathroom the size of Kai's bedroom.

Matthew kicked the door shut. Locked it. "I missed you."

I missed you too. "Yeah?"

"Yeah. It's my new hobby."

Kai grinned like an idiot. He couldn't help it. No one ever missed him. Offscreen and offstage, he felt invisible. "I wanna touch you."

Matthew stepped closer. "Do it."

Kai shoved Matthew against the door and kissed him. He drove his fingers into Matthew's silky hair and tugged, absorbing Matthew's strangled moan. Tongues and teeth, it was one of those perfect, wild kisses, the kisses Kai chased when he slept alone without Matthew curved around him. The kisses neither one of them could control.

Matthew fumbled with the fly of Kai's skinny jeans. Kai

caught his hands, raised them over his head, and slammed them against the door. "Stay still. I'm gonna blow you."

Kai dropped to his knees and tugged Matthew's jeans down his legs. Matthew's underwear was sky blue with a hot pink trim. Tight and small, it was the kind of underwear that usually made Kai pause and giggle, but not now. Now Kai yanked them down Matthew's sculpted thighs without giving them a second look.

Matthew's cock sprang free. Kai caught it in his hand, squeezed. Matthew shuddered, and Kai glanced up to make sure he still held his hands above his head. Matthew gazed back at him, his eyes hooded, his cheeks flushed. "You're gonna make me scream."

Kai smirked, though somewhere in the back of his mind he knew this wasn't quite the place for screaming, drawn-out orgasms. Nah. He wanted something quick and dirty. He wanted Matthew to come like a crashing train.

He took Matthew in his mouth, deep throated him and tugged on his balls. Matthew whimpered and dug his fingers into Kai's shoulders. Kai smiled to himself and grazed Matthew's cock with his teeth, lightly at first, but then with more bite. Over the past few weeks they'd discovered they both got off on a little dash of pain. Biting, scratching, pinching, nothing heavy. They were a good match, and Kai wondered if Cam had known all along.

Matthew tensed and grunted. He was close. Already. High five to me. Kai turned up the volume. Matthew let out a strangled cry and blew his load right into Kai's mouth.

Kai swallowed him down, then sat back on his heels. His own dick was still rock hard, but he felt satisfied, like his work was done. He grinned at Matthew, and Matthew smiled back, lazy, sated and glowing.

I could stare at him all night.

Every night.

Matthew held out his hands and hauled Kai to his feet. They kissed, long and languid, before Matthew pulled away. "You beat me at my own game. I was gonna do that to you."

Kai shrugged. He'd be lying if he said he hadn't read Matthew's intentions and dodged them. Control. He needed to find some, because there was no way he could top Matthew while the other man riled him up so goddamned fast. Their scene would be over before it got started. "I win either way, right?"

"Yeah, me too." Matthew let out a shaky laugh, but then his face sobered. "I can't stay long. I have to get to the airport."

Kai's spirits sank. Matthew was catching a late flight to Boston to spend Christmas with his mom. He'd be gone for ten days. And Cam was sick. Beautiful, wonderful Cam was sick.

Matthew touched Kai's cheek. "What's the matter?"

"Nothing." Kai took Matthew's hand from his face and held it. "I guess I don't really like Christmas. It's kinda lonely, you know?"

"You have me. I didn't get you anything, but we could swap gifts when I get back if you like? Have our own January Christmas."

Matthew's earnest expression broke through Kai's funk. The guy was so sweet sometimes it hurt.

"So what? Are we, like, dating now?" Kai didn't mean it to come out as a negative, but for a moment Matthew looked stung.

Then he rolled his eyes. "You think blowing me in the bathroom is all it takes? Man, I don't know. I just know I miss you when you're not huffing around my place wearing my clothes."

I miss you too. "I don't huff."

"Uh-huh. Now let's go find me some real food before I pass out. You can't blow a guy with an empty stomach. It's not fair."

Kai scowled, but it was halfhearted and laced with melancholy. Matthew really did have to leave, and after a snatched bowl of Mac's special chili, he did just that.

CHAPTER TWELVE

"Are you naked yet?"

Matthew chuckled. He sounded breathless. "Hold on. I need to lock my door."

"At least you have a lock." Kai lay back on his bed. He'd told Matthew he'd taken his clothes off, but in truth he'd left his pants around his ankles, just in case, like he had every time Matthew had called over the three long days he'd been gone so far.

"That's not my fault. I said you could stay at my place."

It was true, and Kai had given Matthew's offer serious consideration, but in the end decided it would feel too weird. He loved Matthew's place—the quiet order, the privacy—but Matthew's presence was what made it special. It wouldn't feel right without him. Besides, Matthew would be gone for more than a week. Who knew what state Kai would find his own apartment in if he left it unsupervised so long.

The clunking sounds at Matthew's end stopped. Kai heard rustling sheets. "There. I'm butt naked in bed. Happy?"

Kai felt his blood heat up. "Is this the same bed you grew up with?"

"Uh-huh."

"So it was the first place you ever jerked off?"

"Um, no." Matthew snickered, and lowered his voice. "I first jerked off in my best friend's basement. We did it together."

That sounded fun. Kai wanted to know more, but a sharp intake of breath distracted him. "What are you doing?"

"Jerking off, duh."

Kai licked his hand and reached for his own cock. He'd been hard since Matthew had broached the ever-present subject of their upcoming scenes. Their "practice" sessions invariably descended into frantic hand jobs, the heat too hot to handle, and they'd decided to cool it awhile. Figure out a cohesive plan, instead of going at each other like wild animals, though that was a whole lot of fun.

Kai rolled his hips up and squeezed his hand a little tighter. His pulse quickened.

"So about the scene..."

Kai bit down on a grunt. "Yeah?"

"Yeah. Jude said we could choose the set, so I was thinking we could use one with the white bed."

"You don't want me to fuck you over the big black couch?"

"No. I want to do it in a bed."

The image formed in Kai's brain. He whimpered. "We'll be on a bed, not in it."

"The first time."

Kai swallowed. Matthew had said a lot of things like that recently, and though it gave Kai a thrill—a rush of craved acceptance he couldn't deny—it also felt strange. Kai was used to getting kicked to the curb, even by his friends. Why would Matthew be any different? "You like it on your belly, right? We'll have to go at the end so the camera can see your face."

"Not if you push my head down. Won't matter then."

Kai arched his back, already close to busting out. How the

fuck did Matthew do that with just his voice? "Like that, would ya?"

"Maybe. I want to feel you touching every part of me when we're fucking. I don't want you to sit back and pound my ass. Tactile, dude. That's what it's all about."

Kai moaned, too riled to grind out a sentence. "Wanna touch you too."

"Where?"

"Your back. Wanna touch your skin. Hook my arms under your shoulders."

"Slide your fingers into my mouth?"

The question was tentative...teasing, and fucking nuclear. Kai growled, equal parts frustrated and too far gone to give a shit. "Gonna come, you fucker."

"Yeah?" Matthew snickered, but it cut off, and Kai remembered that he was jacking off in his mom's house, with his entire family who knew where.

Kai pictured the scene, Matthew naked in bed, flushed, his head thrown back. Pictured him spilling all over his taut stomach. It was enough. Kai came with a groan... A groan he didn't have to repress. "Fuck."

For a long moment, the only sounds between them were harsh breaths. Kai came down slowly, watching his chest rise and fall and the sweat cool on his skin. He felt sated and sleepy, but at the same time, he felt Matthew's physical absence like a stone, sinking through his chest and settling in his belly.

But as always, Matthew's laugh filtered through. "Same time tomorrow?"

Kai licked his lips. Hell yeah.

"Come on, kiddo. It's not that bad."

"I'm not a kid." Kai scowled and pulled his hood further

over his face. It was Christmas Eve, and though Kai couldn't care less about the holiday, he had better things to be doing with his time than letting Mac hustle him to the GED testing center. Yeah, like having phone sex with Matthew...

"What are you smirking about behind that hood?"

Busted. Kai pushed his hood back and peered at Mac. "I'm not smirking."

"You're not a lot of things this morning. What about ready? Are you ready for the test?"

"No."

Mac hung a left, a smile twitching on his lips. "That's not what Matthew says. I called him yesterday. He said you were scoring well on the practice papers."

"That was math. I still suck at reading and writing." Kai turned his gaze out the window and watched the scenery fly by. It was eight a.m., a time of day he rarely saw, and the city seemed cleaner...fresher, than he'd seen it in a while.

Mac's hand on his arm surprised him. The kind smile not so much. "Kai, you've got support, okay? There's gonna be an audio tape for the reading, and you have a scribe for the essays. Just use your brain. I know you've got one."

Kai wasn't convinced, but he'd run out of time to argue.

Mac pulled into the parking lot and shut off the engine. He unbuckled his seatbelt. Took his key out of the ignition. "Let's roll."

"You don't have to come with me."

It was Mac's turn to smirk, though his gaze retained an edge of twinkling sobriety. "Nice try. I want to make sure you go in. Go in and stay in. See it through."

"What if I don't?"

"That's your choice." Mac tapped his fingers on the steering wheel. "But it's a stupid choice. You're already down on yourself. What have you got to lose?"

A bucket-load of self-esteem and respect, as it turned out.

Kai trailed after Mac into the testing center and spent the whole day wrangling with mind-bending words and convoluted sentences, and by the time he emerged six hours later, he had nothing to show for his efforts but a freakin' migraine.

He didn't even know if he'd passed. It would be two weeks before he got the results, and his glum mood was reinforced by the message Matthew had left on his phone. His mom was taking him to see his aging grandma, and he wouldn't be back until way into the New Year. Great. Now it looked like Kai would get confirmation he was a total dumbass long before he got to see Matthew again.

***

I think we should buy each other underwear as gifts
    Xmas gifts?
    Yea
    What kind? Funny or hot?
    Both
    Two pairs?
    No. Two concepts in one
Kai rolled his eyes and tossed his phone on the bed. It was Christmas Day, and he'd been exchanging texts with Matthew ever since the chime of his phone had woken him some time around noon. Matthew had been up for hours, dodging the excitement of his flock of younger siblings, and his messages had ranged from sweet wishes of a merry Christmas to saucy requests for nude pictures.

Kai had obliged on the picture front. His last physical encounter with Matthew, by his own choice, had been one-sided, and as a result he was burning from the inside out. Awake and asleep, he had Matthew on the brain and a permanent boner. Lucky, really, as he was due on stage at Silver that night for the first time since he'd taken a bottle to the side of his head, and somewhere beneath the haze of his ever-growing affection for Matthew, he was fucking terrified.

His phone buzzed. Another message.

Comic books

Kai scowled and tapped out a reply.

Comic book boxers? LAME

Matthew's response was instant.

Who said anything about jock boy boxers?

He had a point. They both had a penchant for briefs, the tighter and brighter, the better.

I'll get YOU comic book underwear, but I want GLITTER... and SPARKLES

You are so GAY

Kai giggled. *Aren't we all?*

Matthew didn't reply right away. Kai swung his legs out of bed. It was four p.m. and time he braved the bathroom to see if there was any hot water left.

Matthew didn't send any more messages for the rest of the day. Kai figured he was busy eating his mom's giant Christmas ham and left him to it. He made the most of his deserted apartment, took a bath, and raided Bianca's room for things that had gone missing over the past few months.

After that, he spent a few hours making himself pretty, but eventually, when he'd run out of ways to procrastinate, he got dressed and headed out to the club.

He slipped past the new, burly security guy guarding the dressing-room door just after nine. He'd left his arrival as late as possible, but even so, he was still taken aback to see Sonny already there. He was even more surprised by his demeanor.

Dancing on the counters? Already?

Sonny leaped like a cat and landed on the balls of his feet, his face inches from Kai's and his eyes dancing with an energy that had been conspicuously absent the last time Kai had seen him.

"Hey, hey, hey. You got your game face on? 'Cause you're dancing with me tonight, both slots. Zeb's called in. Can you believe that? Calling in sick on Christmas Day? That's lame, even for him."

Kai blinked, absorbing Sonny's supercharged chatter. "Both slots? I'm only down for the ten to twelve."

Sonny rolled his eyes and bounced on his feet. "I told you. Zeb called in."

Kai set his bag down and shrugged out of his jacket. Sonny seemed pumped...wired, and his body already bore signs of a wild time on stage. Sweat. Body paint. "Did you go on already?"

"Yep. Mac put me on early slots."

"And he's letting you dance two extra?" That didn't sound right. Silver had always limited the dancers to a maximum of two slots in any one night, and it was strictly enforced. "Where is Mac, anyway? I need to give him his shirt back."

Kai left out the fact that he'd had to wash Mac's designer T-shirt twice to get the smell of Tag's weed smoke from it, or that he'd pressed it within an inch of its life to get it totally perfect.

Sonny smirked like he knew it all anyway. "Mac's not here. Him and Jude went to see Jude's folks in Sacramento. They won't be back until the weekend."

"He'll still find out, you know."

"So?" Sonny danced back to the mirror and held up a bottle of Kai's favorite glittery paint. "Come over here. Let's get you fixed up."

Kai gave in and let the hurricane that was Sonny consume him. Sonny's energy was infectious, and it wasn't long before Kai found himself dancing around the dressing room, wild and free, forgetting that the real world lay just a few feet away in the club, a world where bottles flew through the air and smashed into his head.

Then the new security guy banged on the door and kicked it open. "Let's roll."

Kai jumped and wobbled on the countertop. Suddenly, dancing on any raised platform, let alone the main stage, didn't seem as much fun. He jumped down and grabbed Sonny's can of energy drink. The bubbles fizzed in his stomach. His hands shook.

"We'll be out in a minute." Sonny flitted to the door and closed it in the security guy's face. "Jeez. Who died and put him in charge? Are you ready to go?"

No. Kai nodded. Hot from horsing around with Sonny, he was already stripped down to his underwear, his skin slicked with a light sheen of sweat, his cheeks flushed.

Sonny slapped Kai's ass and threw open the door. He disappeared into the corridor before Kai could stop him. Kai followed at a slower pace. He felt the security guy behind him, sensed his hulking presence. Even the crackle of the radio on his shoulder set Kai's teeth on edge.

The scent of the smoke machines hit Kai at the same time the thumping bass rattled his chest. Nausea rolled in his belly. His vision narrowed, and he stumbled to a stop. Faggot.

Kai stopped dead. I can't do this. "Sonny."

Sonny flung a glance over his shoulder, still walking. Something stopped him. He spun around and came back for Kai. "What's the matter?"

"I...uh." Kai shook his head. "I don't feel well. I want to go home."

Sonny touched Kai's hair, trailed a fingertip over his shorn scalp. He put his other heated palm on Kai's chest. "You're freaking out. Why?"

"I'm not freaking out."

Sonny didn't call Kai out on his bullshit. Instead, he grabbed his hand and yanked him forward. He pushed him into the dark corner between the corridor and the stage.

Kai's back hit the cool wall. He shivered and glanced at the burly security guard, who'd stopped but otherwise remained passive and benign.

Sonny held Kai's face with both hands and stared until Kai squirmed. Sonny had crazy hazel eyes, flecked with gold and mesmerizing, especially when he had something to say. For a moment, Kai thought he was going to kiss him, but he didn't. He ducked his head and nuzzled Kai's neck. The gesture was hot and sweet...familiar. Kai had fooled around with Sonny, on and offscreen, more times than he could remember.

Kai's cock hardened in his tiny underwear. Sonny chuckled and rubbed Kai's chest again with the palm of his hand, as if he could slow his hammering heart with just his touch. His other hand traveled lower, and he gave Kai's dick a squeeze rough enough to make Kai's eyes roll.

"Are you with me?"

Kai nodded. It was a little hard not to be.

Sonny nipped his neck and pulled away. "Let's go. You go first. I'll follow."

"What? No. I don't want to go on by myself."

Sonny held Kai's gaze, steady and sure. "I know. That's why you have to. If you don't go on tonight, you'll reinforce your fear, feed it, and make it worse."

"I'm not scared."

"You should be. Some dumbfuck threw a bottle at your head."

Kai swallowed, dug his teeth into his lip so hard he tasted blood. "What if they come back?"

"And what if they don't? Come on, Kai. They win if you don't go on. Is that what you want? Some fucktard with a bottle to rule your life?" Sonny shook Kai. "Let's go."

Sonny all but dragged Kai along the corridor and shoved

him on stage. Kai tripped over his own feet. The call of the crowd reached him, but the euphoria that usually came with a packed club shouting his name was absent. Kai gripped the pole, scanning the crowd for the assailant he'd never seen. He fumbled on the pole, his hands slick, and the blood roaring in his ears drowned out the bass of the music.

I can't do this.

Sonny spun onto the stage. He caught Kai from behind and put his lips to his ear. "Breathe, Kai. Stay close to me. Let the music take you."

I want Matthew. Kai leaned against Sonny, back to chest, and wound his arms around Sonny's neck. Sonny hummed in Kai's ear, throaty and low, and danced for the both of them, guiding Kai until he found his way.

Flashing lights, swaying hips. Sonny's roaming hands. Kai's favorite dubstep track came on. He closed his eyes and thought of Matthew, thought of the first and last time they'd danced together, before they'd been so violently interrupted. Matthew didn't have Sonny's presence or skills, but for Kai, he had all of his magic...more, and he was fast coming to realize there was nothing else. No one else.

Kai had the dance of his life. Only Matthew's absence stopped the night from being perfect.

He danced with Sonny until the final podium slot came to an end. They spun off the stage together. Their babysitter rolled his eyes and escorted them back to the dressing room. Sonny disappeared into the bathroom, singing at the top of his lungs. Kai laughed and dug out his phone. It was five a.m. in Boston, but he was too buzzed to care. He was flying.

Matthew answered on the third ring. No words, just a sleep-thick mumbled groan that made Kai's bones feel warm.

"If I tell you something, will you remember in the morning?"

"Mmm...yeah..."

Kai wasn't convinced. He'd spent a lot of time watching Matthew sleep over the past few weeks, and the guy slept like a dead man. "Hey, Matthew?"

"Yeah?"

"I wish you were here."

CHAPTER THIRTEEN

Kai studied the laminated menu. "Can I get fried noodles, a double order of orange chicken, egg rolls, and chili prawns? Oooh, and some yellow bean pork. And wontons."

The server at the Chinese restaurant wrote his oversize order on the take-out pad and held out his hand for payment. Kai passed over a roll of notes. He'd ordered enough for six and spent the last of his tips, but he didn't care. His heart still pined for Matthew, but Cam's call had lightened his mood. Kai sent Cam a message every day, right after he sent one to Matthew. He didn't always get a response, but this morning Cam had surprised him by calling him right back. It seemed Cam was feeling good, and craving company and greasy takeout, something Kai was happy to provide.

Kai waited on his order, then walked the final few blocks to Cam's Venice Beach apartment. The January air was brisk, by California standards, at least, and Kai enjoyed the wind in his face. He'd had a good week. Missing Matthew was hard, but he'd found distraction in dancing. He'd followed Sonny's advice and lost himself in the heady bass line at Silver, his residual fears over the bottle incident long forgotten. And, even better, Matthew was due home in a little under forty-eight hours. Kai had bought him his Batman briefs just that morning and couldn't wait to see him in them.

He bounded up the stairs to Cam's apartment with a spring in his step. Cam greeted him with a big smile, an even bigger hug, and a platonic kiss on the lips. "Hey, you. Come on in."

Kai slipped inside and proffered his paper bag of MSG-laden bounty. "Hope you're hungry. I got lots."

"Egg rolls?"

"Yep."

"Orange chicken?"

"Double yep."

Cam grinned and rubbed his belly. "Awesome. I'm starved. Go through, I'll get some soda."

Kai wandered into Cam's living room and dumped the food on the coffee table. He'd been to Cam's tiny Venice Beach apartment a few times, but never sober, and not for a while. He'd forgotten how bare it was, like no one really lived there. He drifted to the window, looked out at the bright lights of the city, and thought of Matthew for the bazillionth time. Matthew's apartment was bigger than Cam's, and he had even less furniture, but it was crammed full of his kooky personality. Comic books, sci-fi posters. Photos of his family and friends. Cam had nothing in his home to show who he really was—no Sasha, no Blue Boy. Not even the riotous twin brothers he so often talked about. Strange for a guy so open and warm.

"Earth to Kai?"

"Hmm?" Kai spun around to find Cam sprawled on the couch, already chewing on an egg roll. "Sorry, I was miles away."

"Jude told me Matthew is too. Missing him?"

Kai flipped Cam the bird, dropped onto the couch, and reached for the first carton of chicken. "He's coming home on Thursday. Where's Sasha?"

"Having dinner with his parents. They're not in town much."

"You didn't want to go?"

Cam shrugged. "His folks are pretty cool, but I think seeing me reminds them of what they went through with Sasha. I can see it in his mom's eyes, and I didn't feel like it today."

"What happened to Sasha?"

"He had cancer too, the same kind as me, but he had it much worse. He had a real hard time."

Delicious, salty-sweet chicken turned to dust in Kai's mouth. He wondered if Cam was picturing himself suffering the same fate, or simply pondering what his life would be like if he'd never gotten the chance to meet Sasha. "He's okay now, though, right?"

Cam smiled. His green eyes gleamed in the soft light from his single table lamp. "Better than okay. He's amazing. Anyway, enough about me. How's that scene coming along? I'm sorry I haven't been around to talk you through it, but Jude said you and Matthew were hitting it off pretty well."

Kai felt the typical Matthew-induced heat flood his cheeks. "Things are good. I don't know if I'll go through with topping him, but I'm not worried about it. Jude said we can do whatever scene we want."

"And what do you want?"

I want to be with him, any way I can. "I don't know. Whatever feels right on the day, I guess."

Cam smiled, like he wasn't fooled. Kai averted his gaze and, appetite restored, started on the wontons. He offered the box to Cam. "Wanna wonton?"

"Nah." Cam waved his own carton of orange chicken. "Sasha can smell that deep-fried shit a mile away."

Kai shook his head, recalled hearing a similar sentiment from Mac. Was that what happened when relationships got serious? Hot guys turned into the food police? Screw that.

Cam interpreted Kai's expression with a wry grin. "Sasha likes all that health food crap—raw food and sushi. He doesn't force it on me, but I've gotta take care of myself while I'm in treatment. Live well, feel well."

"Does it work?"

"When I'm not KO'd after chemo."

Kai made a face. He'd seen the effect chemo had on Cam, and he didn't like it. He didn't like it at all. There was something he'd been wondering about, though. "Can I ask you something?"

"Is it about my dick?"

Kai choked on a mouthful of spicy noodles. "How did you know?"

Cam rolled his eyes. "'Cause it's the first thing every guy asks me when I tell them I've lost a nut, especially fuckin' porn stars."

"So does everything, uh, still work?"

Cam laughed. "Hell, yeah, but I gotta admit, I lost a lot of sleep over it before Sasha put me straight."

"Sasha takes good care of you, huh?"

"The best."

Kai thought on that awhile. Cam had always been cool, generous with his affection and easy grin, but Kai hadn't realized how jaded he'd become until meeting Sasha had brought him back to life. Ironic, much? Yeah, because despite all the crap Cam was going through, he seemed happier than he'd ever been.

"How does Sasha feel about you shooting porn? Are you going to come back when you're better?"

"Maybe. Would have to be the right guy, though. Sasha's cool, but he wouldn't share me with just any—"

A key sounded in Cam's front door. Kai looked around, expecting Sasha's blond hair. Levi's dark, brooding gaze caught him off guard.

"Is Sonny here?"

Cam shook his head, frowning as Levi stopped in the living room doorway. The guy looked beat, like he hadn't slept in days. "Haven't seen him. Everything okay?"

"Fuck if I know. He's been off radar a couple of days. He's not home, not answering his phone." Levi ventured farther into the room, shoved the half-empty take-out cartons aside, and perched on the coffee table, restless, eyes darting, hands twitching. He reminded Kai of a wolf he'd once seen on a wildlife show who'd lost his mate. "He's not dancing tonight, Kai, right?"

"No." Kai curled his legs under him like a cat. "Mac makes him take Thursdays off because he has classes all day Friday."

Levi sighed. "Lucky Mac. I can't get him to do nothin' 'cept come to bed with me. Even then he won't fuckin' sleep. He's never there when I wake up."

"That's not just you, dude. He never stays the night with anyone." Cam said the words with a grin on his face, but it didn't reach his eyes, and he pushed his food away.

Kai frowned. He was relatively new on the Blue Boy scene, but Levi and Cam had been friends a long time. Their bond was deep, and their shared concern for Sonny hurt Kai's heart. In the back of his mind, he recalled the conversation he'd heard Sonny have with Jude the week before Christmas. "Did you guys have a fight or something?"

"Or something." Levi glanced at Cam, who motioned for him to elaborate. Levi blew out a frustrated breath, the kind of breath that told Kai talking about Sonny didn't come easy. "I don't know, man. I know he's swamped with school and shit, but I can't get a handle on him. He's either jumping in my face or sleeping like he don't wanna wake up. I don't get it."

Cam ruffled Kai's hair and got up. He paced to the window and scrubbed his hands down his face. His good mood had evaporated, and in its place Kai saw the weight of real fatigue. "Have you talked to him? He calls me most days, but though he talks a lot, he doesn't say much."

"Sounds about right." Levi snagged an egg roll from the carton on the table and set about picking it apart in a way that didn't fit the personality Kai had mapped for him in his mind. "I try to pin him down all the time, find out what's wrong, but he gets mad and disappears on me. Says he don't want no daddy figure in his life."

"You can't back Sonny into a corner, man. He comes out swinging."

Levi dumped his obliterated egg roll back in the carton. "True that. He's got a crueler tongue than my momma."

The room fell silent. Kai wondered if he should leave, but he was comfortable snuggled up on the couch, and worried about Sonny. He'd noticed Sonny liked to get high—of course he had—but because he'd never seen Sonny actually doing drugs, he'd never considered it a problem. Kai knew plenty of people who dabbled in coke and weed, and none of them had as much going for them as Sonny. Kai felt like he was missing something, and by the look of Cam and Levi, so did they.

"Has he been showing up at the club?"

Kai met Levi's worried gaze and found himself torn. Sonny had missed two slots over the past few weeks and been late for many more, but ratting him out felt wrong.

Cam let him off the hook. "Jude would've told me if he'd bailed too many times. Sonny might be at the library if he's studying. It's open all night. Let me call him." Cam tapped his phone and put it to his ear. The seconds ticked by before he admitted defeat. "His voice mail's full."

"Always is." Levi stood. He went to Cam and put his arms around him. "Don't worry on it. I'll find him. It just freaks me out when he's gone so long."

"He'll be back," Cam said, though he didn't seem so sure.

"I know." Levi hugged Cam, then stepped back. "I'm gonna check the library, then head home. He sometimes shows up when he's run out of steam."

"Call me when you find him?"

"Sure."

"Okay." Cam rubbed his face. "I gotta piss. Speak to you later, yeah?"

Cam wandered off. Levi watched him go, then turned his gaze on Kai. "You're takin' care of him tonight, huh?"

"Not really. Just feeding him."

Levi smiled. "That's all a dude needs sometimes. Stay with him, will ya? Sasha's gone for the night, and I can't worry about the both of them right now."

Kai nodded. That suited him. He didn't feel like going home to his lumpy single bed, and Cam's couch was comfortable enough.

Levi dropped a kiss on Kai's head and left.

Cam reappeared a few minutes later, but his appetite had evaporated. He watched Kai hoover up the remains of their dinner with a distant, amused smile. "Where do you put it all?"

"Hollow legs." Kai gave his standard answer and shoved the empty containers into the paper bag. He got up to dump them in the trash. When he got back, Cam appeared half asleep. Kai went to the apartment's only bedroom and fetched some pillows and a blanket. He dropped them on Cam's lap. "Get comfy. I'll find a movie."

"Huh? Oh, okay." Cam stretched out on the couch, leaving space for Kai in front of him. He grinned at his phone and tapped out a message.

Kai caught the end of it when he came back to the couch. "Pretty little babysitter?"

"Uh-huh. Don't think I don't know Levi pulled his mother hen crap on you. Between him, my pops, and Sasha, I'm lucky they let me dress myself."

Kai spread the blanket over Cam's legs, ignoring his sardonic grin. "What are you going to do about Sonny?"

"Nothing, least nothing I haven't done a thousand times

over. I just feel bad for Levi, you know? They're so right for each other, but Levi can't go through this again."

"Again?"

Cam hummed and rested his head on his arm. "His momma gave him a real hard time before she died. Nearly fucking broke him. Sonny helped him heal but forgot to heal himself. That shit ain't right."

Kai wanted to ask more, but Cam fell asleep before the opening credits of the movie even started. Kai divided his attention between him, Matthew, and Sonny for a while, and then he gave in to his own fatigue, snuggled down beside Cam, and slept until Sasha woke him the following morning, gave him whole-wheat toast and fruit for breakfast, and drove him home.

***

The top of the refrigerator looked like a landfill site. Candy wrappers, chip packets, take-out containers. A pizza box slid free and hit Kai in the face. He cursed but persevered. Some-where in the mess of garbage and fast food debris was the mail... his mail, and though he wasn't expecting good news, he was driving himself mad trying to find it.

He groped around, balancing precariously on the kitchen countertop and clinging to the cooker hood. The dust had already made him sneeze, and he'd dragged his hand through a patch of questionable slime, but his GED results were up here, dammit, and he wasn't quitting until he'd found them. His fingers touched paper. He tensed, hardly daring to look, and tugged on the envelope until it broke free of the junk. He turned it over, saw the logo of the testing center, and jumped down from the countertop.

Kai took the letter into his bedroom and shut the door. He sat on the edge of his bed and stared at it. It was date-stamped a week ago, and who knew how long it had been on top of the refrigerator. It had been three long Matthew-less weeks since he'd taken the test, and he'd all but forgotten about the results. Only a flippant remark from Mac the night before had reminded him to go searching for them.

And now you've found them. Kai bit his lip. His nerves surprised him. He'd studied for the test to get Mac off his back, and later to spend as much time with Matthew as possible. The exam had been hell on earth, and there was little doubt he'd failed, but somehow the benign-looking envelope taunted him.

Kai ripped it open. A sheaf of papers fell to the floor. Kai crouched down and flipped through them until he came to the one with his overall status. He took in the table of numbers. Predictably, his highest score—and it was high—was in math, but that meant nothing unless he'd fudged his way through the rest of the subjects. Kai skimmed the page and found his overall score, and next to the magic number 2950, was the word Kai had never truly considered—Pass.

You've got to be kidding me.

There was no one around to hear Kai's startled whoop. He leaped up from the floor and punched the air. His gaze fell on his phone, abandoned on the bed. He scrambled for it. He had to tell someone. Matthew. He had to tell Matthew. His phone was halfway to his ear before he remembered Matthew was on a plane thousands of miles up in the air and unreachable until he landed at LAX in a few hours' time.

Kai thought of Cam, but he nixed the idea as it entered his head. He hadn't seen Cam since they'd spent the night together on the couch, but Kai knew from Sonny—who'd reappeared without a care in the world from wherever he'd been—that Cam was deep in his chemo cycle and not doing so well this time around.

I could go tell Mac. It was his idea, right? He'd want to know.

Kai pocketed his phone and scrabbled around his room for

his keys and a jacket. He ran a hand through his hair. Over the past few weeks he'd been experimenting with straighteners, but he'd left it wild after his stolen afternoon soak in the tub, and it was a disaster. He covered it with a casual woolen hat and made for the door.

He stepped out into the street and turned in the direction of Silver. It was five p.m., but he knew Mac would already be at the club, checking the books and checking the cleanup crew had done their jobs. Since the bottle-throwing incident, Mac had been a visible presence almost every night, guarding the bar with his hulking presence. Only Christmas had forced him away.

Kai walked briskly in the cool evening air, past the bars and commercial buildings that made up his neighborhood. He kept the envelope in his hands close to his chest, like precious cargo, and as he got closer to the club, felt his legs move faster and faster, until he was running.

Car horns blared as he dodged his way through the busy traffic. He skidded to a stop by Silver's front door and typed in his employee code. Bull, the club manager, called his name as he darted across the dance floor, but Kai paid him no heed. He jumped down the steps to the basement office and barreled right into Mac.

Mac caught him, saving him from a heavy collision with his solid, muscled frame. "Hey, hey, hey. Where's the fire."

"I passed!" Kai wriggled out of Mac's arms and thrust the envelope at him. "I freakin' passed. Look!"

Mac's amused smirk widened to a huge grin. "No kidding? You passed your GED? Lemme see that."

Kai relinquished the envelope to Mac, who held it up to the light. "I don't know if I did good, but I passed. Look, it says right there."

"Hang on a sec, I need my damned glasses. Come in here."

Mac kicked the office door open and retrieved his hunky silver bear glasses. "Let's have a look at this."

Kai thought he might explode while Mac squinted at each sheet of paper in turn. A nagging worry that he'd misinterpreted the words and numbers gnawed at him. He often read things backward. What if he'd seen what he'd wanted to see and gotten it all wrong? Then his feet left the ground and he felt himself being spun around in a pair of couch-sized arms.

Mac hugged Kai hard, squeezing the air from his lungs, before he set him down and noogied his head. "This is awesome, kiddo. Look at this score for math and science. You could go to college on this shit."

"Really?" Kai peered around Mac's torso. "That bit was easy. Matthew taught me all these weird methods to remember the formulas."

"Matthew's a clever kid, and so are you. Have you told him yet?"

"No. He's in the air, on his way back from Boston."

Mac took Kai's precious papers to the printer on his desk and stuck them in the copier tray. "He's gonna be psyched when he comes home to this."

Kai bounced on the balls of his feet. "Yeah, maybe I should surprise him at the airport. Like in that movie on TMC last night... What was it called?"

Mac laughed. "I have no idea, but I'll tell you what..." He pulled his wallet out of his back pocket and held out a fifty-dollar bill. "Get a cab to the airport and grab a pizza on your way home. I'm real proud of you, Kai. Real fucking proud. Go celebrate with your boy."

Your boy. Kai skipped out of the club with a grin so wide his face hurt. *I'm proud of you.* It was the first time he'd claimed any of those words for himself, and damn, it felt good.

He hailed a cab and directed the driver to the airport. On the way, he realized he was still clutching the letter for the testing center tight in his hands, like it would disappear if he let it go, then stuffed it in his pocket. He stared down at it. Overall status—Pass. He read the line over and over. The numbers beside it meant little to him, but those three little words meant everything. He pictured Matthew's grin and bounced in his seat. Matthew had the best grin in the world, and Kai couldn't wait to see it.

Kai ditched the cab and hurried into the airport. He didn't have Matthew's flight number, but when he looked at the big screens, there was only one incoming flight from Boston, and it was due to land in the next ten minutes. Kai made a note of the time, bought a soda, and settled down in the terminal baggage claim area.

He curled up in the hard metal chair and put his chin on his knees. He knew it would take an hour for Matthew to disembark from the plane and pass through security, but even after three long weeks, this last short wait felt like a year. People came and went. Kai watched them, trying to figure out if they looked like they'd come from Boston. Men, women, children. Young and old, Kai watched them all, growing ever more impatient, until finally...finally, he caught sight of Matthew's perfect tousled hair. Kai's heart skipped a beat. Fuck. He's got his glasses on.

Kai slid off his seat as Matthew drifted through the airport, following the crowd, unaware of Kai's watchful gaze. He seemed in a world of his own, intent on keeping track of the bag he was dragging behind him. Kai felt his blood warm up, and realized how cold he'd been without Matthew's presence. He stood, the envelope burning a hole in his pocket.

And then Matthew turned to the woman walking beside him, put his arms around her, and kissed her.

CHAPTER FOURTEEN

I'm home. Do you want to come over?

KAI!!! I got Thai food. Hurry up.

Hellooooo?

Did you get an extra shift? Call me when you finish

Um, so, you either lost your cell, or you're blanking me...

Buzz, buzz, buzz...

Kai groaned and smothered the phone with his pillow. He'd considered turning it off, but the masochistic part of him wanted to see Matthew's name flash up on his screen. Wanted to read the confused messages and watch the voice mails stack up. Matthew's increasing concern felt cathartic, like it could mask the persistent image of him putting lips on a woman. And it worked for a while. Long enough for Kai to fall back asleep, at least.

It was dark when he woke up next, early evening. He reached for his phone and activated the touchscreen before he was awake enough to stop himself. There were no missed calls and no new messages. Kai scowled. Didn't take him long to give up.

Kai rolled over and stared at the ceiling. He'd only slept a few hours and he felt like crap. His eyes felt scratchy from his drunken tears the night before, and beyond that, he felt sore from the inside out. He'd run home from the airport and raided Tag's pharmaceuticals. He'd bypassed the pills and coke—hard drugs weren't his thing—but he'd found enough weed to smoke himself into oblivion, helped along by a bellyful of vodka. Last thing Kai remembered he'd been crying into his pillow, mourning every disastrous relationship he'd ever had and listening to mocking voices from the past.

"It's just fucking, Kai. I never wanted to be with you. Guys don't date guys."

Kai had seen enough of the world since then to know how wrong that was, but the hurt in his chest remained, scratched raw by the image of Matthew putting his lips on that damn fucking girl.

Screw you, asshole. I'm not fifteen anymore.

Kai shoved his hand into his hair and tried to separate the matted curls. In his peripheral vision he caught sight of an ugly dent in the wall and remembered hurling his boots across the room in a fit of petulant rage.

Pathetic, much?

Kai's phone vibrated in his hand. He jumped and stared at the screen, expecting the sweet-sharp pain of seeing Matthew's face. Mac's face made him feel even worse. He sent the call to voice mail and turned the phone off. Mac called every few days, sometimes with a reason...a request for Kai to do something ridiculous, like take a GED test, or come in early and learn how to order liquor for the bar at Silver. But sometimes he seemed to call for no reason at all, and Kai wasn't in the mood to play nice. He'd misread Matthew and pretty much every guy who'd ever been nice to him; why not Mac too? In the cold light of day... evening, it was hard not to feel real fucking stupid. The GED certificate meant nothing compared to the college degrees and hotshot plans the other models had. Of them all, he was the only one who'd never finished high school.

Was there a prize for being the dumbest porn star in town? Kai doubted it. All he knew was the closest he'd ever had to a boyfriend had turned out to like pussy more than him.

Had they all known? Did Mac know? Sonny? Cam? Blue Boy had always been marketed as a gay owned and operated establishment, with no gay-for-pay bullshit, but Jude and Mac had changed everything else; why not this? It wouldn't be the first time Kai had found himself the butt of everyone's joke.

Kai squeezed his eyes closed and tried to go back to sleep. Raised voices reached his ears sometime later. He listened a moment, prepared for apathy. His apartment was party central, and many faces came and went, but though he'd never heard it laced with so much irritation, the soft East Coast accent sounded familiar...too familiar. Kai kicked back the covers and sat up. He stumbled to his bedroom door and out into the hall. There he found Matthew at the front door, firmly trapped in Bianca's clutches.

Bianca was eyeing Matthew with open interest. She had her hand on his arm, her body pressed into his side. "I like your lip ring. Does it feel hot when you make out?"

Matthew wrinkled his nose in answer. Then he saw Kai over Bianca's shoulder and his face relaxed. "Hey, there you are. I've been calling you all day. Did you just get up?"

Matthew's expression was open, his hand already reaching for Kai. Kai couldn't speak. Couldn't move. Bianca took advantage of his silence and slid her hand up Matthew's arm to his chest. "There's a party a few blocks from here. Good booze, good weed. Maybe some X. Wanna come? Show a girl a good time?"

Her choice of words broke through Kai's haze. His hackles rose, and he slapped her hand away. "Haven't you got some skanky manwhore waiting on you?"

"Don't bitch me out, Kai. You're the one who's been crying in his bed all day. Maybe you should let this cutie make you all better." Bianca made a face and slipped past them into the corridor. She backed away with her middle finger raised.

Kai returned the sentiment and watched her go with venom in his gaze. To add to his list of woes, he knew he needed to find a new place to live before he murdered someone.

Matthew touched Kai's cheek. "Why aren't you picking up your cell? I thought you were dead. Are you sick or something?"

Kai shrugged away from Matthew's hand. "What are you doing here? I never told you where I lived."

Matthew caught Kai's tone, read his hostile body language. Absorbed it. "What's the matter with you? Is something wrong?"

"You tell me."

"Huh?" Matthew's eyebrows shot up; then confusion flashed over his features. "Nah. I don't play that game, Kai. If you've got a problem, fucking say so. I'm not talking in circles with you. What's wrong?"

"I saw you."

"Saw me?"

"At the airport."

Matthew frowned. "At the airport? When?"

"Yesterday."

"I don't understand."

Kai laughed, bitter and cold. "I came to meet you, and saw you making out with a chick. Nice, huh? When were you gonna tell me I was just a phase?"

Matthew said nothing. Kai could see his brain working to put the pieces together. Figure out exactly what Kai had seen and come up with a bullshit response.

Kai felt rage bubble up inside him. Felt it merge with twenty-four hours of tears and heartache and become a monster. Fuck you, asshole. There's nothing you can say.

"I wasn't making out with her. I was saying good-bye."

Matthew stepped forward, as if that explained it all. Kai stepped back. No fucking way.

"Good-bye? Why? You gonna miss her now you're not in her bed? Is that why you went to Boston? To sneak off with her?"

"What? No!" Matthew flushed like he'd been slapped. "I was with my mom, my kid sisters, and my elderly grandma. I showed you. You know where I was."

Kai snorted. "Do I? Seems to me I don't know anything about you. Boston, huh? Bullshit. You coulda been anywhere, with anyone... With her."

Bewilderment cleared from Matthew's gaze, and in its place came anger. "Listen, I don't know what the fuck's going on, but this isn't my problem. I told you where I went, why I was going, and when I was coming back. What more do you want from me? It's not like we're together. You've made that fucking clear, and even if we were, I haven't cheated on you."

Kai scoffed. "Whatever. You were macking on that chick. I saw you."

"I kissed her good-bye. She's my best friend."

Best friend. "The same one you used to jerk off with, right?"

Silence. Kai wanted to puke. He'd spent weeks getting close to Matthew, preparing for the scene, and daring himself to imagine what could've come next. *We're not together.* Matthew was right, but fuck, Kai wished he wasn't.

"I don't get what the big deal is. You kiss other people all the time. I've seen you."

"That's guys," Kai spat. "We both do that."

"So? Why's it different? Sonny, Zeb, Cam... I've seen you making out with all of them. Why's it different for me? Is it me? Yeah, that must be it. You can kiss your friends all you like, but I'm just a whore, right? A piece of ass for you to drill in a scene."

Matthew's choice of words hit home. Kai's perspective came

crashing down and punched him in the gut. "You're not a piece of ass."

"Yeah? Don't fucking treat me like one, then. And don't treat me like a punk. If you really think I kiss anyone the way I kiss you, then you don't know me at all."

"But you're not even gay."

"I never said I was."

Kai's stomach turned over. "You dance at a gay club. You're a gay porn star. How can you not be fucking gay?"

"Why do I have to be?" Matthew threw his hands up in the air. "You know what? I don't need to explain myself. I'm tired and you're being a prick. I'm going home, Kai. Have a nice life."

Matthew started to turn away. Kai grabbed his shoulder. "You're gonna walk away? Yeah, that's real fucking mature."

"Mature? Are you kidding me?" Matthew shrugged out of Kai's grip and shoved him hard. "I kissed my best friend good-bye. Yeah, I fooled around with her when I was a kid, but I grew up. Maybe it's time you did, jackass."

***

The next few days passed in a haze of reflection and regret. Matthew gave Kai a taste of his own medicine. Turned his phone off and extended his break from Silver for another week, maybe more.

Kai stewed on their fight for a while, but it wasn't long before he found himself on Matthew's doorstep, ready to eat humble pie. In the cold light of day, Matthew was right. Guy or girl, it didn't matter. They both kissed other people all the damned time. Why was this any different?

The simple answer was that it wasn't, but nothing was ever simple. Kai wanted...needed Matthew in his life, but he couldn't get his head around seeing Matthew with a chick. Was

Matthew bisexual? Who knew? No one but Matthew. Pity he wasn't home. Or answering his phone. Or coming to the club.

Kai spent the next week working bar shifts and dancing late-night slots at Silver. Mac approached him one night while he was setting up the bar.

"Something on your mind, kid?"

"No." Kai dropped a box of mixers on the bar and turned his back on Mac. "Did I do something wrong?"

"Nope. Just wondering why you've had a face like a smacked ass all week. This got something to do with the funk Matthew's in?"

"No." Kai tore the box open and slammed a few bottles down, hoping Mac would get the hint. He didn't want to talk about Matthew, especially not at the club, where his image was plastered on every goddamned wall.

Mac did let him be, eventually, but he came back at Kai later that night, loaded with a hug and a bag of Chinese food to take home, and somehow managed to make Kai feel worse than ever.

The next night, Kai quit his new habit of moping around the apartment and went to the club two hours before it even opened. He expected to find Mac, but Jude was there, and despite seeming to be in an even worse mood than Kai, he took pity on him and wrote him in to dance the early slot with Sonny and Zeb.

"That's if you all bother to show up."

Kai assumed Jude's grouching was aimed at Sonny, so he was surprised when he meandered into the dressing room to find Sonny already there. Zeb joined them a little while later. No one mentioned Matthew, and for a while, everything felt normal.

Then Zeb busted out a bottle of tequila and Kai's mood went south with every shot he threw down his throat.

He sat glumly on the countertop while Sonny and Zeb pranced around the room, singing along to the tunes Sonny was strumming on his guitar. Sometimes Kai enjoyed this part of dancing at Silver even more than being on stage—fooling around with his friends, laughing, making himself pretty, but he wasn't feeling it tonight. Hadn't felt it since Matthew had called him a jackass and turned away from him. Maybe before that. Maybe even since Matthew had left for Boston.

Zeb danced to the door. "I'm gonna swipe some more soda from the bar. Hide the bottle if Jude comes. He doesn't like hard liquor back here."

Kai watched him go through hooded eyes. He felt tired, and the longer he sat hunched on the counter, the less inclined he felt to go on stage and show himself to the world.

Sonny spun to a stop in front of him. "All right, spill. Zeb's got a crush on Jude, so he'll be gone for ages. What's up with you?"

"Nothing." Kai shrugged away from Sonny and stared at the floor. "Why does everyone keep asking me that?"

"Because you're sitting in the corner like your dog just died. Come on, Kai. I'm not cuddly ole Mac. You can't fob me off with puppy-dog eyes. Are you still worried about that scene with Matthew? You can practice topping with me if you like."

Between porn stars and friends, Sonny's offer was sweet, and perhaps something Kai would've taken him up on when this whole saga had begun, but it was too late for that now, way too late. "I don't think it's going to happen now. Matthew hates me."

"What? When did that happen? Last I knew you two were sucking face in Mac and Jude's bathroom."

And the rest. "I fucked up."

"What did you do?"

"Saw him kissing a chick and freaked the fuck out. I was a

dick, blanked him, then threw it in his face." Kai breathed out a heavy sigh. It felt oddly cathartic to admit his sins out loud.

"Oh, boy." Sonny looked thoughtful. "Did you apologize?"

"No. He walked away while I was still being a prick. He hasn't spoken to me since."

Sonny leaned his guitar against the lockers. "What pissed you off so much? 'Cause I gotta say it, dude. You're both porn stars and go-go dancers. If you can't handle sharing him a little, this shit is always gonna blow back in your face."

"It's not about that."

"Then what is it about? The scene? You don't have to do it, you know. Or if Matthew doesn't, and it's an itch you wanna scratch, we can figure something out. Or..." Sonny looked thoughtful. "Hmm, maybe that's not it, though. Maybe you only want to top because it's Matthew. Yeah, that's it, isn't it? You want to claim him."

Kai scowled. Beneath the bullshit there was an element of truth to Sonny's theory. Kai didn't mind the casual affection that came with their shared profession—nah, he loved it—but he did want the whole world to know Matthew was his. Wanted Matthew to know. Kai started to shove Sonny away. "Shut your mouth. I don't want to talk about it anymore—"

Something stopped him, a vibration that seemed to come through the floor and shake his bones. "What was that?"

"You felt it too?" Sonny opened the dressing-room door and glanced up and down the corridor. "Jude must be moving the tables around again. He doesn't like the front bar."

That sounded like Jude. He didn't spend much time at Silver, and whenever he did show his face, he couldn't seem to keep still. Like Sonny, but without the motor mouth. "Where's he gonna put—"

A loud, rumbling groan cut Kai off again. He froze, still sure he was imagining it, then the room swayed, like the club had liquefied, and threw them both to the floor.

Kai landed on Sonny, knocking the breath from his lungs. He rolled over, tried to steady himself, but there was nothing there. The whole world had turned to jelly. He grabbed Sonny, pulled him up to his knees. "Fuck, is this an earthquake?"

"Sure feels like it." Sonny pushed him forward. "Quick, get under the table."

Kai fought for purchase on the shaking ground and scrambled under the dressing table. Sonny followed and squished himself in beside Kai. The building shuddered and groaned, and the dancers' vast collection of lotions and potions crashed to the floor around them. A mounted photo frame fell from the wall and shattered on the ground in a fizzy haze of broken glass. Part of the ceiling landed next to it, then another and another.

Then the power cut out.

Oh, my God. We're going to die. Kai hid his face in Sonny's ribs. Found his hand. Sonny squeezed back, and together they held on for dear life as the club shuddered and groaned. Kai closed his eyes and for a moment was transported back in time to his one and only memory of his mom being maternal. Remembered the fun house attraction at the fairground a few miles from home. Remembered freaking out and his mom coming to get him, holding him, and telling him it was all gonna be okay.

She never said it again, even when they lost their home and moved to the trailer park.

White trash, baby…

And then it was all over. The shaking stilled as suddenly as it had begun. Kai blinked. Felt the abrupt onslaught of energy drain from the earth. Did that really just happen?

Sonny squeezed his hand. "Kai? You okay?"

"Think so." Kai inhaled a shaky breath. "What the fuck was that?"

"An earthquake or a nuclear apocalypse. I'm going to try

and move, okay? Shout if you think something's gonna squish us."

Kai braced himself as Sonny squirmed in their cramped hidey hole. "Are you sure we should move? What if the ceiling falls on us?"

"Then we'll be in here forever, dumbass. Chill, okay? It doesn't look so bad."

Something in Sonny's tone made Kai suspicious, but what was he supposed to do? Wrap his legs around his waist and pin him down? Nah. This was definitely the wrong scenery for that.

Sonny wriggled around and eased his legs out from under the dressing table. Kai squinted in the murky light, but he couldn't see much past Sonny's back.

Jude's voice reached them. "Kai! Sonny! You okay in there?"

Sonny raised his head and looked over his shoulder. "Yeah. We're under the table."

"Can you get out?"

"Think so."

Sonny crawled out from beneath the dressing table and held out his hand to Kai. Kai scrambled to his feet and took in the mess of smashed mirrors and crooked lockers while Sonny searched out his precious guitar. The quake had been short but brutal. The scale of the damage took Kai's breath away.

They picked their way to the door, thankful Sonny had opened it before the quake struck. Sonny looked out and whistled. "Jude? Where are you?"

"I'm right here, guys."

"Where?" Kai couldn't see a thing. The corridor was dark, the air heavy with dust. He craned his neck. Jude stood at the end of the corridor, his way blocked by the crumbled wall supports, his phone pressed to his ear. "Jude?"

"I can't get to you, Kai. Shoulders are too damned wide. You need to come to me, okay? Go slow and stay low."

"Go on." Sonny pulled Kai forward. "You go first, I'll follow."

Kai eyed the trashed corridor with unease. He felt a deep-rooted need to get out of the club, but he had no desire to pick his way through the mess of wires and rubble. "Why do I have to go first?"

"So I can keep my foot up your ass. Come on. Let's go."

Kai dropped to the ground and began to crawl through the wreckage. The lights flickered on and off, and after seeing the carnage around him, Kai decided he preferred the dark. Behind him, Sonny cursed. Kai looked over his shoulder. "What is it?"

"Nothing. Keep going."

Kai hadn't realized he'd stopped. He faced the front and looked for Jude. Couldn't see him, and for a moment, his fragile courage failed. "Jude?"

"I'm here, kid. Just a few more feet."

Kai picked his way over the final few feet of rubble. Jude helped him up and reached out for Sonny.

Sonny scrambled to his feet and winced. Jude turned him around before he could protest, revealing a nasty scrape on his bare back. Kai cringed. The wound wasn't deep, but it looked horrible, and he felt sick. His experience with his own blood hadn't strengthened his stomach.

Jude shook his head, exasperated. "That's what you get for dragging that damn guitar along with you. Come on, let's move. Mac says we need to get out."

Jude led them to the fire exit. Bull, the club manager, met them at the door. Behind him, Kai saw Zeb and a couple of bar staff huddled together on the sidewalk, and realized Jude must have bypassed his own escape to come back for him and Sonny.

Kai looked around and shivered. The street looked strange. People poured out of every building, some dusty and bloody, and a smoggy haze filled the air, rising until it looked like smoke.

Wait, no, it was smoke. The drugstore across the street was on fire. Kai could see the flames flickering in the window.

"Come on, guys. We need to find somewhere safe." Jude ushered them away from the club and to the end of the block. He had his phone to his ear and seemed to be looking for something in particular.

That something turned out to be Mac, who screeched around the corner in his car just as the first sound of sirens began in the distance.

Mac sprang out of his car like a man half his size, strode across the street to Jude, and grabbed him in much the same way he had at the hospital. Smothered him. For a moment, there was no Jude, just Mac's arms around him, keeping him safe.

Kai looked away and took over for Zeb, who was pressing a pad from the first-aid box to the nasty graze on Sonny's back. A breeze caught the air. They both shivered. With Mac and Jude in his eye line, Kai craved the comfort of warm, loving arms, and wondered if Sonny did too. Wondered if he was aching for Levi's arms the same way Kai was Matthew's.

Fuck. Matthew. "Is the quake bad? Did it hit anywhere else?"

Mac released Jude and shrugged. "Doesn't seem too bad. This block must've been close to the epicenter. Phone lines are working. Roads are clear..."

Another wail of sirens drowned Mac out. A stream of fire trucks turned into the street and firefighters spilled out to tackle the growing blaze in the drugstore.

Kai had a thing for men in uniform, but ogling the firefighters was the last thing on his mind. He searched his pockets for his phone, but it wasn't there. He'd left it on the countertop in the dressing room before the quake had struck. Chances were it was smashed to bits.

Mac pulled Kai's hand away from the wound on Sonny's back and whistled. "Ouch. Hurt anywhere else?"

"Nope."

Mac wasn't convinced. "It probably needs washing out. Let me get the club made safe and I'll take you to the ER."

Sonny rolled his eyes but didn't protest as Mac and Jude herded them to an area the firefighters had designated safe. Once there, they took stock of the situation and discovered Kai and Sonny had left all their worldly possessions in the club—keys, phones, wallets. Sonny didn't even have most of his clothes.

"There gonna be anyone at your place to let you in, kiddo?"

Kai glanced at Mac and shrugged. It was Friday evening. Bianca would likely not come home at all, but with Tag, who knew? He split his time between the apartment he shared with Kai and his girlfriend's place across town. Kai wasn't about to tell Mac that, though. "Someone will be around."

Mac turned his attention to Sonny. "What about you? Need a place to crash after we're done at the hospital?"

"He's coming with me."

Kai spun around. Levi stood a few feet away, his truck idling at the side of the road. With the noise of the fire trucks at the other end of the street, no one had heard him pull up.

Sonny stared at Levi, his eyebrow quirked in a challenge that didn't look altogether friendly. "My knight in shining armor?"

Levi held out his jacket. "Just get in the damned truck. I wanna take you home."

Not even Sonny could say no to that. He got in, scooted across the front seat, and kissed Levi's cheek. Levi looked down at him like he was the only guy in the world, and together they drove away.

Kai watched them go, the warmth in his chest bittersweet. However the rest of the night played out, he was going to bed alone, and he had no one to blame but himself.

CHAPTER FIFTEEN

It was late by the time Kai made it home. The street Silver was on had taken the worst of the quake—the rest of the city had suffered minimal damage—but the roads were chaos, and Kai had to wait on Mac. It was past midnight by the time he slipped out of Mac's car a few blocks from home.

He walked the rest of the way in a daze, his legs heavy with exhaustion. He felt like he'd danced every slot at the club and then some. Money worries plagued him too. The club would be shut for the foreseeable future to be repaired, and without the steady income from bartending and dancing, he was pretty fucking screwed. He'd have to pick up some scenes...perhaps even some scenes he didn't really want to do. Or maybe catch a gig with another club. *Yeah, go dance at Sizzlers for pocket change. That'll fix everything.*

"Kai?"

Kai jumped a mile as a shadowy figure loomed out of the alley next to his apartment, a figure with perfect hair and glittery green eyes. "Matthew? What are you doing here?"

Matthew stepped out into the light. He looked as bone weary as Kai felt, but he managed a faint smile. "I called Jude.

He said Mac was bringing you home, and it went so well last time I came here."

Nothing happened for a moment. Matthew stared at Kai, and Kai stared right back, rendered mute by the appearance of the wry grin he thought he'd lost for good. Then Matthew pounced, grabbed Kai, and hugged him tight, hugged him like Mac hugged Jude. Like he meant it, like there was nothing else in the world.

"I saw the club on the news. They said someone died at the drugstore, and then you didn't answer you phone. Fuck, I was so scared."

Kai sagged against Matthew, fatigue, the crazy night, and everything that had come between them weighing him down. "My phone is in the club somewhere. Smashed, probably. The dressing rooms and the corridor collapsed."

Matthew squeezed him hard another moment, then pulled away, seeming to notice for the first time that they were embracing on the sidewalk of a questionable neighborhood in the middle of the night. "That block must have been close to the epicenter."

"The what?"

"The point in the earth above the hypocenter of the quake. It's where the fault line ruptures... Never mind." Matthew shook his head. "Who cares about science, right? Can we go inside? It's freezing out here."

Kai hesitated. He could tell from the lack of music coming from the windows above them that no one was home, and Matthew had been to his place before, but that time he'd hardly gotten his foot in the door before Kai had put his bitch face on. He hadn't seen the filth and the mess. "I don't know if I can get in. My keys are in the club. Tag sometimes leaves the door unlocked, but..."

"Kai, it's cold. You're cold. Just come inside, okay? We need to talk."

As it turned out, Tag had left the door not only unlocked, but wide open too. Kai took a quick glance around for thieves, then beckoned Matthew inside. He shut the door behind them and led Matthew straight to his room, leaving all the lights off until he found the small desk lamp he kept on his bedroom floor.

He flicked it on and shut the door. "This is me."

Matthew took a cursory glance around before he focused on Kai. "Are you okay?"

"I'm fine."

Kai sank onto the edge of his bed. Matthew sat beside him, not touching, but close enough that Kai could feel his warmth. "I've really fucking missed you."

Kai snorted. "You shouldn't be nice to me. I'm a dick."

"I know, but you have dust in your hair and blood on your shirt. Kinda hard to care about much else."

Kai traced the streak of blood—Sonny's blood—with his fingertip. "Sonny cut his back. He's fine, though. Levi took him home."

"Everyone else okay?"

Kai nodded absently. He'd hovered close by Mac while he'd called round all the Blue Boy staff. Some of them hadn't even noticed the quake.

"What about your folks?"

"My mom's neighborhood didn't get hit."

"You never talk about your family."

Kai got up and took the single step to his bedroom's tiny window. "Not much to say. My mom doesn't want me around, and I don't want to be around her."

"What about your dad?"

"Never met him. He was killed in a military accident before I was born."

Matthew absorbed this, solemn and silent. Kai turned his back on him. He didn't want to dwell on the past, and he didn't want Matthew's sympathy. He wanted Matthew's trust...his smile. He wanted his friend back. "I'm sorry I was a prick about your girlfriend."

"She's not my girlfriend. She's a girl and my friend. There's a difference."

"Whatever. I was a prick... I am a prick, and I'm sorry."

Matthew made a frustrated noise, low in his throat. "I can forgive you that, Kai, but first I gotta know why. I wasn't fooling around with Jen, but I am bisexual. If that's a problem for you, I'm walking out that door and I'm not coming back. We're done. Over. I won't be around someone who can't accept me."

Kai turned and took in the fire in Matthew's gaze and realized his flippant response had sounded like he didn't give a shit in the worst possible way. "I do accept you. I don't care that you like girls, I never did. I just...fuck. You caught me off guard. Last time I had a boyfriend he slept with my cousin."

"Your female cousin?"

"Yeah."

Matthew was silent a moment; then he stood and took Kai's hand. "You're not the only one who's been kicked in the face, Kai. Every time you pushed me away, I figured I'd wake up one day to find you gone."

Jon. Shit. Kai kept forgetting about that. "Jon did a number on you, huh?"

Matthew snorted. "Only because I was stupid, and I let him. I can see it for what it was now, but you...fuck. I can't see anything but you."

"You still want me?" Kai kept his gaze on the stained carpet. "Even after all this?"

"Kai, look at me." Matthew put two fingers under Kai's chin and pushed until their eyes met. "I like you...really fucking like you. I feel like I've been walking around in a bubble since Cam pushed us together. I don't cheat, ever, but I won't deny who I am, not even for you. Especially not for you."

Kai felt wet warmth slide down his left cheek. How had

they gotten to the point where Matthew thought he was some kind of bigoted asshole? This shit wasn't right. "I'm scared. I don't fall for guys like this, you know? I have stupid crushes. I'd just about got my head around lov—really liking you, and then I saw you at the airport. It wasn't about the girl, Matthew, I promise. I was being a dick. I am a dick. I'm so sorry."

Kai wiped his face with the back of his hand. Matthew put his arm around him and pulled him close. "You're not a dick, Kai. You're just not used to being wanted for anything other than sex. Do you think I don't notice you freaking out every time I mention us having a relationship that isn't about fucking?"

"I don't do that."

"Yeah, you do, and it's classic porn star behavior. Jude told me."

"Jude?"

Matthew shrugged. "I was doing a little freaking out myself before I went away. You seemed happy when we were together, when you spent every night in my bed, but I felt like we were on borrowed time, that you'd ditch me as soon as the scene was done."

"That's not what I want." Kai spoke to himself as much as Matthew. I want it all...

Matthew reached up and traced the fading scar on Kai's scalp. "You know what I want, Kai? I want to shoot this fucking scene, let you blow my mind, and then I want to get your GED certificate and show you what we can do with the rest of our lives."

* * *

"Are you ready?"

"Think so." Kai glanced over his shoulder at Cam and shot him a nervous grin. "Pass me the glasses."

Cam rolled his eyes but passed over the black faux glasses

Matthew had left on Kai's pillow that morning. "You two have some serious geek kink going on."

"You love it."

"No, I tolerate it because it's cute...like puppies. I like the outdoorsy type of guy."

"Yeah, and muscle men."

Kai ducked as Cam tossed an empty soda bottle his way. He'd spent a lot of time with Cam and Jude over the last few days, figuring out a vague plan for his scene with Matthew, and it hadn't escaped his notice that Cam and Jude had a certain chemistry. It wasn't the deep, loving bond both men shared with their partners, but there was definitely something there, something...unresolved.

"I can't believe you haven't seen Matthew today. It's like you're getting married or some shit."

Kai felt his cheeks flush and smiled to himself. Matthew's absence wasn't deliberate; it had just worked that way. Matthew had classes all afternoon, and Kai had spent most of the day alone, centering himself and garnering some much-needed perspective. The scene was where it had all begun, and if it wasn't to end right here in the studio, he needed to get a grip on himself.

Maybe I should've fucked him at home first. A spark of heat stoked the already smoldering burn in Kai's veins. He'd spent every night in Matthew's bed since they'd reconciled, but they hadn't fucked. Every time they got close, one of them pulled away...put the brakes on, like they were subconsciously saving themselves for this moment.

In the back of Kai's mind it struck him as strange that they wanted to share a milestone so personal with the whole world, but somehow, it felt right. It was right. Here. Now. *This is really happening.*

Cam touched his shoulder. "Enough preening. Let's go."

Kai slipped his glasses on and backed away from the

mirror, admiring the effect. He'd chosen gun-metal-gray under-wear for the shoot, bypassing the awesome sparkly pair Matthew had given him when they'd finally exchanged Christmas gifts, and the black frames contrasted well with his pale skin.

He wondered if Matthew would wear his Batman pair. Kai was saving his own belated Christmas gift for the grand reopening of the club, but Matthew had been coy with his comic-book briefs, refused to even try them on. He seemed like a man with a plan, but as Kai was fast finding out, Matthew's plans were always something Kai liked.

"Kai."

Kai gave in to Cam's impatience and followed him out onto the set they'd chosen all those weeks ago for their scene. It was the white one—dubbed the 'virgin' set—and contained nothing but a king-size bed, a mirror, and a secret stash of extra lube.

And Matthew.

He's here.

He's wearing his glasses.

Kai's heart flip-flopped, and he fought the urge to skip the final few paces and jump on the bed. Somewhere inside him, he knew he was nervous, but with Matthew in his sights the fire in his belly felt good. Better than good.

He took his place on the bed. Matthew grinned, ignored the low catcalls from Cam, and kissed him full on the lips. Kissed him like they were already halfway through the scene. Kai moaned and nipped Matthew's bottom lip. He'd jacked off three times before he'd come to the studio, but the heat between them was incredible.

Jude cleared his throat. "Can I get a minute before you two combust?"

Matthew broke the kiss with a sheepish grin, but a moment or two ticked by before he looked Jude's way.

Jude rolled his eyes and muttered something under his

breath. "Okay. I hope you both know what you're doing, because I haven't got a fucking clue."

Kai laughed. Jude had been saying that for days. He'd given Kai and Matthew free rein and not asked many questions, but behind his sage advice and gentle guidance, Kai could tell not knowing what he was in for was bugging the hell out of him.

Cam threw a strip of condoms onto the bed. Pink ones, Kai's favorite. "Any last-minute issues?"

Matthew shook his head; Kai too. Cam nodded and backed away. It was the first scene he'd mentored from start to finish, and despite a few understandable absences, he'd taken his role to heart. In some ways, he seemed as invested in the scene as Kai was. Kai tried to catch his eye and smile, but Cam was checking the camera angles. The shoot was small and discreet, just Jude, Cam, and a couple of crew. In another first, Jude and Cam would shoot much of the scene themselves.

At Jude's signal, Cam backed away from the set and perched on the arm of a disused prop couch. As Jude raised his hand for quiet, Sonny slithered over the back and linked his arm through Cam's. The glance he shared with Cam was mellow and cool, and it seemed whatever crisis between them Kai hadn't quite understood was over.

Sonny met Kai's gaze with a conspiratorial smirk, his message clear. You want this. Own it.

Jude counted down. Five, four, three, two, one. "Action!"

Kai pounced. He climbed over Matthew and straddled him, tugging on his shirt. "Off. Now."

If Matthew was surprised that they'd hit the ground running, he didn't show it. He pulled his shirt over his head and tossed it away. Then he closed his arms around Kai, and together they fell back onto the bed, kissing, grasping, fighting with denim and belt buckles.

Kai covered Matthew with his body. He'd woken that morning to still-warm sheets and the teasing scent of Matthew's skin, and now he couldn't get enough. He yanked Matthew's jeans down his legs. Took note of the benign black underwear and tossed those aside too. Matthew's cock sprang back, hard and waiting. Kai growled. *Yeah*. He was gonna own this shit.

Matthew caught Kai's mood and smirked, spread himself over the bed, arms open, his grin wide. "I'm yours, baby. Do whatever you want."

Baby. It felt like a dream. The foreplay flowed like water, easy and familiar. Lips, tongues, and teeth on hot, slick skin. It seemed to last forever, but then Kai blinked and it was over. His cock had been in Matthew's mouth, his tongue deep inside Matthew, and he'd missed it all, carried away by the sweetest notion that nothing was real. The condom in his hand changed all that, and he came crashing down to earth in a snap of latex. His cock looked strange sheathed in a condom, alien, like it belonged to someone else.

Matthew took Kai's hand and sucked his index finger into his mouth, teasing it with his tongue. The gesture was sweet and sensual. Warm, and soothing to Kai's hammering heart. He watched Matthew's full lips move around his finger. How is that hotter than watching him suck dick?

He'd probably never know.

Matthew released Kai's finger, opened his legs and raised them gracefully over his head. "Do it. Fuck me."

Kai edged forward on his knees and aligned his cock with Matthew's body. He knew Matthew was ready for him, stretched and relaxed. Sonny had helped him prepare for the scene, and besides, the dude wasn't a fucking virgin.

Still, it had been a while, for both of them. Fate worked in mysterious ways, and since the day Cam had pushed them together, top or bottom, neither one of them had been with anyone else.

Kai pressed inside Matthew, slow and sure, and watched, fascinated, as Matthew's body accepted him.

Matthew gasped and screwed his face up in a brief moment of discomfort. Kai stilled and thought of all the things that eased the strain on his body when he was the one being stretched. He stalled. For a moment, his courage failed. Matthew's rock-hard cock made him feel better. He took a deep breath. He could do this. He could make this amazing for both of them.

He put his hand on Matthew's chest and rubbed a slow, soothing circle; then he bent and sucked on the salty-sweet juncture of Matthew's neck and shoulder. Teasing, light nips at first, but then harder as Matthew began to squirm.

Matthew wrapped his legs around Kai's waist and arched his back. "How does it feel?"

Kai growled again. "You feel amazing."

Matthew raised his arms and gripped the bed frame. The tightness in his face began to fade, and he blew out a slow breath. "Yeah? What does it feel like? Tell me."

Despite the context, Kai wanted to blush, maybe even felt like he should, but he didn't. Instead he leaned down again and put his lips right over Matthew's ear. "Smooth. Hot. Like you were made for me."

Matthew's eyes rolled. He flexed his hips, driving himself up on Kai's cock. "Then make me yours."

Kai didn't need telling twice. He took a subtle glance around, took note of the camera angles, and leaned back on his heels, taking Matthew's leg with him for leverage. Then he began to move, driving in and out of Matthew in a slow, slick rhythm that blew his mind.

He fought a mental battle. His heart wanted to watch Matthew, to see the reactions play out across his beautiful face, but he couldn't look away from the point where their bodies were joined. Kai stared, enthralled. It felt a little strange, but watching his cock slide into Matthew was the hottest thing he'd ever seen.

Kai couldn't help his shit-eating smirk. Holy shit. I'm fucking Matthew.

"What are you grinning about?"

Kai tore his gaze away from his dick and focused on Matthew's face. On Matthew's flushed cheeks, kiss-swollen lips, and hooded eyes. "This. You. You look so hot right now."

"Says you. Anyone ever told you how beautiful you are?"

No. Kai twisted his hips, probing, searching. When he found what he was looking for, the magic angle that made Matthew jolt, he leaned down and kissed Matthew hard, covering his whispered words. "You make me feel beautiful."

The time for talk was over then. Kai hit his groove and shifted them around the bed, following the subtle cues Jude gave him from behind the camera. He fucked Matthew every which way he could think of, until Jude gave them the signal to wrap things up however they pleased.

The air shifted. Something changed. Kai put his hands back on Matthew's hips, flipped him over, and pushed him onto his stomach, his head hanging over the end of the bed. Matthew moaned and raised his ass. "Fuck, yeah. Been dreaming about this."

Kai slid back inside Matthew like a seasoned pro, his nerves a fast-fading memory. Matthew whimpered. His hair was a delicious mess, tousled and damp with sweat. Kai grabbed it and tugged Matthew's head back, exposed his neck for a biting kiss. "You like that, huh?"

"Yeah. Harder."

Matthew's words were choked, and Kai felt them like a sledgehammer. He wrapped his arms around Matthew's neck and molded their bodies together in a sinuous tangle of arms and legs. Matthew said he'd dreamed of this, and he wasn't the only one. Kai had seen them like this over and over, but his fantasies had nothing on reality.

He drove into Matthew hard and deep, and fucked him like

his life depended on it. Held him down, whispered dirty things in his ear. Matthew yelled out and tried to hold himself firm. Kai couldn't see his face, but the sporadic tightening in his body told Kai he was close to breaking point.

Kai felt relief. He'd been on the edge since the moment he'd laid eyes on Matthew...laid eyes on him and really seen him. The scene had flown by, but in truth they'd been doing this for weeks. Dancing around the earth-shattering moment that was finally within their reach.

Skin slapped skin. The bed squeaked and groaned. They fell to the side and held hands around Matthew's cock. Matthew's other hand was clenched tight, fisting the sheets. His muscles tense, straining, desperate for release. Kai sank his teeth into Matthew's shoulder. Matthew cried out and jerked in his arms, spilling out over their joined hands. Kai watched him come with wide eyes, spellbound. I did that. I made him come like that.

His own climax came rushing at him like a freight train. Matthew fell limp and pliant, giving himself over to Kai. Kai drove into him again and again, chasing it down, and then it was over, like a dam had broken. Kai pulled out with seconds to spare and busted his load all over Matthew's back.

Kai collapsed on top of Matthew. He pressed his face between Matthew's shoulder blades, exhausted, his moans fading to harsh, panted breaths. Beneath him, Matthew's torso heaved and his limbs trembled. Kai gave him a moment, then sat up, found Matthew's hands and squeezed.

Matthew moaned. Kai rolled over and opened his arms. Matthew followed, as if pulled by an invisible cord, took off his crooked glasses, and laid his head on Kai's chest, oblivious to the sticky mess they'd created. Kai's heart hammered against Matthew's cheek, but inside he felt calm and sated, like he'd released far more than a few weeks of sexual tension.

He stared up at the studio's utilitarian ceiling and stroked Matthew's face. "You didn't wear your Batman underwear."

Matthew chuckled, shaky, breathless, and wonderful. "Nah. I'm saving them for when I fuck you."

"Yeah? And when are you gonna do that?"

"Later. I want to ask you something first." Matthew shifted and put his chin on Kai's breastbone. "My dad called this morning. He wants me to spend the winter with him."

"In Australia?"

"Yeah."

Kai's heart thudded to a standstill. Saw Jude turn his still camera off and step back from his post by the mirror. In his post-coital haze, he'd almost forgotten the cameras following their every move...every word. "But..."

"But nothing." Matthew pulled himself up and over Kai, took his face in his hands and kissed him, once, twice. "Come with me."

"With you?"

"Yeah. Fuck it, Kai. Be bold. Come with me to the other side of the world."

Bold.

The word echoed in Kai's head as he stared at Matthew. The past few months had been crazy, but if they'd taught him anything, it was that he had nothing to lose by doing shit he'd never dared dream he'd do. Bold. Yeah, Kai could do that. He'd just turned the boy of his dreams inside out. He could do anything he freakin' wanted.

NEWSLETTER

Get a free story!

For the most up to date news and free books, subscribe to my newsletter HERE.

This is a zero spam zone. Maximum number of emails you will receive is one per month.

PATREON

Not ready to let go of the Blue Boys? Or looking for sneak peeks at future books in the series? Alternative POVs, outtakes, and missing moments from **all** Garrett's books can be found on her Patreon site. Misfits, Slide, Strays...the works. Because you know what? Garrett wasn't ready to let her boys go either.

Pledges start from as little as $2, and all content is available at the lowest tier.

ABOUT GARRETT

Bonus Material available for all books on Garrett's Patreon account. Includes short stories from Misfits, Slide, Strays, What Remains, Dream, and much more. Sign up here: https://www.patreon.com/garrettleigh

Facebook Fan Group, Garrett's Den... https://www.facebook.com/groups/garre...

Garrett Leigh is an award-winning British writer, cover artist, and book designer. Her debut novel, Slide, won Best Bisexual Debut at the 2014 Rainbow Book Awards, and her polyamorous novel, Misfits was a finalist in the 2016 LAMBDA awards, and was again a finalist in 2017 with Rented Heart.

In 2017, she won the EPIC award in contemporary romance with her military novel, Between Ghosts, and the contemporary romance category in the Bisexual Book Awards with her novel What Remains.

When not writing, Garrett can generally be found procrastinating on Twitter, cooking up a storm, or sitting on her behind doing as little as possible, all the while shouting at her menagerie of children and animals and attempting to tame her unruly and wonderful FOX.

Garrett is also an award winning cover artist, taking the silver medal at the Benjamin Franklin Book Awards in 2016. She designs for various publishing houses and independent authors at blackjazzdesign.com, and co-owns the specialist stock site moonstockphotography.com

Connect with Garrett
www.garrettleigh.com

<u>Soul to Keep</u>

<u>My Mate Jack</u>

<u>Lucky Man</u>

<u>Finding Home</u>

<u>Only Love</u>

<u>Heart</u>

<u>What Remains</u>

<u>What Matters</u>

<u>Between Ghosts</u>